Lost Lake

Also by Emily Littlejohn

Inherit the Bones

A Season to Lie

Lost Lake

Emily Littlejohn

MINOTAUR BOOKS

NEW YORK

LOST LAKE. Copyright © 2018 by Emily Littlejohn. All rights reserved. Printed in the United States of America. For information, address St. Martin's Press, 175 Fifth Avenue, New York, N.Y. 10010.

www.minotaurbooks.com

Library of Congress Cataloging-in-Publication Data

Names: Littlejohn, Emily, author.
Title: Lost lake : a detective Gemma Monroe mystery / Emily Littlejohn.
Description: First edition. | New York : Minotaur Books, 2018.
Identifiers: LCCN 2018025709 | ISBN 9781250178305 (hardcover) |
    ISBN 9781250178312 (ebook)
Subjects: LCSH: Women detectives—Colorodo—Fiction. | Murder—
    Investigation—Fiction. | GSAFD: Suspense fiction. | Mystery fiction.
Classification: LCC PS3612.I8823 L67 2018 | DDC 813/.6—dc23
LC record available at https://lccn.loc.gov/2018025709

Our books may be purchased in bulk for promotional, educational, or business use. Please contact your local bookseller or the Macmillan Corporate and Premium Sales Department at 1-800-221-7945, extension 5442, or by email at MacmillanSpecialMarkets@macmillan.com.

First Edition: November 2018

10 9 8 7 6 5 4 3 2 1

This one is for David and Carrie, Peter, Bill and John.

Siblings by blood, friends by choice.

I can't imagine my life without all of you in it.

Acknowledgments

I continue to owe a debt of gratitude to my wonderful agent and friend and first reader, Pam Ahearn. Elizabeth Lacks, you took on *Lost Lake,* and Catherine Richards, you saw it through to the end. I couldn't ask for two more lovely editors. To the rest of the team: Nettie Finn, Sarah Schoof, Melanie Sanders; your guidance is invaluable. Kathy (Nana), this book literally could not have been written without you. Mom, David, Carrie, and Ana, I love our daily chats. And, finally, Chris and Claire—everything I do is for you.

Lost Lake

Prologue

Something wakes her in the early hours.

Beyond the flimsy nylon walls of the tent, it is still dark. They went to bed after midnight, so she guesses it is four or five in the morning. The sun will rise soon and with it another day. Another breakfast, another hike, another lunch, another fight.

She listens and realizes the sounds of the lake have changed. Gone is the gentle wind moving through the trees. The bullfrog has stopped its belligerent croak. The ice, cracking against the shore, has settled down.

It was the *silence* that woke her.

She sits up slowly, careful not to disturb Mac. He lies on his back, one hand resting on his stomach, the other hidden in the depths of his sleeping bag. Mac looks like a little boy in sleep: his lips slightly parted, the faintest scowl line across his strong brow.

She hopes he is having a nightmare.

Then she feels bad and wonders if the baby will have his strong brow, his red hair.

She wonders if she cares.

She gently untangles herself from the sleeping bag and then from the tent. Slipping on her boots, leaving them untied, she stands, stretching, scanning the campsite by the little light that remains of the waning moon. She stares for a moment at the red tent pitched fifteen feet away, on the opposite side of the still-smoldering camp-fire pit.

The two people inside the red tent were strangers yesterday; she wonders if the wine and weed and close quarters of the night have left them better acquainted.

Nothing would surprise her anymore.

She walks to the edge of the campsite and stares down at the dark, still water, not daring to go any closer.

Lost Lake.

The air is freezing and she shivers. She hugs herself and looks at the far shoreline. There was a campfire last night, across the water. She is sure of it; she saw the smoke. She wonders who else is here, who else is mad enough to spend the night on this still-frozen ground along the shores of this icy lake.

She moves slowly, heading back toward the warmth of her sleeping bag.

The silence remains.

Chapter One

I stood at the edge of Lost Lake and raised a hand to my forehead to shield my eyes from the bright sun. Accustomed to the gloomy overcast skies of March and April, I'd left my sunglasses at home. But this, the second Saturday in May, was one of those warm spring days when the temperature edged pasty sixty degrees and the sky was blue enough to make the gray winter begin to fade from memory.

My head hurt from a long night of broken sleep with my six-month-old teething daughter and one too many glasses of pinot noir over dinner with my fiancé, Brody Sutherland. I closed my eyes against the glare and instead let the language of the lake wash over me. The crack of the melting ice that lined the water's edge. The young aspen leaves, whispering to one another over the sound of the gentle breeze. The splash of water as an eagle dipped down and plucked an unsuspecting fish from the middle of the lake, the bird's movements as deliberate as a stealth bomber.

It should have felt peaceful, but there was a roughness to the pastoral scene, like a pencil sketch that has been handled by greasy fingers, the edges smudged.

By June, the area would be flush with hikers and fishermen. Both groups would come hungry: the hikers for the chance to see the annual wildflower bloom of lapis and indigo lupines, sprawling up the mountain on the far side of the lake; and the fishermen for the plump trout and bass.

But this early in the season?

The few people hardy enough to try to reach the lake would trek two miles uphill, traversing melting snow and muddy, soggy soil.

There was the ever-present threat of bears, too, just waking from their long winter slumber. Bears that were hungry.

Opening my eyes, I turned from the lake and stared back at the small group huddled around the unlit fire pit.

Why had they come here, to Lost Lake?

There were dozens of camping spots scattered throughout the lower valley, any one of them more accessible than this place. The water was frigid, the wildflowers still in hibernation. It was pleasant now, nearly midday, but without the sun, temperatures would plummet. The ground would have made a cold bed last night.

Yet the group had chosen to come here. And now one of them was missing.

Sari Chesney.

Lost, at Lost Lake.

The ice cracked again. It made an eerie, otherworldly sound, and I left the lake's edge and trudged back to the group, careful to avoid the muddy collage of footprints that seemed to lead both somewhere and nowhere.

They stared at me, the two men and one woman.

The woman spoke first. "I'm very worried that something has happened to her."

Her name was Allison Chang but she preferred to be called Ally. She had told me she was Sari's best friend.

"Has Sari ever done anything like this before? Gone off without leaving word?"

"No, never. Sari's very responsible," Ally said. "She knows we would worry."

Mac Stephens added, "I agree with Ally. I have a bad feeling about this, Detective Monroe."

"Please, call me Gemma."

Mac was Sari's boyfriend, a big bear of a man with messy red hair. He was the only one of the group that I'd seen before; he was a nurse at the hospital in town and had given my daughter, Grace, her first set of shots. He didn't remember me, though; or if he did, he didn't say anything.

"I think someone has taken her," Mac continued. "This place is remote as hell. Anyone could have snuck up on us and kidnapped her."

"Kidnappings are rare, especially in a place like this, with you three right here." I gestured back to the lake. "I hate to ask the obvious, but is there any chance she went for a swim?"

Mac and Ally shook their heads vigorously.

"Sari nearly drowned as a child in a boating accident. She hates the water. She only agreed to come because Mac bullied her into it," Ally said with a troubled glance toward Mac.

He met Ally's glare with one of his own. "That's not true, Ally, and you know it. Yes, Sari hates the water, but she loves hiking and camping. She was happy to come."

I glanced at the second man. Aside from giving me his name— Jake Stephens, Mac's cousin—he'd remained silent, watching the conversation unfold.

"Look, there's no evidence to indicate a crime has occurred. Sari's an adult, and her keys, driver's license, and cell phone are all missing. That's a *good* sign. Everything points to the likelihood that she left the campsite of her own accord," I said, reflecting on the handful of missing person cases I'd worked in my six years with the Cedar Valley Police Department. In each case but one, the individual had turned up within a day. The one person who never returned was later tracked to a commune in Las Vegas.

Ally seemed to have a change of heart and she nodded her head in agreement. Color flared in her cheeks, giving her a sunburnt look. "You know, I bet you're right. Sari can be a little nutty. She's been stressed with work lately. I wonder if she got restless and just up and left in the middle of the night."

"Even though that would mean walking out in the dark, through the big, bad woods?" Jake asked. He stared at Ally, his black hair peeking out from under a blue knit beanie cap. He was in his early twenties, a few years younger than Mac and Ally. His eyes, as dark as his hair, were unreadable behind a pair of thick horn-rimmed eyeglasses.

Ally shrugged. "Maybe. If I was as stressed as she's been, I might do the same."

Another sharp crack of ice drew my attention back to the lake. Once more I squinted against the glare of the sun. A mild spring breeze created gentle waves that should have been soothing. Instead, they beckoned like the hands of a tribe of water sprites, intent on luring us into the lake.

Someone in the group coughed. I turned away from the lake. "You're positive of the timing, that she disappeared in the middle of the night?"

Mac Stephens nodded.

"How can you be so sure?"

"We're sure." Mac scratched at the back of his head. "We went to bed late, close to one in the morning. We'd, uh, had a lot to drink. I got up, maybe about six, to take a leak, and noticed Sari wasn't in the tent. I thought maybe she was going to the bathroom, too. To be honest, I was still drunk at that point. I went back to bed and passed out. When I woke again at nine, she was gone. I mean, she was still gone. So I got the others up and we searched for a while. Finally, Jake hiked out, back to the parking lot to get cell reception. He tried Sari's number first, then when it went to voice mail he called nine-one-one."

I pulled my phone from my pocket and looked at the signal; it was weak, intermittent.

I glanced at Jake. "Did you see anything strange on your hike down?"

Jake had a narrow penknife in one hand and a twig in the other. As he spoke, he took the knife to the wood. Shavings from the twig fell to the ground in a steady stream. "What do you mean, strange?"

I pursed my lips, wondering myself what I meant. "Another hiker, or signs of Sari . . . maybe animal prints?"

Jake shook his head. "Nah, there was nothing weird. But then again, I was moving pretty quickly. I took more time on the way back here, though, after I called you guys. I was stopping every couple of feet and calling Sari's name." He cupped his hands round his mouth, to demonstrate. "Sari! Sari!"

Ally flinched at the shouting and said, "Stop it, Jake. Seriously. Stop."

He shrugged. "Sorry."

I turned back to the best friend and the boyfriend. "While Jake hiked down, what were you two doing?"

Mac said, "We poked around in the woods, in case Sari had tripped, maybe fallen, and was unconscious. Then I searched Sari's backpack. At first, it made me happy, seeing that her wallet and phone were gone. Because that's what you'd grab, you know, when you leave your house. But then I got scared. Where could she go? It's two miles back to the parking lot."

He fished in his pocket and pulled out a keychain. "Look, I've still got my keys. My van is in the parking lot—that was the first thing Jake checked. And no matter what Ally says, Sari is not that brave. She'd never hike out in the dark. It's too big a risk with the mountain lions and bears up here."

He turned to the side, gesturing to the woods around the lake, and I noticed a handgun tucked in the back of his pants, sticking out from under his thick wool shirt.

"Do you have a permit for that?"

Mac looked back at me, surprised I'd noticed the gun. He nodded. "Of course. I've got a concealed carry. It's a 9mm. Do you need to see it?"

Only if I find a body with a bullet in it, I thought.

I shook my head. "Not necessary. Just keep it out of my sight. *Concealed* means concealed. Look, could someone have picked her up at the trailhead?"

None of them had an answer to that.

The thing was, it was odd.

Not suspicious, not yet . . . but odd. Though the fire pit was un-lit, ashes from the night before still smoldered in the ring. There was a lingering trace of marijuana smoke, lending the campsite an air of seediness.

Again I wondered why they'd come here, to this lost lake in the middle of the forest. Finally, I asked the question. "Why here?"

"You mean why did we come here to camp?" Mac said. "I've been coming to Lost Lake since I was a kid. Never this early in the season, though. I wanted to check it out, you know, see what it was like with a bit of snow and ice still on the ground. Jake's new to town and I thought it would be fun."

"I'd never even heard of this place," Ally said. "I guess they call it Lost Lake for a reason."

"You mentioned that Sari has been stressed at work. What does she do?"

Mac smiled proudly. "She is the assistant curator at the Cedar Valley History Museum."

Ally added, "What she is, is exhausted. Sari's been putting in twelve, thirteen-hour days working on the museum gala. There is no way in hell she'd miss the big event. Plus, her boss is a total witch and will fire her if she doesn't show up tonight. And Sari can't afford to lose her job."

The gala was the kick-off event of a week-long celebration of the sesquicentennial anniversary of Cedar Valley. One hundred and fifty years ago, the town's founding fathers had signed the necessary documents to take Cedar Valley from a mining outpost in the mountains of Colorado to an actual town. The local history museum was hosting the gala, while other organizations in town were hosting the rest of the week's events.

I chewed on the corner of my lip, thinking about a seedy campsite and a frozen lake and a missing woman. A woman who put in a tremendous amount of work to prepare for a party, and then disappeared on the eve of the event. It wasn't adding up. The thought of waiting twenty-four hours to open a missing persons case, per our standard police procedure, made me uneasy.

"Okay. Let's go ahead and get Sari reported as a missing person. I'll need a recent picture of her, a description of the last things she was wearing, and any identifying characteristics like birthmarks, tattoos, that sort of thing."

"Damn it," Mac said. The fear in his eyes intensified. "You just said we shouldn't worry."

"Look, here's the thing. Nine times out of ten, a missing person turns up. Maybe Sari was upset or ill. We're over eight thousand feet up here; perhaps she got altitude sickness and woke up disoriented. Or maybe she met up with someone. The point is, in the end, there's almost always a good explanation. However, you tell me Sari's been working on the gala for months, and that she's a responsible person, and needs her job. So, for her to go missing, today of all days . . . I don't think you should worry. But I do want to make sure we're doing our due diligence here."

Mac nodded. "Okay. You're the expert."

A cloud drifted in front of the sun and swallowed the warmth from the day, blocking the light and darkening the landscape. I shivered, then turned around and looked again at Lost Lake, suddenly uneasy having my back to the water.

I watched as, under the dark sky, the lake shifted in color to a murky shade of cobalt ink, and for the first time really noticed the dense woods on the far side of the water. There, a thick grove of Colorado blue spruce trees sprawled along the edge of the lake, a buffer between it and the mountains. As the trees grew up the slope of the mountains, though, they began to thin out. At the tree line, about eleven thousand feet, the spruces were replaced by scrubby alpine brush.

The cloud continued to drift and in another moment, the sun reappeared. Something shiny winked at me across the water from the thick forest of blue spruces. Then I blinked and it was gone.

Another camper? Or a day hiker?

"Did you see that?"

Ally, pulling on a sweatshirt, paused. "See what?"

I blinked again, but the strange light was gone and suddenly I wanted to be anywhere but here. There was a feeling to this lake, a restlessness in the wind, a hardness to the water.

It was a feeling I didn't like.

"Never mind. Just a reflection off the water."

Jake coughed. He rubbed the back of his neck and spoke slowly. "What about the tenth time?"

"Excuse me?"

He removed his eyeglasses and cleaned them on the edge of his sweatshirt. I saw he'd dropped the knife and twig he had been carving. They lay at his feet, next to a plastic water bottle and a half-eaten granola bar. "You said nine times out of ten, the person shows up. What about the tenth time?"

That was a path I didn't want to go down.

"It's too early to think about that. Look, let's get a move on. Pack up your stuff. You can head to the police station to file the official report and give a statement. I'll swing by Sari's apartment and see if she's there."

"Can I come? I have a spare key to her place," Mac said.

"Fine. You can ride with me."

Jake said, "Hey, Mac, I've got stuff to do. Before yesterday, I'd never even met Sari. I've got to find a job soon or my . . . I need work."

Mac ran a hand through his thick red hair, frustrated. "This is my girlfriend we're talking about. I've helped you out more times than I can remember, bro."

Jake nodded slowly. "Sure, yeah. You're right. Of course I'll help." He pulled the blue beanie cap farther down over his ears. "I guess we should pack up."

The three of them split up, tending to different tasks around the campsite. Ally and Mac worked on dismantling the tents while twenty feet away Jake lowered plastic bags of trash and food from the high bough of a thick pine tree. Bears were hungry, curious, and agile climbers; tying food and trash up high might not prevent a determined bear from getting to it but at least it would keep the bear away from the tents.

While they worked, I checked the perimeter of the site, attempting to recreate in my mind the events of the previous night: the roaring fire, the bottles of wine passed from hand to cold hand, the tip of a joint glowing in the dark, a hovering red-hot firefly setting a tiny patch of the black night alight.

Maybe it was the warm spring day, or the lake, once more laid out by the sun like a turquoise egg nestled in a basket of blue spruces, guarded by jagged, ancient stone peaks.

Maybe it was my own fatigue, settling in after the tricky hike and a night without much sleep. I'd had too many evenings recently where a glass of red wine with dinner had turned into a second or third in the hours between meal and sleep.

Whatever the reason, I couldn't see what had happened here at Lost Lake.

All I was able to take in were the slushy, muddy ground and the colorful tents, the four backpacks and the unlit, ashy campfire. The three friends, moving around the site with grim determination.

Later, I would think about the ice cracking that morning, and the eagle, fishing for its breakfast, and the three friends who were once four: quiet and subdued, packing up after a night of indulgence. The three of them silent, like ghosts of their former selves, living in a new world where it was possible for a woman, a friend, to vanish overnight.

Later, much later, I would regret every decision I made that morning.

Chapter Two

In 1837, Harris Theroux, an intrepid scout for the Continental Fur Company, took a respite from surveying the land to follow a twelve-point buck up the side of a mountain through a dense maze of brush and forest. He lost the buck somewhere in the thicket, but as he crested the top of the mountain and gazed at the beauty before him, his disappointment quickly turned to awe.

He marveled that such a place existed outside his dreams.

The lake was half a square mile of deep blue water, as richly hued as a gemstone, nestled in a narrow valley below rocky peaks that pierced the clouds. A thick forest surrounded the lake, sheltering it. Protecting it.

Hiding it.

The scout camped that night next to the water. He practically tripped over the trout, there were so many of them. They were fearless, unaccustomed to being hunted, and he soon feasted on a fat beauty beside a roaring fire. As the sun sank down below the mountains and the moon rose to take its place, star after star appeared in the night sky and the lake in turn deepened from cobalt to indigo to a velvet black.

Harris Theroux's journal stops there.

I like to imagine he wrote those words and then laid back, his belly full, his mind content, at peace with the world.

When Theroux didn't return to the Continental's base camp within the week, three men set out after him. They tracked him to the same spot where he'd seen the twelve-point buck, then they followed his trail up the mountain and back down the other side. It was at the water's edge where they finally found him, mauled and partially eaten by what must have been a very large grizzly bear. The men said a prayer, collected the body, and penciled in the lake on Theroux's map of the area.

They christened it Lost Lake.

Mac took the lead, followed by Ally and then Jake. I brought up the rear, having offered to carry Sari's camping pack. The melting snow and shoe-sucking mud made hiking slow, and it was as frustrating heading down from the lake as it had been heading up to it.

Could Sari Chesney have made it down this trail, in the dark, alone?

Maybe.

Maybe she hadn't been alone.

We hiked in silence. Mac and Ally were the most at ease, nimbly picking their way among the slick rocks and patches of loose gravel. They wore lightweight hiking clothes, easy to breathe in and made for traversing land like this.

Jake struggled. He moved slowly, not exactly afraid, but not confident, either. His leather sneakers were flat on the bottom, without tread, and his shirt was a thin cotton jersey. As he sweated, the shirt stayed damp and he shivered occasionally.

I knew what my partner, Detective Finn Nowlin, would make of Jake. Finn calls them "mountain guppies": inexperienced, underprepared people who (in his mind) inevitably have to be rescued from the mountain they've been foolish enough to try to scale.

Under normal circumstances, Finn might have been here with me, responding to this call. But he was out of town for the weekend. If the call had come in during the week, I might have asked another officer to accompany me to the lake. But as it was, we were shortstaffed, and I was confident in both my hiking skills and my ability to take care of myself.

"Hey, Jake? How'd you end up being the one to hike down this morning?" I asked, carefully wedging myself around a fallen tree.

"I volunteered. It just made sense. Mac knows the terrain; he was the best person to stay and search the woods. And Ally's a chick. I wasn't about to let her run all over the mountain. I'm all for equal rights, feminism, yada yada yada, but at the end of the day, women appreciate a man with some chivalry, am I right?" he said. He stopped and turned around, watching me through his eyeglasses. "Speaking of . . . do you need a hand?"

"I've got it, thanks," I said. "I imagine Ally and Mac were going crazy this morning?"

"Of course they were. We all were. Wouldn't you be, if you woke up and one of your friends had disappeared into thin air?" Jake said over his shoulder.

"Yes, I would be worried."

Fifty-five minutes after we'd left Lost Lake, we reached the parking lot. It was midafternoon; hours since Mac had discovered Sari missing.

I slipped the pack from my shoulders and rested for a moment, one hand on the warm hood of my department vehicle, a battered old Jeep. My Jeep and Mac's van were the only two cars there, but the ground was a mess of tire tracks, slushy snow piles, and mud pits.

If someone had picked up Sari Chesney here, their tracks were long since blended with everything else.

I checked my phone again and saw the signal was strong. Mac pulled his phone from his pocket and dialed Sari's number. After a moment, he hung up, his face grim. "Voice mail."

The rest of the group removed their packs and took a few minutes to stretch weary muscles and sore limbs. They were dusty and dirty, and smelled of fatigue, worry, and sweat.

I gave them a moment, then checked my watch and said, "Ally, have you been to the police station before? Do you know where it is?"

Ally nodded, sweat trickling down her face. Her long dark

hair was a mess, and she struggled to wrestle it up into a ponytail. "I've never been, but I know how to get there. What do I do when I arrive?"

"I'll radio ahead and let them know to expect you. They'll give you some paperwork to fill out. Mac and I will be along shortly. We'll take a peek in Sari's apartment and see if she's there. We'll be, oh, ten or fifteen minutes behind you."

"Okay. I hope she's there."

"Me, too," I replied.

Mac handed his car key to Ally as they walked to his van. He helped load the camping gear, then he hugged Ally and said a few words to Jake. I couldn't hear what he said, but whatever it was caused Jake to flush and Ally to grimace. Then they were climbing in the van and Mac was jogging back to my Jeep.

I was in the car with the engine running by the time he joined me. As we pulled out of the parking lot, I called the department and asked them to get the initial paperwork ready for Ally. Then I got Sari's number from Mac and called her, too. After four rings, voice mail picked up and I left a message with my identification and a request for her to call me immediately.

Mac listened, uneasy, his hands in his lap.

When I was finished with the call, he said, "What do we do if Sari's not home?"

"We'll put a trace on her cell phone and credit cards. We'll also reach out to her family, her other friends, her employer. But I promise you, Mac, the chances are extremely good that she'll turn up quickly."

He nodded and looked out the window as we reached the outskirts of town. He was quiet a moment, then spoke. "Up here, if you cut across Seventh Avenue, you'll miss all the traffic lights on Main Street. Sari doesn't have much family. It's just her mom, Charla. She's sick. With Alzheimer's. She lives in one of those special care facilities. Carver Estates, I think it's called."

"I know the place. And I'm sorry to hear that; my grandmother, Julia, is living with dementia. It's an insidious condition."

"It's been hard on Sari. Thankfully, her mom has some money and good insurance. There's no way Sari could pay for the care Charla needs," Mac said. "Sari can barely afford her own life. She's got expensive taste. Here, turn right. Park up there, by that stop sign. Her apartment is the second door on the left, with the green welcome mat."

I'd barely turned off the Jeep before he was out of the car and barreling toward the front door. Catching up to him, I put a hand on his shoulder. He was a big guy, solid through the shoulders and upper body, and tall.

I struggled to hold him back. "Mac, wait a minute. I need to go in first. If something *has* happened to Sari . . . there might be evidence in the apartment. This could be a crime scene."

Reluctantly, Mac stopped. "Yeah, okay. Be careful. She's got a cat, Barnaby. He's been known to claw strangers."

He held up his keys and separated a bronze one from the rest of the silver keys. "This is the key. There's a bolt and a knob lock, but the one key works on both."

I nodded and used the key to open the door slowly. From somewhere deep inside the apartment we heard a pitiful meow. Mac pushed past me and then quickly shut the door behind us. He started to move further into the foyer, calling, "Babe? Are you here?"

Once more, I put a hand on his shoulder and held him back. I used more force this time, really gripping him. "What did I say? I need you to wait here a minute. Right here, in this exact spot. Let me do a quick walk-through of the apartment."

Mac stopped moving and nodded. "Sure, sorry." The flush in his face was a few shades lighter than his red hair, and I got the sense that he didn't appreciate being restrained.

I walked into a living room with a kitchen off to the right and a narrow hallway to the left. Moving quickly but thoroughly, I checked the rest of the apartment: a darkly painted bedroom with many posters and prints on the walls; a clean, bright bathroom; and a couple of closets.

I found the cat in the bathroom, sitting outside his litter box, looking up at me with big untrusting eyes. Keeping my distance, I peeked around the cat and into the box; aside from a single dropping, it was clean. I backed away and headed to the front of the apartment.

Mac was where I'd left him, anxiously chewing on a fingernail.

"Did Sari have a house sitter, someone to come by and feed the cat?"

"Yes. A neighbor, a teen that lives next door with her mom. This is not good. Sari loves that damn cat; he's her baby. She would never willingly abandon him."

First the gala, now the cat. Mac was right; this was not good.

I took another, longer look around the apartment. It was tidy; there was a single mug, orange and chipped, resting in a drying rack next to the sink. The counters were spotless. The floors were swept and the carpets recently cleaned; I could still see the indentations from the vacuum in the fibers. Even the pillows on the sofa looked recently plumped.

On the far wall of the living room, next to a locked sliding glass door that led to a small patio, I saw a collage of pictures. I studied them. The photos were taken at different times of day and night, in different locations, but they all had one thing in common: the two young women who took center stage and beamed at the camera like they hadn't a care in the world.

I recognized one of the women, and it threw me for a loop.

Mac noticed. He joined me and tapped the other girl. "That's Sari. Uncanny, isn't it?"

I stared at the photographs. Sari and Ally had identical builds—petite and thin—and the same long, thick, dark hair. Up close, of course, it was easy to see the differences: Sari Chesney was Caucasian, with bright green eyes, while Ally Chang was Asian, with dark brown eyes.

"They could be twins, couldn't they?"

Mac replied, "Yeah. It's weird sometimes."

Another series of photographs showed Sari surrounded by a group of young girls.

"And these girls? Who are they?"

Mac pointed at one of the pictures. "Sari mentors them. She's got about six or seven of them at any given time."

"She sounds like a wonderful person."

"She is. Man, I thought she'd be here," Mac continued. He spun around in a slow circle, looking at the floor as though there might be footprints or a clue. "She hasn't been home. This place . . . it smells sterile. Too clean. If Sari had been here, she would have cooked something or at least showered. She likes that smelly stuff, from the beauty shops. This whole apartment smells like vanilla after she showers."

From somewhere down the hall, the cat let out another pitiful cry. Mac called, "Barnaby! Hey, Barney!"

At the sound of his name, the cat crept toward us. He was beautiful, gray with huge golden eyes. As he twisted around my ankle, his cry became a purr. I reached down and patted him on his head. The cat continued to curl around my ankle, and my unease grew.

"You said Sari's mom lives in town, in a nursing home? Any other family?"

Mac shook his head. "She's an only child. Cancer took her dad a few years ago. Sari was bent out of shape for a while. She said she felt 'untethered.' She and her mom are very close, though."

I understood what she meant by untethered. A car accident in the dead of winter had taken my parents when I was a child and left me orphaned, scarred. Scared. It had taken years for the sense that I was suddenly spinning adrift in a world without gravity to abate.

"Are you okay?" Mac stared at me with concern. "You went pale all of a sudden."

I smiled. "I'm fine. Let's feed the cat, and then we'll head to the police station."

"I'm going to take Barnaby with me. Let me grab his things."

I watched as Mac grabbed a grocery sack from underneath Sari's sink and filled it with cat food, a couple of bowls, and a few toys that were tucked in the corner of the living room. Then he retrieved a cat carrier from the hall closet and scooped Barnaby into it. The last

possibility, however remote, of needing to identify a body that was otherwise unrecognizable.

"She's got a couple of tattoos. There's a star on the back of her neck and a four-leaf clover on her right ankle," Mac said. I jotted the information down on the back of the photograph.

"What now?" Ally asked.

"Now, we wait. Or rather, you wait and I work. I'll check out a few things, make a few calls. As I told you before, most people show up within a few hours of being reported missing. Try to remember, it's not a crime to be missing. Maybe Sari just needed to check out for a while."

"Check out of what?" Jake asked. He ate the last chip and crumpled the empty bag, looking genuinely curious.

I shrugged. "I don't know, life, I guess. Haven't you ever wanted to disappear for a few hours?"

Jake smirked. "Every damn day. But that's me."

"Yeah, and you aren't Sari. She's not like that," Mac said. He looked at me pointedly. "We told you, she's responsible. The gala tonight—this is supposed to be her big night."

"And those are the reasons we are taking this seriously."

There was nothing more for them to do at the station, so I began shepherding them out, toward the front door. "All I am saying is try to stay calm. I'll be at the gala tonight. Will I see any of you there?"

All three shook their heads. Mac said, "Sari comped me a ticket, but I gave it to my sister. I'm on call at the hospital."

Ally added, "I wouldn't be caught dead there. A bunch of stuffy, old rich people. Not my kind of crowd."

We left things with me swearing to call them the minute I heard anything, and them giving me the same promise. As I watched them leave the police station, though, something that had been troubling me all morning intensified, and I was finally able to pinpoint what it was.

One of them was lying.

Which one, and about what, I didn't know . . . but I was sure of it.

I looked at the picture of Sari Chesney, still in my hand. By all accounts she was a loving daughter, devoted girlfriend, dedicated employee. A mentor to underprivileged kids and an animal lover.

If there's one thing I've learned in my six years as a cop, it's that no one is that perfect in real life. Each of us has a side that is mean and nasty. I turned around and walked back into the police station, still staring at the photograph, deeply curious to learn what secrets were hidden behind Sari Chesney's wide smile.

At my desk, I started a file on Chesney and decided to start with the mother. It was as good a place to begin as any, especially as Mac had told me that Sari and her mother were close.

I found the number for Carver Estates and called, identifying myself and asking if Charla Chesney had received any visitors in the last few days. The woman who answered, Miss Rosa, asked me to hold while she checked their visitor logs. Twenty seconds later, she was back on the line.

"Detective? Are you still there? Sari came by on Thursday. She stayed an hour."

"But nothing since then? No visits today or yesterday?"

"No, ma'am. We keep good records here. Sari's been visiting her mother two or three times a week since Mrs. Chesney moved in a few years ago. I wouldn't expect to see Sari again now until Monday or Tuesday," Miss Rosa said. Her voice grew troubled. "Is there something wrong? Why are you asking these questions?"

I gave a deliberately vague answer and left my phone number with the woman, in case Chesney showed up. I briefly debated asking to speak to Charla Chesney herself but dismissed the idea; it was much too early to unnecessarily worry her. And if I did need to speak to her, I wanted to do it in person. I had no idea how advanced her condition was, but if she was anything like my grandmother Julia, in-person conversations tended to go better than phone calls.

My second call was to the Cedar Valley History Museum, where I left a message with Chesney's boss, Elizabeth Starbuck, explaining the situation and asking her to call me as soon as possible.

I tackled a few emails and some lingering paperwork from a case I'd wrapped up the previous week, then left for the day. I stopped at the dry cleaners on the way home and picked up my dress for the evening's gala. The gown was black satin, strapless and long, and when I wore it, I felt like a Hollywood actress in a spy movie.

In reality, though, the dress was probably a little too snug to wear six months after having a baby. I'd lost most of the pregnancy weight, but the pounds that remained had migrated from my belly to other locations; my hips were wider, my thighs fuller. I hated that I even cared about such things, but I was accustomed to a lean, athletic figure, not a soft, rounded one.

I carefully placed the dress in the trunk of my car and committed myself to an evening of maximal support wear and minimal intake of cocktails and appetizers. I was lucky to be going to the gala at all; the museum was small, so tickets were limited, and they'd sold out weeks ago. I was attending as the guest of my boss, Chief of Police Angel Chavez. He'd bought two extra tickets and raffled them off at work. I won one; my colleague and fellow detective Lucas Armstrong won the other.

As I drove through town, evidence of the week's coming celebratory events was everywhere. It should have felt festive, but a strange sense of doom coursed through me. I tried to shake it, deciding the unpredictable weather was getting to me. Springtime in the high Rockies is sun-soaked and glorious one minute, overcast and frigid the next.

The clouds that had moved in at Lost Lake loomed over the town now, and an immense shadow darkened the entire valley. The scarlet banners that hung from the streetlamps fluttered in the wind, like flags of an approaching army, and the white event tents that had sprung up in various parks seemed apocalyptic, like fallout shelters in the wake of a disaster.

I slowed as I drove by the museum. It was a large, rambling building, all turrets and gray river rocks and leaded windows. A handful of people were busy setting out bright orange cones, already preparing the empty lot and adjacent street for what was sure to be a headache of a parking situation.

I turned left from the main road and headed up the canyon

toward home, thinking about the morning's events, still trying to shake the sense of despair that had settled over me like the iron-gray clouds that towered over the valley.

At home, I found my daughter, Grace, and our nanny, Clementine Major, lounging in the backyard on a blanket, enjoying the last scraps of the fleeing sunbeams. Our basset hound, Seamus, lay beside them. I scooped Grace up and smothered her with kisses until she started shaking her head at me.

"It's going to rain," Clem said glumly. She was unusually quiet, and I wondered what was wrong.

"I think so. Brody's not home yet?"

Clem tucked a few loose strands of her pink-tinged blond hair back into a purple Colorado Rockies ball cap and rolled her eyes. "He texted about an hour ago and asked if I could stay. Something about a conference call running late. It's fine. It'll cost you, but it's fine. But seriously, it's the weekend. You *both* should be here at home *as a family.*"

"Thank you, my dear. Your wisdom, as always, is appreciated."

She smiled wanly and shrugged again.

I stood there, looking down at the lanky college sophomore with the cut-off jean shorts and the knit sweater that was two sizes too big for her slender frame. She barely looked old enough to be in college, let alone watching my daughter.

"Are you okay? You seem . . . distracted," I finally asked her.

Clem hesitated a moment, then shook her head. "I'm fine. Just some personal stuff. Boy drama."

"Anything I can do to help? I know it's hard to believe, since I'm practically elderly, but I do have experience in that department."

Blushing, Clem quickly looked down at the ground. "I'll handle it. Thanks. So, if you're home now, can I go? I have a nail appointment and then Tori and I are going to park outside the fire station and watch the guys clean the trucks."

Barely suppressing my own eye roll, I said, "Of course. We'll see you Monday. And thank you for staying. Grace adores you."

Clem stood up and to my surprise gave me a hug. "I like you. You are good people. You pay me on time and don't give me any grief about my hair. Plus, you're a cop. A freaking lady cop. You'd be my hero if I had heroes. Which I don't."

As she left, the rain started to come down, first in gentle drops, then in heavy sheets. I put Grace in her crib for a nap and then grabbed a snack. I'd missed lunch and the morning's hike had left me ravenous, though the crackers and hummus did little to satisfy. When Brody arrived home, he found me in the kitchen working my way through a bowl of chicken pasta salad, listening to the rain.

"Sorry I'm late, honey," he asked by way of greeting.

I nodded, my mouth full. He leaned in and kissed me on the cheek.

"This damn contractor in Tokyo got our conference call times mixed up and I had to wait around the office. You'd think with all the technology we have, these things would be easier."

I nodded again, my mouth once more full.

Brody was a geologist by training. After nearly twenty years working in the field, in places as remote as northern Alaska and Mongolia, he'd accepted a job at a local consulting firm that dealt in international mining contracts. While the money was nice, it was even better that he was home most of the time, working a normal eight-to-five job.

Ours was not an easy relationship; an early bout of infidelity on his part had left me with significant trust issues. Her name was Celeste Takashima, and she had an uncanny way of popping into my mind at the most inopportune times. But having him home, beside me in the bed at night, was helping. Of course, watching him with Grace helped, too. Brody was a wonderful father. I hoped that he would make as wonderful a husband; I'd finally accepted an engagement ring from him and we were scheduled to be married in the fall.

Married.

A year ago, the word left me with cold sweats. Now, I was starting to consider dresses, a guest list. Flowers and a cake.

Multiple cakes, if I had my way.

We talked about the things partners talk about: our day, our daughter, plans for a vacation in the summer. The conversation came easy, and when my cell phone rang, I reluctantly answered it. I immediately had to hold the phone away from my head to avoid bursting an ear drum.

"Ma'am? Ma'am! You need to stop yelling," I said in the direction of the phone, still holding it a foot from my face. "I can't understand a word you're saying."

Brody backed out of the kitchen, mouthing "good luck."

A few seconds later, the voice on the other end fell silent. I cautiously brought the phone back to my ear. "Who is this, please?"

"Betty Starbuck. I'm the Director at the Cedar Valley History Museum. You left a message for me earlier regarding my employee, Sari Chesney. I hope she's turned up, because I have a much more serious matter to discuss with you," the woman said. "There's a terrible situation at the museum."

I raised an eyebrow. "What's happened?"

"A rare artifact has been stolen. The Rayburn Diary. I discovered the theft just minutes ago."

I grabbed a notepad from the kitchen counter and began taking notes. "Rayburn . . . as in Owen Rayburn?"

"Yes. One and the same. Cedar Valley's very own founding father. Detective, that diary is absolutely priceless," Starbuck said. She took a deep breath and added, "It is—was—intended to be the showcase of tonight's gala."

"Where was the diary stolen from?"

Another deep breath, then: "Our safe. I threw a small party on Wednesday for the museum's board of directors and removed the diary at that time to briefly show it off. It was a sort of special preview event before the larger gala tonight. After the party ended, I personally returned the diary to the safe and locked it. Only three of us have the combination: myself and two employees, Larry Bornstein and Sari Chesney."

Sari Chesney.

"And Wednesday was the last time you saw it?"

"Yes. I've been out with a stomach bug since Thursday morning. Sari worked Thursday and then took a half day Friday. I expected to see her at noon today; there are some last-minute exhibition tasks to finish before the party tonight. Look, I'm not completely heartless; the fact that you've said Sari is missing is troubling. At least, it was troubling until I discovered the diary is also missing. Now I'm placed in the unfortunate position of hosting a ruined event and being unable to question my assistant curator as to whether or not she knows where the diary is."

"I understand. Look, I'd already planned to attend the gala. I'll come early and we can talk in person. If the diary hasn't turned up by then, I'll take a statement and file a report. We can also do a thorough onsite investigation, check for forensics, but that might mean canceling the event."

I had a feeling what her response to that particular suggestion might be.

"Absolutely not. Come early, by all means, but any kind of formal investigation will have to wait until after the gala. There are thousands of dollars at stake here, and potentially hundreds of thousands of dollars more from future donors who are interested in supporting the museum's mission. I'll see you in an hour," Starbuck said, and hung up.

Disturbed, I went upstairs to grab a quick shower and get dressed. When I'd left Lost Lake this morning, I had convinced myself that Sari Chesney would turn up within an hour or two. I'd started a missing persons file on her, because her disappearance *was* odd, but I'd assumed the case would be over before it started.

Now?

Now a rare artifact had been stolen from the museum's safe. Three people held the combination, and Sari was one of them.

Coincidence?

Not in my line of work.

I turned on the shower and let the water get hot, my thoughts running.

Starbuck had described the diary as priceless . . . in other words, very, very expensive. Money is a powerful motivator, and while the last thing I try to do is jump to conclusions, I couldn't help asking the two questions that went through my mind.

Where are you, Sari Chesney? And what have you done?

Chapter Four

Inside the Cedar Valley History Museum, catering staff in black-and-white uniforms were setting up small cocktail tables and longer serving buffets. After the cool chill of the storm outside, the museum felt warm and smelled of garlic and tomatoes. A posted menu told me the event was to be an Italian-themed evening. My stomach rumbled as a server walked past me, his antipasto tray heavy with glistening olives and a vast array of cheeses and meats.

An older man with a droopy mustache and a starched tan-and-black security uniform pointed out Betty Starbuck to me. She was a diminutive woman with short gray hair, in an emerald ballgown and a gold choker necklace from which hung an opal the size of a robin's egg. Hers was a timeless beauty and I had difficulty telling if she was sixty-five or eighty, though in the end I decided she was closer to eighty.

She was off to the side, near a set of musical instruments and a dance floor, scolding a young man in ripped jeans and a T-shirt. As I approached them, I caught enough of the argument to ascertain that he'd set the stage for the band too close to the dining area. The man's face was beet red. It seemed he'd had enough of her berating him, because as I reached them he gave her the middle finger and stormed off.

Starbuck shook a fist after him and then turned to me. She looked me up and down, and I knew what she saw: a thirty-year-old detective maneuvering uncomfortably in a too-tight black evening gown, long dark hair pulled up in a haphazard knot, an evidence kit clutched awkwardly in one hand and a bejeweled clutch in the other.

"You must be Gemma Monroe. Have you found Sari?"

"No, she hasn't turned up yet." I said, and then stuck out my hand. After a moment, Starbuck grasped and shook it. Her skin was cool and her grip strong.

"That's a beautiful opal."

Her hand went to her necklace and she colored slightly. "Thank you. I don't usually wear such extravagant jewelry, but it felt as though the occasion called for it. My great-great-grandfather purchased the stone in Australia for his wife. He mined the gold here, in the valley, himself."

"A local miner? You've got strong ties to this town, then."

"Well, yes." Starbuck looked at me with a funny expression on her face. "I'm sorry, I just assumed you knew . . . Owen Rayburn was my great-great-grandfather."

"I see. No wonder you're anxious to find his diary."

"Incredibly anxious, for a number of reasons. Come on, I'll show you the safe," Starbuck said.

As we walked, I took a moment to glance around and get my bearings, as it had been years since I'd been inside the museum. The first floor was one enormous open space, with curtains, tapestries, and rice-paper screens serving to distinguish various exhibit halls. Running down the middle of the room was a series of freestanding glass display cases, anchored on impressive granite blocks. Inside each one were the types of object you'd expect to see in a history museum in the West: arrowheads, gemstones, pioneer artifacts.

Starbuck stopped in front of one of the display cases and put her hand gently on the glass. An engraved plaque screwed into the block read simply "The Owen Rayburn Diary" while dim, recessed lights shone down into an empty black velvet–lined box. "This is where the diary should be. This is where it was Wednesday night, at the private preview event. Detective . . . you must understand that beyond being an absolutely horrible loss, the theft of the diary is an incredible embarrassment. We rely on other institutions to lend us their artifacts for exhibits. Not to mention the donors . . . they trust us. Without their support, we'll be finished by year's end."

"Because of one missing artifact?" I asked as we began to walk again. "I find that hard to believe."

"Clearly you haven't spent much time in the museum world, Detective. It's cutthroat. We all need money, and there's only so many donors. Unfortunately, this is the latest in a series of incidents to besiege us over the last few years. The Rayburn Diary is a once-in-a-lifetime artifact. It's priceless. I'll be seen as untrustworthy, sloppy to let such a valuable item disappear on my watch. It's absolutely devastating. Especially given my family connection."

"What makes the diary so special?"

"For one thing, it is quite literally a gold mine of information. Not only was Owen Rayburn one of the six Silver Foxes—the founding fathers of this town—he was also responsible for most of the mining operations. There are detailed maps, scientific recordings, business transactions . . . plus of course personal information, historically important details about Rayburn's life."

Starbuck knocked on, and then opened, a door marked "staff only." I followed her into a narrow, tidy office. A middle-aged man in a sweater vest and bow tie sat at the desk, pecking furiously at a keyboard with his two index fingers. A thin sheen of sweat glistened on his forehead. Aside from the computer and an unopened bottle of water, the only other item on the desk was an industrial-sized bottle of hand sanitizer and a box of tissues.

Startled, the man stood and smiled nervously at Starbuck. "Betty."

"Larry."

I waited a moment to see if Starbuck would introduce us. When she didn't, I extended a hand to the man. He recoiled from my outstretched palm, gave me a jumpy smile in return, and held up his own hands.

"You'll have to excuse me, I'm mysophobic. Germaphobic, if you will. I'm Dr. Lawrence Bornstein. Please, call me Larry. I'm the donor relations director for the museum. Rather, I *was*. What's my title now, Betty?"

Starbuck sighed and leaned back against the wall, her hands tucked behind her back. She looked at Larry, but her words were directed at me. "It's no secret we have experienced significant budget cuts over the last few years. Larry's position was deemed redundant as we had a lower-salaried donor relations development associate. When she resigned, Larry accepted her role."

"Ah, yes. Development associate. Well, if nothing else, it certainly makes me sound like a young person! I perform the same functions as I did before. I'm a bit of a whore, you see, going from donor to donor, begging for a pittance," Bornstein said.

He adjusted his red bow tie and smoothed down his hair, then dispensed a squirt of sanitizer into his hands and began to vigorously rub them together. The air took on a faint chemical smell. "I presume you're here about the theft? Naturally I'll be one of your top suspects."

I raised an eyebrow. "Oh? Why is that?"

"Well, because the safe is here, in my office. And I'm one of the three people who know the code. Ergo, suspect numero uno," Bornstein said smugly, and sat back down. He pointed to the far wall, where a framed oil painting of a field of sunflowers hung. "It's behind that painting."

I went to the wall and pulled on a pair of gloves. Carefully, I swung the painting away from the wall and peered at the safe. There were a number of visible fingerprints along the surface and on the combination dial. There were likely latent prints there, too, which I wouldn't be able to see without an alternate light source.

"I'll call one of our crime scene techs to come and dust this. He can do that much without intruding on the party. In the meantime, don't let anyone else touch it. Is there anything in the safe that you'll need in the next few hours?"

Both Starbuck and Bornstein shook their heads.

"Well, other than fingerprinting the safe, there's not much more I can do without an exhaustive investigation. And as you've already made clear, that would be unacceptable during the gala. What kind of security do you have in place, for the building and the collections?"

Starbuck said, "We have a robust alarm system. It's set each evening, when we close at five, and the first staff member in to work the next morning disables it. But, obviously . . . well, we're a public facility, Detective. We have people coming and going throughout the day. We don't charge admission, so unfortunately, lately, we've seen an increase in some . . . unsavory types. Drunks, the homeless. I feel sorry for them, but we're not equipped to be a social services center. I assume you met our security guard downstairs? He's contracted—part-time, and special events. I wouldn't count on him to chase down anyone, not at his age, but the uniform does seem to deter some inappropriate behaviors."

"White mustache? Yes, I met him. How about this office? Who has access?"

"All of the staff and of course the janitorial service," Starbuck said. "We each have a master key, so that we're able to get into the storage rooms and various other spaces."

Bornstein added, "But there's only four of us. Excuse me, three of us. Three employees. Our fearless leader, Betty; the ingénue, Sari Chesney; and myself, the history nerd. Betty, doesn't Lois have a master key, too?"

"That's right," Starbuck said and nodded thoughtfully. "Thank you, Larry. I'd forgotten about that. Lois Freeman is the president of our board of directors and she, too, has a key."

I turned to Bornstein. "You said four employees, then corrected yourself. Is the fourth person the one who recently resigned?"

He nodded. "Yes. Ruby Cellars. She left to spend more time with her kids. Her husband died a year ago, and she's all they've got."

"You don't change the combination to the safe when an employee leaves?"

Starbuck tilted her head and gave me a small shrug. "We've had the same combination for the last ten years. To be honest, we've never kept many things in the safe. For the longest time, it was used to store duplicate copies of our insurance policies, deeds to the land, that sort of thing."

"How do you possibly run an entire museum with such a small staff?"

Starbuck smiled, toying with her necklace. "We're fortunate to have a wonderful corps of volunteers."

"I see." I turned to Bornstein. "What do you think happened to the diary?"

Bornstein seemed surprised to be asked, taking a moment to smooth down the front of his sweater vest before answering. As he spoke, he took another hit from the hand sanitizer bottle.

"Well, quite obviously it's been stolen. It would be easy work for a safecracker. Either that, or Sari's finally gone and done it."

"Done what?"

"Taken us for all we're worth. You've heard the expression 'champagne tastes on a beer budget'? That's Sari in a nutshell. I wouldn't be surprised if she robbed a bank someday." Bornstein smiled faintly at the thought. "Though she is a very foolish girl if she has stolen it. She won't be able to sell it, not to anyone in legitimate business. She, or whoever stole it, will have to sell it on the black market."

"Is there a black market for such a thing?"

Bornstein tipped his head. "Come now, you're not that naïve. These days, there's a black market for everything." He grew glum. "If we don't get that diary back soon, I guarantee you two things will happen."

"What are they?" I asked.

"First, the board of directors will shut us down. They've been threatening it for years, and this will be the final straw. In fact, Lois Freeman informed us at the last meeting that there is a buyer who is very interested in the property," Bornstein said.

"And the second?"

He stared at me, then smiled grimly. "Someone will die."

Chapter Five

Starbuck practically sneered. "He's talking about the curse, of course."

This just got better and better. "Curse?"

Larry Bornstein nodded. "The curse of the Rayburn Diary. Every person who has ever had it in their possession has died a terrible death. That's partly why it's been locked away in the museum's archives for the last hundred years, save for the past few months when James Curry—our preservationist and book restorer—had it in his shop."

I decided to play along. "Did Curry die?"

Starbuck winked at me. "Excellent question, Detective. Well, Larry? Did James choke on a chicken wing? Or drown in his bathtub?"

Bornstein glowered. "Betty, you know perfectly well that James Curry is alive. That's because he was merely *borrowing* the diary, to ensure it was ready for permanent exhibition here at the museum. The museum retained ownership."

"That's right. You have to *own* the diary for it to kill you," Betty said. She checked her watch, then gestured for me to follow her. Once we were outside Bornstein's office, she said, "My father told me about the curse, and his father told him before that, and all the way back to Owen Rayburn's hag of a second wife, who told anyone in town that would listen to her that it was his diary that was somehow responsible for him catching his leg in an animal trap up in the mountains. He bled to death before he was found. That's bad luck, not a curse.

Of course, it didn't help that one of their daughters drowned a few years later."

"How awful," I murmured.

"Yes. Look, my guests will begin arriving shortly. You can direct your fingerprint person to this office. If I know Larry, he'll be hiding in there for a few hours. He's convinced every other person has the bubonic plague. In the meantime, please, enjoy the exhibits and the appetizers. I need to check in with my volunteers and see if they've found anything suitable to fill the display case where the diary should have been."

I made a few phone calls and, fifteen minutes later, a crime scene tech arrived. He gathered a number of fingerprints from the safe, then left. I kept myself busy in the general vicinity of the food tables, stalking a server arranging breaded mushrooms on a silver platter and chatting up a couple of shopkeepers who were moonlighting as bartenders. They were good for local news and gossip, and by the time the party started, I'd had a glass of wine, seven stuffed mushrooms, three shrimp croquettes, and a chocolate-covered strawberry.

Then I saw the Italian buffet laid out for the main course and immediately tried to figure out where the hell I was going to put Caesar salad, lasagna, garlic bread, and tiramisu.

In spite of the missing diary, the gala seemed to be a success. Betty Starbuck found a flag in the basement that had been carried during the Civil War by a regiment of Colorado volunteers. She draped it in the display case intended for the Rayburn Diary, and while I didn't know much about curating an exhibit, I thought it looked pretty damn good.

After the guests had ample time to arm themselves with a drink or two, Starbuck took to the stage and gave a warm welcome. She explained that the night's real surprise was still under restoration and would be displayed in a short time. There was grumbling in the crowd, and I overheard a few guests mention the words *theft* and *diary*. It was clear that news had spread, though most guests didn't seem as bothered by it as Starbuck had anticipated.

Chief of Police Angel Chavez was among the first of the guests to arrive. I joined him and Detective Lucas Armstrong at an otherwise empty cocktail table and took a few minutes to fill them in on the missing diary. Halfway through my story, Armstrong mumbled something about needing a few hours off from shop talk and drifted away in the direction of the band.

Chavez was relieved that I had, in his words, "handled Betty Starbuck."

"That woman is a real piece of work," the chief grumbled around a mouthful of bruschetta. "We served on the school board together a few years back, and man, if she didn't drive me crazy. We called her Betty the Bulldozer. This is a woman who'll run you over and then sue you for staining her driveway." Chavez lifted his chin. "It looks like she's keeping some interesting company tonight."

I turned around to see Starbuck and Larry Bornstein engaged in a heated conversation with a man I recognized, Alistair Campbell, and a second man I didn't know. Campbell had been in Cedar Valley for nearly six months now. He was an extremely wealthy contractor with a company, Black Hound Construction, that employed mostly ex-convicts. Though I didn't know Campbell well, I didn't like or trust him. Call it a cop's instinct or just plain sixth sense; though I'd never prove it, I was sure Campbell had blood on his hands somewhere in his past.

The four of them—Starbuck, Bornstein, Campbell, and the fourth man—stood off to the side and spoke in hushed tones, but anyone watching them could see by the look on Campbell's face that he was furious. The man next to him—short, about fifty years old, with a scraggly goatee and a pair of rimless tinted eyeglasses perched on a pug nose—raised a finger to Starbuck's face and shook it vigorously, then stormed off and ducked into the men's room. Campbell, too, moved away from Bornstein and Starbuck and joined the crowd mingling around the various display cases.

"The guy with the adolescent beard, who was that?" I asked Chavez.

"James Curry. He owns the used bookstore on Main Street, but most of his business comes from very wealthy, very private international clients. Curry is a world-renowned expert in book restoration and preservation. He moved to town nine, ten years ago."

"Got it. He restored the Rayburn Diary."

"Oh?" Chavez took a sip from his cocktail glass and shuddered. "That's disgusting. What the hell is a paloma? I thought I was getting a gin drink."

"Grapefruit and tequila," I answered.

Chavez gagged. "I hate grapefruit. Be an orange or a lemon, not both. Anyway, you should check out Curry's shop sometime. It's . . . interesting." Chavez wiped his mouth, then discreetly glanced at his cell phone. His dark eyes grew serious. "I checked the logs. What's the story with your call out to Lost Lake this morning?"

"A young woman by the name of Sari Chesney disappeared late last night or early this morning. She was there with a group of friends. She's an adult and there's no sign of foul play but she's not answering her phone and her friends are worried. This is out of character for her. I opened a file and it's a good thing I did, as Chesney works here. At the museum."

The chief raised an eyebrow. "Perhaps you should look at Ms. Chesney in light of the stolen Rayburn Diary."

I nodded. "Absolutely. She's one of the three employees who hold the combination to the safe."

"Lost Lake, huh?" Chavez looked troubled. "There was a group of women who drowned up there, back in the late eighteen hundreds. I think there were five or six of them. Young women, eighteen, nineteen years old."

"How awful. I've never heard this before."

Chavez waved a hand. "It's ancient history. The girls grew up together, here in town. They experienced some kind of mass hysterical illness—sort of like what they think happened in Salem—and the girls made a suicide pact. Over the course of an October, one by one, they hiked to the lake and threw themselves in. At first, everyone thought they'd left town on one of the cross-country trains that passed through in Avondale. The lake froze over, see. No one saw them . . . until the following summer, when the water thawed and some poor fishermen found them. The Lost Girls, they were called. You know, come to think of it, I'm sure one of them was Owen Rayburn's daughter. Isn't that a coincidence? Anyway, the Lost Girls were said to haunt the lake. I think those stories have all died out, though, as people have forgotten about them."

"How awful for the families." I shivered. I don't believe in ghosts, but I couldn't help remembering the sad, haunted feeling I'd experienced at the lake that very morning; the sense that there was some presence, some *being,* inhabiting the woods and the water.

"Tragic." Chavez motioned for a server.

"How do you know all this?"

Chavez shrugged. "After I moved here—and especially after joining the force—I took an interest in local history. I thought I should be prepared. You know what they say, history repeats itself. Look, is there any chance Chesney may have gone in the water?"

"If she did, it's unlikely it was of her own volition. Her friends told me that she nearly drowned in an accident when she was a child. She's apparently been terrified of water ever since. Chief, everything seems to indicate Sari Chesney left the campsite on her own accord. There was absolutely nothing at the lake to indicate anything untoward happened. But when you factor in the theft of the diary . . ."

Chavez nodded. "The mayor would be furious if we sent a dive team up there without probable cause. Between the leak and the fact that we're over budget for the sixth year in a row . . . well, let's just say Mayor Cabot is keeping a close eye on our department."

The leak . . . Over the last few months, confidential information on cases, suspects, even victims had appeared in the local newspaper. Chavez suspected it was coming from inside the police force but had been unable to prove anything yet. Files had been locked down and internal security measures tightened, but the leaks continued. The longer they continued, the lower morale dropped. Mistrust and suspicion were slowly replacing the easy camaraderie and mutual support that had once been the strength of our work force, and it was only a matter of time before an investigation became seriously compromised.

By eleven p.m., my feet were hurting and I needed an antacid. The food was long gone, and many of the guests had moved the party to the bars on South Street. Even the event photographer, a man who had been bustling in and out of the crowd all night, looked weary. I needed a final word with Betty Starbuck or Larry Bornstein, to go over the next steps in the Rayburn Diary investigation, but neither of them was anywhere to be found. I assumed they were with guests and took my leave.

An hour later, I sighed with relief as I finally crawled into bed. Sleep should have come easily, but Brody lay on his back, snoring and making noises that would wake the dead. Seamus had abandoned his own bed for the foot of ours, and his heavy, squat body took up more room than it should have.

I tossed and turned in an attempt to claim a corner of my own.

After what felt like mere seconds of sleep, the home phone was ringing and weak sunlight was seeping through the sheer bedroom curtains. Brody got to the phone first. After a moment he gently nudged my shoulder. "It's for you."

It was Sunday morning, and the clock on my bedside table said 6:40. This couldn't be good.

It was Chloe Parker, our longtime dispatcher, and she sounded panicked. "Gemma? I couldn't reach you on your cell phone. You're up on the roster. There's been a murder."

"Oh no." I was already out of bed and moving toward the closet. "Where?"

"The museum. Chief Chavez is already there. And the techs are on their way," Chloe said.

The museum?

I heard another line ringing at the station, and I knew she'd be off the phone in a flash to answer it. Dispatch typically ran shifts in pairs and, in my experience, calls always seemed to come in when one dispatcher was on break, leaving the other alone to manage the lines. It wasn't ideal, but small-town police departments rarely have the luxury of a large staff.

I remembered Larry Bornstein's words from the previous night, when he spoke of the Rayburn Diary curse: *Someone will die.*

"Chloe—who's the victim?"

But I was already talking to a dead line.

Chapter Six

As I drove down the canyon and into town, I watched the sun slowly climb up a cornflower blue sky. Traffic was light, and I made good time. As I passed a local church, I slowed to read the message on their billboard. It asked "Going the wrong way?" and while it seemed as though there should have been more to the message, that was it.

I was left with a hollow sense that maybe no one knew the answer to the question.

I grabbed a quick breakfast from a gas station and ate it as I drove, immediately wishing I'd ordered a larger coffee. I was running on little sleep. It was ironic that prior to the last few nights, I had been sleeping more heavily than I had in years. Deep, dreamless sleep had been the not-entirely-terrible result of working full time and caring for an infant who blessedly slept through the night from an early age.

In the parking lot, a reporter I recognized sat in a news van. Bryce Ventura wrote for the *Valley Voice* and was no doubt waiting for an official statement from our department.

I wondered if he had heard chatter on the police scanner or if this killing, like so much of our police business, had already been leaked to the press.

The officer lifted the lines of yellow tape that were strung up across the front door like nightmarish tinsel. I ducked beneath them, careful not to touch anything. The corridor was quiet, and I saw little evidence of the previous night's festivities. The space had already been cleaned; the floor was mopped and the trash and recycling cans, which had been overflowing, were now empty. The lights were dim, and my footsteps echoed on the tile floors. Clear of the crowds and food and beverage stations, the museum felt larger, more cavernous, with too many shadowy alcoves and dim corners.

Uneasy, I hurried up the stairs toward the sound of voices.

Chief Chavez, three crime scene technicians, and another uniformed officer stood at the top of the stairs, near an open door, staring into the room beyond with pale, glum faces. I slowed my steps, noting the stockinged feet that stuck out of the doorway, the black high-heeled shoes that lay askew a few inches from them.

Oh, no.

I tried to prepare myself for what lay in the room, for what suffering the woman who wore the black heels had experienced. Staring death in the face, especially violent death, is like a punch in the gut: visceral, breathtaking, severe. I've spent time with cops who have forty years on the force, and with cops who have four months, and the one thing that everyone agrees upon is this: you can't ever forget the dead.

I reached the group, and Chavez stepped aside to let me take in the scene.

I felt the gas station coffee and stale doughnut roll in my stomach. Chavez looked down at the body, his face dark with emotion. "What are your first impressions?"

I crouched down and took a few minutes to do a cursory but thorough study of the scene. Betty Starbuck lay in the doorway of her office. Her gown was ripped and tattered at the hem and sleeves, suggesting a violent struggle. The mess inside the small room further supported this: drawers and cabinets thrown open, papers in shreds, a shattered lamp and overturned chair. In the middle of the floor was a paper bag from the Burger Shack, a cheeseburger and fries soaked with ketchup spilling from it. The ketchup had congealed into a thick, sweet-smelling paste.

In her right hand, Starbuck gripped her necklace, the gold choker with the enormous opal gemstone. The chain was snapped, as though she'd ripped the necklace from her neck, and in the dim light the bright center stone twinkled like a portal to a strange and milky universe.

Her neck . . .

Her neck was a mess of bruises. Blood from the gaping wound on her left temple covered the side of her head. Near the body, stained with what was clearly bodily matter, was a broken ceramic paper-weight.

I stood up slowly, deeply disturbed. "I don't get it."

"Go on," Chavez prodded.

"The room looks ransacked, which suggests that someone was looking for something . . . but what? The museum safe is downstairs, and the most valuable item the museum owns, the Rayburn Diary, is already missing. That necklace in Starbuck's hand? It's got to be worth at least a few thousand dollars. If this was a robbery, why damage and then leave the necklace? Look at her neck, the bruising, the beating. . . . It's a very personal way to kill someone. But if this was an attack for personal reasons, why ransack the room?" I asked. "There's a lot that doesn't add up."

"Those were my thoughts as well." Chavez nodded. "The poor woman. No one deserves this kind of brutality."

I took another look at Starbuck's face. Mercifully, her eyes were closed. Though I'd only met her once, she'd struck me as an intelligent, dedicated woman, and I was sorry to see her become the victim of such terrible violence.

The last time I'd seen her alive, she'd been arguing with three men: the contractor, Alistair Campbell; her employee, Dr. Larry Bornstein; and the rare books dealer, James Curry.

Had their argument turned deadly?

I stepped out of the room and stood in the hallway with Chavez. "Have any of the staff been informed? Dr. Bornstein, or the board?"

"No," the Chief said. "We'll do family first. Betty had two sons. Kent Starbuck is the older. He's been in and out of trouble for years. Last I heard, he was living in North Carolina. After Betty's husband died, she was in a long-term relationship with a man from Avondale until he, too, passed away many years ago. Patrick Crabbe, her younger son, is the result of that relationship. You know him. He owns the Gas 'n' Go station on Seventh and Canyon. Hell of a nice guy."

It was a disturbing coincidence that it was the same gas station I'd stopped at just thirty minutes before. I knew the place well; set back off the road, skirting the woods, it was routinely the target of vandalism. Over the years, Patrick Crabbe had called our department a number of times. Sometimes the vandalism was juvenile slurs scrawled across the bathroom mirrors; other times, it was more destructive—broken windows, smashed lights.

Crabbe, a slim blond man with a meek demeanor and a tendency to avoid eye contact, was always apologetic when he called us, as though the actions of a few punks were somehow his fault.

"I'll inform him when we're done here." It wasn't something I was looking forward to.

Chavez nodded. "Good. Get an alibi for him, too."

"*Patrick?*" I gave the chief a look. "The man would keel over if you sneezed in his direction. You don't honestly think . . ."

"You said it yourself. This killing was personal. Odds are that Betty Starbuck knew her killer, perhaps even intimately. Who's more intimate than family?"

I started to answer, then noticed a young man sitting on the floor behind a pushcart of cleaning supplies at the end of the hallway. He was nineteen or twenty and wore jeans and a light sweatshirt. He sat with his back against the wall, his head in his hands. What looked like dried vomit bloomed across the front of the sweatshirt, and near his feet was a large puddle of brownish fluid.

I turned to Chavez. "Who's that and what's with the spill?"

"The spill with the lovely pine aroma is cleaning fluid. The young man is Jerry Flowers, the janitor. He found the body. Poor kid; it's only his second week on the job."

Flowers glanced up at the sound of his name and stared at us with an intense and slightly nauseated look on his face.

Chavez lowered his voice, turned away from Flowers. "Make sure his story checks out. He called it in, but who knows, maybe he arrived and saw Starbuck working late, thought she was an easy target."

"I'll interview him. Calling in, that doesn't mean much. We've seen it before, perps do the deed then call nine-one-one. They think it's a diversion, that it throws suspicion off them."

"A play like that, coming from a teenager? It's enough to give me chills. Keep me updated, Gemma. I'm going back to the office to prepare a press release. Betty was well known in town. People are going to be asking a lot of questions, seeking reassurance. I want you to dedicate all your resources to this case. Offload your other work to one of your colleagues if you need to," Chavez said. He checked his watch. "And bring Finn in on this as soon as he lands. I think his flight arrives around two. I've sent him a message to come into work this afternoon."

I was already looking forward to getting Finn up to speed. He was a solid investigator, albeit one with a few personality defects: he was chauvinistic and brash and ready to bend the law if it meant nabbing criminals.

"I'll keep you informed, Chief." He nodded and turned away. I watched Chavez walk down the stairs, his shoes treading softly on the tiles, his head lowered. He had the kind of presence that took up psychic space—in a positive way—and his departure from the crime scene was jarring; the museum suddenly seemed both cavernous and claustrophobic. I looked around, taking in the minor details that made up the space: the high ceilings, the polished stair railing, the scratches on the floor from so many shoes moving to and fro.

It had been a quiet spring; until yesterday, when I'd received the call out to Lost Lake, my plate had been relatively empty. Suddenly, I had three active investigations: the stolen Rayburn Diary, the missing Sari Chesney, and the murdered Betty Starbuck.

I glanced around the space again. There was an edgy, unsettled feeling to the building, similar to what I'd experienced at Lost Lake.

Yesterday, it was simply a museum.

But now?

Now it was where a woman had taken her last breath.

Where a killer had taken a life.

Chapter Seven

I sat with Jerry Flowers in a small conference room next to Starbuck's office while he gave me a formal statement. Every time he shifted in his seat, a fetid wave of vomit and sweat rolled across the table and hit me in the face.

"I puked when I saw the body. Then I called the police," Flowers said. He wiped his hands repeatedly on his jeans then finally stuck them in the front pocket of his sweatshirt. He sucked on the insides of his cheeks, breathing hard through his nose, staring at the table, the walls, the ceiling, everywhere but at me. It was obvious I made him nervous, and I leaned back in my seat, tried to adopt as casual a pose as I could under the circumstances.

"You did the right thing, Jerry. Did you touch the body? Check for a pulse, see if she was still breathing?"

"No way," Flowers said. He shook his head emphatically. "I could see she was dead just by looking at her."

I nodded. "I'm sorry you had to be the one to find her. I understand this is your second week on the job. Had you seen Mrs. Starbuck here before, that early in the morning?"

Flowers shook his head. "No, I've never seen that woman before in my life."

I was surprised. "She didn't hire you?"

"No. I work for my dad's cleaning business. He's contracted out by the city. They hired us."

"I see. Jerry, can you please walk me through your routine here? Help me understand what a typical morning looks like for you."

"Yeah, sure. Um, I usually arrive about five a.m. This is the first building on my rotation of places to clean. They gave me the alarm code, so I let myself in through the back door, mop the floors, do the bathrooms, and empty the trash. It's easy work; the museum never gets too messy, and I can listen to my music. I got here early today, because I knew there'd be a lot of trash and extra cleanup from the party last night. I did the first floor, then went upstairs. And that was when I saw her."

"Was the alarm set when you arrived?"

Flowers nodded emphatically. "Yes, definitely. I wouldn't have entered the building if the alarm wasn't activated. It's protocol, and anyway I'm not stupid. I've seen way too many horror movies to make that mistake."

"Have you ever seen *anyone* else here? I mean, coming in that early. . . . Are you typically the only person here or are there others?"

"Sure. That old guy who wears the bow tie and the sweaters. Larry B. He's always here, hanging out in his office downstairs. He's not working, though. I think he comes in early to start his day nice and relaxed; he's usually got the newspaper and a cup of coffee," Flowers said. He leaned forward and hugged himself. Another burst of the sour smell traveled my direction. "We sometimes chat for a few minutes. He likes to talk sports. Listen, can I get out of here soon? I don't feel so good."

"Yes. Let me get your contact information in case there's anything else I need from you."

He gave me his phone number and address, and I jotted them down in my notebook. A lot of cops took notes on their phones or tablets nowadays, but I liked the feel of the small notebook, the stubby pencil. They somehow felt more solid, more real, than the high-tech stuff.

As Flowers turned to walk out of the conference room, I stopped him with one more question. "Jerry, when you arrived, did anything seem . . . strange? Different somehow, other than the murder, I mean?"

The young man thought a moment, then nodded. "Yeah. There

was a beer bottle on the stairs. I almost tripped over it. I've never seen a beer bottle in a museum before. It was a Corona. Half-full. No lime, though."

"What did you do with the bottle?"

"I tossed it in the recycling," Flowers said. "Downstairs, out back. There are big trash and recycling containers. I always empty my bags from the first floor before I come up to the second floor."

I made a note to check the recycling. Alcohol had been served at the gala the night before, but I hadn't noticed if the beer was served by the bottle or poured. There was a set of restrooms near the stairs; the Corona may have simply been placed on the step by a guest who didn't want to take it into the facilities, and then had forgotten to retrieve it.

After speaking with Flowers, I spent the next two and a half hours examining the crime scene and watching the technicians as they photographed the body and room and flagged dozens of spots for evidence. The medical examiner's team showed up early on. I was disappointed that Cedar Valley's usual ME, Dr. Ravi Hussen, was temporarily out of the country on extended leave to visit family in Morocco. I enjoyed Ravi's company and her quick wit, not to mention her insightful and thoughtful manner. Taking Ravi's place was a quiet black man who introduced himself as Dr. Samuel Bonaire, from the Denver ME's office. He was on loan to us for the month that Ravi was away.

Bonaire spent several minutes walking around the body. He worked quickly, moving with the quiet confidence of someone who knows he does his job well. After some time, he knelt next to Starbuck's head and gently touched her neck and skull with his gloved hands.

I crouched beside him. "Find anything?"

Bonaire looked at me. His eyes were an intense shade of green, and he spoke with a warm Caribbean accent. "We'll do an autopsy, of course, but this poor woman died of asphyxiation."

"Not the head injury?"

"Doubtful. The injury appears brutal but was a cursory blow. The vascular nature of the area has led to the severity of the bleeding, not the wound itself. No, I'm fairly confident we'll find her hyoid bone fractured. She was struck, then manually strangled. Tragic."

He stood and went over to one of the techs and asked them a few questions. I took the opportunity to use the restroom and splash water on my face. Before returning to the crime scene, I stared in the mirror and gave myself a pep talk.

The last murder I'd investigated had been just a few months prior. While confronting a suspect, I'd been attacked and nearly killed. I was far from gun-shy, but another killing in our small town, so soon after the last one, was jarring.

Grabbing a handful of paper towels from the dispenser, I dried my hands and face and whispered a mantra to myself that I'd started saying every morning, when I woke.

One step at a time, Gemma. Take it one step at a time.

Bonaire was waiting for me back in Starbuck's office. "Based on the body and room temps, the victim died about one, maybe two o'clock this morning," he said.

"That puts her murder soon after the gala ended," I replied. "There was a security guard working last night. I wonder if he cleared the museum?"

Bonaire shrugged and turned back to the body. I jotted down a few thoughts to follow up on:

Killer at gala and hid? Or entered later?

Did security sweep the building after the last guest left?

Fast food—Starbuck left and came back. Why?

Bonaire came back to my side. "We're ready to move the body when you are."

"As long as the techs have what they need, that's fine. I assume you'll be doing the autopsy today? I'll sit in."

Bonaire nodded. "Yes, I can do a preliminary examination this afternoon. Toxicology and final reports won't be ready for some time, of course, but I'm fairly confident we can get you an official cause of death."

"Excellent. I'll come by the medical examiner's office after I notify the next of kin."

"That's fine," Bonaire said. "Try to have someone come in for the formal identification, if they are willing. If they're not, I'll request medical and dental records and we can go that route. Then we can move on to the autopsy."

I wrapped things up with the techs, then walked to the back of the building. I noted the alarm system—currently disabled—then I opened and examined the back door. The lock was intact. At the bottom of the door, on the interior side, were rubber marks from a nearby stopper, indicating the door had routinely been propped open.

While I'd been inside, another spring shower had moved into the valley, and I walked out into a gently falling rain. I found the large recycling bin next to the dumpsters. Inside it were wine bottles, beer bottles, aluminum cans, and various scraps of paper. I counted at least fifteen Corona beer bottles, making it difficult to know exactly which bottle was the one Jerry Flowers had picked up from the stairs of the museum.

I went back inside and closed the door, then made my way through the museum and out the front door. The same officer who'd let me in sent me off with a tip of his hat. The rain came down harder now, and I hurried to my car and turned the heater on. Then I watched through the mist as the crime scene technicians, followed by Dr. Bonaire, emerged from the museum with Betty Starbuck's black-plastic-shrouded body between them, her form reduced to a small, shapeless mound laid out on a white canvas gurney. They loaded her in the back of an ambulance and then drove off, and all that was left was the same lone uniformed officer, standing out of the rain under an eave, strips of yellow crime scene tape billowing in the wind.

Chapter Eight

Betty Starbuck and her son Patrick Crabbe shared a property in the middle of town, on a quiet residential road three blocks off Front Street. Crabbe lived in an apartment above the garage, while his mother lived in the main house, a small cream-colored Victorian with curlicue arches and square edges. The front yard was tidy, nicely landscaped with native plants and flagstone pavers. An old black tire hung from a thick-limbed tree, swaying gently in the breeze.

It was noon now, and the rain had stopped falling. The air, still heavy with moisture, smelled of clean earth and wet grass.

I parked, then climbed a narrow set of stairs to the apartment and knocked on the front door. Crabbe opened it and sighed in exasperation.

"Oh, don't tell me. Is it more graffiti? It must be very bad for you to visit me at home. I'm so sorry you had to come on a Sunday," Crabbe said. He looked at me, then away, then back again. A hand scratched at his throat then dropped back to his side.

There was never an easy way to say what needed to be said.

"It's not the gas station, Patrick. I'm here about your mother."

I didn't have to finish the rest of the statement. Crabbe could see on my face, hear in my voice, that it was bad news, the worst kind. I watched as first shock then horror flashed in his eyes. He gasped and slumped against the door frame. "Oh dear god. What happened?"

I leaned forward and grabbed his elbow. "Let me help you."

We stepped inside, and I saw with a quick look a kitchen, bathroom, and living room set off a main, narrow hallway. At the end of it was a closed door, likely Crabbe's bedroom.

I led him to a frayed leather couch in the living room then glanced around, surprised. I would never have taken Crabbe for a hoarder. Dozens of newspapers and magazines were stacked in neat towers on nearly every surface. On the shelves surrounding a flat-screen television were hundreds of video cassettes and DVDs. Unopened plastic water bottles were scattered around the room, and I had to move an empty pizza box off the couch before I could sit down.

The room was warm and dusty, and I shrugged out of my jacket.

I unearthed a box of tissues under a stack of months-old television guides on the coffee table and waited until Crabbe was seated before handing him the box. He cried for a few minutes, and I sat next to him, patting him on his shoulder, murmuring condolences.

Finally, he took a jagged breath. "Was it a car accident? I've been telling Mom for weeks that she needs new brakes."

"No, it wasn't a car accident. We're still investigating, but it appears she was . . . attacked. It happened very early this morning, at the museum."

Crabbe flinched. The box of tissues slid from his hands to the ground, landing on the empty pizza box with a dull thud. "Mom was murdered?"

"We should know more details by this evening, but yes, it appears that way," I said gently. "Patrick, is there someone I can call to come be with you? A friend or neighbor? You shouldn't be alone during this time."

"My brother, Kent, needs to be informed. But I can do that myself. He and Mom, they were . . . estranged. Kent is a . . . well, he's difficult. He and Mom didn't speak for years; but he recently moved back to town and they've gotten together a few times. They had both expressed hope that they could make amends," Crabbe said, and he started crying again. "Oh, this is awful. Now they'll never have the opportunity."

"Where does Kent live?"

"He rents a room at that motel downtown, the one with the

extended stay suites," Crabbe replied through tears. "You can't miss him; he looks like me, only older and with a mustache. If he's not in his room, he'll be at one of the nearby coffee shops or up the river, fishing."

"Kent doesn't work?"

"No. He was struck by a drunk driver about six years ago and lives off the settlement. Though it's my understanding that he's slowly running out of funds."

Crabbe stood up and went to a bookcase full of black-and-white photographs, navigating around the dozens of piles of stuff in his way with ease. From where I sat, I could see the details in only one of the pictures: two boys, one younger, one older, arms around each other's shoulders, each wearing a jersey with a large bird blazing across the front.

"Is that you and Kent?"

"Hmm? Oh, yes. Before he . . . before the trouble started. We're five years apart. We both played baseball in school. That was about the only thing we ever had in common. Kent was an incredible player. He could have gone pro, I think, if he hadn't discovered drugs his senior year of high school. He was called 'Slugger' and I was . . . well, I was just Patrick." Crabbe added weakly, "Go Eagles."

I picked up a magazine and fanned myself with it. The heat continued to pour into the room. Crabbe removed a framed photograph off the top shelf. He showed it to me. It was a portrait of Betty Starbuck as a young woman. Then he hugged the picture to his chest. "Oh, Mom. It was your generosity that got you killed, wasn't it?"

It was a strange statement for him to make.

"Patrick? What are you talking about?"

Crabbe set the photograph down and glanced over at me, his shoulders sagging. "Mom had a serious problem. She was constantly giving money away. She would write a check to practically any charity that asked for a donation. Mom couldn't say no. She didn't have the funds to sustain it, though. And over the years, a lot of people in town wised up to the fact that she was so, ah, generous. Some of these people, they're not nice."

He came back to the couch and sat down. To my surprise, he

gently took my hand and patted it. Staring at me out of the corner of his eye, he said, "Thank you, Gemma, for coming here. I don't imagine it's easy, delivering news like this."

His hands were warm and damp, and I was relieved when he moved away. He stood again, restless. A small orange cat sauntered into the room. Crabbe picked the animal up and held it to his chest, murmuring something in its ear.

"Patrick, do you know who any of these people were who approached your mother for money?"

Crabbe set the cat down, and it scampered away. "I saw one of them once. That's how I found out about the checks. It was last September. Mom was here, at home, screaming at a man in the driveway. He left as soon as I pulled up, driving away in an old beat-up black sedan. A Ford, I think. I'd never seen him before, and I insisted Mom explain who the man was and what was going on."

"What did she say?"

"Mom said he was a man who was down on his luck. He'd heard she might be willing to lend him some money. He got angry when Mom refused to give him anything. See, Mom couldn't say no to charities, organized fundraisers, that sort of thing. But she didn't like to give money to individuals. She said that too many of them 'drank their dollars.' Anyway, I should have gone after the man, but I was completely taken by surprise. It's not the sort of thing you expect to see, a man threatening your mother in her own driveway!"

"I would think not. Do you have any sense of how much money your mom gave away over the years?"

"Thousands. Tens of thousands, I think," Crabbe said. He sat down and leaned forward, put his head in his hands. His blond hair was thin and he had a number of freckles on his scalp. "I think it started after my dad died. Mom got lonely. Bored. My parents never married, you know. I think my mom felt an allegiance to her first husband, Kent's dad. I'm sure that Kent threw a fit when Mom and my dad started dating. We all lived together, and Kent was a brute to me from the time I was born. In fact, Kent was such a handful that after my dad died, Mom never dated anyone else. I don't think she had any energy left. Listen to me, going on and on. All families are a little dysfunctional, aren't they?"

I nodded. "Yes, that's probably true. I just have a few more questions, Patrick. I know this is all such a shock. Was your mother in the habit of working late? And did she frequent fast food restaurants?"

Crabbe smiled at the second question.

"Yes to both. Although she's quite healthy, Mom loves a good burger," Crabbe said. The smile faded and his eyes filled with tears. "Listen to me, talking about her like she's still alive. I should have been there, last night, at the museum."

"You didn't go to the gala, did you?"

Crabbe shook his head. "No. One of my night-shift employees at the gas station has been under the weather, and I agreed to cover his hours. I was there from eleven p.m. to seven this morning. One of my other clerks was there as well."

It would be easy enough to check his alibi.

We talked for a few more minutes. Crabbe agreed to notify his brother, Kent, of their mother's death and go to the hospital to make the formal identification. I promised to keep him informed as the investigation progressed. As joint owner of the property, Crabbe also gave me consent to search Starbuck's house.

As I was leaving, he stopped me in the doorway and spoke again. The cool air felt like a salve, and when I turned to look at him, I was struck by the fervor in his eyes.

The fever in his eyes.

"Kent carries a darkness with him. He always has," Crabbe said. His jaw tightened, then he continued in a halting voice, "After my dad died, and after Kent graduated high school and left the area, it was just my mom and me. It's just been the two of us for so long. When I was a little boy, I was scared that something would happen to her, that she would leave, go away and never return. She promised me over and over that if I was a good boy, a good son, she would never leave me. And I *have* been a good son. But she's gone now. That thing, that thing I've been scared of my whole life, has happened. What am I supposed to do without her?"

Chapter Nine

Detective Lucas Armstrong joined me and the crime scene team at Starbuck's house. Patrick Crabbe unlocked the front door and let us know that he was available if we had questions about anything. I thanked him but told him to stay out of the house until we released it back to him.

Once inside, Armstrong and I donned gloves.

"I'm just here to help with the search, then I'm turning this over to you and Finn. Moriarty and I may be tied up in court this week on the park rapist case," Armstrong said. Louis Moriarty was another detective in our squad. The Two Lous, we called them. They'd been partners for years. They'd recently arrested a local community college kid in connection with a series of rapes that had occurred in parks all over town. The defense was screaming entrapment, and both Lous had been called to testify in the trial.

Wiping his brow, Armstrong continued, "Plus, I'm hungover as all get out. I feel like my head is going to explode. I had no idea it was going to be an open bar at the gala last night. And all those servers, passing drinks out like it was Vegas. I couldn't stop."

"It was quite the party. Are you drinking water? Do you need an aspirin?"

He waved away my questions. "I'll survive. Unlike that sweet old lady who was running the show. It's hard to believe someone killed her."

"I know. Look, let's start in the front rooms, then make our way to the back and upstairs."

The house was clean and uncluttered. It was clear that Starbuck had no use for household ornaments or trinkets; the only items on shelves were books and framed photographs, the only hangings on walls subdued landscape paintings. The furnishings were for the most part white, with the occasional splash of color thrown in.

The austerity made our jobs a hell of a lot easier. Though we didn't know what—if anything—we were searching for, at least we didn't have to wade through piles of magazines and prodigious collections and other junk.

"Thank you, Mrs. Starbuck," Armstrong muttered. "This should be quick work."

He pulled back the curtains in the living room, allowing the bright sunshine to pour in. In the light, his crisp white shirt seemed to glow against his dark brown skin, his shoulders broad under the thin fabric. A former linebacker, he kept his six and a half feet of bulk in fighting shape.

We canvassed the downstairs of the house methodically but quickly, making our way through a formal living room, a den, a half bath, and the kitchen. The most interesting thing we found was a stash of vitamins and medicines in a cabinet next to the refrigerator.

"What's she doing, running a pharmacy? She's probably got the cure for cancer in here." Armstrong stepped back and I peered into the cabinet. He was right; it was crammed full.

We moved upstairs. There were three bedrooms: the master, with a beautiful antique four-poster bed, converted walk-in closet, and attached bathroom; a guest room that appeared to see more use as a sewing and craft space; and an office. A narrow bathroom with orange floral wallpaper and a claw-foot tub was squeezed between the office and craft room.

The nightstand in her bedroom held a box of tissue, a few hair pins and a comb, and a bottle of lotion. The sheets on her bed still smelled of detergent, and her closet was well organized, with clothes and shoes lined up by color, light to dark.

"I'm struggling to believe anyone really lived here," Armstrong said. He came out of the bathroom and shook his head. "Nothing much in there, either. Shampoo, soap, toothpaste. Some very expensive makeup—Sonya uses the same brand; it's the only reason I pick up overtime—and a few feminine products. That's it."

"It does feel a little too clean, doesn't it?" I shrugged. "Her son's a hoarder. Maybe this was Starbuck's way of coping with his behavior. Or vice versa—maybe Starbuck's cleanliness and austerity drove Crabbe to hoard."

Armstrong shuddered. "I don't do hoarders. I got a call in Baton Rouge years ago on a suspected animal abuse case. My partner and I showed up at this tiny trailer on the edge of a swamp. It was sick, just sick. The guy must have had seventy-five cats in there. He kept saying there were dozens more he couldn't account for, and the whole time, I'm looking out at this pond behind the trailer. I knew what happened to those other cats."

"Alligators?"

"Gators . . . or snakes."

We hit pay dirt in Starbuck's office. It, too, was minimally furnished: a filing cabinet; desk with a computer and printer; and a stack of correspondence neatly organized with labels such as "to file," "to respond to," "to save." Tucked neatly into the "to save" box was a stack of legal documents.

"Bingo," Armstrong said. He held up the sheaf of papers. "I've got an updated will and trust here, naming Patrick Crabbe and Kent Starbuck as equal heirs to Betty Starbuck's assets. There's this place, a rental property near Buena Vista, her pension, and a trust with a quarter million dollars in it."

I whistled. "That's a lot of assets for a museum director. Maybe she's done well in the stock market. Patrick told me that his mom was quite generous with her money; according to him, she's given away thousands of dollars. Tens of thousands. But Patrick seemed to be under the impression that Betty didn't have much to give. That will and trust would seem to contradict that."

Armstrong read further. "Starbuck changed her will a month ago. In the previous version, Patrick stood to inherit everything. In this version, as I said, it's a fifty-fifty split."

"That could be a motive. But why would Patrick tell me she didn't have a lot of funds? Why lie about something so easy to verify?"

"Maybe he didn't lie. Just because the will lists these assets doesn't mean they're all still viable." Armstrong slipped the pages into an evidence envelope. "You'll have to go through her financial records and see how things shake out."

We searched the backyard last.

It was here that Betty Starbuck embraced, if not chaos, at least color and beauty. It was a gardener's dream. I was only able to identify a few of the flowers already in bloom, such as the pink lungwort; the rest were unusual, exotic varieties that I'd never seen before. The far western edge of the yard was taken up by five garden boxes, their sides lined with chicken wire walls that jutted straight up to prevent rabbits from nibbling at plants.

Inside a shed in the east corner of the yard was a roll of plastic sheeting; a narrow wooden table with gardening tools, including an extremely sharp ax, hung neatly above it; and a thick reference book. A metal stool was tucked under the table and a few pieces of soil were on the ground under the stool.

I flipped through the reference book, stopping to read a few notes in the margin. Betty had jotted down what grew well and when; the whole book was a complete and careful almanac of her gardening adventures.

By the time we'd finished searching the property, we'd collected just enough to fill half an evidence box. There was very little that seemed even remotely tied to Betty Starbuck's murder.

Discouragement must have been written all over my face, because Armstrong patted me on the shoulder and said, "You can always come back, Gemma. If you need to search the place again, you can always come back. We'll leave it secured."

He was right, but it would be impossible to know who might enter the premises in the meantime or to know what items might disappear that could be important to the case. But it was a gamble we'd have to take. It was simply too early in the investigation to know what was unimportant and what was critical. What was a red herring and what was a clue . . . what were merely remnants of a woman's life and what were the keys to her death.

Chapter Ten

It was the middle of the afternoon, and I was famished. I grabbed a couple of shredded pork tacos and an ice-cold Dr Pepper from a food truck in Civic Park. The park, four shaded acres of grass and a small playground, was adjacent to the local community college, and I sat at a damp picnic table under a grove of aspen trees, watching a group of students play Frisbee in the grass.

As I ate, I jotted down notes from my conversation with Crabbe and the search of Starbuck's house. Her extravagant financial donations were new and unexpected developments in the case, though to be honest, I was fairly certain that in the end they would be unrelated to her murder. While it's true that people kill for money every day, the valuable necklace left broken at the scene of the crime seemed to suggest that money was not the motive for this particular murder.

I ate half of my lunch and then pushed the plate away. I'd lost my appetite. Starbuck's murder, coming on the heels of her employee Sari Chesney's disappearance, was disturbing to say the least. Two women who worked closely together, one violently killed, the other missing. Was Chesney dead, too? If so, where was her body? Had she been killed by the same person? To what end? And how—if at all—did the missing Rayburn Diary and/or the museum figure in?

An errant Frisbee headed my way. Picking it up, I aimed it back to the kids and with a flick of my wrist sent the disc flying through the air. The kids resumed their game. The cloudy skies had parted, the morning's early rain forgotten. It was another beautiful day in the

Rockies. All around me were signs of spring, Mother Nature's most glorious display of new life, but I barely noticed it. I had another appointment with death, this time in the form of a phone call to the morgue.

I spoke briefly with Dr. Bonaire. Patrick Crabbe had yet to appear and formally identify Starbuck's body, so I continued on to the police station. The talk there was about the murder, of course. More and more, Cedar Valley was regularly catching the same kinds of crimes that we used to only see in the big metro regions like Denver and Colorado Springs. A television in the corner of the central squad room was tuned to a local station, and the news ticker on the bottom of the screen scrolled highlights from Chief Chavez's press conference earlier in the day: *Prominent citizen murdered . . . Museum director killed . . . investigation proceeding . . .*

My partner, Finn Nowlin, was back from his trip to Palm Springs. His startling blue eyes looked even brighter than normal against his deep tan. I stopped at his desk, and he handed me a small box of chocolate-covered macadamia nuts.

"TSA confiscated the palm tree I stuffed in my suitcase. I figured you'd like the chocolate better anyway."

"You know me so well."

We made small talk for a few minutes as I wrestled with the plastic wrap on the chocolates. Amused, Finn watched me until he couldn't stand it any longer. He grabbed the box of candy and took a letter opener to the wrapper. Then he popped off the lid and handed the chocolates back to me.

I groaned. "Damn. There're only four in here. That's like a tease."

"Portion control, Gem. People in California, they're all about the portion control. So, get me up to speed on the Starbuck murder."

Finn was a good listener, remaining quiet while I spoke, taking notes on the yellow legal pad he favored. In addition to the Starbuck murder, I told him about the Sari Chesney and Rayburn Diary disappearances. I watched as he wrote Kent Starbuck's name and then circled it twice.

It was a lot of information to share. When I was done talking, I sat back and sipped from a water bottle, then finished the box of chocolates and waited while Finn reviewed his notes. He scratched at the base of his neck, and I noticed he was wearing his dark hair longer these days. It didn't suit him, and I almost said something.

Almost.

Finn went first, and his words were unexpected. "I don't think you can assume these three cases are related."

"Seriously?" I raised my eyebrows. "So it's just coincidence that in one weekend, a priceless diary is stolen, a woman disappears, and her boss is viciously murdered?"

"It *could* be coincidence. Here's one explanation: Chesney ditches the boyfriend and the small town for a shot at riches somewhere else, maybe Las Vegas, Los Angeles. The diary is stolen by the guy with OCD. And Starbuck is murdered by some junkie looking for cash to score."

"Larry Bornstein is a germaphobe, not obsessive-compulsive."

"Whatever. Point is, he's one of three employees with the combination to the museum safe *and* he's the only one of the three who is not dead or missing. Out of everyone, he's got the most opportunity and means to both steal the diary and kill Starbuck. Why aren't we looking at him more closely?"

"We *are* looking at him. We're going to look at everyone."

"How does a guy who's scared of germs end up spending his days around a bunch of old, dusty artifacts? I guarantee everything in that museum has been touched by a hundred hands. I find it very strange that he works there," Finn said. "So how do you want to do this?"

"Our priority is the Starbuck murder, obviously. And the stolen diary is just going to have to wait."

After tossing around a few more ideas, we divided up tasks. We were in the middle of finalizing next steps in the investigation when the front desk officer popped his head in.

"Gemma, the medical examiner just called. He's ready for you."

I stood. "Thanks, Tony. Finn, I'll take the autopsy if you want to start gathering the guest list from the gala? We need to interview every person who was there. By my estimate, that's close to two hundred people."

"You got it." Finn looked grateful to skip the autopsy.

I gathered my things, then stopped and looked at him. There was one more thing troubling me, something I hadn't planned on mentioning. But I believed in that moment that by saying it, by bringing it into the light, I'd somehow exorcise it from my mind.

"Have you ever heard of the Lost Girls?"

Finn thought a moment, squinting. "Nope. Who are they?"

"A group of young women who killed themselves in Lost Lake over a hundred years ago. It was a suicide pact. One of them was related to Owen Rayburn." I chewed on my lower lip, hesitant to express the thing that was circling in my thoughts.

Finn said it for me. "You think there's something to this diary curse?"

Hearing Finn say it out loud, I had to laugh.

But the laugh was hollow, and my words felt untrue. "Of course not."

"Good. We've got enough on our plate without worrying about some mumbo-jumbo hex."

Chapter Eleven

As I left the police station, I found and then called the number for the alarm company that serviced the museum. It was a national chain, and I was placed on hold almost immediately. I put the phone on speaker, set it on the passenger seat of my car, and started heading for the morgue. Five minutes later, while I was stopped at a red light, my call was finally picked up. After I identified myself and explained the situation, the man on the other end transferred me to a female supervisor who pulled a few records.

"Yes, Mrs. Starbuck called us last week. According to the notes on file, she wanted override permissions because of a late-night party she was throwing on Saturday. Those permissions overrode the automatic five p.m. alarm. The alarm was set with her code at midnight last night—wait, I guess that's this morning—midnight this morning, then disabled again at twelve twenty-two a.m. and set again at twelve twenty-three a.m. Then the alarm was again disabled at five a.m.," the woman said. "Does that information help you?"

"Yes, thanks so much. So, if I understand correctly, those records show someone—we'll assume Mrs. Starbuck—leaving the museum at midnight and then coming back twenty-two minutes later, disarming the system, and then re-arming it one minute later?"

"You got it. Those codes are assigned to Mrs. Starbuck, and then that next one, the one at five a.m., is a code assigned to a cleaning crew," the woman answered. Having gotten everything that I needed, I thanked her and hung up. I pulled into the hospital parking lot and found a spot near the rear entrance, close to the morgue. I parked, then hurried in, aware that Bonaire was waiting for me to begin the autopsy.

As I changed in the locker room from street wear to paper scrubs, I marveled not for the first time at the sheer number of moments, actions, and decisions that make up a person's life. Were we to trace every second of Betty Starbuck's last day on earth, we'd only be scratching the surface of a vast chasm of time, of seconds and minutes and hours and days, that made up her existence. It was akin to pondering the size of the universe—you're always going to come up short.

The morgue was located in the basement of the hospital. I left the locker room and headed down the corridor to what I'd taken to calling the Death Room. Inside, Bonaire and an assistant were dressed in identical booties, masks, and hair caps. Each wore gloves and a heavy apron over their scrubs. Bonaire also had an earpiece with a microphone that went down to his mouth to record his observations as the autopsy progressed.

The room was freezing, with a sterile quality to the air.

Everything—from the instruments laid out to the grates in the floor—looked cold and unfeeling, yet I knew that, in this room devoted to probing the most intimate human spaces, Bonaire, like our medical examiners, cared very much about the person on the table. They treated the bodies that came in their doors with dignity and care. They were respectful and dedicated to their mission. It was thankless work, and yet somehow, medical examiners were among the most humane professionals I'd met in the field.

Through his mask, I saw Bonaire lift his eyebrows at me. I nodded back at him: I was ready. I stood in a corner, careful not to touch anything. Aside from the rhythmic whoosh of fresh air entering the room through vents set high in the walls, it was silent.

Bonaire and his assistant moved fluidly, comfortable in the chilly environment.

Betty Starbuck lay on a stainless steel table in the middle of the Death Room, draped with a pale blue sheet. While he'd waited for me to arrive, Bonaire—or his assistant—had washed Starbuck's head wound. Without the blood, it was clear the injury was superficial, but now the gruesome bruising around her neck stood out in even more shocking and stark tones.

Bonaire worked steadily and quietly, as he'd done at the museum. He was clinical and thorough, stopping every few minutes to murmur into his microphone and then resuming his work. I was, of course, not an expert, but unlike some of the other autopsies I'd attended, this particular death seemed rather straightforward. I waited for some new piece of information to emerge, but when Bonaire finally took a lengthy break, it was to tell me what he'd predicted that morning: Betty Starbuck, in the plainest terms, had been strangled to death.

"As I initially suspected, the larynx is damaged and the hyoid bone is fractured. Her airway was compressed and the blood flow to the neck impeded. She would have lost consciousness within a minute or two, followed shortly by death," Bonaire said. "There is something strange, though. The bruising on her neck, here and here, suggests that her killer started choking her, only to stop and then start again."

"Maybe he had second thoughts about killing her? Or lost his grip and had to start again?"

Bonaire lifted a shoulder. "Motive is beyond this room. That's your field. I will say, though—strangling someone like this . . . it's a very personal attack."

"Yes. Anything else?"

Bonaire took a step back to the body and lifted Starbuck's right hand. "She has tissue fragments and blood under her nails. You're looking for someone with deep scratches, likely on his or her forearms, possibly on the face."

Bonaire gently set Starbuck's hand down and lifted both of his, putting them together in front of him, mimicking throttling someone. "The victim's right hand was free, and she fought her killer. He, or she, had the victim by the neck—so the surface area on which she could have clawed her killer was limited."

"You'll run the tissue and blood samples through the databases? We could get a match if the killer has a record."

"Of course, that's standard procedure," Bonaire said with a nod. "You are aware results can take weeks?"

I nodded.

"Good. There is one other thing. You saw at the crime scene that the victim had a necklace in her right hand?"

"Yes. I observed her wearing the same necklace earlier in the evening."

"I've submitted the jewelry to your department with the rest of the items she had on her person—her dress, undergarments," Bonaire said. "There are fibers entwined in the chain that don't match the dress she wore. Red and black threads."

"Fibers from the killer's clothes?"

He nodded. "Possibly. Or they may have come from a coat, a jacket that belonged to the victim. They could have come from hugging someone. Point is, they may or may not be important. I'll leave that to your forensics team."

"Got it."

Several scenes ran through my head, visions of the way the killing may have unfolded. Bonaire said the killer started choking Starbuck, then stopped, only to start again. "Maybe the necklace got in the way of the initial choking. The killer stopped and tore the necklace from her throat as she tore at his clothes . . . or she tore at her throat in an effort to breathe and in the process tore the necklace away. Then he started again. The killer was not there for the necklace, so he didn't care that she had it in her hands."

Bonaire slowly nodded. "It could have happened like that."

"Thank you, Dr. Bonaire, for seeing this through, on a Sunday. I know you could have postponed it for tomorrow."

Bonaire frowned. "Yes, I could have. But I would not have been able to look at myself in the mirror tonight, or enjoy dinner with my wife and twin sons. Someone stole this woman's life from her. Every minute that we are not searching for answers is a minute more in the killer's bank."

"That's how I feel, too."

I left the doctor and his assistant to do their strange dance with Starbuck: they manipulating her limbs, her organs; she giving up the secrets of her life and death. As I changed back into my street clothes and tossed the scrubs into a trash receptacle, a thought began to nag at me. Something Bonaire had said, or something I'd seen, scratched at the edge of my mind, but I couldn't for the life of me figure out what it was.

It bothered me immensely, not being able to wrangle my own thoughts.

Frustrated, I stomped out of the locker room and headed to the vending machine that hummed next to the front doors of the morgue. I dropped a few bucks in and was rewarded with a fiber bar and a bag of cheese-flavored chips. Wondering for a moment if they canceled each other out, then deciding I didn't really care, I scarfed down the bar and took my time with the chips, figuring they were maybe dessert.

It was nearly six p.m. and I should have headed home, but instead I sat in my car, watching hospital personnel and members of the public go in and out of the building.

I sat for a long time, thinking about a series of events:

Rayburn's daughter and friends kill themselves at Lost Lake.

Rayburn's Diary is to be the showpiece of a museum.

A museum employee disappears at Lost Lake.

The diary disappears.

The museum director is killed.

How could there *not* be some thread linking these events? Was it the diary? Lost Lake? Or one of the women, and if so, which one: the missing or the dead?

As if reading my mind, Sari's boyfriend, Mac Stephens, called on my cell phone. To my surprise, considering it had been on the news, he hadn't yet heard about Betty Starbuck's murder.

"Oh my god. Sari and Mrs. Starbuck worked side by side," Mac said. His voice grew agitated. "Something must have happened to Sari, too, something terrible."

"We don't know that yet. Mac, what was your impression of the relationship between Sari and Betty Starbuck? Did they get along? I recall that Ally Chang referred to Starbuck as a witch."

Silence on the other end of the line.

"Mac? Are you still there?"

He cleared his throat, then: "Well . . . they were both professionals. But I think they disliked each other, quite a lot, actually. Sari had some great ideas for the museum, cutting edge exhibits, that sort of thing, but Mrs. Starbuck never let her implement any of them. I got the feeling maybe the old lady was jealous of Sari."

"Do you think things could have gotten physical between them?"

Mac snorted into the phone. "You're kidding, right? Like, could Sari have killed Betty? Um, no. Not a chance in hell. Sari wouldn't hurt a fly. She's vegetarian. Although . . ."

"What is it, Mac? Anything you can tell me might be helpful, no matter how small or trivial seeming."

"Well, there was one incident. About six months ago. Mrs. Starbuck blew up at Sari after a board meeting. She belittled Sari. By the time I got off work and met her at a bar, Sari was three sheets to the wind. And Sari's not a heavy drinker. I remember she told me that one day 'that bitch' would get what was coming to her. I didn't pay too much attention at the time—I was more concerned with getting Sari to lay off the booze than with idle comments."

"Did anyone else witness this altercation?"

"No, it was just the two of them. At least, that's what Sari told me."

I heard a muffled voice from a paging system. It was obvious Mac was still at work at the hospital. He said, "Look, I've got to go. Please, call me if you hear anything. She's been gone the whole weekend."

"Of course. Listen, Mac, before you go—did Sari ever mention a diary to you?"

"Oh yeah. She journaled religiously. She'd refuse to come to bed until she wrote in that thing," Mac said. "I called it her second boyfriend."

"No, I'm sorry, I wasn't clear. I was talking about something at work, a diary she was involved with at the museum."

Silence a moment, then: "Sure, the Rayburn Diary, right? She thought it was pretty cool. She said it was cursed, like something out of an Egyptian pharaoh's tomb. Is there anything else? I really have to go, my break is over and I'm on the clock."

We ended the call, and I headed home through a canyon already heavy with violet-tinged dusky shadows. The water in the creek that hugged the canyon was dark and fast moving. On the shoulder of the road, near my turnoff, a few fishermen loaded equipment into the back of a gray truck. One of them, a heavyset man in waders and a checkered pullover, held a string of trout high in the air as his buddy took a photograph. The lifeless fish were dull-colored, their mouths gaping open, their eyes sightless.

At home, I found the baby already fed and fast asleep in her crib. I hated missing her evening routine, especially after being gone the entire day, but there was little to do about it during an active murder investigation. Being a working mother meant I was always sacrificing something, and I hoped and prayed that one day Grace would not only understand why I did what I did every day, but respect it, too.

Brody and I spent a few minutes catching up over a light supper of tomato soup and grilled cheese sandwiches, then he adjourned to the den to watch a movie. I lingered over a second glass of wine and spent a few hours online.

Though the Rayburn Diary's loss alone was a low priority when compared to the Starbuck murder, I felt strongly there was a good chance the theft and the murder were connected. My research started with a narrow focus, but an Internet search of Owen Rayburn led me down a rabbit hole and I was quickly overwhelmed with the sheer amount of information on Rayburn and the Silver Foxes—the wealthy and often unscrupulous men who founded Cedar Valley.

After my head nodded in sleep for the third time, I finally closed my laptop. The last page I visited, on an amateur historian's website, had a black-and-white photograph of the Silver Foxes. The six men were unsmiling, as many of the people in old historical photographs are. Owen Rayburn occupied a spot in the middle. He was a short man with a wide girth, a thick mustache, and flat, dark eyes hooded with heavy, toadlike lids.

I stared at his face, wondering which secrets he had kept to himself and which he had committed to posterity in his diary.

Were they secrets worth killing for?

Chapter Twelve

Monday dawned like an Impressionist painting: a gentle watercolor sky of hazy blues and soft pinks. Seemingly overnight, a thousand white blossoms had appeared on the flowering trees in our yard. I drank my coffee on the front porch, listening to the sounds of the creek moving heavily down the canyon and the staccato cry of a nearby woodpecker.

Brody had an early meeting in town, so I stayed with Grace until Clementine arrived at eight. By then, Grace and I had walked the front yard several times, looking at the blooming flowers and the various insects that were drawn to them. Though Grace was only six months old, she possessed the calmness and serenity of an old soul. When I thought of how fast the months were flying by, a lump rose in my throat. Brody once said that time is both our most precious and our most wasted commodity. I vowed, once again, to find the blessing in each moment I had with my daughter.

In town, Main Street was closed to through-traffic for the day's street fair, sponsored by the arts guild. It was one of the many celebrations planned for the town's anniversary, complete with vendors, food trucks, and carnival-style rides and booths. I took a detour through the west side of town and arrived at work only a few minutes later than usual.

I settled in at my computer armed with one thought: whatever the motive, Betty Starbuck's killing was deeply personal. Standing face-to-face with someone as you choke the life out of them takes enormous will. The victim's eyes hemorrhage; their skin becomes mottled. It's a vicious and ugly way to die, and I knew there was a strong likelihood that we were looking for a killer who was close to Starbuck.

For Betty Starbuck, that meant family—her sons, Patrick Crabbe and Kent Starbuck—and co-workers, Larry Bornstein and Sari Chesney. Friends and acquaintances would need to be considered as well.

Patrick Crabbe had an alibi for the night of the killing, so for the time being I moved on to Kent Starbuck. I planned to interview him as soon as possible, but I wanted to go into the conversation armed with knowledge. Crabbe had made it clear that Kent had a troubled past, and I assumed that might have included prison time.

I entered Kent Starbuck's name into the state and national crime databases. On the monitor, I watched as a number of hits started to return. I had the system consolidate them into a PDF, and then I leaned forward and read. And read. The report was lengthy and troubling.

When I finished, I sat back, disturbed. I looked over at Finn. "Nowlin."

"Monroe." Finn turned his head. "What've you got?"

I read him the highlights from the report. He listened for a moment, then stood up and joined me at my desk. When I finished reading the report, he whistled, hands on his hips.

"*This* is the victim's son?"

I nodded. "Kent Starbuck's been in and out of trouble for years. It's clear from his record that he was escalating, working his way up from petty crimes to the big leagues. Then he fell off the radar after he got out of prison ten years ago. So . . . maybe he's a changed man?"

"Or maybe he's been biding his time and now that he's returned home, he goes after mommy dearest. Go back to the report for a second," Finn said, then he pointed at the screen. "Did you see Moriarty's name here? He was the responding officer on a number of Kent Starbuck's early crimes. They had Lou testify at one of Kent's trials."

"I did see that. I'm not surprised—Lou Moriarty's been a cop here for years." I pushed back from the desk. "I'm going to talk to him."

"You do that. I'm going to finish the warrants for Betty Starbuck's financial records and accounts."

I tracked Lou down in the old jail cell. It was used for storage now and also, apparently, for meals. Lou sat at a narrow desk, wolfing down an onion-laden Italian hoagie with his eyes closed, an expression of utter ecstasy on his face.

I stuck my head in the doorway. "Talk to me about Kent Starbuck."

"He's dead. Or close to it, would be my guess. The last I heard, he was mopping up sweat from a bunch of yogis at some hippie retreat in the backwoods of North Carolina," Lou replied, his eyes still closed. "I can't get a minute of peace. The judge gave us an hour for lunch and look, I'm spending half of it talking about ol' Kent Starbuck. How did you find me, anyway?"

I smirked. "The onions. Kent's not dead, nor is he in North Carolina. He's here in town."

Lou's eyes popped open. "You're shitting me. He was on my list."

"What list is that?" I asked, leaning back into the hallway to get a breath of fresh air.

"You know, the List, with a capital *L*. The perps who will close their careers in some kind of spectacular set of fireworks. I keep a running list in my head of these punks and good old Kenny Starbuck had a prominent place at the top. Assassinate a head of state . . . get a shiv in his throat in prison . . . flee the country with a million dollars in stolen stamps," he said. Lou reached for a large drink and slurped noisily. "It all amounts to the same thing."

"I'm not following."

Lou closed his eyes and shooed me away with a wave of his hand. "The kid was trouble through and through. Kenny was a bad seed, took after his father that way. His old man walked out on Betty and the kid. I seem to recall he died a few years later in a high-speed car chase with the cops out west somewhere, maybe LA. Anyway, like his father, there was never going to be a happy ending for Kent."

"You sound pretty sure of yourself. He's kept his nose clean for the last ten years. Maybe he's a changed man."

Lou swallowed another bite. "I only know what I know, Monroe. And what I know is that Kent Starbuck is a sad son of a bitch—no disrespect to Betty Starbuck intended—who was a waste of oxygen then and I assume still is. He's toe jam, slime. A real slick hombre. Listen, how long has he been back in town? I hope you're looking at him for his poor old mother's murder."

I am now, Lou. I am now.

The front desk officer caught me as I walked back from the old jail cell to the central squad room. "Gemma, you've got some visitors up front. A Dr. Larry Bornstein and Mrs. Lois Freeman. They're insisting on seeing you . . . but I can take a message?"

"No, I'll meet with them. Thanks."

They sat in the small waiting area, talking softly to each other. It was clear Bornstein had been crying; his eyes were painfully red, his nose swollen. I noticed he was careful to perch on the edge of the chair and keep his hands tucked together in his lap. The woman he was with was about fifty years old, petite, with tight red curls that bounced as she moved.

After explaining that she was the president of the board of directors of the Cedar Valley History Museum, Lois Freeman said, "As soon as I heard the awful news, I called Larry and told him we had to come here and speak to you."

Bornstein nodded. "When Lois called, my wife insisted on postponing our special brunch—it's our anniversary, you see—and driving straight here. My wife adored Betty Starbuck. She's waiting in the car for me as we speak, too distraught to come in."

"I'm so sorry for your loss." I looked from Bornstein to Freeman. They stared back at me expectantly. "Well, I'm sure this has all been a terrible shock. There's not much I can tell you, though. We've barely started the investigation."

Lois Freeman exhaled and spoke loudly, her curls whipping to and fro as she shook her head. "Detective, I'm here to give *you* information. I know who killed Betty."

Chapter Thirteen

Once we were settled in the privacy of an interview room, I gestured for Lois Freeman to continue.

"Betty's son killed her, I'm sure of it."

"Kent?"

"Kent?" A confused look came over Freeman's face. "God, no. Is he even still alive? I'm talking about Patrick."

Surprised, I stared and repeated her words back to her. "You think Patrick killed Betty?"

She nodded vigorously, her scarlet curls once more dancing. "Yes. He's a louse who's been mooching off his mother for years. I'll bet she finally threatened to cut him off financially, and he snapped."

"This is a serious accusation. Do you have any proof?"

I'd seen Freeman's type before: full of opinion and bluster, empty of evidence. They typically arrive at the station in the form of a nosy neighbor or a concerned citizen.

"Only what Betty has told me. We'd become friends, you see, over the years. I went to school with Patrick and Kent, here in town. Everyone was terrified of Kent and his temper, but I'll tell you something: I've always been more afraid of Patrick. You notice the way he won't look you in the eyes? It's not right," Freeman said. She leaned forward and whispered, "It's downright creepy."

She tapped Bornstein on the shoulder, and he flinched. "Go on, Larry. Tell the detective what Betty told you."

I turned to Bornstein. He'd pulled a pocket-sized hand sanitizer from his sports coat and gripped it in his right hand as though it were a talisman. His hands were small, pink, and raw-looking, as though the skin had been scrubbed repeatedly.

Knowing his disorder, it likely had been.

Bornstein cleared his throat. "A few weeks ago, Betty approached me at the museum, confidentially. She said she was concerned about Patrick and wanted to know if I could recommend a therapist. She told me that he had been acting . . . well, unusual lately."

"What did she mean, 'unusual'?"

Bornstein closed his eyes, thinking. "She didn't get into specifics, only repeated that Patrick was acting odd. I think she thought he might even be on drugs. She'd have known, after everything she went through when Kent was a teenager. I remember very clearly one thing she said. Betty told me that Patrick kept referring to a 'judgment' that was coming. Only she didn't use that word . . . it was something else, something more exotic sounding."

Lois Freeman offered, "A reckoning?"

"That's it!" Bornstein open his eyes and smiled. "That's exactly the word Patrick used. Anyway, Betty thought I could help. I gave her the name of my therapist, and that was the last I heard of the matter."

"I hate to be blunt here, but all of this can be explained in non-suspicious ways," I said gently. "None of it indicates any kind of implied or stated threat to Betty from Patrick. As far as I know, he has no history of violence."

Never mind the fact that he had an airtight alibi for the time of the murder.

It would be inappropriate to mention that to Freeman and Bornstein, though. Freeman wagged a finger in my direction. "You look into Patrick Crabbe's finances, and Betty's will. I'd bet a thousand dollars that you'll find plenty of motive there. A creepy money-hungry hermit who's experiencing a sudden psychotic episode sounds like a strong suspect to me."

I looked at her steadily. "Of course, we'll be looking into all aspects of Betty's life. Larry shared what Betty told him about Patrick; what exactly did she tell *you*, Mrs. Freeman?"

Freeman straightened in her seat. "She said when Kent came back to town, Patrick grew depressed. She said she'd awoken at midnight to strange noises on more than one occasion. When she went to the window, she saw Patrick standing in the backyard. Just standing there, can you imagine? In the middle of the night?"

"What was he doing?"

"Nothing. Betty told herself Patrick was likely suffering from insomnia, but here's the strange thing: each time, she'd ask him about it the next day. And each time, he'd deny it!"

"And she was sure it was Patrick in the yard? Could it have been someone else?"

Freeman started to answer, then she stopped and her eyes grew wide. "Good lord. You think it was a *stranger*? Or Betty's *killer*?"

"Let's not make any assumptions." I jotted a few notes down. "I'll follow up with Patrick. In the meantime, please know we're doing all we can to bring your friend's killer to justice. I promise."

Somewhat mollified, Freeman stood and smoothed down the front of her dress. "I beg you, take Patrick seriously as a suspect. He was a disaster in high school, and he's a disaster now. Larry? Are you coming? I think we owe your wife brunch somewhere nice."

"Yes, of course," he said. He pocketed his hand sanitizer and made to stand up. I wasn't finished with him, though.

"Dr. Bornstein, could you stay a moment? There's something I'd like to talk to you about."

Lois Freeman started to sit back down, and I glanced at her. "Mrs. Freeman, I need to speak with Dr. Bornstein confidentially. If you'll excuse us?"

She blushed and left without another word.

I turned to Bornstein and gave him what I hoped was a reassuring smile. He continued to look worried. I offered to get him a coffee and he hurriedly declined it, so I got right to it.

"Dr. Bornstein, I saw you and Betty Starbuck talking with James Curry and Alistair Campbell the night of the gala. The conversation looked a little, ah, heated," I said. "Can you share what that was all about? You can imagine, in light of the murder, that anything out of the ordinary that occurred that night might be important."

Bornstein seemed relieved. "Oh that? That was nothing. Simply a difference of opinion on a few matters."

"Owen Rayburn's diary?" I guessed.

He nodded. "That, among a few other things. When they heard the diary was missing, Alistair and James were livid. They both insisted on an immediate investigation of the museum. As you're well aware, Betty had made the decision to postpone any investigation until after the gala. Ultimately, it was her decision as director. Then there were other things we discussed. Alistair's an odd duck. He has offered an obscene amount of money to buy the diary . . . and a man like Alistair just can't believe some things in this world aren't for sale. And James Curry . . . well, James has very little money, but he, too, would like to purchase the diary. Or borrow it, is probably a better way to put it."

"Didn't Curry do the restorations on it? It would have been in his possession for quite some time, I'd imagine." I asked. "Why would he need it again?"

Bornstein shrugged. "Beats me. He's never given us—Betty or me—a very clear answer to that question."

"How long have you known Curry?"

"Years. We travel in the same social circles." Bornstein grew more troubled with his next words. "You must understand, the loss of the diary is a tragedy. We'll lose thousands in donations, and Betty Starbuck, had she lived, would certainly have been replaced."

"I'd say the real tragedy is Mrs. Starbuck's death."

Bornstein flushed at that. "Yes, of course."

"You said she would have been replaced. That seems extreme."

"It is the latest in a series of misfortunes to hit the museum. Of course, hardly any of them were Betty's fault, but nonetheless, as director, the buck stopped with her. The last straw was Ruby Cellars's resignation. She was adored, and the board blamed Betty when Ruby left."

"Ruby Cellars . . . the former employee? Widowed, with a bunch of kids?"

Bornstein nodded. "She was beloved. Many of us assumed she was next in line for Betty's job."

"Who's next in line for Betty's job now?"

His face turned redder. "Well, that depends . . . the board has the right to hire an external candidate, of course."

Something about his tone gave me pause. "And if they hired internally?"

Bornstein swallowed. "That would be Sari Chesney or me. Her background is archival in nature, but mine is administrative . . . but I have seniority. The board is eclectic. They'd likely have been split fifty-fifty."

"Half of them would choose you, the other half Sari?"

He nodded, his Adam's apple bobbing up and down as he swallowed again, his cheeks still flaming. "Yes, that's correct."

We sat in silence for a moment, staring at each other, then Bornstein cleared his throat and stood up. "My wife is waiting for me in the car. As I said, it's our anniversary. If you'll excuse me . . ."

I escorted Bornstein to the front entrance, then watched him walk down the front steps. By the time he reached the parking lot, he was nearly running.

I wondered at his hurry.

Chapter Fourteen

Betty Starbuck's murder was front-page news. Someone had left me a copy of the day's *The Valley Voice,* and I read the article standing at my desk, furious by the time I was finished. There were details in the report, details about the crime scene, that could only have come from this department.

It was clear the leaker had struck again.

Already under pressure from Mayor Cabot and the city manager to solve the murder of one of their more prominent citizens and equally pissed off about the leak, Chief Chavez asked Finn and me for an update.

We briefed him in his office, taking turns talking while he ate from a cup of soup. The shades were drawn and the room smelled of Vicks and chicken broth. The chief apologized more than once for his thick, wet cough. "Kids. They're always bringing germs home from school."

Aside from the coughing, he listened quietly. An outsider might have thought he was paying more attention to his lunch than to us, but they'd have been gravely mistaken.

Chief Angel Chavez was one of the smartest men I knew.

When the chief heard Kent Starbuck was back in town, he held up a hand. "Anyone speak to him yet? Get an alibi? Do we have a viable motive?"

"Talking to him is my next move, Chief. As for motive—Patrick Crabbe told me Kent and their mother had a troubled relationship. Kent's been living off an insurance settlement that is running out, so there may also be a financial motive. Armstrong and I found a revised will in Betty's office that lists Patrick and Kent as equal heirs."

"Authentic?"

I nodded. "Yes, the will was notarized. Also, Crabbe himself has an alibi for the night of the murder. I spoke to one of his employees. She confirmed that Crabbe was there, at the Gas 'n' Go, from eleven p.m. to seven a.m., working in the back office and covering for her while she took her breaks. He normally works the day shift, but one of his night clerks was ill. Crabbe staffs the station with two people at all times, in light of the vandalism he's experienced."

"How about this other thing Crabbe mentioned, about his mom giving her money away—have we confirmed anything there? How about the man Crabbe witnessed yelling at Starbuck?"

"I don't know about the man, but I'm working on access to her bank accounts and financial records," Finn said. "Her will paints a healthy financial picture, which is contrary to what Crabbe told Gemma."

"Okay." Chavez nodded. "Any other suspects? Please tell me you've got something more than this."

"Sari Chesney," Finn responded.

Surprised, I shot him a look and said, "Sari Chesney is not a suspect. If anything, she's a possible victim, with her disappearance tied to the Starbuck homicide. There's been no use of her credit cards or cell phone in the last three days. If she's on the run, she is truly in the wind. No disrespect to Finn, Chief, but the idea that Chesney killed Starbuck is so outlandish, so tenuous . . ."

Finn interrupted me. "Actually, I've had some time to think about this. It's the perfect crime. Chesney fakes her own disappearance, kills Starbuck, and walks away with the diary. No one's the wiser."

"Chief, Finn and I haven't had a chance to vet this . . . hypothesis yet," I said, with another sidelong glance at my partner. I was fuming. He'd been so quick to dismiss a link between the three cases—Chesney, Starbuck, and the diary—and yet here he was, connecting dots and making a case for that very thing.

Worst of all, the chief was nodding.

Chavez rubbed his throat. "How long has she been gone?"

"The middle of the night, Friday, was the last time anyone saw her," I said quickly. "I'd like to recommend we devote more resources to finding her, Chief. It's obvious these women are linked."

"I don't doubt that. The question is *how* are they linked? Finn, you know what I'm going to ask," Chavez said, coughing again. He turned away from us, spat into a handkerchief. "Gah, I'm going to hack up a lung at this point."

"Yes, motive," Finn replied. "Financial is the most obvious. Chesney could sell the diary for a significant amount. In addition, it sounds as though Chesney and Starbuck weren't on the best of terms. Maybe killing Starbuck was the icing on the cake."

"The thing is, the diary disappeared before Starbuck was killed. Why go back and kill her? Could the thief have hidden the diary in the museum, gone back to retrieve it, and encountered Starbuck?" The chief finished his soup and wiped his mouth with a paper towel. Then he leaned back, thinking. "Wherever Sari Chesney is, she's in trouble. If she's guilty of something, if she's on the run, she's not going to get far. Worse, if something's happened to her . . . if she's the victim of a crime . . . guys, you've got to find her."

"We need more manpower, though, Chief. Whatever you can spare. If we're going to find Chesney, we've got to understand who she is first."

"Just a minute," Finn said. "If Sari Chesney is dead, where's her body? Betty Starbuck's killer made no effort to hide *her* body, or alter the scene of the crime. Why hide one and not the other?"

"Finn makes a good point." Chavez said. He looked conflicted. "We're tight on resources as it is, but I'll see what I can do about getting you two more help. In the meantime, talk to Kent Starbuck. What about Betty's other co-workers, this guy with the germs, Bornstein?"

"He's suspicious. He stands to inherit Betty Starbuck's position as director of the museum. Seems an awful reason to kill someone, but we've all seen worse motives for murder. I actually just got out of a meeting with him and Lois Freeman. Freeman—who is on the museum's board of directors—is convinced that Patrick Crabbe had something to do with Starbuck's death because of some concerns Starbuck shared about Crabbe. But as I said, Crabbe has an airtight alibi for the night of the murder."

"I know Lois Freeman by reputation. In the old days, she's what we would have called a busybody. Look, maybe Kent Starbuck and Patrick Crabbe are closer than anyone realizes . . . maybe together they decided to get their hands on their mother's money a bit earlier than she planned." Chavez retched through another coughing fit. "Okay, you two. Keep after it."

Finn and I stood to take our leave, but the chief added, "Gemma, stay a moment, please."

I sat down. Chavez waited until Finn had gone, then he said in a low voice, "I want the turd who's sharing information with the press caught. Yesterday wouldn't have been soon enough. Put your ear to the ground, see what you can figure out."

Taken aback, I said the first thing that came to mind. "Why me, Chief?"

"You're well liked, respected. People trust you, and rightfully so."

I nodded slowly, thinking. "Yet you're asking me to betray that trust."

Chavez tapped his fingers on the table. "Do you think the leak is acceptable?"

"Absolutely not."

He tilted his head. "Then what's the problem? I'm not asking you to do anything dishonorable, Gemma."

"I understand." I asked the obvious question, albeit with a wry smile. "Sir, what if *I'm* the leaker?"

"Let me worry about that." Chavez stared at me, an unreadable expression in his eyes. "Dismissed."

I left the office, upset but trying not to show it. I didn't appreciate being asked to investigate my colleagues. It felt like something a rat would do. I was nearly to the squad room when I came upon Finn, who was lingering in the hall, staring at one of the framed photographs on the wall. Fresh frustration at being blindsided by him in the meeting bubbled to the surface, and I let him have it. "What was that all about?"

He moved away from me, taken aback by the anger in my voice. "What was *what* all about?"

"Your little theory that Sari Chesney killed Betty Starbuck. There's nothing to suggest that she had anything to do with Starbuck's murder. You practically had her on trial back there," I said. I stopped talking as an officer passed us, then hissed, "You're muddying the waters."

Finn pulled his tie from his neck, loosening it with a jerk. "Oh, give me a flipping break. The chief asked for our opinions. The more I've thought about it, the more it seems impossible that the Chesney disappearance and the Starbuck murder are unrelated. You said it yourself, it's too big a coincidence. What do you want me to do, walk back there and tell Chavez you thought of it first? Cry me a river, Gemma. Just because we're partners doesn't mean I have to run every thought I have by you for your approval."

I stared at him through narrow eyes, angry at his unexpected words. This all seemed to be coming out of left field. "No, but partners use each other to vet ideas and theories before they take them to the chief. We looked like fools back there, asking for more resources on the one hand and disagreeing on the other hand about how to approach our cases."

"I had no idea you were so concerned with protocol, with how things *looked*. Maybe you'd do better with a different partner, someone who's as straight and narrow as you. Someone who doesn't like to color outside the lines. You should know by now that my methods tend to be a little . . . risky." Finn started to walk away, then turned around and added, "Life's too short, you know? I didn't become a cop to follow some personnel handbook. Not when it comes to closing cases."

He moved on, down the hall and out of my sight, and I exhaled all the air in my lungs in one big whoosh. Was I too straitlaced, too rigid? I'd thought all along that Finn and I complemented each other, that we brought different strengths and weaknesses to our investigations and that this made us a good team. To hear him, though, I was a puritanical rule player who cared more about staying in my lane than catching the bad guys.

I wondered if there was something else bothering him, something he wasn't saying.

Anyway, he was dead wrong. I didn't care about those things, not the way I cared about solving Betty Starbuck's murder, about finding Sari Chesney.

I went to the photograph that Finn had been staring at. Like the others that hung on the wall, it was a picture of a handful of fresh-faced rookies. This particular one was the previous year's graduating class, from which we'd been lucky enough to snag Sam Birdshead. Sam was a driven young man with a promising career. Tragically, after only a few months on the force, he'd been terribly injured during the course of a murder investigation. Though we would have happily kept him on, Sam resigned from the police department and accepted a position with Alistair Campbell's construction company, Black Hound Construction.

I slowly walked back down the hall, scanning the other photographs of recruits, young men and women who'd joined the force full of dreams and ambitions. Where were they all now? I recognized few of the faces, and stopped walking when I came to my class picture.

It was six years old.

Six years I'd been a cop and, some days, I felt as though I knew no more than the woman staring back at me.

Chapter Fifteen

I met Kent Starbuck at a coffee joint that operated out of what used to be a mechanic shop. The large rolling steel doors that had once admitted cars into the bay were open to catch the gentle spring breeze. It was my first time visiting the shop, and I couldn't help but notice that their baked goods selection was limited to a few dry-looking bagels and a couple of plastic-wrapped slices of what appeared to be banana bread. After my ugly confrontation with Finn, I could have used a slice of cheesecake, or a fresh doughnut—hell, even a stale cookie would have done the trick.

Starbuck sat at a table near the open doors. Though they were half brothers, he and Patrick Crabbe could have been twins, with identical narrow faces, lanky bodies, and thinning blond hair that receded dramatically at the temples. Starbuck had a thick mustache, though, while Crabbe was clean-shaven. And though I'd never seen Crabbe in anything but khakis and dress shirts, Starbuck was dressed casually in faded denim jeans, tan boots, and a long-sleeved checkered flannel shirt.

Starbuck had a voice that sounded like gravel falling from a wheelbarrow, rough and rhythmic at the same time. A cup of coffee and a small, open notebook lay before him. As I sat down, he casually closed the notebook. A young woman came by and took my order, an espresso and a glass of water. A handful of bees buzzed about a row of flower pots that bordered the edge of the patio, and from down the street came the sound of heavy construction equipment. Cedar Valley was changing in more ways than one, it seemed.

Starbuck stared at me expectantly.

"Thank you for meeting with me, Mr. Starbuck. I'm so sorry about your mother. Please know that we are doing all we can to bring her killer to justice," I began.

He nodded slowly. "Appreciate that. Mama was a tough nut. It's hard to believe she's gone. I thought she'd outlive all of us."

"I know this is a difficult time. Do you mind if I ask you some questions?"

Starbuck nodded. "Of course, but I probably won't be much help. I only saw Mama a handful of times in the last thirty years. You should be talking to my brother instead."

The waitress brought my espresso, and I took a moment to sip from the tiny white cup, thinking.

"Are you aware of anyone who might have had reason to hurt her?"

He shook his head. "No, of course not. As I said, I barely knew her. Patrick is convinced that she gave money to some bad people . . . but I have trouble believing that. The woman I knew was righteous. She prided herself on self-control. She thought *miser* was a compliment."

"Did you ever know her to associate with the wrong kind of people?"

He shook his head again. "No, never. She thought finishing a glass of champagne on New Year's Eve was living dangerously. But keep in mind what I'm trying to tell you: *I didn't know her.* Not anymore."

"How about a woman named Sari Chesney? Does that ring any bells?"

Kent thought a moment, then: "No. Is she a suspect in the murder?"

"Ms. Chesney worked with your mother at the museum," I said, and left it at that. I wasn't getting much from him, so I chose my next words carefully. "Patrick told me that you've had a rough go of it over the years. I understand you spent some time in prison."

"Honest Abe, that one," Kent said, and smiled ruefully. "Patty never could tell a lie, even as a child. Detective, if there's one thing I've learned, it's that deception lives comfortably in honesty. Do you understand that? No one ever goes below the surface with honest folks *because they tell you the truth.* Yes, the state determined that I did the crimes and so, as they say, 'I did the time.' That's all in the past, an old scab, long healed. I'm done with that life now. I fulfilled my parole obligations and then I flew away, free as a bird. Like that old fellow." He pointed to a fat gray pigeon pecking at crumbs on the ground, then linked his thumbs together and fluttered his fingers through the air. "Do you want to hear something fascinating? A bird in captivity will live three times as long as a bird that is free. I've traded a long life behind bars for a short stint out on my own. What a deal, huh?"

I was stuck on his earlier words. "Are you saying your brother is not trustworthy?"

"I don't know my brother. Patty and I may be cut from the same cloth, but we are most certainly different suits, if you catch my meaning." Starbuck's expression sobered. "He walks to his own tune. I was five years old when he was born. Mama was in love with Patty's father, and I told her that I would run away from home if she married him. Can you imagine the balls on that little five-year-old? I'm lucky she didn't slap me silly. 'Course, the real tragedy was that she took me seriously. Patty's hated me ever since."

"Why did you come back here, then?"

Starbuck leaned back and pushed his coffee cup to the edge of the table. He looked down at his hands. They were rough and callused, with marks from so many years in the sun and faded scars from long-forgotten injuries.

They were hands that had seen life.

"To be honest, this was the last place I thought I'd ever wind up. I headed east after I was released from parole, spent some time in St. Louis, then Atlanta. I was searching for something, but what that was, I didn't know. At least not then. I ended up in Asheville, doing handyman work at a spa. There was a woman there, Helen, who taught yoga classes. She took me under her wing and helped me see what I was missing, what I'd always been missing. It was balance, Detective."

"And you came here hoping to find it?"

Starbuck nodded. "I started making my way west, not sure where I was going, but called to the mountains nonetheless. I was in Denver on a moonless night in February, talking to a bum at Union Station. I bought him a cup of coffee, and in return he showed me a postcard. The guy had been carrying the card around in his backpack for five years, and it was beat-up, frayed at the edges. It was a photograph of a lake, a deep, clear beautiful lake, surrounded by the most gorgeous peaks you ever saw."

"Let me guess. Lost Lake?"

Starbuck looked surprised. "How did you know?"

"Let's just say it's been a topic of conversation lately."

"I spent weeks up there as a kid, camping, fishing. At the time I saw this postcard, I hadn't thought of that lake in years. Anyway, this bum told me the only thing that kept him going these days was the thought of someday making it to that lake. The very next day, I kid you not, that poor guy died of a heart attack. I took that as a sign of divine intervention. An hour later, I was in a rental car, on my way here," Starbuck said. "I know it sounds crazy but I truly believe someone upstairs sent the man to me as a messenger. I decided there must be something worth returning to. Maybe Mama, maybe Patty. Maybe just some old baseball cards in a shoebox and a dusty jersey in the back of a closet, souvenirs from a dumb kid's dream."

"And was there? Something worth returning to?"

He shrugged, still looking at his hands. "There might have been, at one point. Seems I waited too long to come back and find out. It took five minutes with my mama to remind me why I left. I'm sorry she is dead, I truly am. I can't think of anything sadder than a violent death. How very, very terrible to have fear and pain be the last things you experience on this good earth. But I won't miss her."

"Was she abusive?"

At this, Kent looked up and scoffed. "You've got to be present before you can be abusive. No, Mama was the north star. Distant.

Cold. Out of reach. But always there. All seeing, all knowing. Pro-
phetic. Cassandra of the mountains."

"That's poetic."

"Me, a poet? Imagine that." This got another gravelly laugh from
the man. "Detective, I'm a man of the land, so I suppose in some
ways that's the same thing. Look, I like to watch a ball game and
garden. Drink a cold beer and read a mystery. I'm trying to do more
good in my next twenty years than I've done in the last fifty. I volunteer with seniors and read to kids. I pick up trash when I see it in
the road. I'm thinking of getting a mutt from the shelter. I always
wanted a dog. I think a dumb old golden retriever named Blue sounds
like heaven on earth."

"Those are all noble things," I said, and finished my espresso. The
man before me, a man who had spent years in prison, a man who
by all accounts had been trouble through and through . . . he was
surprising me with his every word.

I decided to peel back the scab.

"You've lived an often violent life. I have to ask, where were
you this weekend, specifically late Saturday night and early Sunday morning?"

Starbuck leaned forward and smiled, and for the first time since
sitting down, I felt a tremor of fear run down my spine. For it wasn't
a smile, not really, but an ugly grimace. His face darkened; his tone
grew harsh. "And so we come to it, the true reason for your visit. You
cops are all the same. You want an alibi? I don't have one. That must
make me a murderer, so go ahead and arrest me. I was at the motel,
in my room. Asleep probably, or damn close to it."

"Were you alone?"

Starbuck smiled the awful smile again. He stood up and put a
ten-dollar bill on the table. "That takes care of my drink and yours,
with something extra for the waitress. I don't have anything else to
say about my mother or my nocturnal habits. My company that night,
as it is every night, was the television and a six-pack of Coors. There
might have been a candy bar or two, but I can't remember."

He excused himself, and I watched him leave. At the door, he waited while two elderly women slowly exited. One of them used a walker, and when she caught it on the doormat, Starbuck helped her free it. The woman leaned over and patted him on the cheek, thanking him.

At the counter, the sad bagels and plastic-wrapped pastries had been joined by a few apples and a lone banana. I bought the banana and ate it on the way to my car, deep in thought. I couldn't get over the differences between Patrick Crabbe and Kent Starbuck: two brothers, born to the same mother, as different as night and day.

Patrick Crabbe, apologetic. A businessman mired in meekness.

Kent Starbuck, unapologetic. A troubled man seeking redemption.

There was one thing I knew to be true, and that was this: nothing—I mean *nothing*—was ever as it appeared to be on the surface. What else lurked in Patrick Crabbe, in Kent Starbuck? Who was ultimately more authentic: the man who lived in meekness and possibly hid a darker side, or the man who walked in darkness and struggled to find the light within?

Tossing the banana peel in a sidewalk trash can, I decided that in the end, the answer only mattered if one of them turned out be a killer.

Chapter Sixteen

I grabbed a quick lunch of a burger and shake from a drive-through and headed back to the police station. The last person I expected to see there was my grandfather, Bull Weston. He stood at the front desk, his back to me, and I took a moment to observe him. His hair was thick and white, his clothes casual. Though his shoulders retained the straight posture of his military days, there was a heaviness to them that was painful to see. A weight was there and, though it was invisible, I knew from where it stemmed—my grandmother Julia's dementia.

I hugged him from behind, feeling his back tense, his body stiffen. "Are you here to visit me? It's awfully early."

When he turned around, I was aghast to see the dark bruising around his right eye.

"Oh, Bull, what happened?" I asked. He winced as I gingerly touched the swollen blue-purple area. "Who did this to you?"

"It's nothing," he said, waving off my hand in irritation. "I stumbled in the dark and fell against the bathroom doorjamb. It'll heal in a few days."

I knew a punch when I saw one.

What I didn't know was why Bull was lying to me.

"What aren't you telling me?" I asked, and looked from Bull to Hank Willows, the officer behind the front desk, then back to Bull. Willows was flushed, embarrassed to be privy to this particular family drama.

"Willows?"

"Oh, leave him alone. He doesn't know anything about this," Bull said with a sigh. "I hoped to avoid getting you involved, Gemma. It's Julia."

Noticing the sudden panic on my face, he added, "Your grandmother's fine. Well, not fine, but *safe*. She wandered off from the house this morning. I woke up about five, and she was just . . . gone."

"Why didn't you call me?"

"I didn't call you because I found her. Unfortunately, it wasn't before this guy found her," Bull said, and jerked a thumb to Willows. "He picked her up just as I got to her. Three streets from our house."

"I thought we had more time, Bull," I said. My grandmother's dementia seemed to be worsening by the week. "We need to look at other options."

"What, put your grandmother in a facility? An old folks' home? Over my dead body. Between the home healthcare nurses and me, we can take care of her. We *will* take care of her," Bull said. He turned to Willows. "Just give me the paperwork, Officer."

"You still haven't told me who punched you."

"I never could pull the wool over your eyes, Gemma." Bull turned around and gave me a small smile. "And I never like to admit when someone's gotten the best of me. Julia was upset yesterday. She didn't like the scrambled eggs I'd cooked, and boy did she let me know, with a hook to the face. Maybe that's why she ran away this morning, she's done with my cooking."

"This isn't funny."

The smile dropped from Bull's face. "No one's laughing."

Something occurred to me. "Why are you here?"

"What do you mean?" Bull asked nonchalantly. I wagged a finger at him and turned to Willows. "How many times have you picked up my grandmother?"

"Gemma," Bull warned.

"No! You don't get to lie to me, not about Julia. How many times?" I said. My voice was raised, and down the hall, one of my colleagues poked his head out of the central squad room. He watched a moment, then decided everything was under control and ducked back into the room.

Willows remained silent.

"How many times?" I whispered. Willows turned bright red and stared down at his desk and whispered in return, "Four."

"Four? Four times you've found my grandmother wandering the street? My god." I turned from Willows back to Bull. "And you. How could you keep this from me? You have no right!"

"She's my wife. We have every right to keep our medical issues private, even from you. Now listen, Gemma. No, listen to me a moment. We both adore your grandmother. And I know you think the best place for her is in some nursing home. But I don't agree. She belongs at home, with me. I can take care of her better than anyone else can," Bull replied. He wiped a weary hand over his face, drawing the skin down. "She's happy at home."

"I've seen the way she lashes out at servers at restaurants, at the post office. It's only a matter of time before she hurts someone else, physically, the way she's hurt you."

At the desk, the phone rang. Willows, thrilled for a reason to excuse himself, turned away to answer it.

Bull had paled at my words. "You don't honestly believe that. Your grandmother wouldn't hurt a fly."

"You're right, my grandmother wouldn't. But Julia isn't the same woman anymore. Don't let her get so far gone that she does something that you and I will regret for the rest of our lives. We'll be the ones living with the consequences of anything she does, not her."

"I taught you a lot of things, including being clever enough to know which battles are worth fighting," Bull said with tears in his eyes. "I'm warning you, stop fighting me on this. As her husband, it's my call to make. I expect you to respect that."

"We'll see about that," I said. I stormed off to my desk. I was shaking by the time I sat down. Bull had every right to his opinion, but he was wrong about this. It was bad enough that Julia was wandering the streets and getting out of the house under his watch; now she was violent, too. The bruise on his face had been a terrible shock for me.

By the time my phone rang a few minutes later, I'd calmed down. Slouched in my chair, I affected a carefree attitude, trying in vain to take the advice I'd read once in a fitness magazine to visualize my stress floating up over my head and out an open window. It helped that Finn had stepped away from his desk, gone to who knew where.

I picked up the phone. "Monroe."

"Detective Monroe? This is Ally. Ally Chang? Sari's best friend?"

Sitting up, I leaned forward. "Yes, hi, Ally. What's going on? Is Sari home?"

"No. No, she's not. I . . . I don't know if I should have called," Ally responded. There was a quiver in her voice, her pitch unnaturally high. "But . . . there's something you should know. At least, I think you should know it. Maybe it's not important. I'm not sure of anything these days."

It was obvious that Ally was in a tenuous state: Push her too hard, and she might hang up. Show too little interest, same result.

Calmly, slowly, I said, "Please, let me be the judge of what's important, Ally. Has something happened?"

"No . . . not exactly. It's just . . . well, I remembered something. From six or seven months ago. Sari and I were on a run and she tripped—her shoe was untied or something stupid like that. She fell and scraped her knee very badly. You know when you fall on asphalt and sort of slide?"

"Like road rash?"

"Exactly. Such a perfect name for what happens." A little laugh from Ally, then a long silence. Finally, "Anyway, she started sobbing. And it was so strange because I've seen Sari be injured much worse. Two years ago she broke her arm in a bicycle accident and didn't even cry."

"She sounds tough," I said. I didn't know where Ally was going with all of this, but I held my breath and bit my tongue.

"She is. Toughest broad I know. But that day, she wasn't so tough. When she stopped crying, she was really embarrassed. We went back to my apartment and got her knee washed and bandaged and had a few beers. After a while, she told me why she was so upset. It wasn't about the knee, that was just the straw that broke the camel's back."

Silence again.

"Ally? Are you still there?"

"I'm here. She . . . she was worried, Detective. She has a gambling problem. Had a problem. Maybe she still has it. I don't know, she said she was going to get help. Anyway, she was worried and scared. She said she was in a lot of debt and wasn't sure how she would pay it all off."

Could she have gone to Betty Starbuck for money?

"Ally, did anyone else know about Sari's addiction?"

"God, no. It took everything for her to confide in me. Mac and her mom don't know, I'm sure of it. And as I said, it's something I just remembered, just now. After that day, we never spoke of it again. With Sari, there were some doors you didn't open. Do you think this is important to the case?"

"It could be. If Sari got into debt with the wrong sort of people . . . Do you remember anything else from the conversation? Did Sari gamble online? At the casinos? Or locally, in private homes? Was her debt on credit cards? Or did she actually owe cash to someone?"

"I'm sorry, I don't recall her saying. In fact, she changed the subject right away. That's when she started telling me about the cop."

"What cop?"

Another long silence from Ally, then, "Sari dated a cop for a few weeks, while she and Mac were on a break. She said this cop got obsessed with her and she had to end things. She called him Blue Bird."

"Was he a Cedar Valley police officer?"

"I think so. But . . . Sari told lies sometimes, for attention. Maybe she made the whole thing up to distract me from her gambling." Ally sighed in the phone. "She could be crazy like that."

"Ally, thank you for sharing all this with me. It might be very helpful to the investigation. Is there anything else you can tell me?"

"No, but I'll call you if I think of anything. I heard what happened to her boss. It's so scary to think that there's a killer out there. In a way, it makes me feel better that Sari disappeared at Lost Lake. Do you know what I mean? Like, she's probably safe somewhere, probably hiding from some prick she played poker with. If she'd been at the gala, she might have been killed, too!"

I hadn't thought of it like that, but Ally had a point.

The cop thing bothered me. We were a small police department with a handful of single men, all of them good, decent guys on the surface. I couldn't imagine any of them becoming obsessive.

A dark thought entered my mind: *Maybe the cop wasn't single.*

We ended the call, and I spent the next few hours on the phone with each of the casinos in Colorado and Wyoming. My routine was simple and straightforward: talk to the highest-ranking security officer onsite. Explain that a young woman was missing. Ask for information.

Sari Chesney was known in half a dozen of the casinos.

They were large, flashy places, all within a day's drive of Cedar Valley. They attracted busloads of people each day, their appeal being cheap hotel rooms and prime rib buffets for under thirty bucks. Over the last few years, Sari Chesney had spent a weekend at each one. When I plotted out the dates of her visits, I saw they occurred roughly every three to four months.

Beyond that, the records got hazy.

I got lucky in one respect: security officers at casinos know a lot about how the house operates, and they're happy to talk about it. The casinos were willing to extend lines of credit to their customers, but unpaid markers were equivalent to bad checks—in other words, prosecutable. If Chesney had outstanding debts, the casinos would seek to get their money back using the letter of the law—say, the local district attorney—and not by use of muscle men.

"The houses don't work that way, Detective," one of the security directors said to me. He snorted, and I heard him unwrap a sandwich or a burger. I had missed lunch, snacking on only the banana and espresso, and I was starving. When the director spoke again, it was through a mouthful of food. "You've seen too many movies. We don't send hired mercenaries out with scare tactics. You should see how much some of these people drop on their visits here. We love our guests."

After the calls, I sat back and made a list of all the local money-lenders and loan sharks that I was aware of. I came up with four names, then turned around and looked across the aisle to Moriarty. Testimony in the park rapist case had finished, and he and Armstrong were back on active duty.

"Lou, what do you know about the bookies in town?"

"Bookmaking is illegal in the great state of Colorado," Lou responded without batting an eye. "You want to make a bet, go to the racetrack."

"Louis, come on. We bring them in, they make bail, or pay their fine, or whatever it is that's needed in the moment, and then they're back on the streets or back in their dens, taking money, same as they did the day before. I know there's a whole network of these rats. Just give me their damn names."

I read to him the list I had, and he thought a moment, sniffed a few times, then added three more names and a warning. "These are good guys, Gemma. Don't bust their balls. They're not hurting anyone."

I shook my head. "That's not my plan, Lou. I have a missing woman who may have owed some or all of them money. You know I've got to follow up with each of them."

"Missing woman? You mean that young lady from the museum?"

I nodded. "Sari Chesney."

"You're going down the wrong path. None of these guys are violent," Moriarty said. "They are serious dorks. I'm talking accountants, number crunchers, computer science kids. Hey, you got any candy, something sweet? Maybe some chocolate? I got a migraine that won't quit."

I found a candy bar in my purse. "You want any aspirin?"

"Nah, that stuff tears up my stomach. But I knew I could count on you, Gemma. Always with the food." He stood up and walked to my desk. "Look, these guys, these bookies . . . they're trying to make a living, same as you or me. They're in it for the money, not to hurt people."

He ate the candy bar in two bites, and I was immediately pissed that I'd given it to him. The chocolate would have tided me over for an hour or two at least.

"That's an interesting attitude, coming from you, Mr. Law Enforcement."

Moriarty shrugged. "You see the same depressing junk I see every day—drugs, child abuse, death. I figure the gamblers are the least of our problems. Anyway, I'm not above throwing down a few bucks myself on a game every now and then. Strictly aboveboard, of course. But . . . I get the appeal. It's a rush, you know?"

"I guess. There's a line, though, isn't there? How easy is it to slide from placing casual bets into a full-blown compulsion? Aren't these bookies taking advantage of gambling addictions? I have to imagine their business models depend on their clients—is that what they're called?—getting their next fix. The house wins most of the time, doesn't it? Same with the bookies?" I asked.

"Sure, it's sad to see someone sucked into the circus, draining their retirement accounts to place hundreds and thousands of dollars on the speed and agility of some college football player who may or may not have been wasted the night before." Moriarty shrugged. "Anyway, your source stinks like yesterday's tuna sandwich. I make it my business to know what's going on in these circles, and trust me, I've never heard Sari Chesney's name come up, not even whispered, not even once."

"What's your interest in this world, Lou?"

Moriarty grew smug. "It's a side hobby. I busted a few punks running a money laundering operation about ten years ago, and it's been an interest ever since."

His cell phone rang and he retrieved it from his pocket. "I've got to take this, excuse me. Thanks for the candy bar."

I sat back, thinking. Maybe Chesney's debts existed in the online gambling world. Or maybe she owed money to someone who operated beyond the local circles, beyond the legitimate casinos . . . someone on the outside.

Someone unknown even to Lou Moriarty.

I was in a tough spot. Because Chesney was merely missing, as opposed to a crime victim or a suspect, it would be difficult to gain access to her financial records. In a strange and twisted way, the longer she remained missing, the easier it would be to investigate her. Another few days and I could convene a search party, put out her photograph on the national wire, start to dig deep into her background.

As it was, there was still the strong likelihood that she walked out of Lost Lake and vanished on purpose. Financial struggles, abusive relationships, trouble with work . . . these were just a few of the reasons why people abandon their lives in search of something better. The reality is that very few missing persons are victims of crime.

Still annoyed about giving up my chocolate, I moved aside my piles of notes to reach a jar of nuts buried on my desk. A handful of almonds later, I opened the Sari Chesney file and reviewed the few notes that were there.

Had she gone to her boss, Betty Starbuck, and asked for money? Based on what Patrick Crabbe told me about his mother's preference to give to organizations and not individuals, Starbuck would likely have said no to Chesney. Did that decision cause her death?

I closed my eyes, trying to imagine a scenario where Chesney could have experienced a rage so terrible it resulted in the murder of another human being.

I couldn't imagine it.

But I didn't know Chesney. I didn't know what she was capable of.

Opening my eyes, I studied the photograph in the file, the one of Chesney and Mac Stephens and Ally Chang. Chesney's eyes were bright and her smile full. In the background, the mountains loomed under a sun-drenched sky. Her red-and-black flannel shirt looked too warm for the weather, but that was Colorado for you—it could be sunny and bright and thirty degrees.

All of a sudden, the thing that had been bothering me since Betty Starbuck's autopsy came roaring to the front of my mind, and I dropped the photograph, cursing.

"Son of a bitch. It was right there in front of you."

I quickly called the medical examiner's office and got through to Bonaire. He listened to my question, checked his notes, then came back to the phone. "Forensics hasn't come back yet, but yes, the fibers could be from a plaid flannel shirt such as the one you describe. The key phrase here is *could be*."

Mac Stephens had made a point to tell me that Sari was wearing the same shirt and boots the night she disappeared.

Was Sari missing . . . or was she on the run?

Was she a victim or a murderer?

Chapter Seventeen

Finn stepped back into the squad room as I ended the call with Bonaire. Though he was the last person I wanted to talk to, he was still my partner.

I cleared my throat as he sat down.

Nothing.

"Ahem," I said. He turned around and stared at me with his eyebrows raised. It took everything I had to adopt the most neutral, professional voice I could to tell Finn about my conversations with Kent Starbuck, Ally Chang, and Dr. Bonaire.

Finn listened quietly, a polite look on his face, his gaze targeting a spot on the wall slightly to the right of my head. He took few notes as I spoke, but when I got to the part about the fibers on Betty Starbuck being a possible match to the shirt Sari Chesney was wearing when she disappeared, Finn got excited.

"All right, all right." He rubbed his hands together. "Finally, something to work with."

"It's weak. Those fibers could be from anything. I'm concerned that Kent Starbuck has no alibi for the night of his mother's murder. And Patrick Crabbe's got an alibi, but there's something off about him. I don't trust either one of them."

"Patrick is scared of his own shadow," Finn said. "He didn't kill his mother."

"How do you know? For sure, I mean? What are the chances that Betty Starbuck let a stranger into the museum in the middle of the night? Isn't it much more likely she met up with someone known to her, like a family member or an employee?"

Finn nodded. "Yes. An employee . . . like Sari Chesney. We have a statement from Ally Chang that Chesney had gambling debts. Her own boyfriend said her tastes ran to the expensive side. So, Chesney steals the diary, kills Starbuck, and 'disappears' from Lost Lake. While we've got our eyes on Starbuck's sons, Chesney is halfway across the country."

"I still think it's a ridiculous idea. Sari's a young woman with no prior history of violence."

The excitement slowly died in Finn's eyes, and the polite, nearly frosty gleam reappeared. He pushed back, though it was mild, reserved, said in the kind of voice you use with a stranger. "Chesney might be a young woman, but you know perfectly well that age has nothing to do with violence."

It was obvious he'd made up his mind.

I said, "I'm going to brief Chavez. You coming?"

Finn shook his head and turned away. "I'm going to keep plugging away at interviewing the guests from the gala. It's a long shot, but maybe someone saw something. I've got the intern working on half the list, and I took the other. So far everyone's got the same story: great party, so-so food, terrible about the murder, didn't see a thing."

"Okay."

The intern was a young man with a name I could never remember and a personality like an index card: plain, square-edged, functional. He'd been with us a few months and so far, he was doing okay.

I found Chief Chavez in his office, his red and swollen nose buried in a stack of budget books. He looked grateful for the interruption, and I took my time briefing him on the latest developments in the Chesney and Starbuck cases.

"Any word on those extra resources, Chief? Finn and I can't be in two places at once. I need more intel on Chesney, but I can't devote much time to her while we've got a killer loose."

"Seems to me her debts are the key here. We've seen it before—

people walk away and start fresh somewhere else. They believe their credit history won't follow them." Chavez peered at me over the reading glasses perched on the tip of his nose. "You've gotten lucky with the fibers, however weak that may be. I think it's enough to justify getting you help. Moriarty and Armstrong are around, aren't they? See what their caseload is like. How about the intern?"

"I'll talk to Moriarty. Finn's already got the intern interviewing attendees from the gala."

"What's his name?"

"The intern? I don't have a clue."

"Damn. Me neither. What about the other thing?"

"Chief?"

Chavez sighed. "The other thing. The leaker. Any headway on that?"

You mean since you put me on it this morning? Inwardly, I groaned. Hadn't I just reiterated to the chief that I was stretched too thin? It was frustrating that he'd asked me to find the leaker in the first place. And it was ridiculous that he thought I should be making headway on that issue while Chesney was who knew where and Starbuck's body was lying in the morgue.

"Well? I know that look, Gemma. Wipe it off your face. You think I'm callous? Dense? Give me a break. Your top priorities are to find Starbuck's killer and find Sari Chesney. The leaker is lower on our list of priorities. *But it's still on the damn list.* Sooner or later an investigation is going to get compromised, and when I say compromised, I mean *screwed*."

"I'll get to the bottom of it."

He dismissed me with a wave, and I left his office, closing the door softly behind me.

When your boss asks you to find the source of the leak in your department, *you find the source of the leak in your department*. Though I had little choice but to obey his order—and make no mistake, no matter how mildly it was delivered, it was an order—I still had mixed feelings about the assignment. On the one hand, I was furious that one of my colleagues was improperly sharing information with the press. On the other hand, I hated the idea of sneaking behind people's backs, investigating them. It felt like dirty work.

I sat at my desk and looked around, taking stock of where things were in the investigations. Finn and the intern were covering the gala guests. We were waiting on further forensic reports. I needed to look into Larry Bornstein's background as well as interview Patrick Crabbe again in light of the information I'd gotten from Lois Freeman and Bornstein. I also needed to tackle a question that had been buzzing in my head since Saturday morning: Just who was Sari Chesney?

There was a lot to do. I shot an email off to Moriarty and Armstrong and begged for some assistance if they could spare it. As I hit the send button, Chief Chavez walked through the room. As he passed my desk, he rapped his knuckles gently on the copy of *The Valley Voice* that lay on top of my files.

I sighed. Message received, loud and clear.

I spent the next hour online cross-checking articles from the paper's archives with cases from the last few months, on guard the entire time in case someone came to my desk and asked me what I was doing. But no one did, and when I was finished, I was pleased to have learned a few things.

The first was that information seemed to be going to a single person: Bryce Ventura, with *The Valley Voice*. He was the author of every article that cited an anonymous source for his information.

I knew Ventura, though not well. He was a meek middle-aged man with doughy, pale skin and ebony hair that he wore combed straight back from his heart-shaped face, reminiscent of Elvis Presley in his later days. In addition to his reporting gig, Ventura was a house painter, and he typically appeared at newsworthy events in jeans and T-shirts splattered with various colors of paint.

"Bryce Ventura," I murmured. "It's a start."

I scanned the squad room again. At his desk, Finn was on his phone, speaking in a low voice. Across the aisle, Moriarty and Armstrong compared notes on some case they were working. The intern walked by me, giving a tentative wave as he struggled to balance three huge boxes of files that he had no doubt been assigned to sort and store.

All of them good people, going about their business.

What motivated someone to leak information to the press? I could think of three things, though I was sure there were others: revenge, concern, money. Revenge for some wrong done to them by their employer, the police department (or a specific individual within it). Concern—perhaps the leaker felt the department wasn't doing enough to solve cases, wasn't working fast enough. Finally, money. This was both the most troubling motive and the cleanest reason— someone was exchanging information for cash.

I glanced around again. Finn moved his arm, and his platinum watch caught the overhead light.

His new platinum watch, the one that he'd made a point of showing all of us.

How many trips had he been on in the last few months? Palm Springs and Las Vegas, at least twice. Then there were the flashy clothes and the new Kimber Custom 1911 pistol, which I knew cost over a thousand bucks.

Finn was a single man living in a rent-controlled apartment with a damn decent salary, but I knew he'd been saving for a down payment on a house and repair work on the speedboat he kept at Horse-tail Reservoir. I also knew he was aggressive with his pension accounts to support his goal of socking away enough to retire at fifty-five and live out his days on the beach somewhere in the Caribbean, a margarita in one hand and a fishing pole in the other.

"*What* is it?" Finn suddenly asked, and I jumped. "You've been staring at me for five minutes."

Flustered, I said lamely, "Sorry. I zoned out for a second."

"Well, knock it off. You're giving me a complex."

I turned back to my desk, my face on fire. Before we were made partners the previous fall, I'd heard enough about Finn to have a healthy mistrust of the guy. His heart was in the right place, but cases are made and broken in the courtroom—not in the squad room, not in the jail cell, and certainly not on the streets. Any halfway decent lawyer with a speck of evidence that the arresting officer mishandled evidence or coerced a witness could get a case tossed in a matter of minutes.

And just like that, the perp would walk.

I sighed. The leaker couldn't be Finn.

Could it?

What I needed to figure out was who had been working at times that would have given them access to the information leaked. But we had dozens of employees across the police department, and we ran a twenty-four-hour, seven-day-a-week operation.

The answer, I quickly realized, was to set a trap.

I could distribute fake information, for a short period of time, and then see if it made its way to Bryce Ventura and *The Valley Voice*. If it did, I would have a much smaller pool of employees to work with. And if it didn't, then I'd move on to another shift, on to another group of people.

But what information should I distribute? It would have to be something that had an air of truth to it, or Ventura would never buy it. Something juicy but harmless . . . something that would, if it worked, send Ventura on a wild goose chase while teasing the leaker to the surface.

The diary curse.

I grinned. It was perfect. It was exactly the sort of thing that Ventura would eat up with a spoon. As I started to jot down ideas, though, the grin was replaced by a frown. I couldn't help but wonder two things: why I'd been chosen for this covert operation, and who was investigating me.

Though it was late when I arrived home, I was dismayed to find that once again I'd beaten Brody. My understanding was that his new job was going to be more of an eight-to-five gig, and yet weekends and now evenings seemed to be fair game for work. My hours were unpredictable enough without adding in an ever-changing schedule from him.

Clementine was good-natured about it all.

"Don't worry, Gemma, Brody texted me. He told me to tell you that he'll pick up dinner and you can eat together," Clem said. She swept Grace off of the floor, where she'd been lying on her back on an activity mat, and handed her to me. Grace felt heavier than she had when I'd left that morning; she was growing like the weeds that sprouted in our driveway, small and fragile one moment, tall and sturdy the next.

"So when's the big day?" Clem asked. "Do I get an invitation?"

I glanced down at the diamond engagement ring on my left hand, realizing that I'd finally gotten used to the feel of it, the weight of it on my finger.

Sometimes I even forgot it was there.

"Actually, I was hoping you'd be a flower girl, Clementine. I'm thinking pink organza and plenty of tulle."

"Barf. You two should elope and save yourselves a bucket of money. I could probably be talked into going with you and babysitting Gracie, especially if we're talking Hawaii or the Bahamas," she said. She smoothed her hair back from her forehead, and I was envious of her smooth skin, her bright eyes. Ten or eleven years separated us in age, but it could have been decades. Her responsibilities were few, her time mostly her own.

I sighed. Looking at Clementine was like holding a mirror up and seeing all the cracks in my own veneer. And yet . . . the look of adoration she and Grace shared was priceless. And I was unlikely to find anyone else willing to work around our increasingly crazy schedules.

After Clem gathered her things and left, I poured myself a glass of wine, then drew a bubble bath and sat in it with Grace. By the time we'd finished our soak, Brody was home. I fed the baby and put her to bed, then Brody and I finally sat down for dinner at nine o'clock. He'd picked up lasagna, garlic bread, and Caesar salad from Luigi's. We sat at the kitchen table and ate on red placemats that matched the thick sauce of the lasagna.

As I loaded my plate, I couldn't help asking, "Is this the new norm?"

"Luigi's? I don't think my waistline could handle it."

"Dinner at nine. You, coming home hours later than expected."

Brody set down his fork. "I'm home late a few nights and you get on my case."

"I'm sorry."

I truly was. I was irritable, easily agitated. I'd been on the go for two full days. A murder investigation doesn't rest easily. "Do you want a glass of wine?"

"I'll get it," Brody replied. He stood and went to the counter. He'd shaved his dark beard, and under the bright kitchen light he somehow looked both older and younger, wiser and more fragile. He held up the bottle to the light, gauging how much of the wine was left, then brought it to the table and sat down.

Desperate to change the subject, I said the first thing that came to mind. "What do you think of Clem?"

Pouring himself a glass of the wine, Brody started laughing. "Now that's a loaded question if I've ever heard one. What do I think of Clem? In what way?"

Shrugging, I went ahead and poured myself another glass. The buzz from the first glass had long since worn off, and I wanted to feel hazy again, hanging out somewhere between caring and not caring. "I'm curious what you think of her, being here, with our daughter. In our lives. Is having a nanny what you expected? Do you think she's working out? Grace seems to love her."

Brody tilted his head and his hazel eyes brightened. "She sure does. I like Clementine, I really do. She's funny as hell and young, you know, energetic. What I wouldn't give to be ten years younger."

"No kidding."

"I'm envious of her vitality. Her youth. Clem's got her whole life in front of her. She's a clean slate. Don't you ever think about what you'd do differently, if you could go back? Start over?" Brody asked. He took a sip of his wine and set the glass down slowly. "There are a lot of things I'd like a do-over on."

"Like what?" I asked, genuinely curious.

Brody sighed. "Well, obviously the . . . my indiscretions. Look at me, I can't even say the word. My *affair*. There're other things, too. I wish I'd spent more time with my dad before he passed away. I thought he was indestructible. It never occurred to me that there'd come a day when he wouldn't be here."

I nodded and started to twist the ring on my left hand back and forth. Brody noticed and paled slightly. "Cold feet?"

"No. No, I don't think so. Maybe an early midlife crisis," I said. "I've felt on edge the last few months. Maybe it's postnatal hormones."

"Do you need to see a therapist again? Dr. Pabst was helpful," Brody said carefully. A pensive look settled over his face. "If we're rushing this . . ."

"No. Brody, you've been incredibly patient with me. I want to marry you, I do. I'll be fine. It's this case. I'm distracted."

He looked down and pushed a last bite of cold lasagna around on his plate, drawing a circle with the pasta. "Just don't shut me out, Gemma."

We cleaned the kitchen and later, in bed, our bodies reached for each other. After, I waited for Brody to say something, anything, but he was silent. I lay in bed, awake, staring at shadows on the ceiling long after he'd fallen asleep.

Chapter Eighteen

"Rough night?"

"I've had better," I said coolly, and dropped my things at my desk. Out of the corner of my eye, I saw Finn watching me. He looked how Finn always looks, polished and put together even when he's had very little sleep.

Today, though, he also looked so hangdog that I sighed. We'd never accomplish anything if we spent all our time fighting with each other. "It's Tuesday, that's always nicer than a Monday."

Finn perked up and joined me at my desk with a mug in his hand. "Truer words were never spoken. Look, about yesterday—"

"We were both out of line. Let's move on."

He nodded. "Absolutely." He picked up a framed photograph of Brody and Grace on my desk, then set it down. "The family's good?"

"Yes, they're fine. How's Cassie? And Roland? I haven't seen them around much."

Cassie was Finn's girlfriend; Roland, her teenage son. The boy had played an integral role in my last case, and though I hadn't seen him in a few months, I kept meaning to look in on him. He used a wheelchair, the result of a tragic accident. Roland was a smart-aleck, too clever for his own good, with an artistic talent that bent toward sketching fantastical and frankly frightening creatures. I liked him a lot.

Finn took a long swallow from the mug and made a face. "How do people drink this stuff? Green tea . . . more like pee tea. It tastes like a wet paper towel. Cassandra is fine. She and Roland and her ex-husband and her ex's boyfriend are in New York. They're looking at colleges for the kid. Talk about modern families."

"Have you met him? The ex-husband?"

"Once. He picked Roland up for the weekend while I was at Cass's place. The guy seems nice enough. He's a short little man. His boyfriend's an accountant with a pencil mustache and box seats for the Denver Broncos," Finn said. He set down the green tea and wiped his mouth with the back of his hand. "Roland barely talks to me."

"What do you expect? He's sixteen years old. You're sleeping with his mom."

Finn looked surprised. "He doesn't know that."

"You're delusional. Of course he knows," I said. "He's not a little kid, Finn. If you treat him like one, he'll never warm to you."

"Like you know so much, Mama," he responded. "How's that nanny of yours? What's her name, Marmalade? Jelly?"

"Clementine," I said, and turned back to my computer.

Finn's phone rang, and he stepped away to answer it. When he returned a few minutes later, he was excited. "That was a man named Tom Lowenstein. He swears that someone who looked like 'that gas station guy but with a big mustache' was loitering outside the museum the night Betty Starbuck was killed."

"Kent Starbuck?"

"I think so," Finn said. "Lowenstein's on his way here to give a statement. He should look at some mug shots . . . think you can dig up a photograph of Kent Starbuck?"

"Yes." I turned to my computer and pulled up the appropriate records. I remembered seeing a picture of Starbuck—albeit a ten-years-younger version—somewhere in his file.

Lowenstein arrived shortly thereafter. He was a nervous middle-aged man with a fringe of red hair around a freckled dome and tiny eyes set into a florid, fleshy face. Heavyset, he smelled of cigarette smoke and blew his nose repeatedly.

"As I told Detective Nowlin, I feel terrible about this. I was out of town on an overnight business trip Sunday through yesterday. I heard about the murder, of course, but it wasn't until this morning when I was catching up on the daily newspapers that I saw the date and made the connection."

"And what do you do for business?" I asked. His answer wasn't necessarily important, but I wanted him relaxed. The way to do that was to talk about things familiar to him.

"Sales. I sell nutcrackers."

Finn started laughing, then stopped short when Lowenstein shot him a cutting glance. "I wouldn't laugh, Detective. It's quite a lucrative business. I collect them from around the world and then sell them online. I made six figures last year. One of them sold for thirty thousand dollars."

"Jesus Christ, I'm in the wrong business," Finn gasped. "Thirty thou? For a tiny doll?"

Lowenstein brushed a speck of lint off his suit sleeve and drew himself up. "This was no tiny doll. It was an original Popov. Three feet tall, carved by hand from a single piece of wood. Only a hundred were ever made. I probably could have gotten forty thousand, but the buyer is a regular client of mine. I wasn't comfortable fleecing him."

I cleared my throat, sorry I'd asked about his profession. "Tell us what you saw that night, please."

"Certainly. I suffer from insomnia and find a midnight constitutional helps quite a bit. I leashed up Buttons and we did our usual route. I live half a mile from the museum, and we typically turn around in the parking lot and return home. An even mile, and at our pace, it's about twenty-five minutes. This was the night of the gala, and by midnight, I'd expected things to be quiet with most if not all of the guests departed for the evening," Lowenstein said. He paused and asked, "Can I smoke?"

I shook my head. "No, it's illegal inside the station."

Lowenstein waved a hand. "No matter. Where was I? Oh yes. We reached the parking lot and I saw a car with security decals pull away. The museum itself was dark, as it usually is. A single light shone at the front entrance, and of course the streetlights were still on. Buttons and I turned to head home, and I noticed a thin, balding man approach the museum from the opposite side of the street. He reached the front steps, looked up at the building, checked his watch, then began pacing. He was dressed in dark clothes, and for a moment, he was clearly illuminated by a streetlight. I thought to myself that he looked just like the man that owns the Gas 'n' Go, but with a thick mustache and an air about him that was utterly suspicious."

"Did you talk to the man or otherwise interact with him?" I asked.

"No. It was late, and aside from my twenty-pound terrier, I was unarmed. As I said, he seemed unsavory."

"But you didn't report him."

"Heavens no, why would I? Here I was, out for a stroll in the middle of the night. For all I knew, he was doing the same. Perhaps I scared him just as much as he scared me."

Finn nodded, conceding the point. "We have some photographs that we'd like you to look at. Gemma?"

I'd printed five other photos from our book of mug shots of men that resembled Kent Starbuck. I slid them and the photo of Starbuck across the table. Lowenstein slipped on a pair of eyeglasses that he'd withdrawn from his pocket and then picked up the photographs one by one. He peered at Starbuck's face the longest. He hemmed and hawed, and Finn and I shot sidelong glances at one another.

Finally, Lowenstein slapped Starbuck's photograph down. "Add a mustache and about twenty pounds, and that was the man I saw outside the museum the night Betty Starbuck was murdered."

We picked Kent Starbuck up at his motel. He was reluctant to accompany us to the police station but ultimately understood he had little choice in the matter.

We were going to talk with him, one way or another.

We sat in the interview room, Finn and me on one side of the table, Starbuck on the opposite.

Finn got right to it. "We have an eyewitness who places you at the history museum near the time your mother was killed, Mr. Starbuck.

This witness saw you lurking about the front entrance after all the guests had departed."

Starbuck sat back and dropped his rough, callused hands into his lap. "Since when is it a crime to be out on the street at night?"

"So you were there."

"Yes, Detective Monroe, I was there. But as I said—since when is that a crime?"

"It's not. But obstruction of justice is illegal. You lied to me. You told me you were home the entire evening. So here's your chance to make that lie right. Just tell us why you were there and we can all get out of here. The museum is four miles from your motel. You don't own a car, Mr. Starbuck. I have trouble believing you were out for an eight-mile round-trip *stroll* in the middle of the night," I said.

Starbuck shot me another of his awful smiles. "What can I say, I'm training for a marathon."

Finn started laughing. "Man, this is going to be fun. I've got no plans for the rest of the day. I don't think Detective Monroe does, either. We're happy to spend the next six hours in here."

"I'm free to leave whenever I damn well choose," Starbuck growled.

"Not if we arrest you for obstruction. We're trying to play nice here, Kent. Work with us," Finn said.

Starbuck drew a hand over his face, considering his options. He must have realized they were few, because he finally said, "Okay. My mother asked me to meet her there, at the museum, after all the guests had gone. She didn't give me a time, but I figured everyone would be gone by midnight."

"Why there, why so late?"

Starbuck lifted a shoulder. His faded denim shirt was threadbare, the stitching coming loose at the seams. He wiped his nose on the edge of his hand. "I don't know. She insisted on it, though. Look, I thought it was strange, too. I took a cab and got there just before midnight, but her car was gone and the whole place looked closed up. I hung around for a few minutes, then left. Next thing I know, she's dead."

"Can you think of any reason she might have insisted on such a strange meeting place and time?" Finn asked. "Why not meet at her house? Or your motel?"

"The only thing I can think of is that it had something to do with Patrick. They were real close, the two of them. If there was something she didn't want him to know about . . . or if she was frightened of him, say, well, then I can see the need for secrecy," Starbuck said.

"There's a big difference between keeping a secret from someone and being frightened of him. Had your mother indicated she was scared of your brother?"

Starbuck thought a moment. "No. I got the sense that she was uneasy about something or someone, but as I told you before, I didn't know her very well. Look, I wish I could tell you more, honestly. Though there wasn't a lot of love between us anymore, I do want to see my mother's killer brought to justice. She didn't deserve to die, not the way she did."

I asked a final question. "Did you see anyone else, or anything at all, while you were at the museum?"

"Just some fat old fart walking his dog."

We let Starbuck go, and then Finn and I sat at our desks, talking things over.

"I think he's lying. Betty Starbuck never called him. There was never any meeting. Lowenstein's account puts Kent Starbuck at the museum within the timeframe of his mother's murder. And all Kent can say is 'We had a meeting scheduled'? Baloney."

Finn rubbed at the back of his neck. "I don't know . . . he sounded pretty sure of himself. What if Betty did call Kent to the museum to discuss Patrick? What if he *was* the man in her backyard, a man she had grown scared of?"

He checked his watch and swore. "I'm late for an appointment."

"I'll pay Patrick a visit at work."

"Good. I'll catch up with you later."

I watched Finn leave the squad room, his broad shoulders tense, his face drawn. I wondered where he was going, who he was meeting.

Bryce Ventura?

I shook my head, turning back to my computer.

It's none of my business.

Working with him these past few months, day in and day out . . . Finn had earned my trust. No matter how much he frustrated me, no matter how much he angered me, he had earned my trust.

Hadn't he?

The possibility that Finn was meeting Bryce Ventura reminded me that I'd come up with a plan to catch the leaker. I left my desk and grabbed a cup of coffee in the break room, thinking through my next steps. The problem was how to make sure that everyone working a particular shift—and only those people—saw the false information. That seemed to be the best way to limit my pool of suspects.

We had three shifts in the department. Three groups of my colleagues . . . three groups of suspects.

I sipped my coffee, scanning the break room, considering and then eliminating ideas. A patrol officer walked in, on his phone. By way of greeting, he gave me a lift of his chin. I nodded back at him. He poured himself a cup of coffee and then left the room. I followed him out, without a destination in mind, and watched as he paused a moment to peruse the Red Board.

The Red Board.

It was perfect.

The Red Board was a small bulletin board on the wall just outside the locker rooms. We called it the Red Board because it was where any critical information would be posted. Sure, most things went out electronically. But if something was deemed a high visual priority— say, a pencil sketch of a suspect, or a photograph of a missing child— it would be printed out and hung on the Red Board. In fact, I'd meant to pin the photograph of Sari Chesney there. Both cops and nonsworn personnel used the locker rooms, and everyone was in the habit of scanning the Red Board on their way in or out.

I could post information and be practically guaranteed that the leaker would see it.

It was perfect.

I frowned. Maybe not totally perfect. Because in all honesty, there was no way to know when the leaker was taking information to Ventura. He or she could work an eight-to-five shift, learn something, then wait a few hours before speaking to Ventura.

As I thought about it more, I realized the answer was to post three *different* kinds of information, one at a time. That way, no matter when the leaker actually went to Ventura, I'd still know which shift the leaker worked. It did mean coming to the station, though, at the beginning or end of each shift and changing out the false information. Checking my watch, I decided to post the first set at the very end of my shift, right before going home.

I sighed and cursed both the leaker and Chief Chavez.

I didn't need to be running around playing spymaster while Betty Starbuck's killer walked the streets.

I had a plan, though. And it would work, I knew it would.

It had to, because I was out of ideas, and if the look on the chief's face meant anything, I was running out of time as well.

Chapter Nineteen

I drove to Patrick Crabbe's gas station under dark skies that threatened to open at any moment. Flowers, orange tulips mostly but some other varieties as well, bloomed in the medians that divided the streets. The city had devoted a lot of money to beautifying the roads, and it showed in the colorful flowers and the shiny new trash and recycling containers that lined the avenues.

Two cars, an older model Camry and a silver hatchback, were parked in the lot adjacent to the station. I'd seen the Camry at Crabbe's house and assumed it belonged to him. As I parked and left my car, a gust of wind moved an empty soda can across the asphalt. The can came to rest against a gas pump, joining torn candy wrappers and crumpled receipts.

The pumps were empty, and for the first time I realized how truly secluded the gas station was. It was set back from the road, close to the woods, in the shadow of the trees that loomed above it. At night, the single streetlight likely did little to illuminate the lot. It was clear to see why the station was the target of so much vandalism; it would be easy to tag the walls and smash the windows without any witnesses.

Another gust of wind set the soda can clanking against the pump, and I hurried inside. Behind the desk, a clerk perused a celebrity gossip magazine. I identified myself and asked for Crabbe. She pointed down an aisle to the back office. "Get yourself a cup of coffee and a doughnut. It's on the house."

"No, but thank you."

"You sure?"

"Well, maybe just one doughnut." I had missed lunch, after all. I chose a warm apple fritter and watched through the front windows as rain began to fall.

The clerk flipped her long red hair off her shoulder and leaned forward, opening her green eyes wide. She was twenty, maybe twenty-one. "Are you here about Patrick's mom? It's so, so sad. She used to fill up her tank here all the time."

"It is very sad. Thanks for the doughnut," I said. "He's in the back?"

She nodded and returned to her magazine, clearly disappointed not to have gotten anything more out of me. Outside, the rain intensified. We both jumped as a flash of lightning lit up the sky. Almost immediately a tremendous clap of thunder followed.

In his office, Patrick Crabbe slumped at a wooden desk that tottered on uneven legs, surrounded by stuff: magazines, empty soda cans, scraps of paper. Boxes of yellowing receipts were stacked on every surface. Two tall bookcases were filled with binders and auto repair manuals. A small trash can overflowing with fast-food wrappers and wadded-up tissues sat square in the middle of the room.

On the desk in front of Crabbe was a single piece of paper that looked like my high school math exams: a mess of notations and scribbles, slashed through with big, fat red marks.

"Mom's obituary," Crabbe explained. He looked haggard, more sunken since I'd seen him last, as though the weight of his mother's death had caused him to cave in on himself. "The paper is asking for something, and I'm having a heck of a time. How do you sum up a person's life in three to five paragraphs?"

I leaned against the door frame. "The *Voice* doesn't have an obit writer?"

Crabbe shook his head. "Nope. They used to, but she died a few years ago. She was smart and wrote her own obituary when it became obvious she was dying. Four paragraphs. The paper sent it over as an example of what they're looking for. What can I do for you, Gemma?"

"I have a couple of follow-up questions. They're a bit delicate, Patrick, so please bear with me and know that I'm asking them because my job is to find your mother's killer. I don't have the time or the luxury to beat around the bush."

He frowned. "Ask away."

"I've had a few reports from people close to your mother telling me that she was worried about you. Maybe even frightened."

Crabbe's frown deepened. I started to speak again, but another tremendous clap of thunder shook the station.

Patrick waited a beat then said, "Storm's close. Who are these people, Gemma, that you've been talking to?"

I shook my head. "I'm sorry, Patrick, but I can't get into those details. Help me understand what your relationship with Betty was like. Did you two fight recently? How's work? Is everything going okay in *your* life?"

He leaned back and stared down at his hands. He was silent so long I was afraid he simply wasn't going to talk, and then all of a sudden, he spoke with a fury so cold I nearly stepped back out of the room.

"Fucking Kent. He comes back to town and everything goes to hell. My business starts losing money. Mom develops this paranoia, I can't explain it, it's as though she's seeing ghosts around every corner. He's like the goddamn Grim Reaper." Crabbe exhaled noisily and looked up at me. "Kent should have died. Not Mom."

"You're upset, Patrick."

"Damn right I'm upset!" Crabbe stood up and shoved his mother's obituary to the floor. "Don't patronize me."

I swallowed. Was he on drugs? Experiencing some kind of manic episode? In my head, I ran through the usual suspects for such an outburst, finally settling on grief and its accompanying stage of anger.

I stood, silent, watching as Crabbe breathed heavily through his nose. The moment passed, and he slowly slid back into his chair. He rubbed at his eyes, took a sip from a water bottle.

Still I waited.

Finally, he said "I'm sorry. I know you're not the enemy. I just . . . it's overwhelming, you know?"

"Yes, I do know. Patrick, one of the things your mom told one of these, ah, witnesses was that she'd seen you in the backyard, behind the house, in the middle of the night. Just standing there. Is that something you've done?"

"Why on earth would I do that?"

"Insomnia?" I offered.

"Well, I have no idea what you're talking about. Your so-called witnesses are lying. My mother never told anyone that . . . *because it never happened.*" Crabbe looked at me, then away. I was relieved to see the rage in his eyes had dissipated. "I'm tired, Gemma. Was there anything else?"

"Just one more question. You hinted that your mom didn't have the funds to be giving money away. We discovered financial paperwork indicating otherwise and a revised will that leaves you and Kent Starbuck equal heirs to your mom's assets. Is that a surprise?"

"Money comes and money goes." Crabbe wearily waved a hand. "My mom had some money stashed away, huh? And she kept it a secret? Great. I'll get back on my feet. Maybe relocate the station to a more appealing lot. And if Kent gets half of Mom's cash, so be it. Maybe he'll take it and leave for good."

"Maybe." I nodded. "Thanks for your time, Patrick. I'll be seeing you around."

I turned around and started to leave, but Crabbe's voice, low and monotone, called me back.

"Excuse me?"

He had moved to a corner of the office. Kneeling, his back to me, he said over his shoulder, "Not if I see you first."

Crabbe slowly turned around. In his hands were reams of old receipts, the print faded, the edges torn. He smiled, and I saw once more how similar he and his brother looked.

"That's an old joke my mom and I had. I'd say 'I'll see you' and she'd say 'Not if I see you first.'"

"Ah. Well, good-bye, Patrick."

I left the station and hurried to my car, holding my jacket over my head in a pathetic attempt to keep dry. By the time I was in the driver's seat, I was soaked. As I started the car and pulled out of the lot, Crabbe's awful smile—the one he shared with Kent—followed me and a chill settled into my bones that had nothing to do with the weather.

Back at the station, I poked my head in the chief's office, but he wasn't there. I ran into his secretary in the hall and she told me he'd already left for the day. I'd wanted to give him a heads-up on my plan for catching the leak but as I thought about it, I realized it might be best if he didn't know all the details.

I had a small window in which to lay the first trap, during the shift change from day to night, so at my desk I quickly typed up a bland summary of the Starbuck homicide. I included information about the missing Owen Rayburn Diary, including rumors of a curse and the priceless nature of the diary itself. Anyone reading between the lines would believe that I was investigating the possibility that the diary, the *cursed* diary, was somehow responsible for Betty Starbuck's murder. I included a picture I pulled off the internet of a worn, brown leather journal. It wasn't Rayburn's, of course, but I asked everyone to keep an eye out for something similar at the local pawn shops.

It was ridiculous. I no more believed in curses than I did in the tooth fairy. And yet . . . it was appealing. Everyone loves a bit of the supernatural, especially a sleazy reporter like Bryce Ventura.

I headed up the summary with a "be on the lookout" alert, then printed and posted it on the Red Board. It was just in time, too. People were suddenly moving in and out of the locker rooms, patrol officers changing into and out of uniforms, nonuniformed personnel retrieving handbags and coats from their lockers.

It was shift change.

It was the end of my day and the start of someone else's.

I was halfway up the canyon when I remembered what day it was. Bull's birthday. I was still stinging from the encounter with him the day before, but birthdays were a big deal in our family and we'd had dinner planned for weeks. I turned around and drove to Chevy's. The pizzeria was packed, and I elbowed my way to the small private room in the back, where I found Bull, Julia, and a dozen of their friends gathered around a long table. Brody came in with Grace a few minutes after I arrived and worked on getting her set up in a high chair.

"I'm sorry," I whispered in Bull's ear as I gave him a hug. He wore a cowboy hat that, together with the bruise on his eye, made him look like a villain in an old western. "What's with the hat?"

"A gift from your grandmother. She insisted I wear it tonight." Bull squeezed me tight, then released me and held me at arm's length. "No apology necessary, honey. We both want what's best for your grandmother. We just have to remember that we're on the same team. The disease is the enemy, not each other."

"I guess it's true what they say: with age comes wisdom. You're practically oozing it from your pores." I smirked. "Not surprising, considering you're a hundred and twenty years old."

Bull rolled his eyes. "Just you wait. Fifty, sixty, even seventy years old . . . those were good birthdays. Milestones. Now? Now the guest list gets smaller and the health complaints list gets longer. I had to listen to that woman talk for fifteen minutes straight about a mole removal. A mole! I told her I'd have taken a pair of scissors to it and saved her the co-pay. She didn't appreciate the comment. Avoid her, at all costs." He pointed to one of Julia's friends, an attractive older woman with a small bandage on her chin. She saw us staring and flushed. Bull held up a hand and made a scissoring gesture. The woman huffed and turned away.

"You're terrible."

"The worst part is she thought I was joking. You hungry?" Bull pointed to the table as servers set out six extra-large pizzas. "We went big."

"Starving."

I sat between Grace and Brody, keeping the baby occupied with toys on the tray of her high chair, talking with Brody about his day in between bites of a mushroom-and-olive thin-crust pizza.

There were few things Brody enjoyed more than discussing his work, and he began telling me in earnest about a contract he was reviewing for a mining corporation in South Africa.

I slowly drifted away, paying more and more attention to Grace's fuzzy, beeping toys and less and less attention to the minutiae of the health standards in some pit on a continent I'd never been to.

"I lost you, didn't I?"

Busted. I dropped Grace's glowing frog thing and turned back to Brody. "I'm sorry, honey . . . but yes, you lost me somewhere between Johannesburg and the Black Plague."

Brody laughed so hard he snorted beer. "Black damp. Not plague."

"Are they different? Wait, wait, it's okay. No need to explain."

"I know it's incredibly boring compared to what you do." Brody wiped his mouth and sighed. "But I think this stuff is fascinating. And it's important to me. It's my career. I appreciate you trying to listen."

"I do try. It's just so . . . technical sometimes. I need the abridged version."

Across the table, Julia stood up and clinked her knife against her water glass. "If you will all stop stuffing your faces for a moment, I have something to say. Today is the day that many, many, *many* years ago, my darling husband, Bull Weston, came into the world. He wasn't supposed to live. He arrived early, a tiny thing, and there were complications. He fought for his life, though, and he's been fighting ever since. In the military, he fought for our country. As an attorney and then as a judge, he fought for justice. As my husband, as a surrogate father for our granddaughter, Gemma, he fought for what was best for our family. And now, as I face down the barrel of this insidious disease that is stealing my memories, stealing my mind, he's fighting for me. So let's raise a glass in honor of the birthday boy. To Bull, the best man I've ever known. The love of my life. May you live to see as many sunrises as inspire you and not one sunrise more." There wasn't a dry eye in the crowd. "To Bull!"

I hadn't heard Julia speak so eloquently, so coherently, in months, and I buried my face in Brody's shoulder to keep from sobbing. *This* was the woman who'd raised me, *this* was the woman who'd begged me not to join the police force and then presented me with my first handgun at my graduation ceremony. Complicated, passionate, a fighter herself.

I pulled away from Brody and caught Bull's eye across the table.

He was happy, content. For tonight, anyway, he was at peace with the world.

Chapter Twenty

Wednesday dawned with the kind of gentle light that comes through stained-glass windows: soft and full of grace. The sky was alive with shades of pink and orange as I left home and headed into work.

My mood was upbeat, with no sense of what the day would hold, of where I would find myself that evening. I arrived thirty minutes early in order to remove the report from the Red Board. I took it down and put in the shredder. It had either served its purpose or not; it was now time for me to come up with some other false report I could post for the next shift.

Then something happened that I rarely experience: I got lucky.

"Hey, Monroe! I think I saw a UFO last night! You want to take a road trip down to Roswell with me?" Barking laughter from the rest of the room. The cop, encouraged by the laughter, continued. "There's a mermaid in my bathtub!"

"What the hell is he talking about?" I muttered to Finn as I set my things down and booted up my computer.

"Bryce Ventura's Twitter feed." Finn pulled it up on his phone and read it to me in a low, angry voice. "*Cedar Valley PD blames museum murder on ancient curse. Missing diary responsible for countless deaths over the years.* What the hell, Gemma? Where did Ventura get this information from? He makes us sound like a bunch of loons."

Holy shit. It worked.

I swallowed a smile. "I have no idea. I'll call him in a bit, get on his case."

"You know what's going to happen next, don't you? We'll get every nutjob in town calling us. Did you know there is a group that meets once a month at the Y just to discuss conspiracy theories? Little green men and the people who worship them."

"There's a group of little green men that meet at the Y?"

Finn made a face and turned away. I smirked, ridiculously proud that my trap had worked. Then I realized what that meant: someone working the evening shift last night was the leak.

And he, or she, hadn't wasted any time in talking to Bryce Ventura.

Did this mean I could eliminate Finn from the suspect list? I started to, then had second thoughts. It would be just like him, sneaky and smart, to act upset about Ventura's Twitter post while in fact he was the one feeding the reporter the information.

I pulled up the shift schedule to see who'd worked the night before and began to jot down the names, when the front desk officer alerted me that Mac Stephens was in the lobby, asking for me. I found him standing in the corner, talking in a low, urgent voice to his cousin Jake.

Mac was angry. "It's been days, Detective. Where is Sari? Why haven't you found her yet?"

I explained that while we'd started to look into Chesney's life, I didn't have any updates for him.

"How can that be?" Mac asked. There were dark circles under his eyes and he'd lost weight. "Someone's taken her, I'm sure of it. She disappears and a day later, her boss is murdered. Something horrible is going on."

"Yeah, you said Sari would turn up," Jake added. He pushed his eyeglasses up on his nose and stared at me. He looked me up and down, sneered. "What kind of a cop makes a promise like that? You said nine times out of ten, the missing person shows up."

"I know what I said," I snapped. His words stung, because he was right.

I exhaled, tried to calm down. My frustrations didn't lie with the two of them. I was spread too thin, running this way and that, seemingly doing a lot but learning little. Progress was slow; it was as simple as that. I was devoting most of my time to the Starbuck case, and rightfully so.

"Look, we're monitoring Sari's cell phone, credit cards, and bank accounts. The fact that she hasn't used any of them is troubling, I'll admit, but if she's left town of her own volition, then she had a plan in place. She may have been stockpiling cash. Mac, I'm sorry to be blunt, but perhaps there's a reason she's gone to all this trouble. Perhaps she doesn't want to be found."

Mac grew angry, his face reddening, his eyes narrowing. He pointed a finger at my face. "This is bullshit. I'm going to have your head when it turns out that Sari's been kidnapped. If she's been hurt . . . that's on you, Detective. This is gross incompetence, plain and simple."

"I know you're upset. I'm worried, too. I have a meeting today with my team; we've gotten additional help to find Sari. We can probably get a few people up to Lost Lake to start canvassing the area—"

"That should have been done on Saturday when we told you she was missing. You suggested maybe she ran away, maybe she met up with someone. I never should have listened to you. Something's happened to her!" Mac yelled.

He stormed out, and Jake followed behind him, a troubled look on his face. Then Jake turned around and opened his mouth as if to speak. But no words came out. He merely shrugged, and then both men were gone and I was left alone in the lobby, my cheeks burning with the unsettling knowledge that there was a chance Mac was right.

"You coming?"

I checked the time, then swore as I jumped up and joined the chief in the hall. He did not appreciate it when people were late to his weekly staff meetings.

I joined the others at the table in our largest conference room. There were seven of us: the chief and his secretary, Moriarty and Armstrong, Finn and me, and the intern. The chief had made good on his promise of extra resources; Moriarty and Armstrong were of-

ficially on the case with us. This meeting was intended to bring everyone up to speed on what we were calling the Museum Mystery: a
lame but appropriate title that captured the Starbuck homicide, Sari
Chesney's disappearance, and the missing Rayburn Diary under one
nickname.

Finn went first. "Between the intern and me, we've spoken to
about two-thirds of the guests who were at the gala the night of Betty
Starbuck's murder. So far, we got zilch. No one saw or heard anything unusual. We've still got about twenty to go—some folks have
been slow in returning our calls, a few others are out of town on business, traveling, and so on. In addition, the intern has also interviewed
all of the museum volunteers and the board members about the
Rayburn Diary. Just like with the murder: no one saw anything. No
one heard anything. Our guy fingerprinted the safe, and that was a
bust, too. All identifiable prints belong to museum staff."

In the corner, the intern nodded along as Finn spoke. I squinted,
trying to read the tiny print on the nametag on the lapel of his suit
jacket, but it was in vain.

Finn continued. "I spoke with the security guard under contract
with the museum. He was broken-hearted about Starbuck's death
and blamed himself. He told us two useful things: he did not do a
sweep of the museum after the final gala guest left, and the last time
he saw Betty Starbuck alive was when he escorted her to her car that
night. She'd given him no indication that she planned to grab a burger
and then return to the museum. Gemma?"

"Thanks, Finn. Guys, we're waiting on forensics from the crime
lab. We have a possible match on fibers found on Starbuck's body to
a shirt that Sari Chesney was wearing at the time of her disappearance. It's weak. Starbuck's opal necklace continues to bother me. It
was valuable and sellable—a hell of a lot easier to sell than the
diary—yet it was left at the murder scene. This, along with the very
personal nature of her murder, strongly suggests to me that Starbuck's
murder was not the result of a robbery gone awry. We've said it from
the start: we're looking for a killer who knew Starbuck. Knew her
intimately." I took a sip of coffee, then continued. "Looking at her

sons, both are suspicious for different reasons. Of the two, Kent Star-buck is the only one without an alibi. Not only that, but he was seen at the museum near to the time of his mother's death. The problem is, it's all circumstantial. We have nothing tying him to the actual scene of the crime."

I started to review the timeline of Chesney's disappearance when Chloe Parker from dispatch interrupted the meeting. She stuck her head in the room, a tense expression on her face.

Chief Chavez frowned. "Yes?"

Chloe shot me a pointed look, and my heart skipped a beat. My first thought was trouble at home, but then she turned back to Chavez and said in a rush, "I'm sorry to interrupt, Chief. We have a situation in the lobby. A couple of guys just came in. They've been fishing at Lost Lake."

She stopped a moment to catch her breath.

Impatient and eager to return to the meeting, the chief was on her in an instant. "Spit it out, Chloe."

"Sir, they say there's a body in the water."

The fishermen were a pair of young locals. Earl Dare and Billy "Chee-tah" Whitehead had parked in the lot of the Haywood Trail before sunrise. Lugging fishing poles, a liter of Coke, a fifth of whiskey, and a pail of sandwiches, they took their time hiking in. They planned to fish until three, then stroll back and be home by six.

They'd just finished their third round of Jack and Cokes when they spotted the body.

Finn and I interviewed them in the conference room. A sick feeling had descended into the pit of my stomach, growing more intense the longer the fishermen spoke. They smelled of sweat and Jack Daniel's and wet wool socks.

"I couldn't believe it," Earl said. He was athletic looking, with a shaved head and eyes bright from adrenaline and alcohol. "At first I thought it was a big log, maybe felled by a beaver. Then I thought it was a drowned deer, or a moose even. Then Cheetah saw the body, too!"

Cheetah chimed in. "I could see how Earl might think it was a moose. The corpse is, uh, bloated looking. Bigger than a body. But it's a body, no doubt about it."

"Is it a man or a woman?"

Earl and Cheetah looked at each other a moment, then Cheetah turned back to me and shrugged. "Can't say one way or another; the hair is long, so maybe a woman? The body is facedown."

"Where is it?" I asked, one hand on my stomach.

Earl considered the best way to explain it. "Well, you have to hike in first. Then, when you reach the lake, go around the right side about a half a mile."

I thought a moment. "Before or after you reach the campsites?"

"Before. But not by far, maybe a dozen yards. We stuck one of our fishing poles in the sand along the lake and tied a bandanna to it. We thought that might help you all," Cheetah said. He was about seventy pounds heavier than Earl, and I briefly wondered how he had earned his nickname. "It's tangled up in some reeds. The body, not the fishing pole."

"That was smart thinking, leaving a marker," Finn replied. "Did it look like the body could break free of the reeds? Could it float away before we get up there?"

"Hell, no." Cheetah said with a shake of his head. "I could see the legs and arms. They're twisted up pretty good in those reeds. I think the body might even be snagged on a submerged log or tree trunk or something. I don't think it's going anywhere."

Earl said, "I'll tell you something, we've been fishing up there since we were kids. And today is the last day I'll ever fish Lost Lake. Not after this."

Cheetah added, "And I don't think I'll be able to eat fish anytime soon. Maybe ever. I know what happens to corpses in the water. They go to the bottom of the food chain."

We finished interviewing the young men, then Finn and I headed to the trailhead. We drove in silence, the sick feeling in my stomach continuing to intensify.

If it was Sari Chesney's body—if she'd been in the water this whole time—how had her friends missed her? Mac and Ally . . . Jake . . . they'd said they had searched the area.

Why had I been so certain she was somewhere safe?

"I should have insisted on a dive team."

"It never would have been approved." Finn glanced over at me, his brow furrowed. His light eyes were troubled. "You didn't know, Gemma. You had no reason to suspect she was in the water."

"Where the hell else would she have been? A woman goes missing from a lake and I assume she's run off."

"This is not your fault."

I swallowed hard. "It might not be my fault she's dead, but it is my fault an exhaustive search wasn't performed of the area. I took Mac Stephens's word for it that he and the others had looked everywhere for Sari."

What if she'd been alive, injured somewhere nearby, as Mac Stephens and the others and I had searched the campsite? I walked through that morning, replaying my steps, my decisions, feeling worse by the minute.

What if there had been an opportunity to save her and I'd missed it, caught up as I'd been in the belief that she'd disappeared of her own accord?

After Finn parked, we took a few minutes to change into hiking boots and grab backpacks from the trunk of his car. We'd loaded them before leaving the station, and they were heavy with flashlights, investigative kits, water bottles, and a satellite phone.

By the time we reached the lake, it was early afternoon. The skies had grown dark with heavy thunder clouds and the wind whipped the water up into whitecaps that skimmed across the lake. The little sunlight that remained danced among the trees, jostling leaves in and out of shadows. Twice I almost believed that I saw a woman in a white dress gliding through the water only to realize each time it was a whitecap.

I didn't like being at the lake.

The Lost Girls had been in this water for an entire winter, their bodies trapped in the ice. Lifeless, frozen in place and time. What a strange and terrible pact they'd made, not only to each commit suicide but to do it here, at this remote and lonely place.

We slowly walked down the trail, eyes peeled for Earl and Cheetah's fishing pole with its marker. The hike in had left me with a sheen of damp sweat that was rapidly cooling into something cold, clammy, and unpleasant.

Eventually, Finn pointed up ahead to a patch of murky reeds that jutted out into the water like a thick finger, exactly as the two fishermen had described it. A fishing pole with a red cloth wrapped around the tip stood out of the ground.

We started picking our way through the knee-high reeds to the water's edge.

I jumped over a nasty-looking section of boggy water, watching where I stepped. Then Finn grabbed my shoulder, stopping me short. "There."

I looked to where he pointed and felt the breath catch in my chest. "My god."

The body was facedown. Long strands of ink-black hair billowed from the head, gently moving with the water like tentacles from some strange new sea creature.

I swallowed and said thickly, "The hair . . . I think it's her."

Chapter Twenty-one

I called it in on the satellite phone.

After a few minutes, Chief Chavez came on the line and said that Valley Mountain Search and Rescue would send a chopper in to retrieve the body.

"VMSR owes us a few favors. I'll catch a ride on the bird with the ME and the crime scene techs," Chief said. "See you in forty minutes."

Finn and I waited at the campground. I tried not to think about all the rain we'd had, the time that had elapsed since Sari's disappearance.

What evidence had been lost, washed away, or removed?

Soon enough, the sound of a helicopter filled the air and the rhythmic whir of the chopper's blades was a welcome distraction. We watched as the aircraft set down in a meadow a hundred yards from us. Chief Chavez climbed out first, his body bent at the waist, his yellow windbreaker incongruously bright. He was followed by two crime scene technicians, Dr. Bonaire and his assistant, and a tall, thin man I didn't recognize.

The group joined us at the campground, and we walked to the water's edge as Chavez made introductions. "Gang, meet Charlie Darcy. Darcy, this is Finn Nowlin and Gemma Monroe. Guys, Darcy is a lieutenant with the fire department and a volunteer with Search and Rescue."

We shook hands and then looked toward Lost Lake. The chief exhaled loudly when he saw the body. "Is that Sari Chesney?"

I said, "Yes, I think so. The hair, the flannel shirt . . ."

Chavez nodded, his jaw tight. "All right, let's get her out of the water."

The crime scene techs were already suiting up in black rubber waders. Together with the medical examiner's assistant, they spread out a dark tarp on the ground. This was followed by a white body bag. The techs then went to the lake and gingerly stepped in, careful not to stir up mud from the bottom of the lake. They reached the body and gently began to untangle her from the reeds, manipulating her limbs with the utmost care.

Disturbed, I watched as they fought the moving water and the stiff body. The flannel shirt snagged on a broken reed. One of the techs, a petite woman, tugged on the shirt, then suddenly slipped, nearly landing in the water but for the saving grip of her colleague.

Cold sweat trickled down my spine.

I'd never seen a body come out of the water before, and I didn't know what kind of damage to expect.

Bonaire called Finn, Chief Chavez, and me over for a conference.

"It will be impossible to establish time of death. I want you to know that, going into the autopsy. I may be able to determine if this was a homicide or a suicide, but please note, I said *may*. Exposure to water for any length of time does a terrific number on organic materials," Bonaire said. Though he was dressed for the environment and weather in jeans, boots, and a windbreaker, the handkerchief he removed from his back pocket was white and silky.

He wiped his brow and continued. "It's critical you understand that. From what the chief has told me, this young lady may be a suspect in the Starbuck homicide. That, of course, changes nothing in my approach to the autopsy, but I do understand that time of death is absolutely crucial. So, I'll do what I can, but I'll tell you now it will be very, very difficult. There may be . . . organisms growing in the body that might help narrow down the time frame, but don't count on it. This water is very cold. Decomposition will have slowed."

Finally, the techs had the body out of the water. Gently, slowly, they laid it face up on the plastic tarp. The flannel shirt was torn at the hem and Chesney's clothes—the shirt and jeans—were heavy with lake water. Liquid seeped from her; like a flood of tears the water ran down to the lake from where it had come.

I took in the blue flesh, puffy with bloat, marred by creatures. Much of Sari's face had been preserved by the cold of the water, but not all of it.

Not the eyes, not the lips.

I had to look away.

To the techs, I said, "Please, check the back of the neck and the right ankle. Are there any tattoos?"

One of them knelt by the body. With a gloved hand, he carefully pushed the wet hair off of the neck and rolled the head to the side.

I waited, my breath held.

After a long moment, he said, "There's a tattoo. The skin is stretched, but I think it's a star."

"Check the right ankle," I whispered.

Another long minute as the tech carefully rolled up the pants leg. "There's a second tattoo. I can't tell what it is, though. Maybe a flower?"

"It's a four-leaf clover," I said.

The girl who loved her mother and her cat was gone. The girl who worked at a museum and had a boyfriend and a best friend had been replaced by this bloated corpse.

Bonaire and Chief Chavez stared at me expectantly. I nodded once. "This is Sari Chesney's body."

Then I swerved to the side and hurled my breakfast into the weeds, retching again and again, until there was nothing more to give.

"Folks, we're running out of daylight. It won't help matters if someone twists an ankle. Let's break for the night and pick this back up tomorrow," Chief Chavez said.

Charlie Darcy, the Valley Mountain Search and Rescue volunteer, offered to set up camp and stand guard over the crime scene. The chief eagerly accepted, then pulled me and Finn aside.

"It's going to be hard to keep this quiet. You know the local news hounds monitor the air traffic, to say nothing of our leaker. They'd have heard the report of a body, the call out of VMSR. I'll try to contain this as long as I can, but I can't guarantee Search and Rescue will do the same," Chavez said. "Get a jump on notifying the next of kin."

I nodded. "Sari's mother has dementia. I'm not sure how much she will comprehend. Her friends, though . . ."

"Yes. Get a move on."

Sari Chesney's body was carefully wrapped and then loaded into the chopper. Chavez, Bonaire, his assistant, and the crime scene technicians followed the body. The pilot started the engine, and I stood watching the aircraft for a long time, first as its blades began to rotate, then as the big bird lifted up and veered east, heading back to town.

"You coming?"

I nodded at Finn. "Let's get off this mountain."

It was full dark when we reached the trailhead and the parking lot. We were quiet on the drive back to the station, each lost in our own thoughts.

Finally, Finn spoke. "You okay?"

I looked at him. He stared straight ahead, eyes on the road, and I saw in his profile the strong set of his jaw, the straight lines of his nose.

"Why do you ask?"

He glanced at me. "I've never seen you get sick before. It's not your first body."

"No, it's not." I turned away from him and stared out of the passenger window as the woods flew by, long swatches of darkness punctuated here and there with patches of white moonlight. "It's the lake. Lost Lake. There's something . . . wrong about that place. It feels haunted somehow. Sinister. When I think of Chesney, in the water, all this time . . . facedown, staring into whatever dark abyss lies under the surface . . . Some cases just hit you the wrong way. I don't know, maybe it's the Lost Girls, too. So many dead women."

We were in town before Finn spoke again. "What do you think happened?"

"Honestly?" I replied, looking again out the window. This time, instead of trees it was houses and shops that passed in a blur, illuminated by porch lights and streetlamps. "I have no idea. Each time I imagine a scenario it seems so wrong, so stupid. Did Ally, Mac, and Jake kill Sari and conspire to cover it up? Did Sari steal Owen Rayburn's diary and kill Betty Starbuck, and then she either committed suicide or was murdered? Did some unknown subject kill her? Maybe she had a stalker. None of it makes sense. What do *you* think happened?"

Finn shrugged as he pulled up next to my car in the station parking lot. "It's always the boyfriend. Every damn time."

"Mac Stephens is a nurse. He's a *healer*."

"He's *human*."

I climbed out of Finn's car. "You look exhausted. Get some shut-eye. I'll notify her friends and family."

He shook his head. "I can't let you do that by yourself."

"Please. I'd like to be alone for a while. Get some rest, Finn. I'll see you first thing in the morning."

Police operations run twenty-four hours a day, but this time of night it was typically quiet inside the station. I said hello to the officer at the front desk and made my way to the squad room.

At my desk, I found the Sari Chesney file.

I was glad to be alone in the room, alone with my thoughts. I stared at her photograph, knowing I wouldn't be able to sleep if the last image I had of her was the terrible thing I'd seen dragged out of the water.

My body felt leaden, heavy with remorse and guilt.

I'd been so certain she would turn up.

After a while, I closed the file. My night was not yet over.

Chapter Twenty-two

Carver Estates was a long, squat building the color of red desert clay, perched high on a hill at the end of a winding road on the east side of town. I parked in the empty visitors' lot, then walked to the front entrance and rang the doorbell. Though it was long past visiting hours and the center was closed, I'd phoned ahead. After explaining the situation, the manager had readily agreed not only to have the on-call doctor meet and escort me to Sari's mother, Charla Chesney, but to be present herself.

A loud buzz sounded, and I entered the care center. The lobby was clean and bright, and everywhere was evidence of the center's specialty: horticulture therapy. Lush green plants and trimmed trees filled the spaces next to white leather couches and wooden coffee tables. I saw a dining hall off the main lobby with floor-to-ceiling windows that, given the location of the center, likely had incredible views of the Arkansas River during the day.

Rosa Martinez, the general manager, greeted me. She was in her midforties, and while her face was unlined, her hair was prematurely white. She smiled sadly as we shook hands. "I remember you—you're the police officer who called the other day, aren't you? I can't believe this. Sari was a wonderful young woman."

"It's a terrible tragedy. Thank you for meeting me."

Rosa nodded. "Of course. Mrs. Chesney is in our A Wing, room 2004. This way, please."

I followed her down a narrow corridor. Along the way, the doctor in residence, Duncan Fields, joined us. He was soft-spoken, with a distinct widow's peak in his coal-black hair. "This is terrible news. I've met Sari on a number of occasions, and she was a lovely young woman. Very sad."

"It is tragic, Dr. Fields. I wanted her mother to be the first to know."

"I have to say, I'm not sure how much Mrs. Chesney will comprehend. She's taken a sudden and severe turn for the worse," he said.

"I'm sorry to hear that," I said. "Is that sort of progression typical?"

Dr. Fields shook his head. "The disease usually moves slowly, but there's so much we don't know about it. Mrs. Chesney may be reacting to some change in her environment. She may even have some underlying health concern that hasn't been identified yet, such as a bladder or urinary tract infection."

"You mentioned a change in the environment. Could it be as simple as her daughter not visiting as regularly this week?" I asked.

We reached Chesney's door, and the doctor hesitated a moment, thinking. "Yes, I suppose so. We usually think in terms of new people—like an unfamiliar doctor or a family member who hasn't visited for a long time—but I don't see why the reverse couldn't be true, too."

Rosa softly knocked on the door, then opened it and called into the dim interior. "Charla? Charla, honey, are you awake? You've got a visitor."

We entered the room. Save for a floor lamp in the corner, the lights were off. A woman in her early sixties sat in an easy chair, her face illuminated by the television a few feet away. It was turned to a game show, and the woman watched it with the volume down, a can of soda in her hand.

She belched softly, then noticed us in the doorway.

"Excuse me," she said with a laugh. "I didn't hear you. Come on in, I'm expecting Paul any moment now, but you three can keep me company while I wait."

"Paul?" I whispered to Rosa.

"Her husband. He died a few years back."

"Hi, Mrs. Chesney. My name is Gemma Monroe, with the Cedar Valley Police Department."

"Gemma, it's wonderful to see you again. You and Sari used to play together for hours," the woman said. "Oh and dear, call me Charla. You always did stand on ceremony."

I looked at Rosa and she shrugged in a kind of *just go with it* gesture.

"Yes, that's right, I'm a friend of your daughter, Sari. I'm so sorry, but something terrible has happened to her," I said in a gentle voice.

Mrs. Chesney waved at me impatiently. "Where's my daughter? She was just here."

I tried again, unsure how to say things. "Mrs. Chesney, I have difficult news. There's been an . . . an accident. Sari was hurt very badly and she died. I'm so sorry for your loss."

The older woman pursed her lips. "Well, she was just here a minute ago. I bet she and Paul wondered off on one of their little adventures. They like to tease me like that, always going places together, leaving me out. I get so mad, but then do you know what they do?"

I shook my head.

"They bring me treats! How can I stay mad when they bring me sweets?" Chesney laughed. "They'll be along shortly, you'll see. That is, if her awful boss doesn't make her work overtime.

"This damn show." She turned darkly back to the television and set her soda can down on a cheap-looking wooden television tray with a heavy thud. "It's got to be rigged."

"Do you know her? Sari's boss, Betty Starbuck?" I asked.

"I did. I read the papers. I saw what happened to that old broad. Good riddance. She got what was coming to her."

"Charla!" exclaimed Rosa, horrified.

I knelt beside Mrs. Chesney's chair. She smelled like cat urine and overripe fruit, though I'd seen neither a pet nor produce.

"What do you mean by that, what you just said about Sari's boss?"

Mrs. Chesney snorted and turned her attention back to the show, keeping one eye on it as she talked to me in a low, confidential voice. "She's made my daughter's life hell for years. It's good she's gone! No one will miss her. I taught Sari not to take guff from anyone."

I took a deep breath and figured I didn't have much to lose. "Do you think Sari hurt this woman?"

At that, Mrs. Chesney let out another snort and spoke in a sing-song voice. "Of course she didn't. Sari is a sweet girl. Such a sweet girl. That man of hers, though," she added. Her voice grew sarcastic, and she snorted again. "Now he's a real winner. Gun-toting redneck thug."

"Mac? You don't like him?"

But it was too late. Mrs. Chesney had slipped away, somewhere deep in the recesses of her mind, and after a few minutes of silence, her head fell forward with a deep snore. Rosa quietly took my arm and led me from the room, closing the door behind her.

"Two tragedies in such a short time has been hard on our guests."

"Two?"

Rosa nodded. "Yes. First Betty Starbuck's death, then this."

"Betty Starbuck wasn't a resident here."

"No, but her son Kent volunteers for us. Or at least, he did. He called yesterday, said it was too upsetting to be around folks his mother's age," Dr. Fields explained. "It's a shame; we struggle to get volunteers as it is."

I needed a minute to process what I'd just learned.

"You're saying Kent Starbuck worked here? Did he interact with Charla Chesney?"

Both Dr. Fields and Rosa thought a moment, then Rosa nodded. "Well, sure. Kent was so popular and so giving of his time that I'd say—no, I'd swear—he's worked with all of our guests."

I asked urgently, "What about Sari? Did Kent and Sari ever meet?"

Try though they might, neither Dr. Fields nor Rosa could answer that. I left them and Carver Estates, my synapses firing at the possibility of a new connection between my cases.

If Kent Starbuck had crossed paths with Sari Chesney, if he knew her, what did it mean? Could they have been partners?

Maybe that partnership turned sour.

We'd already established that Starbuck had motive to kill his mother . . . and we had an eyewitness who placed him at the museum near to the time of her death.

Hadn't Starbuck himself told me that he frequented Lost Lake? Was it possible to place him there on the night of Sari's disappearance, too?

"It's her, isn't it?"

Mac Stephens stood in the doorway of his home. He was pale but stoic, as though he had been expecting this all along. He lived in a small ranch-style house on a narrow street in an older, blue-collar neighborhood on the south side of town.

Through the neighbor's open windows, I heard a television blaring the roar of supercharged car engines and boozy cheers that are unique to a NASCAR race. Somewhere else on the street a dog barked once, twice, then fell quiet.

"Why don't I come in," I replied.

After a brief pause, Mac stood aside. I entered his house and was relieved to see Ally Chang and Jake Stephens sitting on a couch in the front room. It would be easier to break the terrible news to all of them at once. It was past ten o'clock at night, and I was exhausted. My muscles ached, and I wanted nothing more than a hot bath, a glass of wine, and a long slide into oblivion.

Mac's house was cluttered; clothes, magazines, and books covered nearly every surface. Two pizza boxes and a dozen empty beer bottles lingered on the kitchen table. Though the night was mild, a fire burned in the fireplace and the air smelled of burning wood.

I wondered if the campfire at Lost Lake had smelled like this.

The walls were lined with a startlingly large collection of swords: bayonets, machetes, daggers, and other types. The weapons were mounted in locked glass cases and were the only decorations on the walls.

I looked at Mac first, then Ally and Jake on the couch. All three had been crying.

Informing loved ones of the worst kind of loss never gets easy. It's a bleak, raw moment that is so devoid of hope—so empty—that it leaves me feeling physically sick.

When you deliver the news to a room full of possible suspects, that complicates matters.

I took a deep breath and got the necessary words out. Ally gasped, then put her head in her hands and started sobbing. Mac was stoic, nodding, chewing at the corner of his lip. Jake stood up and shook his head.

"That can't be," Jake said. "How can you be sure?"

"Her tattoos confirmed the identification, and her clothes match what she was wearing in the photograph Mac supplied me. I saw her face. It's Sari. I'm so very sorry."

I walked into the kitchen, found a roll of paper towels under a week's worth of newspapers, and took it back to the front room, handing it to Ally. She took one and noisily blew her nose.

Jake continued to pace the room, kicking clothes on the floor out of his way as he went. "This is all wrong. People our age, they're not supposed to die. Why are you lying?"

"Jake, please. I understand this is difficult—" I began. Before I could finish my thought, Mac exploded at the wall with a punch. The swords in their cases clanged, and a hole as big as my fist appeared.

Ally and I both jumped.

The sudden burst of violence was shocking.

"Stop it, Mac!" Ally yelled at him, then buried her face in her hands.

"Shut up, Ally. I *told* you. I told you all. I knew something terrible happened to Sari," Mac said. Jake put a hand on his shoulder, and he brushed it off, nearly pushing Jake backward.

Undeterred, Jake tried again. "Don't listen to her, Mac. She's a liar. A lying bitch."

"Hey," I said sharply. "I know you are upset. But I'm on your side. Calling me names doesn't help anything. Why on earth would I lie?"

"She's right. Sari's gone," Ally said. She lifted her head and looked at the men. Tears streamed down her face. "Can't you feel it? She's gone."

Mac breathed heavily through his mouth. After a moment, the anger subsided from his face and a look of confusion crept into his eyes.

He walked to the fireplace and placed his hands on the mantel, head bowed. "I just don't understand what happened. Why would someone kill her and not kill the rest of us?"

"It's too early in the investigation to have an answer to that, Mac."

"Do you think the same person who killed Betty Starbuck killed Sari?" Ally asked. "It's just too weird that they're both dead."

Ally cocked her head in thought. For a moment, Sari's bloated, waxy face flashed before me, blank spaces where her eyes and lips had been . . . but it was Ally's face, not Sari's, and her eyes were open, staring down into the dark waters of Lost Lake.

I shivered. "As I said, it's too early to know what happened."

"Maybe Sari got mixed up with the wrong kind of people. Mac, you said she had big dreams," Jake said. "Maybe those dreams led to her death."

It was Ally who exploded this time.

She stood up and threw the roll of paper towels at Jake. It hit him in the face, knocking his glasses sideways. "Would you shut up already? You knew her for like five seconds, and somehow that entitles you to an opinion here? I don't think so."

"Please." I held up a placating hand. "Let's all calm down. I need to hear once more, from each of you, how things were that night. The smallest detail might make the biggest difference now, in light of how things have changed."

After a few minutes of silence, Mac spoke first. "We got to the lake about four in the afternoon and set up camp. We thought we'd brought three tents, but there were only two. I said we could do girls and guys, but Ally offered to share with Jake so Sari and I could be together. We got the tents up pretty quickly because it looked like it was going to rain, but then the skies cleared and it was beautiful. It was so beautiful that night."

Mac choked up, so Ally took over telling the story. "We fished for a while, at twilight, when the trout are supposed to be biting, but it got cold and dark quickly. Sari read a magazine in her tent while we fished. She was too scared to get that close to the water. After a while, we decided to just eat the dehydrated food pouches we'd brought. Jake started the campfire and got water boiling."

"No, Mac started the fire. I tried, but my fingers were clumsy from the cold of the lake. Remember? I'd filled everyone's water bottles and collected enough for boiling," Jake said. "But the water was so cold it froze my fingers."

"That's right. I started the fire," Mac said, having collected himself. "And the girls cooked dinner."

"What time did you start drinking?"

The three of them looked at one another, thinking.

Finally, Ally spoke. "It was before we ate. I remember because we were joking about pre-dinner cocktails. So, maybe seven o'clock?"

"And it was just the wine?"

"No, there was whiskey, too. I brought a bottle," Jake said. "We did shots before we opened the wine. Well, most of us did. Ally stuck with the wine."

Ally flushed. "I wasn't feeling well. I had maybe one glass and then stopped drinking."

I pictured the scene, the group warming themselves up with alcohol and the heat of the campfire. The warmth from the alcohol would have faded quickly, though, as the temperatures dropped.

"When did you smoke the weed?"

Again the three of them shared a three-way stare, and then Ally answered. "After dinner. It was Sari's weed."

"Ally!" Mac said, annoyed.

"Well, it's true. What difference does it make now? It's legal, anyway," Jake answered, coming to Ally's defense. He added: "Mac and Sari and I were the only ones who smoked."

Ally nodded. "I don't smoke, ever."

"I'm hardly concerned about the marijuana. Okay, so you set up camp, you fish, then you eat dinner, drink, and smoke. What else?

Did you see anyone at the lake? Hear any strange noises?" I asked. "Were you scared?"

Mac sat up. "Scared? Scared of what?"

"I don't know." I shrugged. "I'm trying to get a sense of what the evening was like. If there was anything unusual that stands out, now, in hindsight."

"You know, there was one weird thing that happened. I'd forgotten all about it," Ally said. She put her hands between her knees and began to rock back and forth. "Sari and I went into the woods after dinner to pee. Not very far, just enough to be out of sight of the guys. We stuck close together, though. Anyway, as we were finishing, we heard the strangest sound. It sounded like a woman's laugh, coming from the water. Do you remember, Mac? Sari asked if you and Jake had heard it, too, but you said no. You said it was likely a loon."

Mac nodded. "Yeah, now that you mention it, that was really strange because neither Jake nor I heard it. But I thought of loons right away. Spring is the start of their mating season, though they are rare."

"Could there have been someone else there? A woman, or a man?"

"I doubt it." Mac shook his head. "Next you'll suggest it was the Lost Girls. Yeah, Sari told us all about *them*. She tried to scare us with that old ghost story. Look, if there was someone else there we would have heard them. Or seen them. It was a clear night."

Ally was the first to connect the dots, and she paled. She went so white that for a moment I thought she was about to pass out.

Mac noticed and leaned over, gently touching her on her knee. "What is it, Al? What's wrong?"

Her eyes filled with fresh tears, and she stammered out: "If we were alone at the lake, that can only mean one thing. One of us did it."

Ally took a deep breath and repeated, "One of us killed her."

Chapter Twenty-three

Midnight in the canyon and the woods surrounding my house were black and still. Somewhere nearby, an owl hooted, his call urgent and insistent. The house was dark, save for a single porch light, its warm glow attracting an enormous moth that flitted about the bulb.

Inside, I quietly rummaged in the refrigerator until I found enough leftovers to cobble together a plate of dinner. While it heated in the microwave, I poured and then quickly drank a glass of cabernet. The wine burned going down and I closed my eyes, grateful for the pain, grateful for the reminder.

I was alive.

I couldn't seem to get warm. Memories from the day continued to assault my senses: the wind-whipped lake . . . the smell of the fetid water seeping from Sari Chesney's body . . .

Her face . . .

I ate standing up, shoveling lukewarm chicken and limp broccoli into my mouth, forcing myself to chew and swallow the food though I'd already lost my appetite. Then I poured a second glass of wine and sat in the living room, in the dark, under a quilt on the couch.

Ally Chang had been correct. If they'd been alone at the lake, and if Sari's death was ruled a homicide, then one of them was a killer.

Ally. Mac. Jake.

Best friend. Boyfriend. Third wheel.

They'd claimed to be asleep, passed out. There was no way to corroborate their accounts . . . but I could check their whereabouts the night of the gala, on the possibility that not only were the Chesney and Starbuck homicides related but that their killers were one and the same. Mac had claimed to have to work that night. What had Jake and Ally been up to?

Though what if they hadn't been alone at the lake that night? What if someone was there, someone who watched them, maybe someone who was fatally obsessed with Chesney . . . or someone with a reason to kill off museum employees.

Kent Starbuck.

Larry Bornstein.

Damn. I'd planned on digging into Larry Bornstein's background today. It was one more thing that had been pushed to the back burner. In light of today's discovery, it was something that needed to happen sooner rather than later.

I had wondered earlier if he could have killed Starbuck to gain her job. At the time, it seemed outrageous, and yet once again, I reminded myself that I'd been involved in cases where the motive was far weaker.

Now *both* of his co-workers were dead. Was he a potential suspect? Or the next victim?

I tried to hold on to that thought, to think through how it could have happened, but the wine was already doing what I needed it to do and a slow-building warmth dimmed the horrors of the day. A creak on the staircase, then Brody was at my side. He sat next to me and rubbed the back of my neck. He smelled of soap and mint toothpaste, and I leaned into his side, closing my eyes against the soft flannel of his pajamas.

"It's late." His hand dropped from my neck to my shoulder, massaging deeper into my tense muscles. "I saw the news. They said the body of a woman was found at Lost Lake. They're saying it was murder. Are you on the case?"

I nodded. "Yes. She was originally a missing person. Now she might be a murder victim. I'm afraid I missed something, Brody. I was there, at the lake, hours after she disappeared. I looked her boyfriend, her friends, straight in the eyes and swore she would turn up. And she did, only she's dead. She's dead."

"Honey, you work harder than anyone I've ever met. But you're only human. You need to rest." Brody gently took the nearly empty glass of wine from my hand and set it on the coffee table. "Come to bed."

"No. I can't sleep just yet. I need to . . . think."

"The dead will wait, Gemma," Brody said. In the dark, it was hard to see his features, but his voice was troubled. "I'm worried. This isn't like you."

"What, the drinking or the sadness? Neither is serious. Just a . . . phase that will pass." Standing up, I took the glass and finished the last swallow. "I'm going to take a bath."

Brody grabbed my hand. I tried to pull away, but he held on tight. "Sweetheart, what if this is more than a phase?"

I was too tired to argue so I simply said the truth, and saying it out loud, for the first time, released the last bit of tension in my body. The words were all that I had left to give, and when I was done speaking, I turned away and moved to the stairs, my eyes full of tears, my heart full of sorrow.

"Sometimes it just gets to be too much, Brody. You said the dead will wait . . . but the dead . . . they're in my mind, constantly. Every case I've worked, every victim . . . It doesn't go away. *It never goes away.*"

He dropped my hand and, in the dark, I heard his breath catch. "I wish I could share this burden with you, Gemma. I wish it more than anything in the world."

In the bathroom, I kept the lights off, afraid to look at myself in the mirror. As the tub filled, I sat on the edge and cried. I was so tired by that point that I didn't know who I was weeping for, the dead or myself.

Finally, I eased in to the bath. The water was just shy of scalding, and I let the heat wash over me as the wine had, loosening muscles, easing joints, dimming the edges of the long, sad day until my mind was an empty well, devoid of thought and feeling.

Chapter Twenty-four

Valley Mountain Search and Rescue operated out of a pair of hangars at the municipal airport on the south side of town. On my way there, I called the hospital and spoke with a supervisor in the nursing department. She confirmed that Mac Stephens had worked an overnight shift the evening of the gala. Then I called Jake Stephens. He picked up on the tenth ring, sounding both angry at the early morning call and extremely hungover.

When I asked him my question, though, he calmed down and grew quiet. After a moment of thought, he said, "I was home Saturday night. I'm living with another cousin, Nicole, until I can afford my own apartment. We went to a party at her friend's house and then came back here. We played some pool and watched a movie. You want her phone number? She's already left for the day."

"Sure, thank you." I jotted down the number and ended the call with Jake. Then I called Nicole, who didn't answer, and left a message.

Though I was nearly to the VMSR hangars, I parked outside a bagel shop and went in. I ordered a box of coffee and a bag of bagels with an extra couple containers of cream cheese. While I waited for my order, I stepped to the side and called Ally Chang.

Unlike Jake, she sounded alert, wired. "I stayed at my parents' house last night. I didn't want to be alone. But they don't want to talk about all this. My mom said it's too sad. She said I should see a grief counselor."

"That's probably a good idea. Hang on a second." I took the bag of bagels and the coffee from the store clerk and set them down on a table in the back of the shop, away from the other customers, where I could continue my conversation. "Ally, I'm collecting as much information as I can in this case. Obviously, we believe there's a connection to Betty Starbuck's murder. What did you do Saturday, after you left the police station? Did you go home? Were you with anyone that night?"

Ally was sharp. "Oh my god, you think *I* killed Sari and her boss?" She started breathing hard and fast. "I'm going to be sick."

"Ally, please, take a deep breath for me. I need you to calm down." I waited while, on the other end of the line, Ally breathed in and out. After a few minutes, she came back to the phone and sounded, if not calm, at least not panicked.

"I went to the grocery store and then I went home. Alone. I spent that whole night looking through old scrapbooks, pulling photographs of Sari, putting together a missing person poster on my laptop. I wanted to be ready in case you asked for something like that, in case she didn't come home and you needed more to find her."

"Did you talk to anyone, see anyone? A neighbor, a boyfriend?"

Ally started crying softly. "No. The apartment next to me has been empty for months. I don't have a boyfriend. And now I don't have a best friend."

"I'm so sorry for your loss. I truly am. I'm going to find Sari's killer, Ally. I swear it."

We ended the call and as I hauled the bagels and coffee out to my car, I couldn't help but wonder if I'd just made yet another empty promise.

Inside the hangar, I found Finn pacing in a small kitchenette.

"You look like hell," he said. His dark hair was tucked under a Red Sox ball cap and his eyes were bloodshot. It seemed I wasn't the only one who'd spent some time the previous night with a drink or two.

"Yeah? Screw you. You want plain or sesame seed?" I dumped the bagels on a paper plate. A couple of VMSR staffers joined us and helped themselves to the spread. They were subdued, with a few questions about the death but not many.

They understood all too well what it meant to recover a body.

"Seriously, you don't look good. Are you getting sick? I've got a weekend fishing trip out to Florida in two weeks." Finn said. "I don't watch to catch whatever you've got."

"No, I'm not sick. What's the story? Are we going to stand around all day kvetching?"

"We're waiting on a few more of our guys." He poured a cup of coffee from the box and tore open a few packs of sugar, adding them and then stirring.

He stirred for a long time, and the sound of the red plastic straw scraping the edges of the cup made me want to scream.

Deep breaths.

"I spent some time this morning checking alibis for Saturday night for Mac Stephens, Jake Stephens, and Ally Chang. Mac worked a shift at the hospital. Jake was with his cousin, Nicole. I'm waiting on a call back from her to confirm this. And Ally was home alone."

Finn raised an eyebrow. "Can anyone verify that?"

"No. Ally was upset, panicked that I even asked. Finn, she's petite but she looks strong, fit. If she incapacitated Betty Starbuck with a blow to the head, she'd have easily been able to then choke her to death."

"What's her motive for the killings?"

It was the same question that was bothering me. "I have no idea."

Twenty minutes later, we were in the air and I looked out over the scenery. The flight would be short, and it wasn't my first time in a chopper, but the experience never gets old. From this altitude, Cedar Valley looked like a dream. In the east, vast tracts of farmland stretched in neat squares, a green-and-brown checkerboard. To the north, the Rockies stretched for miles under towering cumulous clouds.

Finn leaned over and gestured to the clouds. "Thunderstorms," he mouthed. I nodded in reply and turned back to the window. Thousands of feet below me, the Arkansas River sparkled as shimmery and shiny as a dancer's satin ribbon. The water—brilliantly, impossibly blue—ran down from the mountains and then moved south and southeast, headed toward Kansas.

For the briefest of moments, the entire valley was laid out, one long, winding clear swatch in the middle of an otherwise immense and dense forest. As we started our descent, I wondered what it would be like to lose myself in those woods, just for a day or two.

I'd told Brody the previous night that the dead were in my mind constantly, that they never went away. Though a part of me longed to lose them, a larger part knew I needed them. It was their faces, their stories, that kept me moving forward in search of justice.

We landed in the meadow near the campsite and climbed out of the chopper. Charlie Darcy, the fire lieutenant and VMSR volunteer, met us. He said it had been a quiet night at the lake. In the morning light, I couldn't help noticing how fresh and energized he looked. He was a tall, lean man with a charming smile and a wicked scar that traveled in a straight line down his cheek.

He offered us coffee from a pot he'd set up over a low fire in the campground grill, and both Finn and I declined. The other guys in our group accepted, and we spent another few minutes standing around the campsite, murmuring to one another. Darcy and I discovered that we'd graduated from the same local high school, only three years apart, and we fell into an easy conversation.

After a few minutes, Finn interrupted. "Sorry to break up the party, but we should get a move on."

"Absolutely. My chief talked to your chief, and they gave me the green light to stay and help you canvas the area," Darcy said. He pulled off the navy blue wool sweater he wore and replaced it with a lightweight red sweatshirt. "I'm all yours, so just tell me what to do."

I started to speak, but Finn cut me off. "You ever work a crime scene before?"

Darcy shrugged. "Sure. EMS is often first on the scene. Have I collected evidence? No, but I know not to step in anything that has the faintest whiff of importance. That good enough for you?"

"Yes, and we're grateful for the help," I said before Finn could respond. The last thing I wanted to deal with was a pissing contest between my partner and a fire lieutenant. "Charlie, why don't you pair up with the techs. The three of you should go over the campsite. Finn and I will walk the perimeter of the lake. I want to see what's on the other side of the water."

Once again, Finn and I pulled on day packs heavy with water bottles, emergency supplies, and evidence kits. We headed north, moving slowly, not sure what—if anything—we were looking for. Finn traveled to the side, through the woods, while I stayed on the trail. As far as I could tell, no one had yet taken this particular trail past the campsite this season. The ground was slushy with melting snow and mud, and though I could hear Finn, somewhere up ahead, breaking through bush, I couldn't see him.

I saw evidence of bear activity—scat, prints—as well as the distinctive track of a mountain lion. This remote terrain was their territory, and I kept that in mind as I walked, one ear tuned to Finn's movements, the other to the sounds around me. I'd seen a mountain lion just once before, driving home late one night. It was in the canyon, half a mile from my house, and my bright headlights spooked it. The cat had frozen in the middle of the road, then slowly turned away and sauntered down to the creek. It took me ten minutes to exit my car when I reached my driveway; once out, I'd never moved so fast to the front door.

Forty minutes later, we reached the far side of the lake. I stood a moment, under the sentinels of blue spruce trees, breathing heavily, and looked back across the water. I squinted in the general direction of where I thought the campsite was, but all I could see was a seemingly endless horizon of trees.

I dumped my pack and wiped at the sweat on the back of my neck.

Finn, cool as a cucumber with barely a sheen to his forehead, crouched near the base of a spruce that was easily forty feet tall. He brushed dirt and twigs away from an area on the ground.

"Someone's been here. Recently."

I knelt beside him. "How can you tell?"

He pointed out a vaguely rectangular indentation on the ground. "This area, it's from a sleeping pad. It rained last week. This would have been washed away."

I searched the area and found more evidence of what seemed to be a permanent campsite. A thick silver cable was strung between two trees, with carabiners and a pulley system in place. It was rigged for easy hanging of food bags and trash. Near the sleeping area, a pile of rocks with a metal grate on top of it showed grilling activity.

"Someone's staying here on a regular basis," Finn said.

I told him I thought I'd seen someone . . . or something . . . the first day I was called to Lost Lake. "It was the strangest thing. It was like a flash or glint of light, but that's impossible at this distance. Maybe it was the sun reflecting off the surface of the water."

Finn walked the perimeter of the makeshift campground. "Or maybe someone *was* here. Give me your binoculars, would you?"

I pulled them from my pack and handed them to him. He stared through them, across the lake, for a solid minute, then wordlessly handed them to me.

"Take a look."

I lifted them, looked in the same direction he did, and gasped. "That's incredible. The view from this spot is dead straight across to the campground. If someone was here, watching Chesney and her friends that night, he'd have seen everything."

"The worst part is they'd have had no idea they were under observation."

I shivered.

Finn picked up my backpack and handed it to me. "Let's get back to the others. I think when we return to the station we should draft a press release. We can keep it deliberately vague. We'll ask for the public's help, request that anyone who may have seen anything at Lost Lake in the last few weeks come forward."

I nodded and headed back down the trail. This time, Finn walked with me, and I pointed out the mountain lion and bear tracks to him. In light of what we'd found, in light of the fact that someone might have been watching Chesney and her friends, the animal prints were suddenly a lot less frightening.

We talked as we walked. I reminded him that we needed to delve deeper into Larry Bornstein's background and learn as much as we could about the Rayburn Diary. If it, and not the museum, was the link between the murders, then we needed to understand everything about it. Finn liked Bornstein for a suspect, but agreed that the motive of killing someone to obtain her job was a stretch. Still, he, too, had seen people murdered for far less, and we both adhered to Chief Chavez's fourth truth of being a cop: *If you can imagine it, someone's already done it.*

Back at the campsite, we joined up with Charlie Darcy and our guys. They'd been unable to find anything of importance but had dutifully collected samples of soil, lake water, ashes from the campsite, even pinecones and fallen leaves. They'd photographed everything and anything that seemed relevant.

Cold, sweaty, and glum, we piled in the VMSR helicopter and flew back to town, the whir of the bird's blades and the occasional radio chatter between the pilot and air traffic control the only noises.

Chapter Twenty-five

Once we were back on the ground, I phoned the museum and asked Larry Bornstein to join me at the station for a conversation. He was nervous on the phone, in shock about Sari Chesney's death. But he agreed to come by in an hour. I took that time to shower and change into fresh clothes in the locker room.

Bornstein arrived, and Finn and I escorted him to an interview room. Bornstein wore another sweater vest, navy blue this time, over a white long-sleeved button-down shirt and a pair of dark slacks. A maroon bow tie hung askew at his neck.

In his hand was the ubiquitous small bottle of hand sanitizer.

"Thank you for coming in, Dr. Bornstein," I began. "The death of Sari Chesney, coming so soon on the heels of Betty Starbuck's murder, is beyond shocking."

Bornstein nodded. "I just can't believe it. I worked with them for years. To think that they both are dead—not just dead, but possibly *murdered*—is unfathomable. I don't understand why anyone would kill them."

"That's exactly what we're trying to ascertain. Obviously, since both Sari and Betty worked at the museum, our first assumption is that their deaths are related," Finn said. He turned to a fresh page in his yellow legal tablet and clicked open a pen. "Do you have any thoughts about that?"

Bornstein paled as he realized the implications of Finn's question. "My god . . . Am I in danger?"

It was a valid question, and one to which neither Finn nor I had an answer. Bornstein read as much in our faces. He audibly swallowed and said weakly, "Perhaps it's time I take a vacation. I hear Paris is lovely in the spring."

"We'll have to ask you not to go anywhere for a while, Dr. Bornstein. At least not until we have a suspect in custody. Obviously, one of the pieces we're looking at in both investigations is the Rayburn Diary. The fact that it disappeared around the same time as the deaths occurred is troubling and may be the connection we're seeking." I gave Bornstein what I hoped was an encouraging look. "I understand that it's unique, one of a kind. But what exactly makes it so special? Surely the museum has other diaries, other journals of historical importance."

Relieved to temporarily move to a new topic, Bornstein slipped his hand sanitizer into his pocket, sat back, and crossed his legs. "How much do you know about the history of this town?"

I shrugged. "What we learn in school and then some."

Finn nodded. "Same here. I didn't grow up in town, but I'm probably as aware as your average citizen of the local history."

Bornstein tipped his head. "Excellent. Well, of course you're familiar with Owen Rayburn. He was the brother-in-law of Stanley Wanamaker James. James ran the most successful silver mines in the region. He swooped in after the gold mines were tapped out. Rayburn and his family followed shortly thereafter. They arrived from Pennsylvania already quite wealthy. James and Rayburn and four other men established the Avery and Martin Mining Company and built Cedar Valley from the ground up. They were known as the Silver Foxes: Rayburn; James; Peter Johnston Avery; Jeremiah Martin; Thomas Aaron Johnson; and Rico Fioretti. The six of them ruled this town with an iron fist. You've seen the statue at City Hall?"

Finn and I nodded. The statue was bronze, a sculpture of six men sitting on a bench, each holding a mining tool of some kind, such as pick ax or a lantern. It was a popular place for city employees to picnic when the weather was nice.

Bornstein continued. "Of all the men, Owen Rayburn was the most ruthless and the most secretive. At all times, he carried a small leather-bound journal. In it were said to be the locations—secret locations, of course—of the last remaining seams in the valley that contained gold."

I sat back, a smile on my lips. I'd heard these rumors before. "It's been decades since any gold has been found in these hills. Assuming the diary does contain this information, and that the information is true, what would it be worth?"

Dr. Bornstein smiled, too, happy to be on a topic he clearly enjoyed. "Now that's the interesting question. It all depends who you ask. As I've said before, the historical value is simply priceless. The damn thing is chockful of information. Rayburn recorded everything: the weather, maps, details of day-to-day life in the Valley, personal ruminations on life, death, and everything in between. It's a local treasure and, in many ways, a national treasure."

"And did you see any maps to *buried* treasure in it?"

Bornstein's smile grew wider. "In addition to being ruthless and secretive, Rayburn was very, very clever. He considered himself an amateur cryptographer—of course it wasn't called cryptography back then—and loved to encrypt secret messages in his day-to-day missives. If there is a map in the diary to gold in these mountains, it is written in code. That, or invisible ink."

I waited for him to laugh. "You're not joking, are you? Invisible ink?"

Bornstein nodded. "I'm deadly serious. Yes. The man was gaga for encryption and ciphers."

Finn had been taking notes. Now he set his pen down and leaned forward. The talk of buried treasure had caught his interest in a big way. "So theoretically, there are two sorts of people who might be interested in Rayburn's diary. Those who appreciate it from a historical perspective and those who are interested in gold. The scholarly and the greedy."

Bornstein nodded, pleased. *"The scholarly and the greedy.* I couldn't put it better. Of course, there's a third possibility too: those who are interested in the diary purely as an object to sell."

Finn gave Bornstein a small smile. "So which group do you be-long to?"

Bornstein flushed at the sudden attention back on himself. He stammered, "I have dedicated my life to the scholarly pursuit of his-tory. I am an *academic,* Detectives. I resent the implication that my interest in the Rayburn Diary is anything more than professorial."

Finn waved a hand. "Calm down, Dr. Bornstein. Two of your colleagues are dead. Now is the not the time for indignation. Let's switch gears for a moment. Have you been to Lost Lake in the last few weeks? Maybe for a hike or some bass fishing? Perhaps a camp-ing trip with the boys?"

At this, Bornstein practically sputtered. "Are you accusing me of killing Sari Chesney? This is beyond absurd. I'm no longer comfort-able with the direction this conversation is going. In fact, I think I'd like to call my attorney."

I nodded. "By all means. That's your right. Please understand, though, this is not an interrogation. We're simply trying to understand what's been happening at the museum, what's been happening in the lives of these two women, where they may have intersected. You are a common denominator, that's all."

Bornstein ignored me and slid a cell phone out of his pocket. He tapped a few keys then put the phone to his ear. After a moment, he began to speak, and Finn and I looked at each other. We both knew that Bornstein's lawyer would advise him not to say another word. They talked a few minutes longer, then Bornstein hung up.

"Ms. Martin will be here shortly." He pursed his lips. "She's ad-vised me not to say anything more until she arrives."

Eyes widening, Finn coughed into his fist. "Susannah Martin?"

"Yes. Do you know her?"

I watched as Finn compressed his lips and gave a curt nod.

Inwardly, I cringed. Finn had a well-deserved reputation in town as a ladies' man. His past paramours had a funny way of turning up in our cases at inopportune times, and Finn's current expression was not giving me any reassurance that this would be any different. If

Susannah Martin turned out to be another one of Finn's ex-girlfriends, I was going to scream.

"Well, let's break for coffee," I said and stood up. "Dr. Bornstein, can I get you anything?"

He shook his head. "I'll stay right here."

Outside the interview room, I grabbed Finn's sleeve. "Please tell me you and *Ms. Martin* don't have a history. Please tell me she's not going to walk in here with an attitude."

He straightened up, a grim smile dancing on the corner of his mouth. "Gemma, *I'm* not the problem. This town is. There's a serious shortage of eligible women—"

I walked away as he was still defending himself, shaking my head. He needed to move to New York City, or Los Angeles.

But I knew he never would.

Finn enjoyed being a big cop in a small town too much to ever relocate.

Susannah Martin was as I expected, attractive and confident, a willowy blonde with slicked-back hair and serious eyes. She was also a professional, and her demeanor, while cool and reserved, remained steadfastly polite.

Bornstein seemed vastly relieved to see her. Martin took a seat next to him, then folded her hands and placed them on the table. She spoke in measured tones without smiling, her dark gray eyes unblinking.

"My client is here voluntarily, in response to your request to interview him. I understand he's already provided you with information about the Rayburn Diary."

"That's correct," I confirmed. "We would now like to know Dr. Bornstein's whereabouts on the evening of May thirteenth, the evening of May fourteenth, and the early morning hours of May fifteenth, specifically between the hours of one a.m. and five a.m."

Bornstein started to speak, but Martin stopped him by placing a hand on his forearm. She leaned over and whispered something in his ear, then Bornstein nodded. Martin drew back.

"May thirteenth was a Friday. I was home with my wife, Lee. We ordered in a pepperoni pizza and watched a movie on Netflix. I believe we were in bed and asleep by ten p.m.," Bornstein said.

"How can you be so sure? That was nearly a week ago," Finn asked. He looked down at what he'd written, surprised. "'Pepperoni pizza.' I barely remember what I ate yesterday, let alone a week ago."

Bornstein smiled triumphantly. "I remember because Lee and I specifically decided to have a low-key evening at home on Friday the thirteenth, knowing the following night—the night of the gala—would be a long and late evening. Pepperoni pizza with a pesto-stuffed crust is our standard order from Chevy's."

"And how about the gala on Saturday the fourteenth. What time did you leave the museum?" I asked.

Bornstein thought a moment, then said, "About eleven o'clock, with most of the other guests."

Finn asked, "Did you go straight home?"

Bornstein shook his head. "No. Lee was engrossed in a conversation with Mayor Cabot, and we were invited to join the mayor and her companion for drinks at the bar at the Tate Lodge Inn. We saw a number of other guests downtown, continuing the party at various bars. We left the Tate close to one a.m. and were home soon after."

I took a moment to think. Susannah Martin stared at me, the expression on her face unreadable.

"Besides your wife, can anyone corroborate your whereabouts the night of Friday, May thirteenth, and your actions after you left the Tate on the night of the fourteenth?" I asked. "Maybe the pizza delivery man?"

Bornstein shook his head. "No. Lee answered the door for the pizza. On the fourteenth, we drove straight home from the Tate. Frankly, I find these questions insulting. I had nothing to do with Betty's murder or Sari's death. You're wasting your time."

Martin nodded in agreement and stood. "If there's nothing else,

Detectives, we'll be on our way. You can call me directly if you have further questions for my client."

She stood, opened the door, and beckoned Bornstein to follow her. They left without a word, but as he passed through the doorway, Bornstein turned and met my stare.

The arrogance and triumph in his eyes was shocking.

Then he was gone and I sat back, uncertain if I'd really seen what I thought I'd seen.

Finn exhaled and ran a hand through his hair, then leaned back. "That went better than I expected. I half thought she'd come in with a glass of water and throw it in my face. Suzie and I didn't end things on a good note."

"Why am I not surprised?"

Finn started to respond, and I cut him off. "It doesn't matter. Bornstein's wife is his alibi. We'll get no further with him unless forensics comes back with hard evidence."

Chapter Twenty-six

I warmed up a cup of coffee and microwaved a bag of popcorn, remembering just as the popcorn finished that the chief had asked us to avoid it as the smell filled the whole station.

"We're not a movie theater," he'd written in a department-wide memo that some smart-ass had photocopied a dozen times and plastered all over the break room.

"Chief's going to have your butt," Armstrong said as he walked into the kitchen and grabbed a handful of the popcorn.

"Yeah, I forgot."

At my desk, I returned a call to the medical examiner's office and spoke with Dr. Bonaire at length. Because Finn and I had been canvassing Lost Lake, neither of us had attended the autopsy of Sari Chesney.

Given the condition of her body, I wasn't sorry to have missed it.

Bonaire was officially ruling the death a homicide and he shared with me his preliminary findings. "In the final moments, the victim's cause of death was drowning. There are a few other things that you should be aware of. At some point before she went into the water, the victim suffered a significant head injury. In addition, there are scratches and lacerations on her face and forearms that occurred before death."

Face and forearms . . .

"She was dragged?"

"It appears so," the doctor said. "Facedown, by the feet, for a distance of say, a few dozen yards over a terrain with small rocks and twigs."

"That sounds like a match for the area around the lake, on the trail, and at the campsite," I said, picturing the land. "And the head injury?"

"Hard to say how it was sustained. Something collided with her skull, but what it was, I don't know. She might have been unconscious when she was placed in the lake," Bonaire stated. "Let's hope she was. It's a terrible thing all the way around."

"Yes. Any defensive wounds?"

"No, nothing to indicate she put up a struggle. I'll call if I find anything else."

I thanked him and hung up, then wrote up notes from our findings at Lost Lake and the conversations with Bonaire and Bornstein. All of it would go in the murder book, the thick black binder that contained all the evidence and information to tell the story of Sari Chesney's death. If we caught her killer, the book would help prosecute him or her.

I was finishing up as Moriarty walked in. His thick white hair was brushed back from his lined forehead, his eyes bright. He bit into an apple, chewed, and swallowed. "Guess who I just picked up for a drunk and disorderly?"

"I have no idea."

"Kent Starbuck."

"What?" I sat back, surprised. "What happened? And how did you get dragged in instead of patrol?"

"Dave Zusak called it in," Moriarty said. Zusak was the owner of the Crimson Café, a coffee and wine bar a few blocks off the downtown strip. The Crimson was popular for its homemade cinnamon taffy and generous pours.

"I was a few blocks away, on my way here, so I responded. Zusak and I play ball at the rec center on Thursdays. Anyway, I found Starbuck three sheets to the wind. He'd entered the café ready for a fight. He knocked over a newspaper stand, called one of the waitresses a 'whore.' Zusak refused to serve him and asked him to leave. Starbuck went ballistic. He threatened Zusak and said, quote, 'Don't you know who I am? I'm a convicted felon. I've done terrible things.' That was when Zusak called us."

"It's the middle of the day. Kent must have started drinking early."

"No kidding. He came with me easily enough. By the time I booked him, the guy was weeping. He spoke of the waste of trying to make amends, the fatigue of convincing people you're something they think you're not."

Moriarty sat down at his desk and rubbed a hand over his jaw. For some reason I'd never noticed the pale scar on the back of his right hand. "Some people never change."

I stretched my legs out in front of me and clasped my hands in my lap. "My first year here, as a rookie, I busted a little old grandmother for poisoning her neighbor's dog. The dog barked too much, she said. The neighbor was this big, burly, bald motorcycle dude, easily three hundred pounds, all muscle. He cried like a baby over that dog. And the grandmother? I brought her into booking in pink hair curlers and a muumuu. Her children and grandchildren refused to appear in court on her behalf. Mr. Motorcycle had fifty people lined up in the back of the courtroom, all testifying how much he loved the dog."

"What was the sentence?"

"Funny, I can't remember. Probably wasn't long enough."

"It rarely is. Listen, I got a bad feeling about Kent Starbuck," Moriarty said. He rubbed his jaw again, then moved his hand through his thick hair.

"You've had a bad feeling about him for thirty years," I replied.

Finn caught the tail end of our conversation and joined us. "Lou's got good instincts. I still believe Kent is the perfect suspect for the Starbuck homicide: He's got a violent past and he stands to inherit a tidy sum. He was observed at the scene of the crime, and he's obviously got an attitude problem. I got to say, I think we need to push harder on him."

"That all sounds great in theory, but the location of the murder troubles me. Why would Kent kill his mother at her office, in the middle of night?" I asked. "Even if Betty Starbuck had summoned him to the museum, it still would be a hell of a lot easier to kill her at home, some other time . . . unless the killing wasn't planned at all. If Kent's unstable . . . maybe they got into an altercation?"

Moriarty stepped out, and Finn was about to respond when his eyes moved to something behind me.

A look of dismay flashed in them, and I turned around.

The Squirrel stood behind me and grinned, his long teeth gleaming in the pronounced overbite that, together with his last name, had earned him his infamous nickname.

He moved to the side of my desk. "Gemma, Finn."

"Squ—Richard. What's up?"

Field Parole Officer Richard "the Squirrel" Nuts looked down at me with watery eyes, his basketball-sized paunch hanging dangerously close to my bowl of popcorn. The parolees he oversaw for the Trenton County Justice System called him Dick Nuts. A recent unwillingness or lack of care to wear deodorant didn't help things for the Squirrel, and some on both sides of the law had decided Stinky Nuts was an even more appropriate nickname.

Suffice it to say, the man was not well liked.

"How's it hanging, my lady?" The Squirrel helped himself to a handful of popcorn. "I thought Chief Chavez forbade this stuff."

"Yeah, I forgot," I said, and leaned back, stretching. I stopped stretching when I realized the Squirrel's eyes were starting to taking an elevator ride down from my face to my chest.

I gritted my teeth. "Eyes up here, Dick."

He snorted. "No one calls me Dick."

Not to your face.

He stood there, waiting for more conversation. I knew he wouldn't leave until we made at least a bit of small talk, so finally I asked, "So, how are things in Trenton?"

He shrugged and talked around another mouthful of popcorn. "You know what they say."

I didn't know and, to be frank, I didn't care.

The Squirrel had a territory of sixty square miles, coordinating parolees who took up residence in Avondale, Cedar Valley, Black Rock, Trenton, and Jasper Lake. He reported to the warden at the penitentiary. The Squirrel was the worst kind of administrator, a lazy bully.

He continued, "Well, I'd love to stay and chat, but I'm doing rounds and I have a date in Black Rock tonight. Joanie and I met on Tinder."

"Tinder?"

"It's online dating," Finn explained with an eye roll. I knew he'd die before looking for love online.

I laughed. "I know what it is. I'm just surprised it works."

Raising his eyebrows up and down in a manner that I believed he thought was suggestive, the Squirrel said, "Some of us aren't lucky enough to work with such fair specimens of *both* sexes. We have to look for romance outside the workplace."

"As should we all," I quickly said. "Do you have something for us?"

He nodded and deposited a piece of paper on my desk. It was a list of names of parolees who had moved into one of our fair towns. Many would move out as soon as their parole was met, getting as far away from the system as possible, disappearing into the wind. But for now, if they didn't want to get their parole revoked, they played by the rules.

We didn't do much with the list; it lived in a file folder and, every once in a while, one of us would cross-check it against any local crimes. It was a formality. For the most part, we respected the system: as Kent Starbuck had put it, these men and women had done the crime and done their time.

"Thanks." I took the list and put it on top of a stack of other papers on my desk. I moved the nearly empty bowl of popcorn closer to the Squirrel. I wasn't about to eat any more, not after he'd had his fingers in it. "Please, finish it."

"Don't mind if I do," he said and, perching on the edge of my desk, took the last handful. He snickered as he ate it.

The Squirrel was the only person I'd ever met who actually snickered in real life.

"You can tell Chavez I brought the popcorn in. But it'll cost you. Dinner?"

"Um, thanks anyway, but I'll take my chances with the chief," I said, and checked my watch. "Well, it's getting late."

The Squirrel reluctantly slid off my desk and hoisted his pants up under his belly. "Another day, another dollar, am I right?"

Finn and I nodded. Finn added, "Right as rain."

Finally, the Squirrel moved away from the desk and, with a farewell waggle of his fingers, he was gone.

"I can't stand that guy." I gave a mock shiver. "I want to jump in a chemical shower every time he comes near here."

"No kidding. I feel dirty just breathing the same air," Finn said. He jerked his chin to the parolee list. "Long list?"

I picked up the paper and glanced at it, shrugging. "The usual."

I scanned the names and stopped short halfway down the list. "Son of a bitch."

Finn leaned over and plucked the paper from my hands. He read over the names and then looked at me with surprised, round eyes.

"Well, well, well. The plot thickens."

When Jake Stephens didn't answer his phone, I called Mac, who gave me their cousin Nicole's address. Finn and I drove together and, as we parked, I noticed a black sedan with tinted windows slowly pass us then speed up and take a right at the next street. The back license plate was smeared with mud and I could only make out the last two letters: AT.

"What's up?"

"That car. I think it was following us." I jotted down the partial license plate in my notebook, then climbed out of the car.

"You recognize it?"

I shook my head. "It's probably nothing."

The home was a narrow townhouse on the east side of town, nestled among a dozen other homes that looked as though they'd been built in the 1980s. The tiny front yard was tidy, recently mowed. A battered old blue Ford pickup with California plates was parked next to a sleek black-and-chrome motorcycle under the shade of a beautiful blossoming cherry tree.

"Nice bike." Finn whistled.

"Yeah? I don't know much about motorcycles."

I picked up a few days' worth of newspapers from the front stoop then knocked on the door. Jake answered in a pair of plaid boxer shorts and a long-sleeved T-shirt. His eyes looked heavy and tired behind his eyeglasses.

I held up the newspapers. "Special delivery and a few questions, if you've got the time?"

"Uh, sure. Let me just put some pants on," he said. "I was taking a nap."

He gently closed the door. Finn and I waited on the front stoop, enjoying the warm breeze. We'd already decided that I would handle most of the questions. After a long five minutes, Jake returned and invited us in. He'd put on jeans and a ball cap. I introduced Finn to him, and they shook hands.

"Do you want some water? Or juice? I'm on a bit of a health kick. I don't even have any coffee to offer you," Jake said. The house had an open floor plan and he moved into the kitchen.

He opened the refrigerator, staring into it. "There's some sparkling water."

"We're fine, thank you. So, no coffee, but alcohol and marijuana are okay?"

Jake pulled his head from the fridge and looked back at me. The quizzical look on his face made him look more like his cousin Mac than I'd yet seen. "Huh?"

"You all drank quite a bit up at Lost Lake. Drank wine, and smoked weed," I reminded him as I walked around the living room, checking out the place. Finn took a seat in a corner armchair. The couches were brown leather, the coffee and end tables granite. An enormous flat-screen television took up most of the south wall and scattered all around were framed photographs of exotic locales.

I moved closer to one, a full shot of a great white shark's mouth. The photo showed one of the shark's eyes, and I stared at the black rimless orb.

After a minute of silence Jake responded. "Oh yeah. I never thought of that, but yeah, you're right. Well, isn't that life for you. One step forward, two steps back."

I moved from the photograph of the shark to a picture of a tiny purple frog balancing on an electric-green leaf. "What does your cousin do?"

"Nicole is a freelance nature photographer. These ad companies, they fly Nicky out to awesome places—Bangkok, Egypt, Dubai—all expenses paid. All she has to do is point and click," Jake said. "Can you believe that? And she's a woman, no less."

I turned from the photographs to watch as Jake came out of the kitchen with a glass of water. "What's that supposed to mean?"

He took a seat on one of the couches and flushed. "Ah, come on, don't bust my balls. Those are dangerous places for a chick."

A tall woman with stunning red hair suddenly appeared behind Jake and gently hit the back of his head. She looked more like a super-model than an adventurous nature photographer.

"Hey, watch it," he whined. "What are you, my mother?"

"If I were, I'd kick you out for all that sexist crap you say," the woman said. She turned to Finn and me, giving Finn an apprecia-tive once-over. "I'm Nicole Stephens. You two cops?"

We nodded and introduced ourselves. I said, "I left you a message this morning."

"Yeah, sorry, I got it and then accidently deleted it. I couldn't remember your name, and I was too embarrassed to call the police and explain all that. I figured if it was important, you'd track me down. So, what is it?"

Jake stood up. "Nicky, they want to know about Saturday night."

"Last Saturday night? What about it? We left my friend's party early because it was lame. Jake fixed up my pool table and we played a few rounds, then watched a movie. I think Jake went to bed around one, and I was probably up until three. I'm a night owl," Nicole said. She gave Jake another thump on the back of the head. "What's the screwup supposed to have done, anyway?"

"It's not a joke, Nicky. They're here about Mac's girlfriend, Sari. And stop fucking hitting me," Jake said. He raised a hand then quickly lowered it. "We're not kids anymore."

"Poor Mac," Nicole said, and sobered up. "I can't believe Sari's dead. I really liked her."

"You knew her, too?" Finn asked.

She turned to him and once more gave him a look that was way too suggestive. "Sure. It's a small town, and we're a close family. Sari was fun. She had a lot of positive energy. We liked the same sorts of things, nice dinners, weekend trips. Mac's other girlfriends were all so boring."

Nicole glanced at her watch. "Damn, I'm going to be late. Listen, if you need anything from me, *anything at all*, don't hesitate to call." She handed Finn a business card and, with a swish of her red hair, left through the front door. A moment later, the motorcycle outside roared to life.

"So, did you get what you need?" Jake sat back down on the couch. He shot a glance at Finn, who gazed back, a neutral, relaxed expression on his face. "Can I go back to sleep?"

"No. Detective Nowlin and I learned something very interesting about you this morning."

A look of wariness crept into his eyes. "Oh yeah? What?"

"Prison, Jake? Really? You didn't think to mention this when we first met at Lost Lake?"

He stood up. "Ah, man. Come on. I served my sentence. I'm trying to do things right. I'm looking for work, I'm checking in all the goddamn time with Stinky Nuts, my parole officer . . . I didn't think it was important to say anything. I haven't *done* anything, so why *say* anything?"

I stared at him and raised my eyebrow. "Assaulting a woman is a serious crime, and when you are involved in a case where a woman has disappeared, you mention these sorts of things to the responding officer. Because when you don't, that makes me angry. It makes me wonder if I can trust you."

"But the whole thing was an accident! It wasn't my fault," Jake whined. "I was in the wrong place at the wrong time. It's the goddamn story of my life. Nicole got lucky, her old man paid for photography classes . . . Mac's a damn humanitarian . . . And me? I'm the fuckup. The black fucking sheep of the family."

Finn spoke for the first time since entering the house. He muttered, "Wrong place, wrong time . . . I've heard that before. It's a weak excuse for poor behavior."

Jake slammed his glass of water down on the coffee table. Water sloshed over the rim and spread across the granite surface, but he didn't seem to notice. "It's the truth. I wasn't supposed to be in LA that night. My buddy Clark told me about this sick night club where the booze was cold and the girls hot. We must have dropped five hundred dollars that night, but this bartender, this chick with short black hair and muscles like a dude, she wouldn't let up on Clark. He served in the Marines, and this bitch, after she saw his corps tattoo, she would not shut up. She kept going off on Gitmo, torture, blah, blah, blah. I tried to get Clark to pay the damn tab and get the hell out of there, but he was too proud."

Jake took a breath. Calmer now, he shrugged. "And, well, you know the rest."

"Not quite. The report said you spent six months in county jail for misdemeanor assault. How did you end up knocking out the bartender's front teeth?" I asked.

"This stranger, this random dude, he tried to pull Clark back from the bar. Clark has PTSD and he lost it, man, just lost it. A punch got thrown, and then all hell broke loose. I could see the bartender creeping up behind Clark with a bat, and I shoved her. Harder than I meant to. She fell against the bar and that was it," Jake said. He drew a hand over his tightly drawn mouth. "I'll tell you what, though. Those six months in jail are all I'm ever going to do. I'll die before I go back.

Jail is no joke. I made friends really quick with an Aryan Brother-hood gang, so I was protected, but the stuff I saw, well it scared me straight. I'm a changed man."

"What happened to Clark? The report didn't mention him."

Jake exhaled. "Clark was not so lucky. During the fight, some-one got Clark in a headlock and broke a few bones in his neck. He's in a wheelchair and lives with his parents in San Diego. I haven't seen him in a while."

"That's awful."

"Yeah, well, it's over now and I'm here, just trying to live my life. Okay?"

"Sure, whatever you say," I said. "So what did you think of Sari?"

Jake seemed relieved by the change in direction of the conversa-tion. "I didn't know her. I'd only met her that day, that day we went camping."

Finn jumped in again. "Come on, man, you spent the whole eve-ning together, hanging out with Mac and Ally. You and your cousin, two hot chicks. You must have formed *some* kind of impression."

"She was fine, I guess. I got the sense that she made Mac happy," Jake said after a moment's thought. He stood up and paced the length of the living room, parting the curtains at the front window and peer-ing out, then coming back and sitting down again.

"Do you think Mac made Sari happy?"

At this, Jake smiled knowingly and pointed a finger at me. "Now I see it."

"What do you see?" I asked.

"Why you're a good cop. I wasn't sure before, but it's clear now. You ask the right questions. Trust me, I've spent a lot of time with cops, and there's good ones and bad ones. Did he make her happy?" Jake replied. "I don't think so."

"Why?"

Jake paused a moment, thinking. Then he moved to the photo-graph of the great white shark and pointed at it. "See that? The shark is what's called an apex predator. This guy is at the top of the food chain. That was Sari. Beautiful, smart. Mac is chum compared to that. Of course he couldn't make her happy, not for very long. Not after she had her way with him."

Finn stood and straightened out his arms, adjusting the cuffs of his suit jacket. In a bored, almost detached voice he asked, "So what do you think happened at Lost Lake?"

"Me?" Jake asked, removing his eyeglasses. He cleaned them on the hem of his T-shirt and then replaced them. "I think someone else was there. Someone we never saw, never heard. A silent killer."

Chapter Twenty-seven

I've never been a big fan of cemeteries.

There are three of them in Cedar Valley. The Latham Group owns and manages the largest, Latham-Windsor Cemetery. Latham-Windsor is a sprawling, open space of gentle rolling hills and verdant green lawns, with sleek flat grave markers, marble memorials and headstones, and stately mausoleums. It's conveniently located near two churches and one synagogue and prides itself on being the area's premiere burial ground for all religious backgrounds (that is, according to their ad in *The Valley Voice*).

The next largest is Cedar Valley Cemetery, a municipal cemetery that's owned and managed by the city. My parents are buried at CVC. Every year on the anniversary of their death, I lay a dozen roses on my mother's grave and play a recording of "Ode to Joy" from Beethoven's Ninth Symphony over my father's grave.

Years after my parents had died, I came across an old video recording of them from before they were married. In the video, the two of them are in an art studio somewhere on the college campus where they met. My father is painting, but the easel is turned away from the camera and I can't see the artwork. My mother is standing next to him, her hand to her mouth, a look of concentration on her face. A radio is playing in the background, soft classical music. A familiar Chopin tune fades and "Ode to Joy" begins. My father flings the painting to the ground, jumps up, and picks up my half-screaming, half-laughing mother and proceeds to twirl her around the room. I don't know who was filming, but whoever it was, was laughing so hard the camera shook.

I hope that wherever my parents are, they're still dancing.

River Street Methodist Church has the third and smallest cemetery, and it was there that I headed after receiving an urgent and cryptic summons from one Ruby Cellars, the church's current caretaker and the Cedar Valley History Museum's former employee. The message had been left on my voice mail while Finn and I were interviewing Jake Stephens.

One of the oldest buildings in Cedar Valley, the historical church was situated on a dozen acres at the foot of Mt. James, just half a mile from the remains of the original mining camps that had come to define this entire stretch of the valley.

In the daytime, the simple white clapboard structure glowed as though lit from within against a stunning background of grassy meadows, colorful wildflowers, and the conical peak of the valley's tallest mountain.

But it was dusk when I arrived, and the church was dark. The single bell tower rose into the blackening sky, mirroring the look of the hundred or so tombstones that filled the graveyard next to the church. Half a dozen horses moved in the shadows in a corral near a weather-beaten wooden barn.

Nearby, light spilled from the windows of a small two-story house. A tiny woman stood on the front porch and waved to me. I pulled up alongside the porch, parked, and climbed out of my car. The air smelled of hay and horse manure, pine trees and rich earth.

"Mrs. Cellars?"

"Please, call me Ruby. Thank you for coming."

Barely five feet tall with tawny-colored eyes set deep into a narrow tan face, the caretaker wore the clothes of a cowboy or a cattle rancher: jeans, boots, a long-sleeved button-down shirt, and a Stetson, which she removed as we stepped into the house.

"Can I offer you a glass of water?"

"Thank you, yes."

She moved into a narrow galley kitchen, and I took the opportunity to glance around what must once have been the parsonage. It consisted of a main living space, with the kitchen and what I assumed to be a bathroom or closet tucked in the corner. A set of stairs led to what were likely a couple of bedrooms and a bath or two on the second floor.

The living room was decorated in a classic Western style; a long-horn cow skull hung over the stone fireplace, where a small fire offered a warm and ambient glow, and the soft suede couches were accented with brick-red cushions. The bookshelves were lined with worn paperbacks, thick hardcovers, and children's books. I vaguely recalled that Cellars was a widow, with kids, and I wondered where they were at the moment.

The house was awfully quiet.

"Here you go," Cellars said. She handed me the water. "I'm on a private well. Best water you'll ever have."

I took a sip, nodded. She was right: it was delicious. "Thank you. I must admit, your message was . . . unusual."

"Please, have a seat. I'm sorry about being mysterious, but it couldn't be helped. I've learned the hard way that some folks just don't want to buy what I'm selling."

She sipped from her own water glass, and I waited for her to speak. Suddenly, a flurry of activity and noise erupted from upstairs. What sounded like a herd of dogs flew down the stairs and, within seconds, I was surrounded by four little girls, all blond hair and blue eyes and nightgowns in varying shades of sherbet.

"Girls, settle down. This is a detective from the police force. She and Mama need to talk for a bit," Cellars said. She smiled as the kids grew quiet.

One of the girls asked with wide eyes, "A *lady* police officer?"

"Yes, my love," Cellars replied. She lowered her voice and said to me, "They are going to be talking about you for weeks. Their favorite game to play is Cops and Robbers."

"Mama, Mama, can we play outside?"

Somewhere in the house a clock chimed. Cellars and the girls kept count, mouthing one . . . two . . . three . . . And when the clock finally stopped, Cellars pointed to the front window. All six of us watched as night fell and the world turned dark. We were a few miles from the nearest streetlights, and I guessed that when I stepped outside after we were finished the stars would be breathtaking.

"But, Mama—"

"You know the rules. Play outside when it's light, quick inside when it's night. Now off to bed with you, all of you. Teeth and pee. I mean it."

The girls trudged upstairs in single file, moving like small soldiers who'd been expecting to win a battle in the bedtime war only to be ambushed by an enemy who looked and sounded an awful lot like their mother.

Cellars waited until the last little one had rounded the corner and moved out of sight.

"Well, I suppose I should get right to it," she said, and rubbed her hands together. "Do you know that I used to work at the history museum?"

I nodded.

"I was horrified to hear of Betty Starbuck's death. To then hear that Sari Chesney is dead, too . . . I worked with those women day in and day out, for years. I'm so sorry they're gone. Then I read online that you think the deaths are related to the missing Rayburn Diary. That all of this, all this death, has something to do with the Rayburn curse. And I knew."

"Knew what?"

Cellars's eyes gleamed. "That you're a believer, too."

"A believer?"

"I want to show you something." Cellars stood and went to the bookcase, retrieved a thick binder. She flipped through it. "Ah, here we go."

I stared at the black-and-white photograph she handed me. Five young women, dressed in long skirts and high-collared blouses, stood in front of the River Street Methodist Church. Their arms were linked, their faces lit with smiles.

I flipped the photograph over and whistled when I saw the date: September 1897.

"Old picture. Who are they?"

"The Lost Girls. It's the only known photograph of all five of them, at least as far as my research shows me. And I've done *a lot* of research. Within a month of this photograph, all five were dead." She paused. "Look at their faces. Look at their smiles. Do these girls seem unhappy?"

"Appearances can be deceiving." I studied the photograph. "But . . . no. No, they look happy."

"They're buried in my churchyard. When I first arrived in Cedar Valley, about six years ago, I made a point of walking the graves. Seemed only right that if I was going to be the caretaker of the church, I should get to know my neighbors, so to speak. Right from the start, there was something . . . magnetic about their particular graves. I'll show you, after we're done talking, and you can tell me if you sense the same thing."

Cellars added another log to the fire, and the dying flames roared back to life with a crackle and hiss. "Anyway, along with the parsonage and the church, I inherited a large amount of old records, historical things. Aside from the girls, the horses, and a bit of maintenance work here and there, I've got some time on my hands, and I love to read. Especially in the evenings. So I started looking into a few things, and I have a theory. It doesn't make me very popular at the local watering holes, but I've made peace with that."

I set the water down on an end table and leaned forward. "I'm all ears."

"I don't think those girls wanted to die. I think they were driven to kill themselves. And I think it's happening again."

Cellars saw the skepticism on my face. She sat down and clasped her hands together. "Please, just hear me out, and if I haven't convinced you after that, then fine."

I nodded to indicate that I was still with her. Relieved, she took a deep breath.

"Okay. For lack of a better title, I've taken to calling it the Sixty-Year Event. In 1837, Harris Theroux was mauled to death at Lost Lake by a large grizzly bear . . . never mind that grizzlies had never before and have never since been seen in these parts. In 1897, the Lost Girls experienced a so-called mass hysteria and drowned themselves. In 1957, three hunters died in a grotesque murder-suicide a quarter mile from the lake." Cellars shifted in her seat on the far end of the couch. "You see where I'm going with this, don't you?"

"Yes. There's a sixty-year span between the deaths. Sari Chesney's death fits your timeline. What about before 1837, before the fur traders and miners claimed this land as their own?"

Cellars frowned. "That's been harder to determine. Something happened at the lake in 1777, something that is only hinted at in the tribal histories I've found. After the event, the Ute avoided Lost Lake, even though its waters were flush with fish and the land around the lake was fertile. As to what occurred before that—well, my research has hit a wall."

"You think Harris Theroux was killed by a man?"

"Let's just say I'm skeptical it was a bear."

I was quiet, thinking. Outside, one of the horses snorted loudly, and Cellars cocked her head, listening. After a moment, though, the night fell silent again, and she relaxed.

"A mountain lion's been sniffing around the property this week. I think I'll put the horses in the barn tonight. I'd hate for the cat to tussle with one of them."

"Ruby, you've convinced me that an unusual pattern has occurred over the last two hundred years. But surely there have been other deaths at Lost Lake . . . heart attacks, maybe? Wayward hikers succumbing to the elements?"

She shook her head. "Honest to god, I've checked with the city clerk and the town archivist. Any free moment I had at the museum, I was researching the lake. I've scoured obituaries going back to the

first edition of *The Valley Voice*. Aside from the deaths I've mentioned, there have been no others at Lost Lake."

"You said the Lost Girls were driven to kill themselves. Driven
by what or whom?"

Worry clouded her eyes. "That's the missing piece of the puzzle.
I'd say by the lake itself, but that's crazy. And yet . . . I've been up
there, poking around. It's easily the most beautiful lake I've ever seen,
but there's a presence there. When I walk the shores, I feel as though
there's someone or something watching me. Truth be told, I stopped
going a few years ago. I'd hoped this year would pass by without any
deaths, and yet here we are."

"Yes, here we are . . ." I said slowly.

The whole thing was incredibly bizarre, and yet hadn't I felt that
same presence at Lost Lake? Didn't the very thought of returning
there put an ice-cold rock in the pit of my stomach?

Her eyes widened. "My god, you've felt it, too."

"I don't know what I felt . . . Could there be some poison in the
water, a fungus in the soil? Something organic that causes a reaction
in humans or animals?"

"Possibly."

"Surely you have a theory?"

Outside, another snort from one of the horses. I watched as Cellars's shoulders tensed, but once more, the night fell silent and she
relaxed.

"This damn mountain lion's got me on edge."

"You have a rifle?"

"Yes, but the cat would have to be practically on my neck before
I'd shoot it. This is her territory, her land. The horses and me and
the girls, we're just renters. A theory? Sure. I've got half a dozen. There
are rumors that the Silver Foxes were members of a satanic cult. In
exchange for fabulous riches and the opportunity to rule Cedar Valley,
they sacrificed a young man. The cult is still in existence and, every
sixty years, a fresh sacrifice is required. That's one half-assed theory.
Another is that a backwoods interbreeding family of mountain folk
are living up in the woods by the lake, killing people according to

some strange astrological calendar. Zodiac killers, maybe. I've got other theories, but I'll stop there. Suffice it to say, I *believe*, Detective."

"What am I supposed to do with this, Ruby? I can't flush out the forests in search of some incestuous tribe."

Cellars looked crestfallen. "I thought . . . I thought there would be *something* you could do. Warn people, maybe. Put up a perimeter. Close off access to the lake. You and I will be dead and gone when the next sixty-year event occurs, but think of future generations. Think of my daughters. Do you have kids? You have an opportunity to save lives, Detective."

I stood, uncomfortable with the sheen in her eyes, the flush that had appeared on her cheeks. "I appreciate all of this, I really do. I'm going to take it back to my team, and we'll look into it."

Cellars suddenly stood and crossed the room to the door, putting a hand on the knob. "Please, come with me to the graves."

"Now? It's pitch black outside."

"I'm begging you. If you don't sense what I sense, out there in the churchyard, I'll never bother you again. But if you do . . . if you do sense it, then maybe I'm not crazy," Cellars said. She jammed her Stetson on her head and grabbed two large flashlights from a shelf next to the door.

Finally, I nodded. I'd come this far already.

She grinned and handed me one of the lights. I switched it on and followed Cellars across the meadow, comforted in the darkness by the twin beams of light and the soft snorts and whinnies of the horses in the corral.

As I'd thought, the stars were brilliant in both their number and their luminosity.

We skirted the church itself and entered the graveyard through a rusty gate that screeched like a wounded owl.

"Another thing on my to-do list," Cellars muttered. "Careful where you step; there are some low-to-the-ground headstones. I'd hate for you to trip."

She led me to the back of the graveyard. We were far from the church now, far from the familiar noises of the horses and the warm glow of the house. I shivered, regretting that I hadn't grabbed my jacket from the car. I wondered, not for the first time, at the strange places my career took me.

"Here we are." Cellars played her light over five identical tombstones, lined up in a row. "Though their deaths were judged suicides, the good Reverend Elias Rayburn granted burial rights to all five women. No doubt his decision was due in part to the mass hysteria—or temporary insanity—thought to inflict the poor women and in part to the fact that one of the women was his very own niece, Roberta Rayburn."

"The reverend was Owen Rayburn's brother?"

"Yes, his only sibling." Cellars's light dimmed. She shook the flashlight, and the bulb went out with a soft sizzle. "Damn. Let's not linger. That mountain lion could be anywhere, and while I have confidence that the horses would alert us to its presence, we may have just enough distance between us and the horses to make that confidence . . . inaccurate."

While I had no desire to test that theory, something kept me rooted in place.

I shone my flashlight over each tombstone, reading the name, the birth and death dates. The air here was warmer, and though it was impossible to see anything beyond a few feet, the downward slope of the ground told me this particular section of the graveyard was sunken and likely protected from the wind.

Cellars suddenly spoke, and I jumped, aware that some minutes had passed.

"You feel it too, don't you?" She moved a little closer. "It's . . . magnetic. Or hypnotic. I haven't decided which. Let's head back now. If I may lead the way?"

She took the flashlight from my hand, and I followed close behind her. We parted ways at my car and, as I pulled away, she moved to the corral and ducked between the wooden slats of the gate, moving like a small ghost in the immense darkness.

Chapter Twenty-eight

I was exhausted and unnerved by the time I got home. As I pulled into the driveway, I was surprised to see Clementine's car next to Brody's truck.

As I stepped into the front hall, reaching down to scratch Seamus's back, I stopped short.

Brody's rolling suitcase, a carry-on bag, and his laptop case were stacked in a neat pile next to the door. Frowning, I called out, "Honey?"

Brody came out of the kitchen, Grace in his arms. "Oh good, you're here. Clementine's got to leave soon."

I set my things down. "What's with the luggage?"

"I've got to be on a flight to Beijing, leaving Denver at five a.m. I'll drive to the airport tonight and crash at one of the hotels." He checked his watch and swore, his hazel eyes darkening. "In fact, I need to leave very soon."

"Excuse me, what? You're driving to Denver now? And then flying to China?" I was so surprised, it was hard to get the words out. "What are you *talking* about?"

"The Chinese have questions, technical questions, about some of the clauses in the contract. You know, the one I was telling you about a couple of weeks ago? Anyway, they're asking for me. I worked with a few of them, years ago, in Mongolia. Look, there's twenty million dollars on the line, Gemma. I have to go. I owe it to Harry," Brody said.

He put the baby in my arms and leaned in for a kiss but I turned away, burying my face in Grace's neck, inhaling the sweet, innocent smell of her skin, desperately trying not to lose my temper.

Brody sighed. "Babe, I'll only be gone a week, two at the most."

"*Two* weeks? This is crazy. What the hell am I supposed to do with the baby? I'm in the middle of two homicide investigations."

"Harry took a chance hiring me, Gemma. I have to go. We knew travel might be part of the deal." Brody was amped up, excited to be headed back out into the field. "After we hammer out the contract, Harry wants me to fly to the western part of the country and check on operations."

"Is Harry going, too?"

"No, just me. He's tied up with the courts this week."

I rolled my eyes. Harry was on his third divorce, and rumor had it that this one might just clean him out for good.

Brody finally seemed to notice that my mood had darkened. "I'm sorry, honey. I can't say no."

Taking a deep breath, I nodded. I shifted Grace to my other hip and nudged Seamus away with my foot so I could stand closer to Brody and give him a hug.

"We'll be fine. What can I do to help?"

He leaned in and nuzzled my cheek. "Nothing. I love you. I'll call when I land."

Brody picked up his luggage and walked out the door. I called out after him, "Text me when you reach Denver. I don't want to worry all night that you've crashed in a ravine somewhere."

"Will do. I love you," he called back with a wave.

I slowly closed the front door and stood in the hall for a long moment.

Clementine appeared, wiping her hands on a kitchen towel. "Dinner's in the oven. I take it I should come a little early tomorrow?"

"That would be great. Something smells wonderful; did you cook?"

"Are you kidding? I threw a frozen potpie in the oven and cranked the heat. Should be ready in twenty minutes. I figured you'd be hungry."

"What would I do without you?"

Clementine shrugged. "Beats me. I have a feeling you'd live on vending machine food for a while, then your teeth would fall out and your pancreas would shut down and you'd die. It would probably be both painful and slow. Not a great way to go."

"Agreed. How is everything else going? School . . . your boy problem?"

"School's good, nearly wrapped up. And I ended things with Joe. He turned out to be a stage-five clinger. It's too bad, he was a nice guy. Until the calls started."

I frowned. "What's a stage-five clinger?"

"Someone who gets too attached too fast. Like, you go on two dates with them and suddenly they're looking at wedding china and naming the babies you'll have together. That was Joe. Clingers are . . . well, they're emotionally needy."

"God, I had no idea there was a term for this. I hope I haven't been a clinger."

Clementine burst into laughter.

"What's so funny?"

"You are so not a clinger. You're like the total opposite. I don't even think they have a word for what you are . . ."

Suddenly I wasn't sure if she was complimenting or mocking me. She left, still laughing, and I took a moment to glance in the hall mirror after I shut and locked the door.

Did I look like a clinger?

I quickly fed Grace, then put her straight to bed. After she was asleep, I spent a long time sitting on the living room floor, flipping through a photo album stuffed with pictures of Brody and me, marveling at the winding and often broken road our lives had taken thus far.

Beijing.

It was a hell of a lot closer to Tokyo than Cedar Valley was.

Closer to the university where Brody had spent a semester as a guest lecturer, where he'd been wined and dined and seduced . . .

I tried to slam the door on that train of thought, but an image of Celeste Takashima, with her long dark hair and eyes the color of amber, barreled into my mind anyway. After Brody had confessed their affair, I'd made him tell me everything. I even searched for her online and found a picture. She was ten years older than him and, when she wasn't rappelling down glaciers and hiking up volcanos, she lived in a small apartment in Tokyo.

They were colleagues at the university, and a dinner party with a few of the other professors ended late. Brody had too much to drink. One thing led to another and another and another.

For ten weeks.

Before the affair, I'd never thought of myself as a jealous person. But after?

Until you've lived through a betrayal like that, you don't get it. You don't understand how quickly trust can be gone. How slowly it can come back. Your confidence shatters, and if you're tough enough to put the pieces back together, you find you've become fragile.

Brittle.

Breakable.

I slammed the photo album shut. Downstairs, I scanned the contents of the liquor cabinet and settled on a plum brandy. Seamus whined at the back door, and I let him out, opening the door wide, inhaling the cold night air. Then I curled up on the couch and sipped the brandy and waited for Brody to let me know he had arrived safely in Denver, my thoughts as jumbled and mixed up as an overturned box of puzzle pieces.

Chapter Twenty-nine

In the early morning hours on Friday, I sat in my car outside Sari Chesney's apartment waiting for Finn. The first time I'd been here, with Mac Stephens on the day Chesney disappeared, we'd been hopeful she would return. I'd taken a cursory glance around her home, nothing more. Now that her body had been found and her death determined to be a homicide, a proper search of her apartment was in order.

I passed the time sipping from a cup of coffee and reading an article by Bryce Ventura in the day's edition of *The Valley Voice*. It was a few short but potent paragraphs that criticized the lack of progress on the Betty Starbuck case and, to my shock and horror, posed the question of why Kent Starbuck was not being investigated as a suspect.

The article listed Starbuck's transgressions, including his time in prison and a photograph of him from his trial twenty-some years ago. The story went on to say that while Starbuck had been questioned, it was clear the Cedar Valley Police Department was treating him with kid gloves and being over-cautious with his rights due to fear of a lawsuit.

I threw the paper in the backseat of my car, fuming. Not only had the leaker struck again, but the whole article was written in a way to stir up emotions and not in a way that shared truths. We had no hard evidence tying Kent Starbuck to his mother's homicide; all we had was a collective gut feeling that he may have been involved, a strong motive, and the fact that he'd been observed outside the museum.

Enough was enough. As soon as I was back at the station, I'd go through the list of people who were there when I'd posted the fake report on the Red Board. And somehow, I'd figure out a way to whittle away at the list until I had the leaker in my crosshairs.

Finn pulled up next to me, and I lowered my window, asking, "Did you see the paper today?"

"It's bullshit. Let it go."

He slid into the empty spot ahead of me and parked. As we walked to Chesney's apartment, he was quiet. I shared with him my strange evening at the River Street Methodist Church and Ruby Cellars's theories. As I'd suspected he would be, Finn was dismissive.

"Sari Chesney's death was a homicide, plain and simple. The lake's just a lake, it's not triggering murderous rages in people."

"I know it sounds nuts. But you have to admit it's odd that every sixty years, there is violent death at Lost Lake. What if there is a family, some kind of tribe, living in the woods? And part of their tradition is a sacrifice to the waters?"

Finn groaned. "Do you know how crazy that sounds?"

"Yes."

We arrived at Chesney's apartment, and the manager greeted us. After he unlocked the door, I withdrew a penknife from my bag and sliced through the yellow tape that secured the premises. The manager was a timid man with scarred olive skin, deeply disturbed by Chesney's killing. He told us he was praying for her soul, and Finn thanked him, not sure what else there was to say.

Inside the apartment, the air was still.

While Finn stood at the kitchen counter and rifled through a stack of old bills, I spent several minutes in the living room, staring at the photographs on the wall.

Once again, I was struck by how closely Chesney and Ally Chang resembled each other. I wondered, too, who had the grim job of explaining to the girls that Chesney had mentored why she would no longer be in their lives.

I peeked out onto the narrow patio and saw a mountain bike

chained to the railing. Two rusty lawn chairs and a small table with a few dying potted herbs took up most of the space.

We didn't find anything of note in the living room or kitchen, so we moved on to the bedroom. The drawers in her dresser were filled with designer clothes, many with the tags still on. I recognized a few of the labels and couldn't understand how she could afford these on her museum salary.

A few minutes later, Finn found a stack of credit card bills. "She was living high on the hog. Chesney was in debt to the tune of thousands of dollars."

"I'm guess I'm not surprised. She had gambling debts . . . why not credit card debt, too? In fact, it's probably one and the same. A lot of cards allow you to withdraw a cash advance. I bet that's what she was doing: withdrawing cash against her balance, then blowing it at the casinos."

Finn read through the bills. "That's exactly what she was doing."

I opened the closet door and found more designer clothes, along with an impressive number of shoes. The closet had a single high shelf with a leather suitcase and a cardboard hat box. I stood on my tiptoes and was just barely able to reach them.

Inside the hat box was a delicate black crushed velvet hat, adorned with flowers and ribbons. I admired the handiwork for a moment, then put it aside and opened the leather suitcase.

Jackpot.

Inside the suitcase were five journals, along with a stack of photographs, concert ticket stubs, and other memorabilia. It was the sort of stuff that a person collects over the course of a lifetime.

Chesney's suitcase would forever remain half-filled.

She was a dedicated diarist; each notebook covered a year—no more, no less—and she appeared to have started the journals six years ago. Before diving into them, I scrutinized the dates and realized that the most current volume was missing. The fifth journal in the set ended at Christmas of last year.

Mac had told me that Chesney was obsessed with her diary, writing in it every evening.

So where was this year's journal?

Finn joined me at the kitchen table, and we split the diaries; he took the oldest, while I started with the second most current.

Sari wrote prolifically, in a kind of shorthand that made more sense the more I read.

A typical diary entry: *November 2, mild fifty degrees. Snow on the horizon. Slept undisturbed—no dreams! Movies tonight with Ally Cat. Hope to discuss My Sweet with A. My Sweet is getting fat—work stress? I'm losing the attraction. He struggles to get it up sometimes. Sigh. We can't all be hot all the time. Oh wait, yes we can! It's called "get off your lazy ass, dude."*

Ally Cat . . . Ally Chang? And My Sweet . . . MS . . . Mac Stephens?

I read through the diary, fervently wishing I had the most current one. The year started off well enough; Mac and Sari seemed to be enjoying a particularly blissful time together. The two of them spent a lot of time traveling on the weekends, cheap camping trips and road trips to Vegas and Arizona. Sari spoke of needing more money but sounded content with her current situation. Ally accompanied them for a lot of the trips, and I got the sense that Mac thought she was a third wheel; or rather, Sari got that sense based on things Mac said.

In the summer, the couple hit a rough patch and decided to separate. They discussed seeing other people, but Mac wasn't keen on the idea. Sari pursued it. In numerous entries for August, she referenced seeing someone new in town, someone she nicknamed Blue Bird or BB.

Blue Bird.

Sari's cop, the one Ally Chang had told me about on the phone.

BB and Sari dated for a few weeks, then she broke things off when she decided to get back together with Mac. Blue Bird wasn't happy. Sari wrote that she was finally so fed up with BB she threatened him, promising to call his boss and report him for harassment and stalking.

My blood went cold when I read the next few lines in her journal.

*Little BB isn't happy with me. I told him I'd call Chavez person-
ally and tell him that the newest bird in the nest couldn't keep his hands
to himself. Blue Bird squawked but I know he'll leave me alone now.
He won't risk his career.*

Blue Bird . . . Sam Birdshead. He'd been the only recruit to join
our force last summer, wearing the blue uniform of a patrol officer
for just a few short months before the hit-and-run accident derailed
his career and left him disabled.

Sari and Sam?

"Holy shit," I whispered.

Finn jerked his head up. His eyes were glazed, and it was obvious that reading the diary of a twenty-something woman was hardly
his cup of tea. "Got something?"

I read out loud what Sari had written. A muscle in his jaw began
to twitch. When I finished, he sat back and rubbed his eyes.

"We have to drag Sam into this now, too?"

"Yes." I realized I hadn't seen Sam in a couple of months. After
his accident, he'd left the force and joined Alistair Campbell's Black
Hound Construction. Sam ran with a different pack now, one I didn't
trust. Was it possible that Sam was more like the Black Hounds than
I could have known?

Could he have been harboring a jealous, murderous streak for
the last eight months?

Did he stalk Sari and her friends to Lost Lake, and then kill her?

The Sam Birdshead I knew couldn't hurt a fly.

But how well did I really know him?

Before we left the apartment complex, we stopped at the small storage unit assigned to Chesney in the underground parking garage.
About the size of a walk-in closet, the unit was locked with a rusty
padlock, and Panetta, the property manager, didn't have a spare key
for it. He did have a bolt cutter strapped to his utility belt, though,
and in a few minutes, Finn had the padlock cut and the door to the
unit open.

An atrocious smell hit us, and we all took a step back.

"Good lord," I said, and covered my mouth and nose.

The landlord waved a hand in front of his face and puckered his lips. "We had a rat problem a few months back. Smells like one of the critters got in there and died."

Finn shone his flashlight into the dark unit, moving the beam over a bicycle wheel, a spare tire for her Honda, a vacuum with a cracked canister, and five-gallon jugs of paint. A thin layer of dust covered all of it, including the desiccated rat nestled in between the paint and the spare tire.

"Chesney hasn't opened this unit in months," Finn said.

The landlord coughed. "You guys still need me? I'll call our maintenance guy, get this rat cleaned out."

"Please leave it for the time being, Mr. Panetta. Don't touch a thing until we give you the green light, okay?"

Panetta looked at me like I was crazy, then shrugged and said, "You're the boss."

Finn and I split up in the parking lot. He had a court appearance on an unrelated case. As he drove away, I called Sam Birdshead. He was free, and we agreed to meet at the Silver Creek trailhead in twenty minutes.

I parked on Main Street and walked to the trailhead, arriving first. I took a minute to admire the view. The creek was an arm of the Arkansas River that meandered through town at a gentle pace, and the trail that paralleled it was shaded and popular. A few cyclists sped past me, their faces shielded by helmets and sunglasses, their bodies lean and hunched.

"Hey."

I turned around and smiled at Sam. From a distance, his denim-blue eyes and tousled blond hair made him look hardly older than a teenager. Up close, though, those eyes were haunted and the hair shot through with gray.

"Hey yourself. Been a while."

"Sure has."

Our hug was awkward and reserved. I hadn't told Sam why I

wanted to meet with him, but the grim set of his jaw told me he might have an inkling.

We walked the trail, Sam's gait slow and steady. He wore a prosthetic leg, and I was happy to note he moved better with it than he had with the crutches I'd seen him use in the past. Sam's leg had been amputated below the knee the previous September, after a hit-and-run accident during a case we were investigating. He'd had a long road of healing, one that he was still on.

"This is about Sari, isn't it? I saw the news in the paper this morning," he said. "I can't believe she's dead. The article didn't give many details. Was it an accident?"

"We're still investigating."

Sam nodded. "Of course. Since you're talking to me, though, I'm going to assume this wasn't a natural death."

I tipped my head slightly. "Your name came up in a journal Chesney kept. It wasn't exactly flattering."

Sam picked up an empty Coke can and crushed it in his hand, looking around for a trash bin. "I hate people who litter. Selfish pricks. Sari and I went out a few times last summer. Before my accident. She wanted more than I was willing to give, so we broke it off. She was looking for marriage, a family. I wasn't ready."

He stopped walking and aimed the crushed can at a recycling bin six feet ahead of us, then tossed it. He missed, and the can landed on the ground with a clatter. As we passed by, he sighed, picked up the can again, and placed it in the bin.

I chose my words carefully, knowing Sam was no longer a cop. In fact, based on Sari's journal, he could almost be a suspect.

Almost.

But he wasn't. Not yet.

"Sari recorded a slightly different version of events. She said it was her idea to break things off and you resisted. She wrote that you only left her alone after she threatened you, promised to go to Chavez."

Behind us, a bell rang, and we both moved to the right to allow a pair of cyclists to speed past. Sam started laughing, but it wasn't a humorous laugh. There was disdain there.

"This is going to be a fun game of 'she said, he said,' isn't it? Only I'm automatically guilty because I'm alive. I'm alive, and she's dead."

"You know that's not how I work, Sam. I know you. I'm doing my damnedest to keep an open mind here."

He stopped walking and took a step back. There was coldness in his eyes. "Why do you think you know me? Huh? We worked to-gether, what, a few weeks. You *don't* know me, you don't know what I believe, how I think. You have no idea what I'm capable of. So stop making assumptions based on a handful of interactions."

The vehemence in Sam's voice took me aback. After a few deep breaths, he pushed the blond hair off his forehead and started walk-ing again. I joined him, and he continued talking.

"Like I said, Sari wanted more of a relationship than I was will-ing to give her. I don't remember her taking it particularly badly. Seems like we talked things over one night at dinner and agreed to go our separate ways. If I remember right, there was an ex-boyfriend in the shadows, Matt or Mike or something like that. I can't imagine she stayed single for too long after we ended things."

"Mac," I said absentmindedly. I couldn't reconcile Sam's version of events with what Sari had written in her journal. I assumed Sam was telling the truth but if he was, it only created more questions. What reason would Sari have to lie in her own personal journal? Was she a pathological liar? Did she do it to make herself feel better?

Could I trust anything she wrote?

Perhaps she wrote her diaries for someone else's reading pleasure, someone else's benefit.

More chilling was the thought that perhaps Sam wasn't telling me the truth.

He was still talking. "That's right, Mac. He's a nurse at the hos-pital. Big Mac, she used to call him. I couldn't tell if that was meant to be derogatory or not. Knowing her, it was probably an insult." He puffed out his cheeks and then exhaled. "Anyway, I'm not sure what else I can tell you. Although . . ."

"What?"

"Well, she mentioned this guy a couple of times. She called him the Bookkeeper."

"The bookkeeper? Like an accountant? Or a bookie?"

Sam nodded. "She only talked about him when she was drunk, and honestly, it was just two or three times. I only remember because I asked her what kind of a name that was, and she laughed and said it was her pet name for him. She said something about how if anyone was going to help make her dreams come true, it was him."

"Do you remember anything else about him? Was he someone she knew through work, or friends?"

Sam shook his head, looking genuinely sorry. "No, I'm telling you, she talked about him in passing. She could be guarded that way. I remember she never let me come to her apartment. We always met up at bars."

"Was she scared of this man?"

Sam thought a moment. "No, it didn't seem that way. She was . . . smug when she talked about him. Like the cat that swallowed the canary."

I tried to reconcile Chesney's debts, the mentoring she did of young women, her work at the history museum, her often cruel journal entries. She presented a complex personality, on the one hand generous and fun loving, on the other hand struggling with addictions and demonstrating a mean, closed-off streak.

"Sam, there are elements of Chesney's life, her personality, that don't add up. What was your take on her?"

We neared a fork in the trail. A fire truck screamed past us on the nearby road, its sirens and lights running. Sam gazed after it with an unreadable glint in his eye, then checked his watch. "I've got to be back soon. Let's turn around up here. Look, obviously she was beautiful. Beautiful, attractive. There was this sort of . . . passion about her, you know? But like I said, we only dated a few weeks. I knew it wasn't going anywhere, so why invest the energy? Anyway, it was clear her long-term plans didn't involve Cedar Valley. She was going places, and this is my home."

"Makes sense." I'd gotten as much as I could from him about Sari, so I changed the subject. "How's work going?"

Sam looked at me out of the corner of his eye to see if I was being sarcastic. It was no secret that I thought his resigning the police force was a huge mistake, especially to join Black Hound Construction.

He saw I was asking in earnest, and he brightened a bit. "Work's awesome. It's good, honest work, Gemma. Campbell is a great man. He's got big plans for Cedar Valley, for this whole area. *Progressive* plans."

"Like what?"

"Well, take the museum. Under Campbell's stewardship it could become a real tourist mecca. A genuine money maker. Cedar Valley's dying, Gemma, whether you see it or not. Ten years from now, unless we innovate, we'll be a joke, a pit stop on the highway," Sam said. "We have to capitalize on whatever we can. For us, that's our mining history and our ski resort."

We reached the trailhead and our cars.

"It's good to see you, Gemma. Let me know if I can be of further help. If you narrow down a time for Sari's death, I'm sure I'll have an alibi."

"I doubt that will be necessary, Sam. You know I have to follow up on all leads. You're not a suspect."

"Not yet, anyway," he said with a tight smile as he pulled out of the parking lot.

Chapter Thirty

As I walked back to my car, I passed James Curry's used and rare bookshop. Nothing pointed to him as a suspect in either of my murder investigations and yet, like Larry Bornstein, Curry had worked with both Betty Starbuck and Sari Chesney. He'd also worked on the Rayburn Diary and, if Bornstein had told me the truth, was interested in buying or borrowing it.

I entered the store, a tinny bell announcing my arrival.

Dusty stained-glass windows let in weak light. Curry had a small selection of new books in the store's front windows, but the bulk of the inventory was made up of used books of all kinds: paperbacks, hardcovers, children's books, even textbooks. The store smelled of dead air and cat urine, and I wasn't at all surprised to see an enormous tabby lounging on the floor, his big head resting on a battered copy of the Oxford English Dictionary.

Curry himself was seated behind the counter. He rose quickly, his chair scraping along the floor as an electric tea kettle behind him whistled. He switched it off, then turned to me. He was a short man, about sixty years old, with broad shoulders and bowed legs. He wore rimless tinted eyeglasses, a scraggly goatee, and a sweater with moth holes in the sleeves. His eyes were small and pale and they moved over my face quickly and frantically, like a mouse staring down a cat.

I introduced myself. "I understand that you worked with both Betty Starbuck and Sari Chesney."

"Terrible, terrible business. I didn't know Sari all that well. But I've worked with Betty, and others at the museum, for years now. She was a lovely woman." Curry wiped at his nose with the sleeve of his sweater and stared at me. "Now. What do you want with me?"

"I have some questions about Owen Rayburn's diary."

Before I could go further, Curry let out a loud moan. "Don't remind me about that, please. I haven't slept a wink since the gala. If only they'd let me keep it here, I'd have kept it safe, secure. That's my life's work, you see . . . keeping priceless artifacts like that safe."

"Most people I've talked to blame Betty Starbuck for the diary's disappearance; her, or Sari Chesney."

"Yes, but should they? Those on the shore always blame the captain when the ship goes down. The rats know to jump ship before it leaves the dock."

I lifted an eyebrow. "What are you saying?"

Instead of answering, he scuttled to the far end of the counter, dove into a file cabinet, then remerged with a sheaf of papers in his hand and hurried back to me.

"Look at these."

I held them close to my face, then moved them back a few inches and squinted. I'd left my reading glasses back at the office. Curry noticed and, with a flourish, handed me a pair from a tray of glasses for sale.

"Thanks," I said, discreetly brushing off a wad of orange cat fur. Even with the glasses, it took a few minutes for me to realize what I was looking at. "It's a map, isn't it? Of the valley? But why is everything mixed up on it? I see the river, the mountains . . . but none of it is in the correct location."

Curry nodded, pleased. He said smugly, "I photocopied those pages from Owen Rayburn's diary. Do you notice anything else strange?"

Looking closer, I saw what appeared to be tiny symbols strewn about the map.

"These little arrows, or are they trees? What do they mean? What kind of map is this?"

Curry stared at me. "It's a treasure map."

"Come on." I burst out laughing. "You're a believer, too, huh?

These hills have been tapped out for years. There is no secret vein of gold or stash of silver. Next you'll tell me that you too think the diary is cursed."

"I can't speak to a curse." Curry snatched the pages out of my hands and scowled. "It is a treasure map. The problem is that it's all in code. And the cipher is in that diary."

"You're a clever man. I have to imagine that if you photocopied *some* pages from the diary, you photocopied them all."

The little man gave me another sly look from the side of his eye. "Now who's the clever one? Of course I did. I was just doing my job, making sure I had pages lined up, that sort of thing. But you see, I've come to believe the key to the cipher is actually somewhere in or on the diary's cover. Which I neglected to photograph."

"What exactly had you been hired to do?"

Curry removed his glasses and wiped at them with his sweater, taking his time to answer. When he put the glasses back on, they were just as smeared and greasy as before. "I was tasked with a number of things. First, establishing provenance. Was this truly Owen Rayburn's diary and not a fake? It had been in the basement of the museum for decades. There was no doubt in anyone's mind that it was authentic . . . but it's best practice to establish this totally and definitively. Second, was it in good enough condition to go on display? Was it legible, free of mildew and mold, that sort of thing? You can't put something out that's disintegrating. And third, I was asked to type out the contents. I believe the plan was to eventually digitize the whole thing. You know, put the diary online, on the museum's website. Having me do it, as opposed to the museum volunteers or staff, helped limit the number of fingers in the pie, so to speak."

"Who did you work with on the project? Sari Chesney?"

"No, Sari was strictly in charge of the curating side of things. I reported directly to Betty."

"Do you think the murders and the missing diary are connected?"

Curry shuddered. "Now there's an awful thought. If the diary was stolen with the intent to sell, there's a very small market for it. A black market, if you will. As I understand it, Betty was killed *after* the diary went missing."

"What other purpose would someone have to steal it, other than to sell it?"

At that Curry smiled a humorless smile. "There's an equally small market for collectors of that sort of thing."

It was the same thing Larry Bornstein had said.

Before I could respond, the bell over the shop's front door chimed and we both turned to watch a young man and woman come in. They blinked in the dim light, then moved to the textbook section.

"So you truly believe there is treasure out there?"

Licking his lips, Curry nodded. "What exactly it is, I couldn't say. Gold, silver . . . There are rumors that at least one Spanish conquistador made it this far north. Perhaps there are gemstones, valuable emeralds or rubies."

"Do you have Advanced Chemistry?" the young man shouted toward us. "Or Calculus?"

"I'll be right there," Curry shouted back. To me, he said in a low voice, "I'm not the only one interested in that diary. You should talk to the black hound."

"Alistair Campbell?"

Curry nodded, a glint in his eyes. "He offered me *quite* a lot of money for a copy of these pages."

"Did you take the money?"

Curry stepped back and moved toward the young couple. "What I do and don't do is my business. I think I've 'shared' enough with you, Detective."

"I can get a warrant for the information I need, Mr. Curry."

"Then do so!" he whispered furiously, and made a shooing motion at me.

As I walked to my car, I chewed on a cuticle. Alistair Campbell's name had a funny way of popping up in my murder investigations.

Perhaps it was time I paid him a visit.

Chapter Thirty-one

As I drove north to Campbell's office, I noticed a black sedan with tinted windows and mud-smeared license plates following me. The sedan hung a few cars back, but it turned when I turned and changed lanes as I did. The driver was clearly an amateur and, while I could have lost the tail, I decided not to screw around. Instead, I cursed myself for forgetting to run the partial license plate number I'd collected outside of Jake Stephens's house and then pulled a sudden right turn. It might not have gotten me very far, but it would have been a start.

Three cars back, the black sedan made the same turn, moving slowly, cautiously.

Thinking quickly, I ran through options. It was Friday, and the roads were already heavy with people cutting out of work early and parents hustling for carpool pick-up. I could use the traffic to my advantage.

Approaching a streetlight, I slowed my speed. The black sedan had moved up and was now two cars behind me. Perfect. As the light changed from green to yellow, I increased my speed and moved through the intersection before the light changed again to red. Then I quickly made a series of right turns.

In a matter of minutes, I was four cars behind the black sedan, smiling grimly as it slowly cruised down the road, its driver obviously scanning the side streets for me. I slapped my dash light and siren on and, one by one, the cars between us moved to the side.

After a brief moment during which time I wondered if the black sedan was seriously going to attempt to flee, the driver pulled over and killed the engine. I lifted my radio microphone and spoke through it, glad I was in a department vehicle and not my personal car.

"Get out of the car with your hands in the air. Now."

After a long minute, the driver's-side door opened and Bryce Ventura of *The Valley Voice* clambered out, his face red and sweaty, his blue jeans caked with long streaks of blood.

"It's not blood. It's Glossy Currant. I'm painting old lady Washburn's master bedroom," Ventura whined. "She's going for a bordello effect."

"You think I give two hoots about Janet Washburn's brothel bedroom?"

"Bordello. Not brothel. There's a difference," Ventura said smugly. "See, in the bordello—"

"Shut up. Why are you following me?"

Ventura hung his head. We stood on the side of the road between our two vehicles. Passing cars slowed to check out the drama, and I could see he was embarrassed. He rubbed his hands together and started to speak.

"And don't lie to me. I'll know if you're lying, and your day will get a whole lot worse."

Ventura nodded, and his ebony black hair moved like it was an entity separate from his head. "Okay, okay. I was following you. You're working the two hottest cases in town, Monroe. I want the scoop."

I glowered. "Seems to me you're already getting the scoop, Ventura. Who's your source in the department?"

"Huh?"

"Have you got peas in your ears? Who is sharing confidential information with you?"

"Ah, that. Well . . . you know I can't tell you that." Ventura's expression grew smug. "Journalistic integrity and all."

I waited until a group of giggling, gawking middle-school children on the sidewalk had passed us, then took a deep breath and tried to calm down. "Have you ever considered the damage you might be doing to an active investigation when you prematurely include information in your articles? What if a killer goes free because he's been tipped off by something you write?"

Ventura chewed his lip. "If a killer goes free, that's on you, not me."

"Bullshit."

"No, it's true," Ventura insisted. "It's up to you to get these guys before a prosecutor with enough evidence for a conviction. It's up to *me* to keep the citizenry informed."

"Spare me the philosophical debate, Ventura. I read your article this morning. Prematurely naming a person of interest, which is exactly what you did, jeopardizes everything. This is still America. We still adhere to the fundamental belief that a person is innocent until proven guilty. You practically tried and convicted Kent Starbuck with a few—poorly written, by the way—sentences. Now who's your damn source?"

Ventura seemed to feed off my anger and grew smarmier with each word. "Tit for tat, Monroe. If you promise me a scoop when you catch the Museum Murderer, I'll give you two clues who my informant is. That's the best I can do and still walk away with my integrity intact."

Surprised, I found myself considering his offer. When we caught the killer or killers, Ventura would write about it anyway. What did it matter if he got the scoop, as long as I was that much closer to catching the leaker? My anger and frustration at him, and at the leaker, began to fade at the prospect of some answers.

"Deal."

He grinned, and I felt as though I'd just struck a bargain with the devil. Ventura rubbed his hands together, excited. He thought a few minutes, then said, "Your first clue is this: what gets hit over and over and keeps coming back for more?"

"Ventura, that's a goddamn riddle. You can forget about the scoop."

He scoffed. "And you can forget about your second clue. Now, *Detective,* am I under arrest? I have a bordello bedroom to finish painting."

"Get out of here. Don't let me catch you following me again. Nothing more than an ambulance chaser," I muttered, and walked back to my car. I climbed in and slammed the door, equally furious and curious.

What gets hit over and over and keeps coming back for more?

What gets hit . . . a boxer? Finn boxed in his free time. He and ten other guys in the department.

I started the car and pulled away from the curb, struck by a sudden, disturbing thought.

What if the leaker was more than one person?

I checked my watch and saw I'd missed lunch by hours. I headed to a drive-through and ordered a vanilla milkshake and a chicken sandwich with a side of fries, remembering Clementine's dire prediction for my health. Parking in the lot, I scarfed the food down and then continued on to Alistair Campbell's offices.

I'd seen him across the room at the gala, but it had been months since I'd last actually spoken to Campbell, and my opinion of him remained unchanged: I was suspicious of his motives, pure and simple. On the surface, he appeared to be a generous contractor, giving ex-convicts a second chance through legitimate employment with his company, Black Hound Construction. Cedar Valley was small potatoes, though, and I believed he had ulterior motives, still to be seen, for being here.

Campbell rented a suite of rooms on the third floor of a law firm on the north side of town. There, a receptionist took my name and then spoke to Campbell on her phone. After a moment, she hung up and directed me down a short hallway to a closed door with Campbell's name on a discreet placard next to it.

I knocked, then slowly swung the door open.

Campbell sat behind a heavy-looking oak desk, and I took a moment to glance over the surroundings. On the wall behind him were bookshelves lined with what appeared to be legal tomes and complete sets of revised statutes going back dozens of years. A vase of drooping pink tulips, a black telephone, and an overturned glass were the only items on the desk.

Campbell was as he always was: impeccably dressed, his thick white hair flowing back from his temples like a lion's mane. His face lit up when he saw me.

"My, my, it's been a while."

I nodded to him. "Mr. Campbell."

"You've got yourself a new scar, I see," Campbell said. I resisted the urge to tuck my arm behind my back; in my short-sleeved blouse, the straight narrow slice down my forearm was a visible souvenir from a run-in I'd had with a fire poker brandished by a murderer in a previous case. The damaged tissue had faded from angry red to vulnerable pink.

Something suddenly moved in the overturned glass on Campbell's desk, and I peered closer. A black spider crawled to the far side of the glass and angrily beat its forelegs against its prison wall.

"Black widow. They aren't nearly as deadly to humans as their name and reputation suggest."

Campbell lifted the glass.

The spider scurried across the desk, gaining six inches of freedom, before Campbell lowered the glass once more.

I took a step back. "What are you doing with it?"

"Doing with it? Nothing. I caught it this morning, and now I'm faced with a moral dilemma. Should I kill it? Or release it and risk someone getting hurt? I'm curious, what would you do?"

"Kill it."

"Perhaps I'll go that route. Or perhaps I'll keep it, as a pet. I'm sure my employees would get a kick out of a new mascot."

I took a seat in one of the two chairs on the opposite side of the desk, choosing the one farthest from the trapped spider. "What's your interest in the history museum?"

"That's my girl." Campbell smiled widely and tented his fingers. "Right to the heart of the matter, without preamble. I respect that, I truly do. Terrible about Mrs. Starbuck. The last time I saw her was the night of the gala. In fact, I've just gotten off the phone with a marvelous young man, an intern with your police force. I regret I didn't catch his name. As I told him, I didn't notice anything amiss that night. Though now I understand there's been a second death? Another museum employee?"

"Yes. A young woman named Sari Chesney. Did you know her?"

Campbell frowned, shook his head. "No. Most of my dealings with the museum were with Lois Freeman and Dr. Larry Bornstein."

"I understand you've offered to purchase the museum? To what end?"

"Would you like a cup of tea, Gemma? I was just about to have one myself when you arrived," Campbell said. He lifted the telephone and spoke to someone. A few minutes later, the receptionist entered with a tray of bagged tea selections, a carafe of hot water, and two bone china teacups.

She grimaced at the spider as she quickly set the tray down and left the room.

"Please." Campbell gestured. I leaned forward and helped myself to an herbal blend. "Yes, I've made an offer on the museum. I'm quite aware that you've looked into my background, Gemma. Does it really surprise you that I have a soft spot for those cultural institutions that preserve our local histories? I was an orphan, kicked—quite literally—around dozens of foster homes in Scotland. Do you know what that means? *I have no history of my own.*"

Campbell made himself a cup of tea, sipped at it, then made a face and added another splash of cream. I noticed a tremor in his hands that I hadn't seen before. "I thought you'd be pleased."

"Me? What do I have to do with it?"

Campbell's eyes twinkled as though enjoying a private joke. "Don't you want to see Cedar Valley prosper?"

"I think we've been doing just fine. Our ski season revenues have been on the upswing for the last twenty years. Our tax base is strong."

"For now. The nature of your police work demands that you live among details. You dwell in the small things of life. You're many things, Gemma Monroe, but a visionary you're not. I'm talking five, ten, twenty years from now. This town can't survive on ski lift tickets and souvenir T-shirt sales. You are sitting on a gold mine, and no one's done a damn thing to drill it."

Was he right? Was I naïve to think that Cedar Valley could continue on as it had for years, without significant growth and development? I set my cup down, went to a large picture window on the wall, and looked out over the fancy houses and boutique shops.

"And you're the man to do it?"

"Yes."

"I saw you at the gala, Mr. Campbell. What did you argue about, you and James Curry and Betty Starbuck and Larry Bornstein?"

He chuckled.

I turned from the window and went back to my seat. "What's funny?"

"You. Always on the case. I wouldn't say we argued. We disagreed on a few things. Curry and I thought the gala should have been canceled in light of the disappearance of the Rayburn Diary. We pushed for a full-scale investigation. The diary is too valuable to leave the theft uninvestigated, even for just a few hours. As I understand it, there still hasn't been a serious investigation launched."

"That's not entirely true. We've looked into the matter. The diary seems to have disappeared into thin air. Anyway, we've been kind of busy with our murder investigations. They seemed more important than a lost journal."

Campbell shook his head. It was his turn to rise, go to the window. He gave it a gentle knock. "Hear that?"

"What?"

"That sound, when I knocked on the glass. It's quality construction. When you're building something—anything—you must start with a solid plan. Without it, things develop haphazardly. Opportunities are missed, costs double. People get hurt. Do you believe all this—the town, this valley—just happened? That one day there was a mine and the next day an actual city? No. This town was built on someone's plan."

"And you believe that someone was Owen Rayburn. Is that your interest in his diary?"

Campbell returned to his seat and his cup of tea. His hand shook as he picked up the cup, and he saw me watching him. "Parkinson's. I have a few years left, and I intend to use them wisely. You've always been honest with me, so now I'll be honest with you. I believe there's gold still left in these mountains. I believe Rayburn's diary holds the key to finding it."

Buried treasure, again. A legend for children and thrill seekers. I'd wasted enough time already on the topic

"I see," I said, checking my watch. "Well, I've kept you long enough. I appreciate your time. By the way, did you enjoy the gala?"

"Very much. In fact, James Curry and I continued our shared fascination with the Rayburn Diary in a conversation at the local pancake establishment. Flap Jack's, is that what it's called? Delicious. Do you know they serve pancakes all night long? If I recall, we closed down the place around three in the morning. We left the waitress a very large tip," Campbell said with a tight smile.

He lifted the glass and the spider tried again to make an escape. The glass came over it once more. "That's really what you're after, isn't it? Hmm? My alibi for the night of Betty Starbuck's murder? I do wish you'd learn to trust that I'm not a bad person, Gemma."

If Campbell's story was true, then Flap Jack's would be able to confirm it. And if Curry was there, too, then that took him as well out of the running for killing Starbuck.

I gathered my things and, at the door, turned back and answered Campbell's last words. "I don't believe in 'bad' people, Mr. Campbell. I believe an equal measure of good and evil lives in each of us and on any given day, that balance can tip one way or another. Thanks for your time."

With a sudden jerk of his wrist, Campbell flipped the glass and brought it down on the spider with a heavy thud.

"You're more naïve than I thought. Evil, true evil . . . it exists in this world. It walks among us," Campbell called out as I moved quickly through the door, eager to be away from him. "Evil is here, Gemma. It's always been here."

Chapter Thirty-two

Talking to Finn was the last thing I wanted to do, but I called him anyway and briefed him on my conversations with Sam Birdshead, James Curry, and Alistair Campbell.

When I finished, he groaned. "More buried treasure. And now a mystery man . . . the Bookkeeper. Sounds like something out of a Hollywood mafia flick."

"No kidding. Look, Chesney had debt. Betty Starbuck gave away money. Maybe the Bookkeeper is the connection we've been looking for. Maybe he links the two women beyond their work at the museum. He could be an accountant, or someone involved with the casinos. There was no mention of him in Sari's journals, but I bet she talks about him in the one that's missing, the current year's journal."

"Maybe Mac's got the journal . . . or Ally."

"Good thinking. We'll ask them."

Finn said, "The intern wrapped up the interviews with the gala guests this afternoon. As I predicted, it was a waste of time. Have you heard anything further from forensics?"

"Not yet."

We spoke a few more minutes, but the longer we talked, the more tension I felt both in my shoulders and from the other end of the phone. It was obvious something was bothering Finn. Finally I said, "Okay then. I'll be in tomorrow. You?"

"Hell, what's tomorrow, Saturday? Yeah," Finn said. "Yeah, I'll be in."

He hung up, and I checked my watch. It was nearly five o'clock.

I headed up the canyon toward home. A few minutes later, Bull texted with an invitation for dinner. I called back with a grateful acceptance and told him Grace and I would stay the night with them in town.

Clementine was in a rush to leave. She and a girlfriend had tickets to a show in Denver on Saturday night and would be gone the entire weekend. Before she left, she offered to stay at my house the following week, overnight.

"Don't you have classes?"

"School is almost out, and I've already turned in my final assignments. I can do what little homework I'll have here just as easily as I can at home. I know you're working the museum murders and with Brody gone, I bet you could use the extra help."

"That would be wonderful, Clementine. Thank you."

She left, and I packed overnight bags for myself and Grace. Seamus ate his dinner, and I scooped a few cups of his dry kibble into a plastic container for his breakfast. Then I got the baby and the dog loaded into the car and headed back into town, to the old Victorian house I'd grown up in, with its cracked concrete driveway and purple irises that bloomed every spring and antique wooden flower boxes that were painted to match the trim.

Bull met me at the front door.

"Is Brody joining us?"

I shook my head. "He's in China. Emergency work trip."

Bull started to say something in response, then decided to remain quiet. He took the overnight bags and dog food from my arms while I went back to the car for Grace and Seamus. The dog bounded from his seat and made a beeline for the side gate. I opened it and he trotted into the backyard, beginning his loop of the familiar space, his nose to the ground for any new scents.

"Julia's in the kitchen," Bull called back over his shoulder as he walked upstairs to put the bags in my old bedroom. "Keep an eye on her, would you? Your grandmother's liable to burn the house down."

"No kidding," I muttered under my breath, and kicked off my shoes in the direction of the front closet. Barefoot, with Grace in my arms, I padded down the hall to the kitchen, passing the pale green living room where I'd spent hours practicing the piano, and the narrow dining room, with its oversize table where I'd done my homework.

It's an odd thing, spending time in your childhood home as an adult. Rooms appeared smaller, and the shine had gone out of things that used to sparkle, like the chandelier and the crystal vases Julia collected. But what remained—the wonderful memories, the sense of place—made the house feel large and rich.

Suddenly I missed Brody very much. If he were here, he and Bull would have already cracked open two cans of beer and pulled out the chess set.

In the kitchen, my grandmother Julia stood at the stove, her thin frame casually draped in a pink cardigan and blue jeans. She wore no makeup, and her fair skin seemed paler than normal, nearly translucent. She slowly stirred something in a large pot while Laura, her caregiver, sat at the kitchen table with a deck of cards, playing solitaire.

I peeked into the pot. "Are we having water for dinner?"

"Don't be a smart-ass. We're having spaghetti and meatballs. The water needs to boil," Julia said. She noticed the baby and cooed. "Sweet angel. May I hold her?"

"Of course. Let's move away from the stove."

We went to the couch and sat down. Slowly, with complete concentration and care, Julia took Grace from my arms. After a moment, they both grinned. Eyes locked, they seemed fascinated with each other.

"Is she yours?" Julia suddenly asked. "She's beautiful."

I nodded, blinking away sudden tears. "Grace is your great-granddaughter."

"She's so heavy! I don't think I can keep her. My husband doesn't let me have any fun anymore," Julia whispered to me. She shot Laura a dark look, then added, "Neither does that one. They act like I'm sick. But I'm fine, really. Just a touch of the flu."

"That must be frustrating," I whispered back.

"Sometimes I get so mad," she continued. "It's terrible when no one understands me."

Julia gently bopped Grace on her knee until the baby spit up, at which point Julia quickly handed her back to me. Laura tried to take her leave, but by then Bull had joined us in the kitchen and he convinced her to stay for dinner. He took over the cooking. A bottle of red wine appeared and, shortly after, a platter of spaghetti with red sauce and meatballs the size of my fist.

After dinner, Julia decided she wanted to watch television on the big flat screen in the master bedroom. Bull joined her, and I took the opportunity to speak to Laura in private. She was responsive to my concerns regarding Julia's increasing aggression.

"Your grandmother is in the middle stages of the disease, Gemma. Her behavior will continue to worsen, although it may be years before we get to the late stages. She will only need more and more care. As it is, she still bathes and dresses herself. But . . . I've noticed there is confusion there, as well. As far as the aggression goes, we rule out pain and discomfort and then try to respond as best we can," Laura said. "I've discovered it's also very easy for Julia to get overstimulated. So we watch that, too. In addition, we've installed more locks on the doors and windows."

"When was the last time she saw her doctor?"

"A few days ago. He's reluctant to change her medications at this point, so we'll continue to monitor the behavior and if the aggression worsens, we'll re-evaluate," Laura said. She crossed her sturdy arms over her stout body and fixed me with a steely gaze. "I know this is stressful, Gemma. Bull told me you saw him after Julia punched him. He was upset about your comments. I talked with him, helped him understand your point of view."

"I'm glad he listens to you. It sounds as though you agree with him, that we don't need to move her yet to a twenty-four-hour care center?"

She gently shrugged. "That's a decision you'll need to make with your grandfather and with Julia, too. I've seen many patients get to the point where that is the kind of help they themselves express needing."

"So status quo for the time being."

"Unfortunately, with this particular disease, there is never a status quo. But yes—I think it is okay for her to stay here," Laura said.

She left, and I joined Grace in my old bedroom, me in the bed, the baby in a spare crib that we'd picked up at a consignment shop. I watched her sleep, wondering if she would remember Julia and Bull, if they would live long enough for her to form memories of them.

I was grateful that when my parents had died, I was old enough to know them. As time passed, though, I found my memories of them were fading. It was difficult to remember the bark of my father's laugh, the softness of my mother's skin. I touched the scar that wrapped around my neck. It was long and narrow, the width of a pencil. I'd gotten it in the same car accident that killed my parents, and every time I looked in the mirror, I felt the slow slide of the old station wagon on the black ice, heard the breathless scream of my mother and the frantic shout of my father.

Then came the silence, and that was the worst part of all.

The buzz of my cell phone beckoned me out of my melancholy reverie, and I smiled when I saw who it was.

"Hi."

"Hi, honey. I tried the house phone first. Where are you?"

"We are staying the night at my grandparents'. How's Beijing?"

"Crowded. Loud and crowded. I'm making coffee in my suite and wishing my girls were here, but I think we'd best save China for when Grace is a little older." He started the coffee pot, and from thousands of miles away I heard the familiar drip of hot water hitting glass. "You know what I realized on the flight over?"

I lay back in bed and rubbed my eyes with my free hand. "That you hate Chinese food?"

"Funny. I've never been away from Grace for longer than a night. It's unsettling."

"So you're not going to come home and tell me you're applying for field jobs?" I asked, half joking. "Or tell me you have to stay in China for a month?"

"Nah. I got everything I need in Cedar Valley. Don't you worry, babe. I'm coming home."

We chatted for a few more minutes then said good night. I snuggled in under the covers, feeling cozy and content and loved. Sleep should have come easy, but it didn't.

I dreamed I walked along the shores of Lost Lake, watching a woman on the far side of the water. Her back was to me. When she finally turned around, I saw it was my mother. Opals filled the space where her eyes had been, and the water beneath her was as black and deep as an abyss, and suddenly she was *running* across the water toward me, her arms outstretched, her mouth a twisted grimace.

Chapter Thirty-three

I left Grace in Bull's care and reluctantly headed back to the police station. Weekends . . . holidays . . . it didn't matter, when I was in the middle of an active murder investigation. I couldn't be fully present with my family until my cases were wrapped up, one way or another.

I picked up a box of doughnuts from my favorite café downtown, Four and Twenty Blackbirds, then took the scenic route to the station, driving parallel to the Arkansas River. The midday sun shone high in the sky, and a few brave souls kayaked down the still-icy waters. I put the windows down and turned up the radio, humming along to an old U2 song.

I took the pastries to the break room, calling out as I did so. The on-duty officers were excited to see them, and I had to fight to claim two chocolate doughnuts for myself. I finished them before I reached my desk and immediately regretted having the second one. Wiping sticky glaze from my hands, I swore to quit all junk food, cold turkey.

"Morning, Fatty!"

Flushed, I turned around, then breathed a sigh of relief when I saw Chloe Parker waving hello to Thad Fatioli, our mail room clerk. Though he couldn't have been more than a hundred and fifty pounds soaking wet, everyone called him Fatty.

Relieved that the two doughnuts I'd eaten hadn't been the impetus for my colleagues to start calling me names, I sat down and tried to decide where to start.

I stared at my notes, willing two increasingly complex murder investigations to somehow simplify themselves. Closing my eyes, I pictured the Betty Starbuck crime scene and then worked backward, as though watching a film in reverse. Betty returning from a fast-food jaunt, holding the meal in one hand, setting the alarm with the other . . . locking herself in.

Locking a murderer in?

It would have been dark in the museum, dark and hushed. I remembered the way my footsteps had echoed in the cavernous space. But Betty had done this before, working late, alone in the big building.

Did she ignore the odd creak that night? Brush off a feeling that someone was in the museum with her?

Or was she taken by complete surprise, attacked in her office out of the blue?

All at once I realized something and called Finn. He answered on the second ring, his tone sharp. "I'm on my way in. Can it wait?"

"No. How did the killer get out of the museum? Betty Starbuck activated the alarm system when she returned from the Burger Shack. We've been focusing on the theory that either the killer came in with her—i.e., someone she knew—or the killer remained inside after the last of the gala guests had left, hiding somewhere, like a restroom or an alcove. What we haven't determined is *how did the killer leave after he or she murdered Betty?* The building stayed alarmed until Jerry Flowers arrived at five a.m."

"He must have hid and then escaped at some point later in the day. The museum was searched, wasn't it?"

"I assume so."

"*You assume so?* What the hell does that mean? You're not sure if it was cleared?" Finn was angry. "Jesus, Gemma. The killer could have been there all along."

"I wasn't first on the scene. By the time I got to the museum, the chief and the techs and even the goddamn media were there. So lay off me. I'm going to call Chavez, see what he says."

I hung up and dialed the chief's number.

Chavez picked up on the first ring. "This better be good. I'm about to play the eighth hole, and I've got a hundred bucks against the mayor on this game."

"I'll be quick, Chief. Did you or anyone else do a sweep of the museum, the morning Betty Starbuck was killed?"

"Of course we did a sweep. Jerry Flowers was scared to death when he called it in. Chloe instructed him to find an office or a closet and lock himself in until we arrived. Hell, we had no idea what we were walking into. Fred Newman and I did the sweep ourselves," Chavez said. "There was no one there."

He covered the phone and shouted something that sounded suspiciously like an insult directed at someone's mother. "Gemma? I've got to go. The mayor's about to go ballistic."

I called Jerry Flowers next. His mother answered and, after I introduced myself, she asked me to hold while she woke Jerry up. I checked my watch—it was one in the afternoon.

Must be nice, I thought.

Then I remembered that the kid had been waking at four in the morning to start his cleaning job by five and felt sorry for disturbing his sleep.

"This is Jerry."

"Hi, Jerry. I'm sorry to bother you, but I have a few more questions for you, about the morning you found Mrs. Starbuck's body."

"Yeah, sure. What do you want to know?"

"Talk to me about the alarm system."

Silence, then Jerry said, "Well, like I said earlier, I have a code. I enter it into a panel on the back door, wait for the beep, then go inside and reset it. When I leave, I do it in reverse."

"Only you didn't reset the alarm that Saturday."

"I didn't?" Jerry sounded confused and more than a little afraid. "Are you sure?"

"I called the alarm company to find out when Mrs. Starbuck had used her codes. They pulled the records and explained that she left the building and then returned, disarming and arming the museum along the way. When you arrived, you disabled the alarm but never armed it again. I believe that is how the killer exited the building."

"Oh my god, I think you're right," Jerry gasped. "There was so much trash, I could see piles of it as soon as I got there. It's such a pain in the ass turning the alarm on and off every time I haul a load of garbage out to the back bins that I must have thought 'screw it' and just left the alarm off."

My heart sank. Though it was what I'd expected, it added a new dimension to the case.

Another moan, then, "So you think I was in there with a killer? I didn't hear or see anything, I swear. If someone else was there . . . they were quiet. Jeez, I could have been killed!"

"Better not to think about that, Jerry. If it makes you feel better, I believe Mrs. Starbuck was targeted. I don't think you were in any danger."

"Oh thank god," a female voice responded. Then Jerry shrieked, "Mom! Get off the fucking phone!" and I swallowed a much-needed laugh.

"Thank you both. I'll call back if I have any further questions."

I stood and paced the squad room, then glanced in the break room and saw a lone doughnut remaining. It was a strawberry glaze, pale pink with rainbow sprinkles. I wondered if anyone would notice that I'd eaten three doughnuts in the space of an hour.

Then Chloe Parker rushed in. Her husband, Bud Parker, owned the Midnight Alley, and the bottle she filled at the tap was shaped like a bowling pin. "Hey, Gemma. I heard you brought doughnuts! Are you going to eat the last one?"

"Help yourself. I like your water bottle."

"Thanks. I'll bring you one on the house. Got to run." She headed out as quickly as she'd come in, and I continued pacing, treading over the same narrow circle, walking in the footsteps of the countless cops who'd walked this same floor before me.

If the killer had escaped the museum the way I thought—through the disarmed doors—then he or she was incredibly lucky. There was no way to know that Jerry Flowers would leave the building unlocked. It meant that the killer likely didn't know about the alarm system until he or she had tried to leave the museum after Starbuck's murder but before Flowers's arrival and then was forced to hide and wait somewhere.

It was the first real inkling I had that perhaps Betty Starbuck's murder wasn't planned after all; perhaps it wasn't the work of a cold, calculating killer but rather the tragic end of an act of passion, a moment of rage.

If that was true, it gave weight to the possibility that the Chesney and Starbuck murders were unrelated. And if *that* was true, we could remove the museum as the common link and look for suspects unique to each woman.

In Betty Starbuck's case, I felt that brought us squarely back to Kent.

Back at my desk, I set aside the cases and turned to my unofficial assignment, finding the source of the leak in the department. Bryce Ventura's Twitter post had gone out on Wednesday morning. I pulled up the master roster and started cross-checking names and dates. Eventually, I had a short list of employees—both sworn personnel and civilian—who had worked the night shift on the previous Tuesday and would have seen my false report on the Red Board.

The worst thing about the list was that I knew every one of the people on it. Chloe Parker, Lucas Armstrong, hell, even the intern had pulled a late shift and worked a double. No matter who the leaker turned out to be, this would be personal.

This would hurt.

I groaned as I realized something else that should have struck me much earlier. Because of the way shift change worked, there were usually a few people who overlapped due to meetings running late, emergency call-outs, that sort of thing. I'd need to include on my list all the people who worked the day shift on Tuesday, too.

Damn. My genius plan to narrow down the suspect pool wasn't so genius after all.

"Gemma." Finn was suddenly hovering above me, staring at me with an odd and somewhat formal expression on his face. "Can I talk to you, in private?"

"Sure," I said. "What's up?"

He didn't answer and instead walked to the conference room. Once we were both inside, he closed the door and lowered the blinds.

"You're acting weird, Nowlin." I took a seat on the edge of the table and let my feet swing back and forth. "What gives?"

Finn stared at me, his blue eyes darkening. "Gemma, I know."

I stared back at him, suddenly uneasy at the look on his face.

"I know you're the leaker."

It was the last thing I expected to hear, and I burst out laughing. "You're kidding, right?"

"I wanted to know your side of the story before I go to Chief Chavez. Look, people make mistakes all the time. Maybe there's something else going on, something at home, that's screwing with your head. There's no way you can keep your job, but perhaps the chief will handle this quietly." Finn stuck his hands in his pants pockets and looked away, embarrassed for me. "He likes and respects you. At least, he did."

The smile slid off my face. "So you're the one. You're the one investigating me. I should have suspected it. This is ridiculous, Finn. *I'm not the leaker.* In fact, there's a lot of evidence pointing to you."

"Oh really? So Chavez has you on the case, too? Come on. You've worked every shift that there's been a leak. I saw you talking with Bryce Ventura on Friday afternoon." Finn finally looked back at me. Though his tone was mild, there was deep anger in his eyes. "People trusted you. *I* trusted you."

"Okay, I'll play along. What's my motive, Finn?" I was angry now, too. "Huh? You got that all figured out?"

"That's the one piece I don't have. Why don't you tell me? You'll feel better getting this off your chest. I thought the cases were getting to you . . . or you and Brody were having trouble again," Finn said. "But it's all become clear now. You've got a guilty conscience. I can see it all over your face."

"I don't have to listen to this crap any longer."

I stood up and walked to the door, then turned around. "You're making a big mistake, Finn. If you go the chief with this pathetic theory, he'll laugh you right out of the office."

"I'm not wrong, Gemma!" he called after me as I walked down the hall, my head pounding, my stomach in knots, my face on fire.

We'd been partners for six months.

Finn was chauvinistic and pig-headed, quick-tempered and sarcastic. He also cared very deeply about the same thing I did, which was getting justice for victims of crime.

Lately, too, the son of a bitch had made me laugh.

The two of us had grown into a comfortable relationship, the sort you dream about when you're first in the academy and you start understanding just how deep the trust must be for a police partnership to be successful.

In many ways, the partnership becomes as intimate as a marriage. After all, this is the person who's supposed to have your back when the shit hits the fan.

I sat at my desk and clenched my hands together in my lap, the nails biting in to my palms.

Bastard.

Chapter Thirty-four

Determined not to let Finn spoil the entire weekend, I took advantage of Sunday's warm weather and cooked out in the backyard, inviting our closest neighbors over for dinner. I picked up half a dozen trout fillets at the fishmonger and grilled them next to foil packets of cubed potatoes heavy with butter and seasoning. A couple of six-packs of beer, a green salad, and a carton of strawberry ice cream rounded out the meal.

Our neighbors were a young couple. Elsa was twenty-three years old and made six figures working remotely for a tech firm based in San Francisco. Her husband, Eduardo, was two years older. Originally from Colombia, he was a paramedic in town, and he and I had over the years worked a number of accident scenes together.

I envied what appeared to be an easy love between the two of them. We sat in the backyard in shorts and summer tops, passing the baby around, refilling our plates and enjoying the lazy day. Elsa and Eddie were both entranced by and terrified of Grace.

"Isn't it a lot of work?" Elsa asked. She lowered her straw hat over her eyes, then raised it again and winked. "I love my downtime. Napping, catching up on shows. When do you relax?"

"You mean with the baby? I don't think I've relaxed since before I was pregnant. Parenting is both exhausting and exhilarating," I said, and hastily added, "but worth every minute, of course. Just look at that smile."

Elsa and I looked over at Grace who grinned at us from Eduardo's arms. The baby grunted, and Ed's face took on a look of concern. Then, "Oh hell," and he held the baby out from his body.

"She, uh, needs some attention in her drawers," he said. The concern on his face grew to a grimace, and he gagged. "Oh god, it stinks. Someone, please. Take this monster away."

I started laughing. "Don't you deal with blood and guts all day?"

"Blood and guts are one thing. Poopy diapers are another thing," Eddie said. "Please, the smell . . . I'm going to be sick."

Still laughing, I set his plate down and took Grace. To Elsa, I said, "The trick is getting Dad used to doing diapers from day one."

"Yeah . . . maybe we're good with just the cat for a few more years."

Later, we cleaned up the dishes from dinner and then Grace and I said good-bye to Elsa and Eddie as they began the quarter-mile walk down the canyon to their house. After the baby was in bed, I grabbed a sweatshirt, then took Seamus out to the front yard and watered the flower boxes. I tidied up the porch, brushing leaves from the seats of the teal Adirondack chairs and shaking dust from the woven welcome mat. Seamus found a large stick with a knobby end and contented himself by gnawing on it.

I found myself thinking about Eddie and Elsa, and what appeared to be their easygoing relationship. I was envious. Though I was sure they had their struggles just like any other couple, they seemed so in love and so . . . kind. How many times had Brody and I been short-tempered with each other? How many times had we chosen a quick retort over a kind one?

Brody was a good man. He was a good father. And he'd make a wonderful husband. I just couldn't escape the niggling doubt in the back of my mind that wondered if he'd make a wonderful husband *for me*.

I sighed. Brody was everything I'd always wanted in a partner: loving, attentive, kind, intelligent, with a sense of humor and patience in spades. That's what ultimately made his betrayal so devastating. It was like finding out your golden retriever had the personality of a wolverine.

Seamus barked, and I looked around. It was twilight, my favorite time of day in the canyon. Our driveway is long, our house set back from the road, and in the encroaching darkness it was easy to believe we were in an enchanted forest. In the sky, there were already twinkling stars, and I watched as the fast-moving lights of an airplane sped past them. Inside the house, the lone light I'd left on in the front window shone through the screen door. I softly hummed a lullaby that we'd taken to singing to Grace.

I tried to think of a word that described the scene, the hushed woods sheltering our little home, the night insects beginning to sing, the rapidly cooling air, and the only word that came to mind that felt like it did justice to the evening was *peaceful*.

As the last trace of sunlight blinked out and darkness settled in for the night, the house phone rang.

I ran in and picked it up before it could wake the baby. Then I took the call outside, not yet willing to give up the fresh night air.

It was Patrick Crabbe. He spoke slowly, his voice full of a wooziness that comes from illness or alcohol. I turned off the garden hose and sat down on the front step, looking out over our gravel driveway and our cars, neatly parked by the garage door. The short lanterns that lined the drive illuminated the tall pines and shorter juniper bushes, giving their usual green color a golden glow.

"Patrick? Patrick, I'm having a hard time understanding you. Where are you?"

"Home," he answered. "I'm always home. I read in the paper that my brother might have killed my mom. Is that true?"

"Patrick, I can't go into details with you. But please, I'm begging you, please put your faith in us instead of Bryce Ventura and his hack reporting."

Silence, then Crabbe quietly said, "Okay. There's more, Gemma. I found something disturbing in my mother's office. I've been cleaning out her files, and there's some scribbling on the back of a utility bill. I don't know what to think about it."

"What does it say?"

"*I'm afraid. I'm going to lock my door tonight for the first time in years.*"

A chill went through me. "Is there more?"

Another long moment of silence, then, "Yes."

"Read me all of it, Patrick."

"He's changed. There's an anxiety in him, as though he's . . . as though he's waiting for something. Or someone." Patrick's voice shook. "Gemma, who was my mother talking about? Why did she scribble these thoughts down?"

Well, Patrick, I'd say there's a damn good chance she was writing about you, I thought.

"Hello? Hello, Gemma, are you still there?"

"I'm here, Patrick. I don't know why your mom wrote those things. I think sometimes . . . sometimes things happen, and it helps to get them out of our heads and commit them to paper. I don't keep a diary, but I'll often jot things down either to help me remember or to purge them. What's the date on the utility bill?"

He read me the date.

The bill was only a few months old.

At the end of the drive, a lone blue spruce tree stood by the road. I'd always liked the tree, the way it signaled our turn from the road, the way it stood, straight and proud. Now the tree reminded me of Lost Lake, and I thought of Sari Chesney's body in the water, the way her feet had pointed across the lake toward the spruces on the other side. A dark thought flitted across my mind: we all come out on the other side, one way or another.

Patrick and I arrived at similar thoughts.

"Kent. This was right around the time Kent came back to town," he breathed. I heard him open a cupboard or a door and then close it with a slam. "It's just like in my nightmare. Every night it's the same."

I pinched the bridge of my nose with my free hand. "Do you want to talk about it?"

A clarity returned to his voice. He told me about his dream, and I was glad for the sweatshirt I'd grabbed, glad to be home, with the warm light spilling from the front windows and my dog, my most loyal companion, by my side.

"Mother came back. I opened the oven door to put in a frozen pizza and she was there, curled up. Her skin was charred. It hung in tatters from her bones. She had waited for me. I screamed and she climbed out. When she tried to hug me, I lost my mind. I ran outside, but everything was different. Earth was gone, it was like we were on another planet. And everywhere I turned, Mother was there, waiting. Kent stood behind her, his face in shadows, his hands raised to the heavens. She kept asking me why I let her die."

"Her death wasn't your fault, Patrick."

"Sure it was." Another cabinet door slammed shut, then, "I'm her son. I'm supposed to look out for my mother. I'm the *good* son. Do you want to hear a secret?"

"Yes."

"On second thought, it's best I don't tell you." He started laughing. "I'm going to go now, but I'll be seeing you soon."

"Wait, Pat—" But it was too late. He'd already hung up.

When I called him back, the line was busy. After a minute, I tried again with the same result. I got in touch with a patrol officer at the station and requested someone run a wellness check on Patrick Crabbe at his home. It was obvious he'd been drinking, but there was something else there, something darker and more disturbing than simply one too many beers.

By the time the officer got to Crabbe's house, Crabbe and his car were gone. I spent the rest of the evening praying he wasn't drinking and driving.

In the early morning hours of the next day, it was obvious I'd been praying and hoping for the wrong thing. They say hindsight is 20/20, but in my heart of hearts, I'm convinced I should have known what was coming.

Chapter Thirty-five

Monday morning.

In the east, the rising sun was obscured by a quilt of clouds, patched together in shades of dove gray and dirty white. To the west, the mountains loomed out of a heavy mist that left a sheen of moisture over the world.

I was nearly to the station when a frantic voice came over the police scanner and said shots had been fired downtown at the Crimson Café. I waited for more information to come, but the dispatcher merely repeated the call.

It was five minutes to eight o'clock: the start of business hours and carpool drop-offs.

God.

Wilson Elementary School was three short blocks from the café.

Heart racing, I pulled a U-turn in the middle of the road, against the angry horns of oncoming traffic. I slapped on my red dash light and sped toward the Crimson, praying the dispatcher had been wrong in her call. We'd never had an active shooter event in Cedar Valley before and, though we participated in quarterly trainings, I knew we'd never be ready, not really, for such a situation.

If there were hostages . . .

Two minutes later, I slowed to a crawl and took a left on Second Street. At first glance, the street was quiet. This time of day the traffic should have been brisk, the sidewalks crowded. In addition to the Crimson, there was a breakfast diner, a couple of retail shops, two banks, and a small branch library. I pulled over and parked three buildings down from the Crimson, and it was then that I realized the street was quiet because everyone who had been on it had sought shelter.

Terrified faces peered out of storefront windows. Three bikes and a tipped stroller lay on the sidewalk, abandoned by their owners. A blue-and-green crocheted baby blanket spilled out of the stroller, and my stomach dropped at the thought of what might be happening in the Crimson.

In the distance, the sound of police and ambulance sirens grew loud. I spent precious seconds sitting in the car, torn between my instincts—run to the Crimson and offer aid—and my professional training—sit in the damn car and wait for backup.

There is absolutely a time and place for a single-officer response; this was not it.

The sirens were on top of me now, their shrill call punctuating the cool, wet air, and I watched in my rearview mirror as a sedan pulled in behind me. It was Louis Moriarty and Lucas Armstrong. Two ambulances pulled into the street and hung back, idling.

I slid out of my car, weapon drawn, and crept backward, keeping my eyes on the Crimson. Moriarty and Armstrong joined me on the sidewalk. We stayed down, crouching on our knees, using the car as a shield between us and the café. Moriarty and Armstrong were breathing hard, and I realized to my surprise that I was, too.

We were scared.

"I heard the initial call and nothing since. Is this still an active shooter event?" I asked. Nodding my head toward the shops, I added, "We've got civilians in the stores."

Armstrong said, "Three shots fired. We have one person confirmed dead. The suspect is contained."

"What do you mean contained?"

"He's being held at gunpoint by the Crimson's owner and a customer."

"Okay." I took a deep breath, willing my heart to stop racing.

Though the situation was somewhat under control, we still did things by the book: single-file approach, weapons drawn, watching our front and back. Armstrong was first into the café, and I followed him, watching as his neck and back muscles visibly relaxed. He holstered his weapon. Then he moved to the side, and I saw the scene for the first time.

I gasped. "Oh no. Oh, my god."

The back of the café was taken up by a long glass display case with a short service counter at the south end. A single bullet had punctured the glass, shattering it and exploding pastries and pies.

Slumped down in front of the case, his head tilted and resting on his right shoulder, sat Patrick Crabbe. His eyes were open and vacant, his breathing shallow. His skin was a pasty, pale color.

Five feet from his right leg was a Smith & Wesson 9mm handgun.

Two men stood over him. One of them was Dave Zusak, proprietor of the Crimson. He loosely held a handgun of his own, and though it wasn't pointed at Patrick Crabbe, it was obvious that Zusak was ready to go there if needed.

The other man was a young guy in a tweed jacket and jeans, his forehead soaked in sweat. He stood over the Smith & Wesson, not touching it, but also clearly ready to move it farther away from Crabbe if needed.

Zusak's eyes, wide with emotion, slid to the right, to something behind me, and for a moment sheer panic walloped my chest.

Had we gotten it wrong?

Was Crabbe a victim and the real shooter behind us?

But Zusak's eyes didn't hold fear. They held sadness.

Armstrong and Moriarty noticed, too, and together, moving as one unit, the three of us turned and took in the awful scene. Quick images flooded my mind, and I knew I would relive this day, again and again, in the weeks to come.

A young blond waitress in khaki pants and black polo shirt holds a glass carafe of coffee in her violently shaking hand. She moans as her eyes meet mine and I try to smile reassuringly, but what comes over my face is a grimace. She drops the carafe, and the sound of shattering glass fills the room.

Kent Starbuck sits at a small, round table. His back is to the door.

A napkin covered in blue writing and a painted porcelain cup occupy the table top. The cup appears to be white with scarlet paint abstractedly applied, and then I realize it's not paint at all, but blood. The back of Kent's head is an open trauma of wet blood and crisp bone and gray brain matter. The bullet is somewhere in there, inside his head, and next to me, Lucas Armstrong is gagging, his large body shaking violently with dry heaves.

As if in a dream, I moved to the table and read aloud the last words of Kent Starbuck, a self-described "man of the land": *"I am the one who travels by moonlight, a chosen witness to God's own dreams. Around me are silences more deep than the oceans, broken only by the shrill cries of the creatures that inhabit the shadows. They are furtive things—the cries and the animals—and I ride alone; fast; with purpose. I am a journeyman of the dark."*

Moriarty called it in. He requested emergency medical services, to treat Patrick Crabbe for suspected shock, as well as the medical examiner, and a team of crime scene techs. Lucas Armstrong secured the handgun on the floor while I crouched in front of Patrick Crabbe, mindful of the mess around us from the exploded pastry case.

"Patrick?"

At the sound of my voice, Crabbe roused. I watched his eyes grow fearful, hysterical. He began to babble, and his voice was that of a man who's been haunted by ghosts of his own creation for so long that he struggles to discern reality from fantasy.

I was deeply sorry I hadn't seen this coming in the short time we'd spent together.

Perhaps, somehow, I might have prevented Kent Starbuck's death.

Crabbe used words I'd never heard before, stringing them together in sentences upon sentences. He spoke without swallowing, and spittle pooled at the edges of his mouth, spilling forward, wetting his chin and neck.

I tried to calm him. "Patrick, shhh now, it's all right. Everything's going to be okay."

Crabbe furrowed his brow, and his eyes became unreadable. Suddenly, he leaned forward and growled. Surprised, I fell backward, landing on my rear. Crabbe put his hands on the ground in front of him and began to crawl toward me. I tried to scoot back, but I was caught in the sticky mess of pastries and I couldn't gain ground.

Moriarty was on Crabbe in less than a second. He gently but firmly pushed him facedown and secured handcuffs on him.

"You okay?"

I nodded, picked myself up, and brushed crumbs from my rear. Shaken by the look in Crabbe's eyes and the hatred in the growl, I took a moment to compose myself.

"He should have been cuffed the minute we walked in."

"Yeah. He seemed comatose," Moriarty said. "Goddamn situation we have on our hands. I always knew Kent Starbuck was going to end up in a bad way. I never figured it would be his own brother who would do him in."

"Patrick believes Kent killed their mother," I replied. "This was a revenge killing."

"That's ridiculous."

We turned to the young waitress. She knelt on the floor with a brush and dust pan, slowly collecting shards of glass from the shattered carafe. She dropped the brush and wiped away tears then looked up at us, a heartbreaking expression on her face. I was sorry that she'd had to witness this. Murder is a terrible thing to see at any age but especially for someone so young.

"What do you mean, 'ridiculous'?" I asked.

"Kent's a good man. He's been coming to the Crimson twice a week for ages. He's sweet, polite. Tips well and always asks how school's going," she said. Her voice was heavy with conviction, fierce. "I know he's got a drinking problem, but he can't be a killer."

"Sweetheart, you're what, seventeen? This guy may have been a nice customer. That doesn't mean he was a nice guy," Moriarty said.

The waitress stood and straightened her shoulders. She looked Lou Moriarty straight in the eyes. "Sir, I was taught to believe that the character of a person shines brightest in how they treat the people who serve them. I don't see how my age plays into this. And I'm not your sweetheart. I'm not anyone's sweetheart."

She turned away and Moriarty flushed. "Everyone's a critic."

I looked again at Kent's body, the way his sightless eyes seemed to take in the room, the same way his mother's eyes had.

I excused myself.

In the restroom, I stood under the light of a single, bare bulb, staring into a streaky mirror that both softened the lines on my face and enhanced them. After a moment, I bent over and ran cold water into the sink. As I splashed it on my face, one thought kept rolling through my mind.

Had we been chasing the wrong brother all this time?

Had we missed something along the way?

Had I sat in a murderer's apartment and offered him a damn box of tissues?

"What the hell is happening?" I whispered to my reflection. Then I grabbed a handful of paper towels, dried my face, joined the macabre party out front, and got back to work.

Chapter Thirty-six

Patrick Crabbe was evaluated by paramedics at the café, then released back to our custody. Chief Chavez arrived, and we secured the café. Armstrong and Moriarty carefully placed Crabbe in the back of their squad car and then headed to the station to book him on murder charges. By then, the crime scene unit had arrived, and they got to work flagging evidence.

The media descended quickly. Chief Chavez gave a brief press conference outside the café, praising the quick actions of Dave Zusak and the lone customer in containing the situation and likely preventing further deaths. I watched long enough to see Bryce Ventura and a handful of citizens hound the chief about the increase in violence in Cedar Valley, then I turned away and collected official statements from the witnesses and pieced together the timeline of the killing:

At 7:52 a.m., Crabbe had entered the café and fired three shots: one at the glass pastry case; the second at the floor; then the final, fatal shot at his brother. Then he'd dropped the gun, taken a step back, and collapsed. The customer had called the police while Dave Zusak grabbed his own weapon and stood guard over Crabbe. Between the second and third shots, the brothers had exchanged words, but no one was close enough to hear what was said.

As I was about to leave the café, I got a call from Moriarty.

Patrick Crabbe had begun to complain of chest pains en route to the station. Armstrong was driving, Moriarty on the passenger side, Crabbe in the backseat. Armstrong looked in the rearview mirror and saw that Crabbe's lips were an unnatural shade of blue. He pulled a hard right and headed to the hospital. By the time they arrived, Crabbe's breathing was labored and he was doubled over in pain.

I met Moriarty in the lobby of the hospital.

Moriarty didn't mince words. "Massive heart attack."

"Oh no." I groaned. "Is he going to make it?"

Moriarty shrugged. He pulled a mint from his pocket and unwrapped it. Before popping it into his mouth, he said, "He's stable, whatever that means. One of the nurses told me if we'd gotten here any later, Crabbe would be dead."

"When can we talk to him?"

"Who knows?" Moriarty moved the mint back and forth in his mouth, making a clicking noise with his tongue. He pointed to a tall man in blue scrubs striding toward us. "That's Crabbe's doctor. Pompous asshole. Good luck getting through to him."

The doctor was dour, with red chapped lips and a thick Texas accent. "I'm placing Mr. Crabbe in isolation. I don't want anyone talking to him until he's ready to be released. Three days minimum, probably more like five. The last thing he needs is additional stress and excitement. He's lucky to be alive."

My jaw dropped. "You do realize this man killed someone, right? We have to talk to him, as soon as possible."

The doctor shrugged. A faint smile danced on his lips. I felt like wiping it away with my boot. "No one is talking to him."

Moriarty responded with "You ever hear of obstruction of justice?"

The doctor crossed his arms and took a step forward. He was inches from Moriarty and mimicked his sarcastic tone. "You ever hear of the Hippocratic oath?"

"Gentlemen, please. This isn't helping anything," I laid a hand on Moriarty's arm. "Come on, Lou. We'll get a court order."

Moriarty backed down, the red slowly fading from his face. "Yeah, sure, Monroe. Whatever you say."

The doctor turned to me. "Monroe? Are you by any chance Gemma Monroe?"

I nodded.

"Why didn't you say that in the first place?" He withdrew a folded piece of paper from his pocket. "Before he went into surgery, Crabbe insisted my nurse write this down. He said no one should see it but you."

I reached for it, but the doctor held it back. The scowl dropped from his face and suddenly he looked immensely weary. "You should know that the patient asked to die, Detective. As we prepped him for surgery, he asked me not to save his life but instead to execute him. Whatever this man did—whatever that note says—you're dealing with someone who is unstable. His actions, however heinous, may not have been under his control."

"I'll keep that mind. I spoke with Patrick Crabbe last night. He was disturbed, frightened. But when he recovers, as I'm sure he will under your excellent care, he will be arrested for murder."

The doctor shrugged again. He handed me the note and walked away, his hands clasped behind his back, his head down.

"Well?" Moriarty asked. "What's the damn note say?"

I unfolded the piece of paper and stared down at the neat, cursive writing.

I was mistaken.

"That's it? What the hell is he talking about? What mistake? Killing his brother, or something else?" Moriarty's face again grew florid. "What a fucking mess. The man I saw in the café couldn't put two sentences together . . . Then his heart stops and suddenly he confesses? Three homicides in a week. When does it stop?"

Moriarty's words gave me pause.

Cedar Valley is not inherently a dangerous place. There is death—car accidents, domestic abuse, hunting mishaps, ski fatalities, and of course heart attacks, strokes, cancer, and the like—but murders are outliers and three in one week was, as he'd put it, "a fucking mess."

Betty Starbuck . . . Sari Chesney . . . Kent Starbuck.

Once again, the sense that I'd honed in on the wrong brother hit me.

I recalled the receipts in Patrick Crabbe's office, the hoarded old papers. Was Crabbe the Bookkeeper? I thought it through, trying to imagine how it could have happened. Maybe he and Sari met at the museum, through his mother. Sari was young, attractive . . . Patrick was alone, lonely. Did she scam him? Promise him love, affection in exchange for money? Did she then withdraw that love, and did he then kill her?

Patrick Crabbe murdered his brother in cold blood. . . . Who knew what else he was capable of?

"Talk to me, people. What's the latest?"

We sat in the conference room, the chief at the head of the table while Finn, Moriarty, Armstrong, and I took seats in the middle. At the last minute, Finn had pulled in the intern. The young man sat in the corner of the room, taking notes on a tablet. He looked a little green around the gills, and I realized that from where he sat, he could see the photographs of the café scene, of Kent Starbuck's body.

I hadn't spoken to Finn since our fallout on Saturday. I'd asked Moriarty to brief him on the shooting specifically so he and I didn't have to talk.

Chavez glowered. "Well? Don't everyone speak at once."

I started. "Chief, Crabbe is sedated. We've been unable to interview him. There's a guard posted outside his hospital room, in the unlikely event that he recovers enough to attempt an escape. The murder itself is open and shut—we've got eyewitnesses to the entire thing. But before Crabbe went into surgery, he left me a note that simply reads 'I was mistaken.' Hell of a mistake, if he's referring to murdering Kent Starbuck."

Finn added, "We've got to be careful not to assume anything. Patrick Crabbe could have been referring to any number of things."

"Good point, Finn," Chavez said. "Let's set aside the note for a moment. Why the hell did he shoot his brother?"

My turn again. "In Friday's *Voice,* there was an article naming Kent Starbuck as a person of interest in his mother's death. Crabbe read the article; he told me as much. He hated his brother. Imagine how he felt once he believed Kent killed their mother?"

"When I find out who the leaker is . . . if this death is on their hands . . ."

I continued. "Kent Starbuck is the obvious suspect for Betty's Starbuck's homicide. No alibi, the eyewitness at the museum, the strong motive, and the history of violence. We've been over all this. But here's the thing: remember how Betty Starbuck told both Lois Freeman and Larry Bornstein that she was scared of Patrick? He called me at home, late last night. He said he'd found cryptic notes in his mother's things indicating she was terrified of someone. Based on Freeman and Bornstein's accounts, that someone was likely Patrick *himself*."

"But he didn't recognize himself as the person his mother wrote about?" Chavez's frown deepened. "How does Sari Chesney fit into all this?"

We fell silent, no one wanting to be the first to say what we'd all concluded, which was that we'd hit a wall.

"They say silence is golden. 'They' have obviously never been in a room full of cops. Your silence is worrying. Usually you're fighting one another to share information with me." Chavez stood and began to pace the room. "So why don't I talk awhile and you all nod, tell me if I'm on the right track. At one point in the past few days, Kent Starbuck was our prime suspect in his mother's death. Now we like Patrick Crabbe for it instead? And we're saying he's gone off the deep end?"

"Maybe," I said in a low voice.

"Damn it, 'maybe' isn't good enough," the chief said. "Patrick has an alibi, doesn't he? He can't have murdered his mother."

Finn said, "The problem is that we've got no forensics linking Kent or Patrick to the Starbuck murder, *but* we can make a strong case for either of them being Sari Chesney's killer. The connection's there, somehow. We just can't see it yet."

"The murders are connected," Chavez said, frustrated. "That's yesterday's news."

The chief stopped pacing and took his seat. "Get out there, all of you, and come back when you've got something more. Gemma, a moment, please?"

I stayed seated. Once the room was cleared, Chavez said, "Where are we on that special assignment I gave you?"

I swallowed. "Making progress. I hope to have a name to you very soon."

"Good, good. You know I don't condone violence, but when I get my hands on this jerk's neck—"

"May I ask you a question?" He looked surprised at the interruption but nodded. "I know you assigned both Finn and me to investigate the leak. Finn thinks it's me. I thought it was him . . . but it's not his style, is it?"

Chavez leaned back in his seat and began to rock. The chair squeaked loudly, and I wished he would stop. "No, Finn's not the type to undertake covert sabotage of the PD. Neither are you. And make no mistake, that's exactly what the leak is: sabotage. Finn hasn't come to me, by the way. To accuse you, I mean. I think you should know that."

"It's only a matter of time. He was confident on Saturday . . . Chief?"

"I know what you want to ask me, Gemma. You think I pitted the two of you against each other. You're wondering why."

"Yes. It seems cruel, and you're not a cruel man."

"I had to be sure you weren't the leaker." Chavez sighed. "The fact of the matter is that you and Finn are two of my best detectives. There's no one else I'd trust to get the job done. It's that simple."

Though in his mind it was simple, the reality was that the chief's decision might have caused irreparable damage to my partnership with Finn.

"Is there anything else?"

I shook my head and took my leave. In the hall, I once more passed by the photographs of recruits. In the glass, my reflection looked haunted. It was hard to acknowledge that for the first time in my career, I felt disappointed in the chief. I felt let down, and I realized that there is no sound, no telltale rumble in the ground, when an idol falls.

It just happens, and all you are left with is a dry taste in your mouth and the longing to go back to the time before, before you knew.

Chapter Thirty-seven

After what felt like mere minutes at home—enough time to grab dinner, spend a few hours with Grace, and get some much-needed sleep—I was back to work early on Tuesday morning. I left as soon as Clementine awoke, driving down the canyon as the sun rose and the radio promised it would be another glorious spring day in the Rockies.

I ran into Chloe Parker in the women's locker room, and we spent a few minutes chatting.

As promised, she'd brought me a water bottle from her husband's bowling alley.

"Thanks, Chloe. This is great."

She smiled brightly. "Sure, we've got dozens. Anytime you want to bowl, let me know and I'll give you a coupon."

I had to laugh. "I appreciate that. I think it will be a while before I get around to it, but thanks for the offer. Things really hit the fan yesterday."

The smile slid from her face. "What a tragedy. How is Patrick doing?"

"He's in the hospital, under sedation. He'll be there for a few days, maybe a week. The shooting was awful. Not only does it throw a major wrench into our investigation, it's just plain sad. First the mother dies, then one brother shoots another," I said, fiddling with the cap on the water bottle.

Chloe nodded. "Horrible, just horrible. I've known Patrick for years. He and my husband go way back. I would never have imagined he was capable of something like this. I know you can't go into all the details, but do you know what happened?"

"I don't think we'll know for sure until he comes to and we can interview him. We think an article in Friday's edition of *The Valley Voice* might have triggered Patrick's actions. Patrick saw that Kent was a person of interest in their mother's death, and he may have decided to take matters into his own hands."

"Oh, that's terrible," Chloe gasped. "Patrick's always been such a sweet, kind soul. This is such a tragedy."

She glanced at her watch. "Shoot, I've got to get to the phones. Gemma, let's get a drink or lunch soon, okay? We gals have got to stick together."

I nodded. "I'd like that."

Finally settled at my desk, I was surprised to see more than a dozen voice messages waiting for me. I listened to the first and then remembered that we had listed my name as the primary contact on the press release asking anyone with information from the Lost Lake area to come forward.

I grabbed a coffee and a stale bagel from a communal bag in the break room and then started in on the messages, wishing I had some cream cheese. Even jelly would have made the dry bread more palatable.

The first three calls were pranks; each referenced seeing the Lost Girls prowling the lake the week of Chesney's murder. The next eight weren't helpful, either; I listened half-heartedly to them as I sipped my coffee, occasionally pausing and rewinding one to make sure I hadn't missed something. As I'd thought, they were from misguided people who meant well. An example: a couple hiking on the Haywood trail a few days before witnessed an aggressive mother bear and two cubs. They were certain the bear had killed Chesney.

Uh-huh . . . killed her without leaving any evidence and then dragged her into the lake.

The last message was the most promising, and I listened to it twice, hopeful we'd finally gotten the break in the case we so desperately needed.

The man said his name was Virgil Salt. His voice was deep, with a hint of a Midwest accent. In his message, he said he'd seen a couple of people having a violent argument at Lost Lake a few weeks prior. He hadn't thought much of it at the time, but seeing as there had been a murder, he figured he should report it. Not only did Salt sound rational and serious, he stated that he worked with the Parks and Wildlife Association. The local chapter of the PWA was, in my experience, a solid group of straight-shooting nature lovers with about as much imagination as a roll of quarters.

I checked the time Salt had called and saw it was six this morning. It was now nearly eight, so I dialed the number he'd left. When he didn't answer, I left a message and asked him to stop by the police department at his earliest convenience. Then I joined Armstrong and Moriarty in the conference room to discuss the cases.

We made small talk, waiting for Finn to join us.

I hoped to hell that Finn was sleeping poorly, racked with guilt over the accusations he'd hurled at me. But when he finally arrived, a few minutes after eight, he looked refreshed and well rested. If anything, there was an extra spring in his step.

He took a seat across from me and studiously avoided eye contact.

"All right, kids, here's the thing. Chavez sweet-talked the hospital administrator into allowing us to talk to Patrick Crabbe," Armstrong said. "We interviewed him late last night. Gemma was correct: Crabbe was convinced that Kent Starbuck murdered their mother to get at the inheritance money."

"You said 'was.' Has Crabbe changed his mind?" I asked.

Moriarty nodded. "Yes. Unfortunately, this change of heart happened as he pulled the trigger to release the bullet that ended up in Starbuck's skull."

"We know from witnesses that just before Crabbe shot Starbuck, the two of them exchanged words. Crabbe told us that after he accused Starbuck of murdering their mother, Starbuck merely shook his head and said, 'I loved her, too.' And just like that, Crabbe knew. He knew Starbuck wasn't the killer," Armstrong said. He leaned forward and set his elbows on the table, rubbed at his tired eyes. "But it was too late. He'd gone to the Crimson with the intent to avenge his mother's death, and his synapses were already firing that gun. Kent Starbuck's death was a foregone conclusion the minute Patrick Crabbe left his house Monday morning."

"Did you search Crabbe's house?"

Armstrong shook his head. "Not yet, but we did a walk-through of Betty Starbuck's home office again and found the utility bill that Crabbe described to you. The writing on it matches Betty's handwriting. She was scared of someone, there's no doubt about it."

Finn sat back and crossed his arms. "I think this is all bullshit. I think Crabbe killed his mother for her money and then pointed the finger at his brother, steering our attention that direction this whole time. Then he killed his brother. He should do hard time in prison. If he's insane, he should be locked away at the state mental hospital in Pueblo."

I stared at Finn. "Crabbe's got an airtight alibi for the night of Betty Starbuck's murder. I checked it myself—it's his clerk. He can't have killed her."

Finn finally met my gaze, and his small smile was triumphant. "I spoke with that clerk yesterday at the Gas 'n' Go. Very helpful. She told me that Crabbe spent most of the night in the back office, with the door shut, emerging every few hours to chat with her and grab a fresh cup of coffee. She can't be one hundred percent certain he was there from eleven p.m. to seven a.m."

"She told me he was there. She insisted." Stunned, I sat back. Something awful occurred to me. "You're lying. You never talked to her."

Beside us, I felt Armstrong and Moriarty stiffen and exchange tense glances.

Finn's face reddened. "I did talk to her. I just probed a little deeper than you, I guess. It was the work of five minutes."

"Shit." I pushed back from the table. "Then we're back to the drawing board. I'm going to get some air."

I left the room and walked the length of the station, reaching the front door and shoving the push bar with an anger that left me nearly in tears. I was furious at Finn for accusing me of being the leaker and for going behind my back to re-interview a witness. If he'd had any doubts of Patrick Crabbe's alibi, he should have informed me, and together we would have taken a second look at things.

I set off down the street, not headed anywhere in particular, just certain that if I didn't keep walking I was going to scream. One thing was for sure: once I wrapped up these cases, I was going straight to Chief Chavez to request a new partner. There was no reason Finn and I had to be paired up.

Lucas Armstrong, Louis Moriarty . . . either of them would be a pleasant change from Finn. Maybe I could talk to Brody, swap my day shift for nights. Then I could spend my days at home, with the baby.

I reached the end of the street and looked left. Cars, a transit bus, and a few bicyclists sped past me, their movements mere blurs. Life went on, one way or another.

A couple of deep breaths and an eighth of a mile later, I was back at the station, calm and collected.

The front desk officer grabbed my attention with a wave of his hand.

"Monroe. There's a guy here talking to Nowlin, says he got a call from you to come in. His name is Virgil Salt. They're in conference room A. He's been here just a few minutes."

"Great, thanks."

I hurried to my desk and grabbed the Sari Chesney file, determined not to let Finn spend much time alone with a potential witness.

He was a big man, close to seventy, with a white fringe of hair and bright, curious eyes.

"Gemma Monroe, this is Virgil Salt," Finn said. "Gemma, Mr. Salt was at Lost Lake. That campsite we found, on the far side of the water? He regularly uses it. He wasn't there the night of Chesney's murder, but he saw something a few weeks ago. Mr. Salt, why don't you tell Detective Monroe what you told me."

"I'd be happy to. Detective, I'm a volunteer with the state's Parks and Wildlife Association. I've been going to Lost Lake for years, decades now, every spring. I spend one or two weekends each month camping and monitoring the beavers, checking for illegal traps," Salt began. "Well, I was there two weeks ago and I witnessed a strange argument between a man and a woman. Now, I'm not the nosy kind, but the woman, she was a lot smaller than the man. He was huge, a bear of a man. I was worried their argument might get physical, violent. So I sort of stayed close by. Just in case."

"Could you hear what they were arguing about?" I leaned forward. "Did they know you were there?"

Salt shook his head emphatically. "No to both questions."

"How can you be sure they didn't know you were there?" Finn asked. He'd taken a place against the wall, arms crossed, a curious look on his face.

Salt blushed. "Because the argument turned amorous rather quickly and I got out of there at that point."

"I see." I thought a moment. "Mr. Salt, there's nothing unusual about a couple arguing and then making up. Something must have made you wonder if the argument you witnessed had anything to do with the Sari Chesney murder."

Salt nodded. "Yes. In all my years at Lost Lake, that's the first time I've seen anyone else camp in the area that early in the season."

"Thank you. That's an excellent, logical reason, and we appreciate you coming to us with this information. I have a photograph that I'd like you to look at, Mr. Salt, then you are free to go." I opened the Sari Chesney file and withdrew the photograph of Mac Stephens, Sari Chesney, and Ally Chang.

I pointed to Mac Stephens first, then Sari Chesney. "Are these the two people you saw arguing?"

Salt looked confused. "Well, no. No, they aren't."

Deflated, I sat back. It must have been another couple he saw. I was disappointed; Salt would have made a strong, compelling witness. I started to put the photograph away when I realized that Salt was still staring at it.

"No. It was him and her, this other girl in the photograph, that were arguing and then having . . . doing the other thing."

Forgetting our mutual anger, Finn and I locked eyes then I turned back to Virgil Salt. "Are you telling me that you saw this man and this woman fight and then have sex at Lost Lake two weeks ago? You're positive it was her, and not this one?"

Salt nodded. "I may be old, but I'm not senile. That girl, the one I saw at the lake, she's Asian. Looks Japanese maybe. The other girl in this photograph is white, isn't she? I've never seen this one—the white girl—before in my life."

"You're absolutely certain?"

He nodded once, twice. He was sure. "Boy oh boy, they could almost be twins, huh?"

Chapter Thirty-eight

"It's the oldest tale in the book," Finn said after Virgil Salt had left the conference room. "The best friend and the boyfriend, screwing around behind our girl's back. Then one or both of them decide to take her out of the picture."

We momentarily set aside our anger, both excited at a possible break in the case, unable to keep our thoughts from tumbling out.

"It's a long road from infidelity to murder. You didn't see Mac and Ally that morning at Lost Lake. They were genuinely worried about Sari. When I told them her body had been found, they were devastated."

"Guilty consciences. It makes the most sense that Sari was killed the night she went missing, by one of the people she was with. If not them, who?"

"Finn, just because Mac and Ally were screwing around does not make them murderers. There may have been someone else up there that night. The Bookkeeper. Or Kent Starbuck. Or Patrick Crabbe. Or maybe Larry Bornstein's full of crap and *he* was up there."

Finn stood up and headed back to his desk. I followed him. He said, "Hell, for all we know the Bookkeeper character is a figment of the girl's imagination. You said it yourself, her diaries may not be trustworthy. Or maybe Sam's the killer and he made up the Bookkeeper to throw you off his scent."

"Woman."

"What?"

"Woman. Sari Chesney was a grown woman. Stop calling her a girl, it's insulting."

Finn reddened. "Sure. Let's start with Mac."

"I can't wait."

Twenty minutes later, after having taken separate cars to the hospital, Finn and I stood behind Mac Stephens. He sat at a desk on the third floor, in green scrubs, with his head down, studying a medical chart. A row of computer monitors, each with a series of colorful valleys and peaks running across it, beeped steadily.

The irony was not lost on me that two floors above us, Patrick Crabbe continued to recover from his heart attack and subsequent surgery.

"Mac," I said in a low voice.

The big man jumped.

"Dude! You almost gave me a heart attack. Seriously, not a good idea to sneak up on people like that," Mac said. He rearranged himself on the stool. "Do you have new information on the case?"

"Well, yes," I said. "This is my partner, Finn Nowlin. Is there somewhere private we can talk?"

Mac looked around with a shrug. The corridor was empty. "I'm on duty, so I've got to stay by the terminals. Anyway, here's as good as anywhere else. We've got a light schedule today."

I nodded. Best to get right to it. "Mac, are you having an affair with Allison Chang?"

Gripping the arm of his chair, he turned pale, then flushed bright red. "I . . . I don't see how . . . No. No, I'm not. And I resent you asking."

Finn pulled an empty stool from behind Mac. He took a seat, then swiveled around once, twice, whistling a nameless tune.

Mac stared at him, perplexed. "What are you doing?"

"Playing with myself." Finn stopped swiveling. "Like you're playing with us. Stop wasting our time. Your girlfriend's dead. We pulled her decomposing body from a half-frozen lake. Her eyeballs were gone, *dude*. If that isn't enough to compel you to tell us the fucking truth, then you're a harder man than most."

I leaned back against the counter and waited. After a moment, Mac let out a choked sob and started shaking. Finn leaned over and patted him on the back. "Calm down, kid. That's it, big breaths."

After he'd composed himself, Mac said in a rush, "Ally and I started seeing each other about six months ago. But we broke it off in February. We were sick of the lies, sick of keeping things from Sari. I loved Sari with my whole heart. I always will."

"How did the affair start?" I asked, curious.

I'm always curious how affairs start.

Mac wiped his eyes and shrugged. "I don't know. I don't really recall."

"Sure you do," Finn said with another encouraging pat on Mac's back. "You don't forget that sort of thing."

"I think . . . yeah, it was a Friday. We were at a bar and Sari got sick. She went home early. But she insisted we stay out and celebrate. It was Ally's birthday, and Sari felt terrible for ruining the party. So we stayed downtown. Ally and me. And, well, we drank. A lot. One thing led to another," Mac said. He raked his fingers through his red hair.

"How long did the affair last?" Finn asked.

"About three months."

I crossed my arms over my chest. "So one thing led to another *for three months?*"

Finn stared at me, warning me.

Don't make this personal. Don't make this about you and Brody.

Mac hung his head. "No. It all became quite intentional, quite quickly. Things were different with Ally. Sari and I had a lot of struggles, just like any other couple. With Ally . . . I was free."

"Free. Uh-huh." I nodded. "Okay. Well, that's very commendable that you ended things in February. Was that the last time you and Ally hooked up?"

Mac nodded vigorously, stared up at me. "Yes, ma'am."

"Ma'am, I like that. Don't you think that's sweet, Finn?" I leaned forward and put my hands on the table in front of Mac. "You know what's not sweet, Mac? The fact that you continue to lie to our faces.

I have a witness who puts you and Ally at Lost Lake the weekend before Sari disappeared. The weekend before she died. This witness, he watched you argue. He saw you make up."

Mac fidgeted, stood up. He paced between Finn and me. He picked at the hem of his top, rubbed his hand over his beard.

We waited patiently.

Finally, he sat back down and laughed.

Finn raised an eyebrow. "This isn't funny."

"Sure it is." Mac laughed again. "My life is one big fuckup after another. Ally is pregnant. We were at Lost Lake to, ah, discuss options."

It wasn't the answer I was expecting. "Let me guess. She wants to keep the baby and you're pushing for an abortion."

Mac shook his head. "No, actually it was the opposite. It's not the baby's fault any of this happened. I think Ally should keep the baby. I thought we could co-parent and I could still have my relationship with Sari."

"Wow, talk about having your cake and eating it, too. Good for you. I mean that," Finn said. "No, seriously. Way to believe in happy endings."

I asked, "Were you planning to tell Sari about the affair? The baby?"

"*Of course.* I did tell her, I told her the night she disappeared. She was furious, but she forgave me. We decided to try to make things work. She is—was—the one I want to be with. Now she's gone. And I can't help but think that I'm being punished for my sins."

Mac jumped as a loud beep sounded from one of the monitors behind him. He swiveled on the stool and punched in a few keystrokes on the computer.

"I need to check on a patient," he announced, and stood up. He put his hands out. "Relax. Mrs. Dunleavy needs another dose of morphine. Room three one six. I'll be back in literally one minute."

Mac slowly backed away, then turned around and quickly walked down the corridor.

"Think he's going to run?"

I shook my head. "No. Where would he go?"

"What do you think about his story?" Finn asked.

"I think he's telling us the truth. We'll confirm the affair and pregnancy with Ally. What we can't confirm is whether or not Mac in fact told Sari all about it the night she disappeared."

"Does it matter?"

"It might. Let's say she took the news badly. . . . Maybe Mac killed her. Or maybe Sari attacked Mac, or Ally, and they fought back a little too hard. . . . Maybe they're both in on it together."

"I'm going to get a soda. Do you want one?" Finn stood. I was surprised he'd offered, and I could tell by the way that he glanced off into the distance that he'd made the gesture out of habit, nothing more.

He fished for change in his pocket. "You got a quarter?"

I found a handful of loose coins in the bottom of my purse. "Nothing diet."

"Be right back."

While he was gone, Mac returned and sat down. "Where's your partner?"

"Getting a soda. Did Sari ever mention a man she called the Bookkeeper to you?"

Mac thought a moment, then, "No, I don't think so. Who is he? Is he a suspect?"

"His name has come up as part of the investigation, that's all. Obviously the Bookkeeper is an alias for someone. Mac, I want to ask you something else. When we searched Sari's apartment, it became obvious that she carried a lot of credit card debt. As I understand it, she also had debt from a gambling addiction. Do you know anything about that?"

Mac sighed. "I'm not surprised. I know she liked to hit the casinos. I didn't know it was that bad, though. She was very private about her finances."

Another beep on the monitor, and I waited while Mac checked it out. "False reading."

"Mac, is there any chance Ally could have hurt Sari?"

"No way. They were best friends. Nearly sisters."

Finn returned with three cold cans of cola. He handed me one, then offered Mac a can. Surprised, Mac took it and murmured thanks.

I snapped my fingers. "I almost forgot. Do you have Sari's diary? We found previous years' journals but nothing for this year."

"No, I don't have it. I'm surprised it wasn't in her apartment."

"Could she have brought it camping? Maybe it's in her backpack," Finn said.

Both Mac and I shook our heads. I said, "It's not there, either. I searched her backpack at the lake."

Mac drank down the soda in three long swallows. "Thanks, I needed that. I can't sleep. I keep seeing Sari's face everywhere I turn. It's like she's watching me."

"Well, you know what they say, Mac," Finn said.

Mac smiled at Finn, eager to be in his good graces. The soda had gone a long way toward building amity. "No, I don't know. What do they say?"

"They say that innocent men are rarely haunted. I think you had motive and opportunity for murder, Mac Stephens. I can't prove it, not yet, but I promise you, if you killed Sari Chesney, we will find out. We will find out and prosecute you to the fullest extent of the law."

We left Mac slumped on his stool, his face pale, his limbs limp, a rag doll whose stuffing has been sucked out.

Chapter Thirty-nine

Back at the station, I had a message from one of my favorite techs in the Crime Scene Unit. I returned her call and as usual she cut right to the chase. "I've got findings for you from the Starbuck homicide. Chavez has been breathing down my neck for me to rush these. Like I told him, you can't hurry greatness."

"Of course not," I said.

She ignored me and continued. "I was specifically asked to compare the fibers found on Starbuck with fibers from a sample of Sari Chesney's shirt. It's not a match."

I exhaled. Chesney wasn't Betty Starbuck's killer.

"I didn't think it would be." I jotted down a note, nearly missing what the tech said next. "Say again?"

"The fibers are a match to soil from Lost Lake."

Confused, I said, "Of course they are. That's where we found Chesney's body. She was dragged across the ground before going in the water."

"No. I'm talking about Starbuck's body."

I stood up so fast I knocked an empty coffee cup to the floor. "Are you saying that the fibers on Betty Starbuck came from someone who had been at Lost Lake?"

"Someone or something. We've been working the evidence from the Chesney homicide, and a routine aspect of that is of course environmental analysis. I won't bore you with the technical details, but we analyzed the composition of the sand trapped in her clothes and matched it to Lost Lake. Routine procedure to prove she wasn't dragged in from some other location. I dabble in petrology here and there, you know. Anyhoo, Lost Lake is a unique region because of the glaciers and the mineral concentrations," the tech said. "So, naturally I noticed it right away under the scope when I looked at the Starbuck fibers. I'll send over the report if you want the specifics."

My mind was racing. "You said 'someone or something' . . . What did you mean by that?"

"Transfers. Think of a towel on the beach. You shake it out at the end of the day and you throw it in the trunk. A week later, you're loading groceries and there's sand everywhere. It's the same concept. Maybe Starbuck camped at the lake or picnicked up there. Awfully cold to do either, though. What I'm saying is, don't get hung up on thinking these fibers came from someone's clothes," the tech explained. "Because maybe they did, maybe they didn't. We're still analyzing exactly what kind of fibers they are. I got a backlog a mile long."

"Got it."

She continued. "There's more. We recovered a large number of prints from the Starbuck scene but none from her body. Her killer wore gloves. The prints in her office have all been matched to Starbuck, Sari Chesney, a Lawrence Bornstein, and the cleaner. There are dozens of others that we'll just have to assume are the cost of doing business in a public space."

"Of course. How about any other physical evidence, hair or blood?"

"We did recover hair. If you get a suspect, we can sample for DNA and make a comparison. At this point, all I can tell you is that it is male hair. And I can't tell you if it's from the killer or not. It was found just outside the office, against the door frame."

I pictured the crime scene. "Almost as though someone slid into the room? Hugging the door?"

"Possibly."

"Anything else?"

The tech said no. She explained that while they were nearly finished with the Starbuck scene, they were still working through the

evidence on the Chesney homicide. Things were made more difficult by the fact that the body had been in the water. She promised
to send over the Starbuck report via courier, and we ended the call.
I shot an email to Finn and copied the chief, updating them with
the information from the tech.

I ended the message with a final thought that I couldn't yet prove
but that felt as true as anything else I'd come across in the investigation thus far: *We're looking for one perp. It's always been one person.*

It had been a hell of a day.

When Finn intercepted me in the parking lot, I figured it was
about to get a whole lot worse.

But he surprised me.

"I know you're not the source of the leak, Gemma." He'd changed
into jeans and a black sweater. As the sunlight began to wane, he
toyed with his car keys, clearly uncomfortable.

I stared at him. "You sounded pretty sure of yourself on Saturday."

"I was wrong." He shrugged. "You're much too straight and narrow
to leak confidential information to a two-bit hack like Bryce Ventura.
It's not your style."

Funny, hadn't I said the same to Chief Chavez about Finn?

"Yeah, well, you're right. I'm not the source of the leak."

Finn nodded. To my shock, he looked like he was about to cry.

"What is it?"

He cleared his throat. "I don't, uh, have the best track record with
partners, Gem. I'm so sorry I accused you. You didn't deserve that. I
was an asshole."

"That's nothing new."

This got a surprised laugh from him. "Friends?"

I stuck out my hand. "Friends. Got any plans for the evening?
How about a pint at O'Toole's?"

"Actually, I was considering camping at Lost Lake tonight," Finn
replied. "I've been thinking about what you said, about Ruby Cellars's

theories. We've only been up there in the daytime. But everything seems to happen at night. Want to come with me?"

"You're joking. You think her theories are insane."

Finn shrugged, then casually tossed his keys high in the air and caught them. "You scared?"

"Of course not." The truth was that the lake did scare me, but I've never been one to back away from a challenge. What if Ruby Cellars was onto something; what if there was a supernatural force operating at the lake? It was ridiculous . . . wasn't it? But if we spent the night there, maybe we would see something. Or hear something. Didn't we owe it to Sari Chesney to exhaust all leads?

I realized Finn was grinning at me. "I dare you."

This was crazy. I bit my lip, considering, then said, "I'm in if Clementine can care for Grace. Unless you hear otherwise, I'll meet you at the trailhead in an hour. I'll bring dinner."

Finn nodded. "It'll be dark by then. Make sure you've got a few extra flashlights."

At home, I talked with Clementine. She was comfortable staying alone with the baby, and I realized as I packed that this would be the first full night I'd spend away from Grace. I was both excited at the prospect of making progress in the case and nervous about leaving her, but I trusted Clementine implicitly.

I packed quickly but, by the time I reached the parking lot and met Finn at the trailhead, it was dark. A full moon provided some light. Finn howled up at the sky, then grinned, and his even, white teeth glowed in the darkness.

"Scared?"

"No. Just chilly. Let's get a move on."

We hiked in silence, listening to the noises of the forest as our flashlights lit the ground in front of us. Part of me wondered just what the hell we were doing. We'd be lucky not to break our legs.

Finn set a face pace, and we reached Lost Lake forty-five minutes after we'd left the trailhead. As I'd expected, the campgrounds were deserted. The surface of the lake was black save for the places where the moonlight touched it. The forest was quiet, as though our sudden arrival had sent creatures scurrying for shelter. Then a strong gust of wind blew through and suddenly there were noises everywhere: the leaves rustling in the trees, the wind itself whistling a steady tune.

We set up our tents and then, starving, got going on dinner preparations. Finn built a fire in the pit, and soon the night was alive with the glow of red flames and the sound of logs burning and shifting against one another. In the meantime, I put together a bear bag and, after a few attempts, got a rope over the thin branch of a tree two hundred feet downwind of our campsite.

The fire provided a sense of normalcy. I boiled water and then poured it into pouches of dehydrated beef stew. Finn and I ate side by side, the fire between us and the lake. Somewhere, a loon cried out, its eerie scream sharply piercing the night and then slowly fading away.

Finn scraped the last bite of stew from his pouch and set it aside. "This is heaven on earth."

"It's beautiful," I agreed. "Though I'm a little disappointed that I haven't seen or felt anything suspicious. Have you?"

"Nah." He checked his watch. "It's early, though, only nine o'clock. The boogeymen only come out to play at midnight."

"You don't really believe in any of this, do you?"

Finn shook his head. "Not really. Sure, there *might* be something unusual happening here after dark but I believe in what I can see, what I can touch, what I can hold. Evidence. Hard facts. Murder is a bloody business, Gemma. It's a flesh-and-blood business. This? What we're doing tonight? It's like an episode of *The X-Files*. I'll be shocked if it's anything other than fantasy."

"Maybe. As you said, it's early. Finished?" I stood and stretched. A yawn escaped, and I groaned. "Damn. I forgot dessert."

Finn stood as well. "Never fear. I know you have an insatiable appetite. I got it covered."

He took the trash to the bear bag and then ducked in his tent. After a few minutes, he emerged with a bag of chocolate chip cookies and a flask.

"And Finn saves the day, once again."

He gave me the cookies and took a healthy swig from the flask. "Whiskey?"

After a moment, I nodded. He handed me the flask and I took a small sip, then a larger one. The alcohol burned going down, and I felt a warmth in my chest and a flush in my cheeks.

Finn took the flask back and drank again. "Come with me."

I followed him down to the edge of the lake. We stared out across it, both of us looking to the far side where we'd found the makeshift campsite, but all we could see was the dark swath of forest.

I shivered, both from the cold and from the taste of the whiskey still burning in my throat. Finn noticed and edged closer. He passed me the flask. I took another swallow, then coughed.

He laughed softly. "Not a whiskey drinker?"

"Red wine's more my style. But the whiskey was a good idea." I knelt and trailed my fingers in the water. "It's so cold."

"It's so beautiful."

The wind picked up and I shivered again and stood up. "I'm going back to the fire."

"I'll be up in a minute," Finn said. He continued to stare out across the water. In the moonlight, his face looked soft and serious and I realized, I think for the first time, how good looking he really was. No wonder women constantly threw themselves at his feet.

I ducked in my tent and grabbed a wool cap, then went to the fire. I found a small log on the ground and fashioned a seat for myself. By the time Finn joined me, my feet were propped and I'd made a serious dent in the bag of cookies. The dessert, combined with the heat of the fire and the whiskey, had me feeling comfortable.

"Are there any cookies left?" Finn stood near the fire, rubbing his hands together.

"Here you go," I said, and tossed him the bag. "I think there's two or three. Finish them, please."

He caught the bag. "You look nice and cozy. What are you thinking about?"

"The case. I wish there were some way to know if Mac Stephens really did tell Sari Chesney about the affair."

"There might be a way," Finn said. He took a seat beside me and took another long swallow from the flask. We were shoulder to shoulder, and then Finn adjusted the log behind us and we reclined against it, somewhat sheltered from the wind. "We've got a witness who likely knows more than he's telling."

"Virgil Salt?"

"Not Salt . . . I'm talking about Jake Stephens. Sound carries up here. If Mac and Sari argued, Jake would have heard. For that matter, Ally would have, too," Finn said.

"Let me see that flask." To my surprise, it was half-empty. We'd had more to drink than I'd thought. "So why hasn't one of them come forward?"

Finn sat up and threw a fresh log on the fire. Flames shot up, sending dozens of sparks into the air. He leaned back. "Loyalty. They could all be in on it together. One of them kills Sari and the other two agree to cover it up out of some sick sense of allegiance. Jake and Mac are blood; Ally is carrying Mac's baby. Is it so hard to believe that all three have a stake in keeping Sari's murder quiet?"

"That might be, but did you read my last email? Forensics came back with a match to the fibers on Betty Starbuck's body. But they didn't match to Sari Chesney's shirt. They matched instead to someone who'd been at Lost Lake. We're looking for one perp. One person killed both Starbuck and Chesney. Mac and Jake have alibis for the night of Starbuck's murder. And I can't think of a single reason why Ally would kill Starbuck."

Next to me, Finn blew out his breath in one long sigh. "That's that, then. So we look at Larry Bornstein again. Maybe James Curry, too, and Campbell."

"Let's start with Ally, though. We heard Mac's side. I want to hear Ally's tomorrow."

Finn pulled the flask out of my hand and took another long swallow. His eyes were bright in the glow of the fire, and I realized I was buzzed. If anything suspicious did happen in the next few hours, neither of us would be in a good state to handle it.

Finn tipped his head back and looked up at the stars. "Let me play devil's advocate again. It's what I'm best at. Coincidences happen all the time. That's the nature of our universe. Is it so hard to believe that Betty stumbled into something at the museum, say another robbery, and was killed while across town—across a mountain, for Pete's sake—Sari was killed for some other reason?" Finn asked.

"Okay, if we're playing that game, who's to say the lake itself wasn't responsible for Sari's death? What if Ruby Cellars was right?"

"Come on, Gemma." Finn groaned. "I know you've got some wacky ideas, but this is just a lake. Secluded, private, beautiful. There's no one for miles. We should be enjoying it, not trying to make it into something it's not."

I shrugged, and Finn turned his head to look at me. We were inches apart. He started to respond, then stopped and simply stared. I froze, sure he could see my heart suddenly thudding in my chest.

Slowly, he lifted a hand toward my face.

I couldn't breathe.

Then he flushed and his gaze moved from my eyes to the side of my head. He pulled his hand away.

"I thought you had an ember on your hat. I didn't want you to get burned." Finn coughed and got to his feet. "I'll be back in a sec. Too much water on the way in."

"Watch out for bears!" I softly called after him. My heart continued to pound, sending blood coursing throughout my body.

What just happened?

I exhaled and put a cold hand to my cheek. I was warm, flushed from more than the whiskey, more than the heat of the fire. Desperate for a distraction, I picked the flask up and finished off the whiskey.

I wasn't sure what scared me more: the fact that Finn wanted to kiss me or the fact that I didn't know if I would have stopped him.

Chapter Forty

We broke camp early.

I'd spent a restless night tossing and turning, listening first to the wind and then to the sound of Finn in his tent softly snoring. As soon as the sun rose, I was up, getting the fire going again and boiling water for coffee. My head pounded from the whiskey. I felt tired, achy.

The water was calm, flat as a pane of glass. In the early morning light, I saw wildflowers just beginning to bloom along the edge of the trail. The whole area seemed to be suffused with a softness that made it difficult to believe this was the site of so many deaths.

"There's nothing here," I whispered to myself. Then I went into the woods to pee and saw fresh bear tracks on the trail. I went about my business quickly and when I'd returned to the fire, Finn was there. I didn't know how he did it, but he looked rested and ready for the day.

I told him what I'd seen.

"I heard him huffing and puffing. Must have been midnight."

"Was he close?" I handed Finn an orange and a protein bar.

He nodded. "Fifty feet, maybe. He sounded like a big guy. I must have fallen back asleep. The next time I woke up, he was gone."

The fact that Finn could fall asleep while a bear stalked the campsite, after a flask of whiskey and our near romantic encounter, was impressive.

A thought occurred to me: Had I read too much into something that wasn't there? Had I imagined the look in Finn's eyes, the way his hand seemed as though it was going to fit perfectly against my cheek?

"You okay?" Finn stared at me, his brows furrowed.

"Never better. Let's get out of here."

We doused the fire and then left. As we hiked, we discussed the weather, summer vacations, even television shows we were enjoying. We talked about everything except for what had almost happened the night before.

At least things weren't awkward. If anything, the conversation flowed better than it had in days, and a part of me wondered what that meant.

As we reached our cars, Finn said, "I don't know if you were hoping to see something at the lake or not, but I'm sure glad it was a quiet night. You had me convinced a werewolf was lurking in the woods."

I grinned. "I never said anything about werewolves."

"See you back at the station?"

"Yes. I'm going to get cleaned up and check in on the baby. I'll see you soon."

At home, I showered quickly, reluctant to step out of the hot water but wanting to spend an hour or two with Grace. She was excited to see me, and we played on the rug in her room as Clementine went for a run and then took her own shower.

I didn't know what I would have done without Clementine. With Brody away, she'd been holding things down on the home front and keeping Grace happy with what seemed to be an unlimited supply of energy.

She handed me a small black sack as I was gathering my things. "What's this?"

"Lunch. I found the bag in the back of your pantry. There's a turkey sandwich, apple slices, string cheese, and orange juice," she said. "I know you like soda, but I thought the juice might do you good."

She lowered her voice. "I threw in a few aspirin, too. You looked like you could use them."

Blushing, I thanked her. "I'm going to be spoiled at this rate, Clem."

"Don't worry. I'm keeping a running tally of all the extra things I'm doing for you. I'll invoice you when Brody's home," she muttered. She gently lifted Grace's arm up. "Wave bye to Mommy! Wave bye!"

At my desk, I called Allison Chang and explained that I had a few questions for her. I was deliberately vague, and when she asked if the conversation could be handled over the phone, I said no. "Let's talk in person, Ally. It's easier for me to take notes that way."

"Sure, I understand. I can come by after work? About five?"

"Great. See you then."

I hung up and then swore as a reminder popped up on my computer calendar that my yearly fitness test was coming due. I'd been slow to reach my pre-pregnancy fitness levels; early morning runs and a lean diet were so much less appealing than extra cuddles with the baby and second servings of ice cream.

But the yearly fitness test was something I had to pass.

Groaning, I pushed back from my desk and headed to the women's locker room. I kept a small bag of workout clothes, toiletries, and extra sneakers there for exactly this purpose.

I changed and walked to the small gym that was annexed to the back of the police station. A couple of guys were doing timed sprints on the treadmills, so I moved to an exercise bike in the corner and slipped a set of headphones on. I needed serious motivation and only one artist would do: Janet Jackson, circa the early nineties.

I was eleven miles into a preset workout that was heavy on the hills, sweat pouring from my forehead, quads trembling, when Chief Chavez appeared in the corner of my eye. I wondered if he could smell the alcohol that seemed to be seeping out my pores.

"Chief," I gasped. I pulled out my headphones and hit pause on the bike. "You're just in time. I think I'm dying."

I laughed, but he wasn't smiling in return. He laid a hand on my forearm. "Gemma, there's been an accident. It's your grandmother."

Julia sat in the back of an ambulance, face scrunched up as a paramedic applied butterfly bandages over a cut on her forehead. I parked and opened the car door in time to hear him tell Julia that she really should go to the hospital.

Bull stood nearby, talking with two patrol officers. At one point, all three glanced over at my grandmother's yellow Mercedes, and Bull shook his head sadly. Julia had ended her escapade on the front lawn of a brick ranch house, her car crumpled against a stately ponderosa pine tree.

A woman in a pink terry cloth bathrobe stood on the front porch, a small white terrier at her feet. The dog kept up a constant yap at all the excitement and, as I joined my grandmother and the paramedic, Julia shouted, "If someone doesn't shut that rat up soon, I'm going to light a fire under its ass."

"You love dogs, Grandma. And you quit smoking twenty years ago."

"So? Your grandfather still enjoys the occasional pipe. I'll borrow his matches. And excuse me, but *that* is not a dog."

"Are you badly hurt?"

"I'm fine, darling," she said. "Such a fuss over nothing. Doc here is worried about my heart. He thinks I've had a sudden stress."

She mocked the paramedic with her tone, but he continued to apply the bandages to her head, seemingly ignoring her.

Bull joined us and, when I glanced at him, he merely shrugged.

I took a deep breath. None of this was his fault, and it was unfair of me to punish him. He was trying to do the best he could in a situation that had no positive outcomes.

"What happened?"

He gave a wry smile. "Your grandmother finally pulled a fast one on Laura while she was in the restroom. I was in the backyard and didn't hear a thing."

"How did Julia get the car keys?"

"Beats me. She must have had a spare we didn't know about. I've got them all locked in the—well, you know where they are."

"And the front door?"

"We're not Fort Knox, Gemma. The door is kept bolted, but we're not living on lockdown. She got out."

"She could have been killed, Bull."

Julia squeezed my hands hard. I pulled them away. "Ouch, Grandma."

"Please don't talk about me like I'm not here, Gemma. You all are acting like I'm some common criminal. I didn't do a damn thing wrong." She crossed her arms and frowned. "I'm supposed to be at the ballet, and I'm a mess."

I stared at her clothes: bowling shoes and satin pajamas. Bull just shook his head.

The paramedic finished. "Are you sure I can't give you a ride to the hospital, ma'am?"

"There's absolutely no need. I'm *fine*." Julia slid off the ambulance's back step and stood. "See? Just fine."

The paramedic said to Bull in a low voice, "I can't force her to go. She's in your hands now, buddy. Good luck."

As the ambulance and the patrol officers left, a tow truck arrived. We watched as it slowly extracted the Mercedes from the ponderosa pine, the three of us cringing as we saw the flattened front end, the flaking paint. The car was totaled. It was a miracle that Julia hadn't been badly injured. As it was, she'd likely have a nice scar as a reminder of this adventure.

I followed them back to their house, where an upset Laura scolded Julia, then forced her to take a nap.

Bull grabbed two cups of coffee and joined me in his "chambers," the small study just off the front living room. He handed me a coffee, then took a seat behind his desk.

I stood, scanning the framed photographs and newspaper articles that lined the wall behind the old brown leather couch. When he was a judge, Bull had been something of a minor celebrity in town. It seemed everybody wanted to be friends with the man who one day might run for mayor . . . maybe even Congress. But politics had never been Bull's passion, and the longer he spent in retirement, the more time he spent here, at home, with Julia and Laura as his most constant companions.

I sat on the sofa. Bull faced me, his face grim, his fingers tented together and resting on the desk blotter.

"This is serious, Bull. What if a child had been in that yard? You and Laura . . . you can't keep her here, not safely, not anymore. It's too big a burden."

He lifted a finger, pointed at me. "It's not a burden. It's a gift to be able to care for her."

"Burden, gift. I don't care what you call it. It's too much. What about her social life? She doesn't go out with friends anymore, or see people other than her family. Don't you think it might do her some good to spend time in the company of others like her? I visited Carver Estates. A resident there is the mother of one of my murder victims. It's a nice place, Bull. It's affordable and safe and, most important, Julia could be with people who understand her." I sipped my coffee, set the mug down. "She's only going to get worse. What will it take for you to admit that?"

He put his head in his hands, rubbed his scalp. "I pray every night, Gemma, that your grandmother has only peace and love in her last few years here on this earth. Shoot, we might not even have years. It might be months. I feel like we're staring down the barrel of a loaded gun, waiting for it to go off. I'd give anything to trade places with her. What am I going to do after she's gone?"

"I don't know. We'll get through it, though, I promise. As a family. But right now, we have to consider what's best for Julia. And for you. You'll run yourself into the ground if you keep going like this, and we need you to be here, to be strong. Brody, Grace . . . we need you in our lives, Bull."

He looked up at me with tears in his eyes. "You do?"

"Of course we do! We love you, and I've only ever wanted what is best for you and for Julia. And I have to say, I think we're at a point where what's best is a move to an assisted living facility. You will still be her guardian, her voice. Nothing will ever change that, Bull." I handed him a tissue from a box on the end table, and he blew his nose mightily. "We don't have to make a decision today. But please, give me your word that you'll think seriously about this. After my cases are done, you and I can tour Carver Estates. If you don't like it, there's another care center in Avondale that has an excellent reputation."

Bull nodded, his throat too thick with emotion to speak.

I stood up and sniffed. "Is that homemade bread I smell?"

Bull cleared his throat and smiled gently. "Laura bakes when she is stressed out." He patted his belly. "Where do you think this extra fifteen pounds came from? Her specialty is cinnamon bread with raisins and walnuts. Let's go talk with her in the kitchen. I'd like her opinion of this Carver place."

Chapter Forty-one

It was ten after five when Allison Chang arrived at the police station. I walked down the hall and greeted her. Now that I knew she was pregnant, it was easy to recognize the tiny bump she sported under her striped blue-and-white blouse for what it really was. I took her to the conference room and left her there a moment while I got us a couple of bottles of water from the vending machine.

When I returned, she was staring at her cell phone, frowning. I closed the door, then took the seat next to her and pushed a bottle across the table.

"Sorry, I'm trying to respond to this email," she explained. "It's for my job. . . . But your wireless connection doesn't seem to be working."

"What do you do?"

Ally brightened and set her phone down on the table. "I teach fifth grade at Burnham Elementary in Avondale. We've got a few more weeks before summer break, and it's a crazy time of year for us. There are a lot of things to wrap up."

"How long have you taught there?" I didn't take notes as she spoke, hoping to keep the conversation casual, a warm-up for things to come.

"Gosh, it's been seven years now. Sometimes it feels like seventy years," she said with a laugh. "I love it, though. I can't imagine doing any other kind of work."

A knock on the door, then Finn stuck his head in. "Ally, right?"

She nodded.

He entered the room. "I'm Finn, Detective Monroe's partner. Mind if I sit in?"

Ally looked uncertainly at me. I smiled. "Finn's working on Sari's case with me. It's best if he joins us."

Finn took a seat, and I explained to him that we were just chatting about Ally's job.

"And you grew up here, right? You and Sari were what, neighbors?"

She shook her head. "We met in first grade. We didn't live close to each other, so our parents were constantly driving us back and forth. We were born three weeks apart at Memorial General. Neither one of us ever wanted to leave this place, even when all our friends were going away to colleges on the coasts," Ally said. Tears welled in her eyes. "I still can't believe this is really happening."

I nodded. "I can only imagine. Ally, we know about the affair between you and Mac. And the baby."

Ally flinched and knocked over her bottle of water, which splashed against the table and all over her jeans and shoes.

A pink flush crept over her neck. "Damn it!"

I calmly reached across the table and grabbed a box of tissues. She took a few and dabbed at her clothes. By the time she was done, the flush in her neck had moved to her cheeks. Tears welled in her eyes.

"My parents are immigrants. They moved here in the eighties, with just a few hundred dollars in their pockets. I'm their only child," Ally said, dabbing at her eyes with a fresh tissue. "They worked two, three jobs at a time to give me the best life they could. I've never wanted for anything. And what do I do? I betray everything they stand for with my best friend's boyfriend. Who does that? I'm a monster."

"No, you're a human being," I said, careful not to meet Finn's eyes. "People make mistakes. Why don't you start at the beginning?"

Ally's story mirrored Mac's: the birthday party celebration, a late night out on the town, one thing leading to another. It was when I pressed her on Sari's knowledge of the affair that their stories diverged.

"No, absolutely not," Ally said, shaking her head emphatically. "Sari would never have forgiven me or Mac. So no, no I don't believe you. Or rather, I don't believe Mac. There's no way he told Sari about us."

"Why would he lie?"

Ally shook her head again. "Beats me. Like I've said before, Sari had a temper like you wouldn't believe. She would have had his balls for breakfast."

"Mac also said you are planning to keep the baby?"

"Yes, that much is true. Lord knows how we are going to do this. We're not meant to be together. But he'll want to be involved as a father. He'll be a good dad."

Finn asked, "Do you think he could have hurt Sari?"

"Absolutely not," Ally said. She answered quickly, but there was the slightest doubt in her eyes and I touched her arm very gently.

"Ally?"

Tears filled her eyes, and she nodded. "Mac can be . . . rough. At first, it was exciting. He knows how to play the bad boy. But sometimes, he takes it too far."

"Sex?"

"No. And he's never gotten physically abusive, at least not with me. And not with Sari, that I'm aware of. It's more his attitude. He has a mean streak that he keeps well hidden, but it's there. A few times, he's scared me," Ally said. "You saw the weapons in his house, his gun. He keeps a shotgun in his van, too. He's . . . paranoid, I guess is the right word. Sari once told me that Mac's dad was pretty rough with the family; beating up on his mom, that sort of thing. I guess Mac wants to be able to protect himself."

"How did he scare you?"

"Just, you know, wondering how far he'd go if push came to shove. That sort of scary."

"Did he ever threaten you?" Finn's voice was tight.

Ally shook her head. "No. Like I said, he keeps the meanness hidden. Overall he's a really good guy."

We talked a few more minutes, but I had the sense that I'd gotten all I was going to get from Ally. I had one final question, and I asked it of her as Finn and I walked her down the long hallway of the police station and back toward the entrance.

"Ally, you said Sari would have been furious at Mac for the affair. And you also said she would never have forgiven you. Do you really believe that?"

Ally touched her belly, just once, very gently, and I felt a pang in my chest. I remembered doing the same thing when I was newly pregnant, that universal gesture of wonder and acknowledgment of the new life developing inside me. Though my baby was only six months old, it felt like a lifetime ago.

"Yes, I really believe that. Sari would have killed me."

As I packed my things to leave for the day, I couldn't find my house keys.

I retraced the steps I'd taken over the course of the day and realized they must have fallen out of my purse, in my locker, during my earlier attempt at a workout.

It was dark in the locker room. I flipped on the lights and, as the fluorescent bulbs flickered and hissed, a voice cried out in surprise.

I froze. "Who's there?"

Another cry, this one more subdued. Then a shaky voice said, "It's me. Chloe."

I rounded the corner and found her sitting on a bench, her head in her hands. I sat next to her and touched her lightly on the back. "What is it?"

She sobbed in response, and I glanced around, unsure what I should do.

I knew Chloe in that way that you often know co-workers: superficially, with enough knowledge to make conversation. In fact, I could list what I knew about her on one hand: she'd been with the department about nine years and had a couple of kids in high school. Her husband, Bud, part-time trucker, full-time bowling alley owner, held the town record for the highest number of hot dogs eaten in one sitting (Cedar Valley Fourth of July Festival, 1997: seventy-three hot dogs) and bragged about it every chance he got.

"Is it the kids? Or Bud?"

"No," Chloe said. She finally raised her head and looked at me. Her cheeks were pale and streaked with tears. Thick gobs of wet mascara clung to her eyelashes. "They're fine. They're perfect."

"Do you want to talk about it?"

Chloe thought a moment, then nodded. "I might as well. I can't keep going like this. It's killing me."

I waited patiently while she took a deep breath. She ran a hand through her short blond hair and dried her eyes with the hem of her shirt. "It all started in February. You'd just finished the Fuente case and things were quiet in town. I was at the grocery store, minding my own business, when my credit card was declined. It was so embarrassing, Gemma. Bud's been struggling with the business. He can't compete with that new arcade in Avondale. No one wants to bowl anymore except that old fart Jethro Dodge and his cronies. Anyway, I guess we'd missed a few payments. No big deal, right? I wrote a check to the market and walked out. Well, next thing I knew, Bryce Ventura sidled up to me as I was loading my groceries into the car. He slipped me a business card and whispered, 'I'm very good to my friends. Let me know what you hear, Chloe.'"

She stopped to blow her nose—also on the hem of her shirt—and I felt my stomach drop. I had a bad feeling I knew where all this was going.

Bryce Ventura's second clue suddenly made sickening sense: What gets hit and keeps coming back for more?

Bowling pins.

Goddamn bowling pins.

"So a few weeks went by and then there was that terrible fire at the apartment complex on Second Street. Remember that? Thank god no one was hurt. Well, I just happened to overhear the fire chief tell Chief Chavez that they suspected arson. And I thought, well, that's something the public ought to know about! By then, we'd missed another credit card payment and Bud was getting very nervous. He talked about taking on another job, but he's already had three heart attacks . . . anyway, it seemed so innocent at the time. I convinced myself it wasn't a big deal to call Bryce and tell him what I knew. And wouldn't you know it, the very next day an envelope with two hundred dollars in it was delivered to my house," Chloe said. She wrapped her arms around herself and rocked a few times. "Two hundred dollars might not sound like a lot of money, but when you're trying to keep a roof over your head and feed three growing boys, every cent counts."

"Chloe, this is not good."

"Don't you think I know that?" She choked out another sob. "Why the hell do you think I'm in here, crying like a ninny? I may be responsible for Kent Starbuck's death. I adore the chief. I've worked for the man for years. How am I supposed to look him in the eye and tell him what I've done?"

I sighed. "People make mistakes."

She sat up, straightened her shoulders, and wiped away the smeared mascara from under her eyes. "You know what Chief Chavez hates more than anything, right? It's disloyalty. He can forgive stupidity, carelessness, and arrogance. I don't think it's in his bones to forgive betrayal. Do you want to hear the worst part of it all? Bud sold the bowling alley at a nice profit to a developer two months ago. I didn't need to keep sharing information with Bryce. But I did."

So that was that.

Chloe Parker was our department's Deep Throat. No, scratch that. Deep Throat had myriad motives for leaking information to Woodward and Bernstein. Chloe had been motivated purely by money. She'd jeopardized investigations and her actions might have led to the death of Kent Starbuck.

I'd wasted precious time and attention getting dragged into Ruby Cellars's theories about Lost Lake being a site of some kind of curse or supernatural activity. After all, if I hadn't set up a trap to catch the leaker, Bryce Ventura never would have tweeted about the diary curse and Ruby never would have called me.

And I most definitely never would have spent the night at Lost Lake with Finn.

In hindsight, it should have been so obvious.

As a dispatcher, Chloe was first to hear of anything going on in town. She had the full run of the station, access to memos, files, all of it.

Chloe patted me on the hand, reading the disappointment written all over my face. "Thanks for listening, Gemma. I'm sorry for what I've done. I'll be lucky if the chief lets me resign. He may press charges, and if he does, I deserve whatever punishment I get. I know in my heart I'm not a bad person. But I've done a bad thing. And to be honest, I'd do it all over again if it meant keeping my family safe and fed."

"I don't agree with what you did . . . but I understand why you did it. Do you want me to go with you to talk to Chief Chavez?"

Chloe stood up and shook her head. She paused a moment, then removed her name tag and pressed it into my hands. "I wish you the best, Gemma. I've always liked you. Hold on to that, will you? It's too sad to keep it at home, and I can't bear to put it in the trash. Consider it a reminder to keep your chin up and your nose clean."

I sat in the dim locker room, listening to a dripping faucet, staring at that name tag, for a long time after Chloe Parker walked out.

Chapter Forty-two

The following day, Chief Chavez sent out a department-wide email, the heading of which was *Personnel Changes*.

I read the short message with mixed emotions. Chavez wrote that Dispatcher Chloe Parker had resigned, effective immediately, after nearly a decade with the police department. He thanked her for her years of public service and shared that he would seek to fill her position as soon as possible.

The chief left out any mention of the fact that Chloe had been sharing confidential information with Bryce Ventura, and my respect for him, already high, went up another notch. I could only imagine how uncomfortable and awful the meeting between him and Chloe must have been.

I sighed and tucked her name tag into a drawer in my desk. With any luck, as time passed, the memory of the department's leak would fade. People would soon forget all about the hard months when we'd looked at one another with suspicion.

There was at least one person who read between the lines of Chavez's memo.

Finn pushed back from his desk and came over to me. In a low voice, he simply said, "Chloe?"

I nodded and bit my lip. "She confessed to me last night, after I stumbled on her crying in the locker room. She must have gone directly to the chief after that. In the end, she was brave. Brave and apologetic."

Finn snorted. "I hardly think she was brave. She was going to get caught sooner or later. It was just a matter of time. The chief should have pressed charges."

I shrugged. "I don't know, Finn. You didn't see her face. You weren't there. She was sorry for what she had done."

Finn nodded. "There's that, I guess. Look, I've been thinking—taking a step back, trying to approach this from a new direction. Who benefits from Betty Starbuck's death and who benefits from Sari Chesney's death? Setting aside the fibers on Starbuck's body for a moment—because we can't be certain that they did come from her killer—let's assume in the first scenario there's one killer who did them both and in the second, there's two killers. And if no one benefits, then we have to assume we're dealing with a random psychopath who just happened to target two women who worked together."

"And we both know that's a stretch and completely unlikely."

"Agreed."

We moved to the far end of the squad room. There, an enormous blank whiteboard took up the length of the wall. I grabbed a couple of dry erase board markers. I made two columns, one for Betty Starbuck and one for Sari Chesney. "Let's run through this, starting with Starbuck. I want only the names and possible motives of the people who *also* had means and opportunity to kill her."

Finn, perched on the edge of a table, nodded. He thought a moment, then started calling things out. As he talked, I wrote on the board.

He started with family. "Kent Starbuck, motivated by an inheritance and/or revenge, had means and opportunity. He had no alibi and was observed at the scene of the crime. Patrick Crabbe's alibi didn't hold up. His motivations were also financial, and/or whatever this psychosis is that he's experiencing. Moving on to colleagues: we have Larry Bornstein, looking for a promotion; Sari Chesney, also perhaps seeking a promotion, or revenge, or she did it as part of some connection to the still missing Rayburn Diary."

"Good, this is good. But I don't buy Chesney for Starbuck's killer." I crossed her name out. "Although we won't ever know for sure, we have to move forward under the assumption that Sari was killed in the early morning hours on Saturday, May fourteenth so she can't have killed Betty Starbuck."

"Okay, that's fine. Let's add James Curry to the list as well. His motive is perhaps the murkiest of all the suspects: we know from Larry Bornstein that Curry wanted access to the diary. He could have stolen it, and perhaps Betty Starbuck suspected him, even confronted him. Curry then killed Starbuck."

We paused a moment and looked over the names on the board. "Are we missing anyone?"

Finn shook his head. "I don't think so. Except . . . let's go ahead and add 'unknown subject.' I hate to make things even messier, but what if Larry Bornstein and Lois Freeman are in on this together? Maybe they concocted that story about Betty confiding her fears of Patrick to them. Maybe the note Patrick found in his mom's house wasn't written about him or his brother. Maybe there is an unknown subject at play here."

I exhaled. "You're right, of course. A lot of our movement in this case has been based on secondhand accounts from unreliable witnesses. Now let's do Sari Chesney. Both Mac Stephens and Allison Chang had motive, opportunity, and means, either independently or together, to kill Chesney. The affair, the baby . . . it's compelling."

"There's the Bookkeeper, too."

"Right. What about Sam Birdshead?"

Finn shook his head. "Sorry, but no. Sam is not a killer. There's just no way."

I chewed on the end of my pen, reluctant to say what I was about to say. Finn sensed it and said, "What? You disagree?"

"It's a classic he said, she said. We want to believe that Sam is not a lovesick stalker. We want to believe that he could never kill someone. What if we're wrong? I just hate to dismiss Sari's diaries so quickly. Why would she lie? There's nothing in her background to suggest she's a liar. She had a gambling problem, sure. Addiction. A mean streak, perhaps, based on the nicknames she used in her diaries. And she was secretive. But a liar? Where's the proof?"

Finn scratched at the back of his neck.

Chief Chavez strolled by, a cup of steaming coffee in his hand. He stopped for a minute and scanned the board, then looked quizzically at me. "You've got the columns reversed."

I stared at him. "What are you talking about?"

"Sari disappeared—was killed—before Betty. Sari's column should be on the left, in the first slot, then Betty's should be on the right. You started with Betty, probably because you have more suspect names for her, and because her body appeared before Sari's, but you should have started with Sari. Her murder came first," Chavez said.

He moved on with a curt nod and I stared first at the whiteboard, then at Finn, thunderstruck.

"It all starts and ends with Sari Chesney," I whispered. "We know the fibers on Betty Starbuck came from someone who'd been at Lost Lake. They came from Sari's killer. One killer, two murders, some connection we haven't figured out yet. But all along, we've been trying to make Starbuck's killer work as Chesney's killer. We've been working backward. We should be looking at Chesney's killer for the Starbuck homicide. And if we stay with that thought, we have three viable suspects who had motive, means, and opportunity to kill Sari Chesney: Allison Chang, Mac Stephens, or a third subject, either known to us or not."

"Well, we can eliminate Mac Stephens. He couldn't have killed Betty Starbuck because he worked an overnight shift at the hospital the night of the gala," Finn said, reading from his notes. "You verified that."

"Yes." I stared at the list of names in both columns.

Something was there, something we'd missed along the way. It niggled at the back of my mind, something I'd heard or seen but hadn't realized the importance of in the moment. But what?

I replayed conversations from the last few days in my head. Patrick, Kent. Mac, Ally, Jake. James Curry, Alistair Campbell.

Jake.

I didn't need to glance at the board to know his was the only name not there.

Why?

Why had we not considered him a suspect? He had the means, the opportunity, and a history of violence . . . but he'd just met Sari Chesney that day.

What reason could he have to kill her?

Out of all the suspects, Jake made the least amount of sense.

Still, to be thorough, I added his name under the Sari Chesney column.

Finn frowned. "Sure, Jake could have killed Sari . . . but he didn't kill Betty Starbuck. Remember? His cousin Nicole is his alibi for Saturday night."

"You're right." I drew a line through Jake's name and stepped back.

I read the name that remained.

"Ally?"

"Maybe. Maybe Mac did Sari and Ally did Betty Starbuck." Finn went to the board and tapped Jake's name. "I want to talk to him. He knows more than he's telling us."

Chapter Forty-three

We found Jake Stephens at a tavern on the south side of town. The Jukebox was dim, with stale air that smelled of dusty peanuts and beer. The early afternoon crowd was mostly male, mostly blue collar. Jake sat in the corner booth, a half-eaten burger on the table in front of him and a rough-looking blonde in a halter top next to him. The woman slid out of the booth when she saw us coming and Finn murmured, "Tanya Green. She's a working girl. I picked her up a few months ago for solicitation."

Green slunk past us, studiously avoiding eye contact with both Finn and me, leaving a trail of musky perfume and pungent hairspray in her wake.

We reached Jake's table.

"Mind if we join you?" I asked, and took a seat across from Jake. Finn eased in next to him and folded his hands on top of the table, a neutral expression on his face, his eyes scanning the crowd. Jake shrank back against the far end of the booth, putting as much distance between himself and Finn as possible.

"Are you going to eat those?" I asked, pointing at an untouched pile of crispy, curly sweet potato fries. There was a small bowl of what looked like gorgonzola cheese nestled in the basket.

Jake shook his head. "Help yourself."

"What's the matter?" Finn turned in the booth and stared at Jake. "No appetite?"

"Not really. I can't stop thinking about Sari. Imagining her in the water . . . knowing that she was scared of drowning. It's awful."

I dipped a couple of fries into the cheese and ate them, then pushed the plate away and wiped my fingers on a paper napkin. "Those are good. You should try them, Jake, before the cheese gets cold. You know what I can't stop thinking about?"

Jake peered at me and shook his head. "I have no idea."

I smiled and grabbed another sweet potato fry. "I think you know more than you're telling us. We know about the affair. We know Ally and Mac have been seeing each other for months."

"Affair? *Ally and Mac?*" Jake's jaw dropped and, behind his thick glasses, his eyes grew wide. "What are you talking about?"

I leaned in over the table, holding Jake's gaze. "We're talking about motive for murder, Jake. We're talking about a cold night at an even colder lake, and a young woman discovering her beloved boyfriend has been sleeping with her best friend."

Finn added, "She's upset, maybe she threatens Mac. Or maybe it's Ally that she gets into it with. Things turn ugly, and Sari ends up in the water. She dies, Jake. *That* is what we're talking about."

"And now," I said, "would be a great time for you to tell us what you know. What did you see that night, Jake? What did you hear?"

"I didn't see anything! There is no way Mac could have killed Sari."

"You didn't hear a scream in the dark? A strange noise? Maybe it woke you up and you lay in the tent, wondering if you were dreaming?" Finn asked.

He edged closer to Jake.

In response, Jake shrank even farther back into the booth. "No! This is crazy. It was supposed to be a fun camping trip. Now someone is dead and you think her boyfriend—my cousin—killed her. That's horseshit. I'm telling you, Mac couldn't hurt a fly, much less Sari. Mac was in love with her. The idea that he'd hit her . . . drown her . . . it can't be true."

He looked genuinely aghast, and I felt a cold trickle of doubt crawl down my spine. Were we wrong? Had we gotten so focused on the affair that we'd somehow missed something?

Finn asked Jake, "So what about you?"

"Me?"

Finn nodded. "Yeah, you. You were at the lake that night. You've got a record for assault. Maybe we should be looking at you?"

Jake paled, and his shoulders sagged. "I'm never going to get away from that stupid mistake. I haven't done anything. I'm fulfilling all the requirements of my parole. Talk to Stinky Nuts, he'll tell you. I'm clean."

"Good for you." Finn leaned back, thinking. "Okay, you're certain about Mac. How about Ally?"

"I barely know her! I met her for the first time the day of the camping trip. She struck me as a snooty, stuck-up bitch. That doesn't make her a killer! I'm telling you, there was someone else there that night. There had to have been," Jake said. His voice got low. "I've been doing some research into the history of this town, and I've read the stories about the Lost Girls. I'll tell you this much: you couldn't pay me to go back to that lake. That place isn't just haunted. It's evil."

"Well, at least the fries were good," I said as we exited the Jukebox into the bright light of day. We both pulled sunglasses out and slid them on.

"I've never met anyone who thinks about food as much as you do. You're lucky you've got a fast metabolism. At the rate you eat you should be four hundred pounds. You should have your own television show," Finn said. "You could make a fortune."

"That's mean."

"What?" Finn protested. "I meant it as a compliment. *Gemma Does the Buffet.*"

"Will you quit. I'll drive."

Back at the station, I was surprised to see a wrapped package waiting for me on my desk. I read the attached note. It was from Bryce Ventura, and it was an apology for how he'd behaved.

"Jerk," I muttered under my breath. With Chloe Parker out of the picture, Ventura's connection in the police department was gone. If this gift was the weasel's way of trying to get in my good graces, he was going to be sorely disappointed the next time we saw each other.

I opened the box and lifted out a gorgeous hardbound book. Flipping it open, I saw it was a commemorative album of photographs, commentary, and clippings from the previous week's sesquicentennial celebration. All week long, photographers for the paper had staked out the various events in town, capturing the gala, the street fairs, the band performances.

It was actually a lovely gesture, and it made me think of something that might help our case.

I called Ventura.

"I considered flowers but decided this was more appropriate."

"It's beautiful, and thank you. But there's no way in hell I'm going to share information with you," I said.

He laughed. "Believe me, I'm not going to ask. I just want us to be friends. Okay, okay, maybe not friends. But respected professional colleagues. I see a lot of things, Detective. We should be able to help each other out."

"I'm so glad you think that, Bryce. I'd like access to all the images taken the night of the gala by your paper's photographers. I know there was at least one guy stationed at the museum."

Ventura hemmed and hawed and finally realized it would be futile to resist me. I could get a court order, but if I had to waste my time doing that, I'd be angry . . . and his little gift would be for naught.

"I'll bring you a flash drive. It's too big a file to send electronically, and I'm not giving you access to our servers," Ventura said. "I just hope you remember in the future how helpful I am."

"I'll remember. I'll see you in ten minutes."

"Twenty. I'm not your toady. I don't hop to at your every command."

"Fifteen and you get the scoop on the museum murders."

"Deal."

Ventura was as good as his word; he arrived twelve minutes after we ended the call. He handed over the flash drive, and then I made him leave. I didn't have time for small talk.

"What's that?" Finn asked as I started to scroll through the photographs on my computer.

"A little gift from Bryce Ventura. Pics from the night of the gala. There were photographers at the event, and in town, taking pictures all week. I got to thinking, what if they captured something? Something important?"

"Want some help reviewing them?"

"Sure."

Finn pulled up a chair and, together, we scrolled through picture after picture. My eyes grew heavy, and twice we stopped for a break. The second time, Finn ran to the gas station and brought us back cherry slushies. The sugar helped, and we moved from one image to the next, not sure what we were looking for, but we had faith that we'd know it when we saw it.

"There. Is that who I think it is?" I stared at the screen and rubbed my eyes.

Finn squinted. "Can you enlarge it?"

I moved the mouse and hit a few keys on the keyboard, and suddenly Jake Stephens's face filled the screen. It was a blurry photograph, but it was definitely him, in a bar downtown, the night of the gala.

Finn took the mouse from my hand and moved the arrow to the bottom right of the screen. "There's a timestamp. Eleven thirty p.m. And look what he's drinking."

It was a bottle of Corona.

I sat back. "Nicole Stephens lied to us. She said she and Jake were home, watching a movie, playing pool. They fell asleep sometime after midnight. She lied to us, Finn."

He stood up and checked his watch. "What are the chances that Jake's still at the bar?"

"The man has nothing else to do. Finn, this doesn't mean he's our guy."

"I know. But it means *something*."

Chapter Forty-four

As we drove back to the Jukebox, I thought through our earlier conversation with Jake Stephens. He'd been shocked by the affair . . . defended Mac . . .

Then it hit me, and I pounded the steering wheel in both frustration and exhilaration.

Sari's killer had been right in front of me the whole time.

From the first day I was called out to Lost Lake, he'd always been there.

"It's Jake. Jake's the killer." I parked outside the Jukebox. "He admitted as much. Come on."

Jake groaned when he saw us. His food had been cleared and a fresh beer sat on the table in front of him, the foam still high in the pint glass. We took the same seats we'd taken before, Finn sliding in next to him, me across the table.

"My food's long gone, lady. You want something, order it yourself."

"I've lost my appetite, Jake. See, the thing is, something you said earlier stuck with me. You said you couldn't imagine Mac—your cousin, the nurse, the all-around good guy—hitting or drowning Sari."

Jake nodded. He picked up his beer and took a deep swallow. "You're right, I did say that. Because it's the truth. There's no way he did that."

"I know he didn't. Mac didn't kill Sari," I said. I caught Finn's eye, and he nodded, suddenly knowing exactly where I was going with this. Jake must have seen something pass between us because the color began to drain out of his face.

"See, here's what I'm struggling with." I stared at Jake. "How the hell did you know she was hit?"

Jake's mouth moved like a fish, open and shut, but no words came out. Then suddenly Finn was grimacing, and I saw a glint of silver in Jake's right hand as he pushed the gun harder into Finn's side.

Damn it.

"I'm not going back to prison." Jake pushed his eyeglasses up his nose with his left hand and sniffed. "You'll have to kill me."

"Don't do this, Jake. There's no need to make matters worse for yourself," Finn said in a low voice. "There are a lot of people here, innocent people. Let's take this outside."

My mind was going a million miles an hour, trying to figure a way out of this situation with the least collateral damage.

Jake grinned. "That's an excellent idea. Nice and slow. Ladies first. Hands on your shoulders, like you're giving yourself a massage. Then Detective Nowlin. Anything funny and he gets a bullet to the spine. From what I hear, that's worse than death. You'll be in a chair the rest of your life."

Finn and I nodded. What choice did we have? We had to get Jake and his weapon out of the crowded restaurant, away from these people. He was a loose cannon and there was no telling what he'd do. As we moved through the restaurant, I tried to catch the bartender's eye, but he was comparing shoulder tattoos with a burly biker at the bar.

Just outside the front door, Jake said, "Stop a minute. I need to think."

Finn and I waited. We were both carrying our service weapons, but it had been too risky to draw them inside the restaurant. I slowly lowered my hands.

"Hey! Put them back up. Jesus, you think I'm an idiot? I know you've got a gun. Both of you do. So unless you want to see your partner split in two, keep those hands where I can see them," Jake said.

I took a deep breath, showed him the palms of my hands. "Let us help you, Jake. You're making a bad situation worse. Put the gun away and let's go to the station, where we can sit down and talk—"

"*Shut up!* I told you I need to think!" Jake howled. Finn tensed up as Jake pushed the gun against him, hard. "Why the hell do women talk so damn much? You're all the same! Where's your gun?"

I lifted my jacket, showed him my hip holster. Finn watched my every move, and I saw in his eyes that he wanted me to draw on Jake. But I couldn't risk it. In that moment, there were too many factors out of my control.

Jake smiled. "Take it out slowly. Slowly. Now throw it in the bush."

I did as he said.

"Now do the same with Finn's weapon."

"It's a shoulder harness," I replied. "I'll have to get close."

"Forget it," Jake said. He kept his gun trained on me while he reached for Finn's. In a moment, he had it, and he threw that one, too, in the bushes. "Now, each of you, take one foot and lift up your pants leg. Then the other. Good, no ankle weapons. Very good. Where's your car?"

I looked at Finn. We were disarmed, but if we were going to make a stand, this was the place to do it. Once we were in the car, there was no predicting what would happen.

"I said, where's your car? You think I'm playing games here?" Jake screamed. The bartender must have heard him, because he stuck his head out the front door. When he saw Jake's gun, he ducked back in, and I heard him bolt the door. I prayed he was calling the cops.

"My car is right there, Jake. Just put down the gun—"

Before I could finish my sentence, there was a loud pop. Finn fell face first to the ground with a single, heart-stopping cry. He went still.

I dropped to my knees beside him.

"Ah, fuck! Fuck!" Jake screamed. "He moved and the gun went off! Ah god, I've killed a cop!"

I rolled Finn over. He was pale but alive. Blood seeped into the dirt and, above me, Jake let out another scream. Finn tried to sit up, then fell back to the ground.

"Finn, honey, don't move, it's going to be okay. You're going to be fine. Where are you hit?" I was talking a mile a minute, willing myself to stay calm when all I wanted to do was stand up and blow Jake's head off.

"My . . . my side. Don't think . . . it's too bad," Finn gasped. I pulled my hand away from his body and felt my throat lurch when I saw how much blood there was. It was serious.

"It's over. Drop the gun. He's alive but hurt badly. You still have a chance to make this right."

Jake was shaking his head, nearly hyperventilating. "You and I are getting in your car. Come on."

"I'm not leaving him."

Jake pointed the gun at my head. "I'm not going back to prison. I'll kill you and shoot him again and then myself. Get in the car now. In the driver's seat. Do it, and if we get far enough away, I might let you live."

"Go," Finn whispered. I had to lean forward to hear his next words. "Keep the clock ticking, Gem."

He passed out and I knew his last words had been right. As long as I kept moving Jake forward, as long as we just kept moving, I had a chance.

"Why did you do it?"

I had to know and, at this point, Jake had nothing to lose by telling me. We were twenty miles outside of Cedar Valley. It had taken every ounce of willpower I had to stand up and leave Finn on the ground, bleeding, possibly dying.

The only thing that had gotten me into the driver's seat of my car was the gun held firmly against my head.

Jake said "Drive," and so I drove. I headed north on the highway, going ten miles above the speed limit per his instructions. My gas tank was nearly empty and, when I looked in the rearview mirror, I saw a smear of blood on my cheek and the eyes of a woman I didn't recognize.

"Do what?" he asked. He rested the gun in his lap, pointed up at my chest, nervously looking out the window, checking behind us. But there was nothing: no sirens, no lights, no indication that help was on the way. Only a green blur as we sped past the trees and a hollow sense that I should have hugged Grace a little longer that morning.

Another semitruck thundered by, one of the dozens of vehicles that had passed us in the last fifteen minutes.

"Why did you kill Sari Chesney?"

Jake sighed. "It was an accident. A stupid accident. It's Ally's fault. I liked her, okay? I liked Ally, and she was such a bitch. I kept complimenting her, offering to do nice things like rub her back, get her more water. I knew she didn't feel well. But she just kept getting meaner and meaner. We were sharing a tent and when we finally went to bed, I crawled in and made a joke, or something, about how someone was getting laid. I meant Mac, but Ally must have thought I was going to attack her. She said if I spoke to her again or touched her she would have me arrested."

"And you couldn't have that, could you?" I asked. "Not with your record. Your parole officer would have had a fit."

"Mac had mentioned my arrest. She knew all about it and took advantage of that."

I glanced over and saw Jake's face sour.

He kept talking. "I curled up in my sleeping bag and moved as far away from her in the tent as I possibly could. When I woke up, it was dark. I climbed out and took a leak. Then I sat by the water, staring at it. It was beautiful. The lake was so black, with these spots of ice that kind of glowed in the moonlight. The air was cold, and I'd never seen so many stars in the sky. I felt so lonely. Then who should appear but Miss High and Mighty Herself, Ally. She didn't see me. She went in the woods, to pee I think, then came out and stared out at the water. And I . . . I was still pissed off at her, you know? So I decided to scare her. I wanted to see her upset, just for a minute or two. I snuck up on her. I tried to be quiet, but she heard me and freaked out. I mean, really freaked out. She ran away, but her shoelaces weren't tied. She tripped and fell. I heard her hit her head and, from the sound of it, knew it was bad. I got to her and she was facedown and not moving. When I rolled her over, that's when I saw."

"Saw what?" I asked.

"That it was Sari and not Ally. And that she was dead."

Stunned, I drew in a breath. "Did you feel for a pulse? How did you know she was dead?"

"It was obvious," Jake said. "She was gone. The wound on her head, it was bad. There was a lot of blood. Her eyes were half open. I just knew. I panicked. All I could think about was being sent back to prison."

"What did you do next?"

"I rolled her back over and dragged her to the water. Then I pushed her body in and out, toward the middle of the lake. I waited until I saw her start to sink, then I went back to where she'd hit her head. With the light of my cell phone, I scooped up all the dirt and leaves with blood on them and then dumped them in the lake, too. Then I wiped out the drag marks with my feet, which was easy since it was so muddy. The last thing I did was pull down her backpack from the bear line and remove her wallet and cell phone. I saw that once, on a mystery show, where the bad guy hid his old lady's car keys and wallet. It screwed up the investigation and he ended up getting away. Anyway, then I crawled back into the tent. I lay there, sick to my stomach, until I heard Mac shouting Sari's name," Jake said. His voice took on a whining quality. "You have to understand, this was an accident. It's Ally's fault. She's a bitch, just like the rest of your whole sorry sex. But I am sorry."

"I don't think you're sorry at all." I risked another glance at him. He didn't look good; it was as though shooting Finn had triggered something in Jake akin to shock.

"You don't understand. I wasn't . . . I was sick. Things happened so fast. It was all so fast. I would give anything to take it back. What was she doing, anyway, sneaking around in the dark like that? She probably would have tripped over that damn log even if I hadn't frightened her. It's like a bad dream I can't wake up from."

I was tired of hearing Jake's excuses, and it was unacceptable for him to attempt to shift any blame to Sari. I swallowed hard. He needed to understand the full scope of what he'd done, but that didn't make it any easier to say what needed to be said.

"Jake, Sari was alive when she went into the water. She didn't die from her head wound. She drowned. The head injury? That was survivable. You could have saved her. Instead, you killed her."

"No. That's not possible. She was dead."

"She wasn't, Jake."

I glanced at him again and watched as anger darkened his face. Anger at the cards he'd been dealt, anger at his whole life, the way everything seemed to turn to dirt for him. Then he laughed.

"What's so funny?"

He snorted, on the edge of hysteria. "All of it. It's a fucking Shakespearian tragedy, is what it is."

"And Betty Starbuck? How did she play into this?"

"I went out drinking that night, the night of the gala. I was so depressed about what I'd done. Mac was at work, and I couldn't be alone with my thoughts. Around ten p.m., all these rich people started pouring into the bars. A few of them were talking about the big party at the museum. I recognized Betty Starbuck's name; Sari had been bitching about her boss at the campsite. These people, they were talking about a diary that had been stolen from the museum. They all seemed to blame Betty Starbuck for its disappearance.

"Look, I was nearly drunk by then. I thought Sari's body would never be found, you know? That it would decay in the water or whatever. I figured if I went to the museum and made it look like Sari had been there it would throw you all off track. I didn't know what I was going to do once I got there, I swear. But I took my beer and strolled over and waited until I saw this old lady and a security guard at the front door. They were talking, looking at something on the front lawn, and while their backs were turned I snuck in. It was that easy. Everyone was gone. Then all of a sudden the lady came back in! I hid behind a curtain and watched her set an alarm on a panel near the door. And I knew I was fucked. I hadn't counted on being locked in the goddamn museum. Thank god I had my beer. Anyway, I poked around and then I found Starbuck's office. It was unlocked. I went in and started trashing it. Then the old lady came back! Again! She walked in with a bag of food, and she started screaming. You have to believe me, I never meant to hurt her, either. But she wouldn't shut up."

I felt sick to my stomach. Two women dead because of one man's terrible, awful decisions. "So you strangled her and then made your cousin Nicole lie for you."

"The old lady got this look in her eyes. It wasn't fear. It was rage. It scared me, and I stopped choking her. Then she started screaming again. She called me pathetic, a loser, a thug. I couldn't take it. I hit her in the head with a statue and then finished the job. Then I went downstairs. I nearly ran out the back door, but I saw another alarm panel and figured she'd set it when she came back in. So I hid. Finally, this kid showed up. A janitor. There was so much trash he propped the door open. I waited until he'd gone back into the museum and then I slipped out. I ran the whole way home." Jake started crying. "No one is born wanting to be a screwup. This isn't the life I had planned for myself. Every time I get close to making something of myself, some asshole interrupts my plans."

"You're the asshole, Jake. When we get out of this car, I'm placing you under arrest for the murders of Sari Chesney and Elizabeth Starbuck."

"That's not going to happen. I told you I'm not going back to prison."

I looked around. We were halfway between Cedar Valley and Trenton. "So what's your plan? I'm nearly out of gas. We have to stop at some point. We'll be lucky if we make Trenton."

"We'll make Trenton. If we don't, I'll hitch a ride."

I looked over at him and was alarmed to see he no longer looked in shock or angry. He looked at peace.

"And me?"

Jake lifted the gun until it was level with my head. "Just shut up and keep driving."

I swallowed. Jake had nothing left to lose and I didn't have a clue if backup was nearby or miles away. There was no telling if the bartender had called the police. Finn had passed out before Jake and I left the parking lot; he'd have been unable to tell anyone which direction we were headed. My mind went to worst case scenario: if I ran out of gas, Jake would kill me. He would hide my body in the trunk and catch a ride with a trucker. My colleagues would find me in a few days, and by then Jake would be halfway across the country.

I wasn't going to let that happen. But what to do? I couldn't take my hands off the wheel to grab his gun, or go for his eyes or punch him in the throat.

The wheel—I did have one thing under my control. The car.

But that was crazy . . . use the car as a weapon?

Jake shifted in his seat and, from the corner of my eye, I saw that he wasn't belted in.

Perfect.

This might be a suicide mission, but there was no way I was going to wait for a bullet from Jake. I'd go out fighting, with my eyes open and on my own terms, just as I'd lived my life.

Thinking fast, I realized that I'd been on this road before. Somewhere up ahead, four or five miles, around a curve, there was a section of guardrail that was busted up from an old car wreck. The rail had done little to protect the car from going over the edge and sliding down a steep ravine. I slowed my speed.

Jake leaned over and looked at the speedometer. "Get your speed back up. Now."

I silently said a quick prayer and thought briefly of my parents, of the terrible accident we'd all been in when I was a child.

Maybe it was my fate all along to die in a fiery crash.

Maybe all these years I'd just been living on borrowed time.

They'd died, and I'd lived, and I was about to recreate the whole awful thing.

"Sure, I'll speed it up." I pushed down on the gas pedal and watched my speed creep up to sixty, sixty-five, seventy.

Jake leaned over again. "Hey, that's fast enough."

"I don't think it is. Fuck you, Jake Stephens." I pushed harder on the pedal and watched as Jake realized he wasn't wearing a seat belt. He struggled to keep the gun pointed at me and pull down the shoulder strap at the same time.

"I'll shoot you!"

"You shoot me and we both die," I said. Up ahead, the busted guardrail appeared. Jake saw it as I turned and aimed the car at it head on.

"Holy hell," he breathed.

We left the road and time stopped.

Chapter Forty-five

A trucker on a long haul from California to Missouri saw the whole thing. He watched as my car slipped through the wide opening in the guardrail and did a nose dive into the ravine. He called it in and then left his truck and walked to the edge of the road, careful to stand back, sure the car would explode. But we'd been running on fumes, and I'd counted on that in the minute or two I'd had to hatch my plan.

A boulder the size of a sedan had stopped our descent into the ravine, and so we'd come to rest ten or fifteen feet down a rocky, shrub-covered slope.

The paramedics were first to arrive. After he heard what happened, Lieutenant Charlie Darcy turned white and said I was either incredibly lucky or incredibly stupid. Then he apologized and said that no, he was sure I was incredibly stupid. I thought he'd been right the first time: luck and stupidity played equal parts in the whole damn thing. He examined me in the back of an ambulance, shocked I was as unharmed as I was. I had contusions on my face and an abrasion, a burn really, on my chest from the airbag, but I'd be okay.

The same could not be said of Jake Stephens.

I imagine I'll live with the image of him sliding headfirst, screaming, through the windshield for the rest of my life. As the paramedics evaluated him, it was obvious to everyone that his spine was badly damaged, and an enormous wave of guilt left me breathless. Though Jake had given me little choice but to try to save my own life, I was nevertheless responsible for his injuries.

In that moment, I understood all too clearly that I'd made a decision that would haunt me in the days to come.

After Darcy finished examining me, I insisted on using his radio to call the station. Dispatch put me through to Chief Chavez. He'd already been briefed by Trenton PD, which had arrived on the scene shortly after the paramedics.

"You could have been killed, Gemma. Don't ever do that again."

"I don't plan to, Chief. I was out of options." I hesitated, unable to voice the question that had been forefront in my mind for the last hour.

Chavez must have felt something in the silence. He sighed deeply. "Finn is going to be fine. It was a clean shot. He'll limp for a few months, but he'll be just fine. I can't believe it—I haven't lost a cop yet on my watch, and today I almost lost you both. To a snot-nosed punk, no less. Before he was wheeled into surgery, Finn told me the gist of things."

I cleared a sudden lump in my throat. "Are you there? At the hospital?"

"Of course I'm here. Where else would I be? One of my own goes down with a bullet, you bet your ass I'm at the hospital."

"Tell Finn I'll be there soon. There's someone I need to see first."

I'd made Charla Chesney a promise, and I intended to keep it, whether or not she was able to understand my words. My car was totaled, so Charlie Darcy gave me a ride back to the police station where I picked up a loaner car, then drove to Carver Estates. It was late and once more, Miss Rosa escorted me to Charla's room.

Then she left me to deliver the news in private.

Charla sat in the same lumpy armchair in the corner of her bedroom, watching a soap opera. I took a seat in a rocking chair next to her and spoke softly. "Hi, Mrs. Chesney. My name is Gemma. Do you remember me?"

She nodded her head and smiled brightly. "Gemma. You lived down the street from us in Los Angeles. You and my daughter played together quite a bit when she was a child. Sari. That's my daughter."

"Yes, Sari is your daughter. Mrs. Chesney, we got him. We got the man who hurt your daughter."

"Hurt? Sari's fine. She was here this morning. Such a silly girl. It's practically summer, and the whole time she visited, she complained about how cold it was," Mrs. Chesney said. She pursed her lips. "Darling girl needs money. I wish I could help her more."

I bit my lip as tears suddenly welled in my eyes. She noticed them.

"Oh heavens, don't cry. Why are you crying? This is just a silly show," she said, gesturing at the television. "It's all make believe, honey. You can't take it so seriously."

I nodded and looked around the room, desperate for a distraction. I took in the faded watercolor paintings on the walls, the dusty novels on a leaning bookshelf, a glass vase with dying red roses on the small kitchen table.

The water in the vase was murky and brown. A few petals floated on the top of the water, their softness and beauty changed to slime and decay.

Like drowned girls . . .

I stood up abruptly. "Can I give your flowers fresh water?"

Mrs. Chesney glanced away from the television. "Please. I'm sorry, I've forgotten your name. My daughter, Sari, gave me those flowers. She brought them with the books."

Half listening, I took the vase to the sink in the corner and poured the slime down the drain. The flowers were beyond saving, but I added fresh water to the vase anyway and replaced it on the table.

"That was sweet of her. Do you like to read?"

The woman laughed. "These books are *secret* books, honey. Sari made me promise to keep them hidden. Gosh, you and Sari used to spend hours hiding in the backyard. The two of you would play all day. Oh, the fun you had! You kept her secrets all these years, didn't you?"

I stepped away from the table, the flowers forgotten.

Access to the museum . . . expensive tastes . . .

"Where are these secret books, Mrs. Chesney?"

She pointed to the leaning bookshelf. "The red one, there, and the funny old brown one next to it."

Holding my breath, I walked to the shelf and pulled the two she pointed at. "These?"

But her attention was already back on the television.

I looked down at what I had in my hands. They weren't published books and the final piece of the puzzle fell into place.

They were journals.

One was red vinyl, filled with Sari Chesney's familiar handwriting, an account of the last five months, starting with January first and ending on the Wednesday before her death.

I set her journal aside and turned to the Rayburn Diary, running a hand over the engraved leather cover, feeling the symbols and soft leather under my fingertips. Flipping it open, I read the name on the inside and shook my head, wondering if there was a curse on the damn thing after all. Had this book—this collection of thoughts and observations and secrets—been the catalyst that started this whole chain of events?

Chapter Forty-six

I stood at the edge of Lost Lake and lifted a hand to my forehead as a visor. I'd forgotten my sunglasses again, and I cursed both the brightness of the sun and my own stupidity.

It was a windless day, and the water was calm. June had come and gone and the hot July weather had drawn scores of visitors to the cool, turquoise lake. Most were hikers and fishermen, though one determined couple had, incredibly, hauled inflatable stand-up paddleboards up the trail. The couple floated on them now in the middle of the lake, bobbing in the gentle waves.

Turning from the water, I watched as a young family with three boys set up camp near the spot where Sari had slept on the last night of her life. The mother and father argued as they struggled with the poles of the tent. The boys raced back and forth along the water's edge, daring one another to touch the lake.

I wanted to call to them, warn them to be careful, but I held my tongue.

The water, the running . . . all of it was no more dangerous than the decision to get out of bed in the morning. We are, each of us, born with a bull's-eye on our back. Death is the price we pay for life, and when our time is up, that's it, folks.

And if Ruby Cellars's theory was correct, Lost Lake would be the safest place for miles around . . . at least for the next sixty years.

Still, the lake made me uneasy. From the scout who had discovered it to the Lost Girls to Sari Chesney, the waters demanded a terrible price for their beauty.

I hadn't been back since the night I'd camped with Finn. It was hard to believe that had been two months ago, though the reality was that after what I was calling my "road trip from hell," things moved very quickly in the investigation.

Between Jake Stephens's confession in my car and Sari's journal, we were able to piece together the rest of the story. James Curry was the Bookkeeper, an obvious nickname in hindsight. Though he'd had the Rayburn Diary in his possession for months in order to restore and authenticate it, he wanted it for longer.

He wanted it forever.

Knowing that Betty Starbuck would never allow it to be sold, Curry went after Sari Chesney. Somehow—Sari was never sure how—he discovered her money woes. And he used those woes to lure her in, promising to make her rich beyond her wildest dreams.

Together, they hatched a plan practically the first week that Curry had the diary. The theft was months in the making. Curry agreed to pay Sari a quarter million dollars in exchange for the diary. It was more money than she would otherwise ever see at one time, and it would be enough to let her leave Cedar Valley and start fresh somewhere else. She stole the Rayburn Diary the Wednesday before her death, the night of the special preview party. Then she'd hidden it and her own journal in her mother's apartment for safekeeping.

We arrested James Curry at his home. When confronted with the evidence, he confessed quickly. He accepted a plea deal with the district attorney in exchange for a reduced sentence.

Larry Bornstein assumed the position of Director of the Cedar Valley History Museum. He was thrilled to have the Rayburn Diary back, and there was talk of renaming a section of the building the Elizabeth Starbuck Hall and installing the diary there permanently. Between the curse, the theft, and the recovery of the diary, there was enough material to fill ten articles in *The Valley Voice*, which was exactly what Bryce Ventura did. The media coverage sparked enough interest in the museum to attract the attention of a bigwig donor in Denver. The last time I talked with Bornstein, he beamed as he told me that as long as he was director, he'd never sell the museum.

I'd paid Ruby Cellars another visit at the River Street Methodist Church. She'd been in the corral, working one of her horses, when I pulled up and parked. In the light of day, the graveyard seemed smaller than I remembered, more peaceful somehow. Her little girls ran around the headstones, playing tag, their white cotton summer dresses and blond hair making them appear, when the sun hit exactly right, like little ghosts.

When I told Cellars that a person—a real, live, flesh-and-blood man—was responsible for the murder of Sari Chesney, a thoughtful look came into her eyes. I said in a joking tone, "Perhaps your theory is wrong after all."

She replied in all seriousness, "Detective, there are still eight months left in the year. This isn't over yet."

The only remaining mystery was Betty Starbuck's utility bill, with its cryptic message indicating she'd been afraid of someone. I felt strongly that it was Patrick Crabbe; he'd admitted to Moriarty that he did in fact spend time in his mother's backyard, in the middle of the night, when he couldn't sleep. I never did figure out why he lied about that to me. Subsequent requests to speak with him were turned down on advice of his attorney. Crabbe was awaiting trial in the Trenton penitentiary for the murder of Kent Starbuck, and I was okay with letting that business drift further and further away from Cedar Valley, away from me.

And, of course, we never did learn why Betty Starbuck had requested the meeting with Kent the night of the gala. Kent's theory was as good as any other: his mother had feared Patrick and wanted to keep the meeting secret.

The last I heard, Mac Stephens and Ally Chang had moved in together. To everyone's surprise, they were having twins, and I wished them well. Whatever mistakes they'd made, they deserved to start fresh . . . especially with two children soon entering the picture.

And though Jake's trial wouldn't start for a few months, already word on the street was that he would get life in prison for his crimes.

We'd solved the murders and returned a priceless diary to its rightful home at the history museum. Morale at the police station continued to rise as the leak in the department faded from collective memory.

Every loose end that could be tied up had been . . . so why did I still feel so disquieted? Part of it stemmed from the sheer awfulness of it all.

Sari's death . . . Betty's death . . . Kent's death.

I knew part of it stemmed, too, from Jake Stephens himself. He would spend the rest of his life in a wheelchair, paralyzed from the waist down. It was a terrible fate.

Did he deserve it? Probably. He probably deserved a hell of a lot worse. He killed two women and, though he didn't pull the trigger on Kent Starbuck, his choices had caused Kent's death, no doubt about it.

Three dead, and for what? It was madness to try to assign meaning to such tragedy, and yet it was human nature to do so.

I looked down at my left hand, watching the way the stones in my engagement ring captured the sunlight and changed it, reflected it back as a thousand colors in a million directions. Brody and I had settled on a wedding date, and I wondered if my continued unease was a result of that. Maybe the ring was a metaphor: life before marriage appeared as one thing, life after as something completely different.

Maybe I was being ridiculous.

After all, it was just a ring.

And a lake is just a lake, I thought, as I turned from the deep blue water and headed back to the trail that would lead me home.